Nicole trailed a lazy finger on the wall as she made her way into the storage hold of Derek Sutherland's ship.

She walked over to inspect the shining silver barrels of water. Sutherland had so many advantages over them. But that would make the win that much sweeter, she assured herself as she turned—and collided with Sutherland's unyielding chest.

"Going somewhere?" He gripped her arm and raked his eyes over her. "What the hell are you doing down here? And do not think of lying to me!"

Think . . . think! How long had he been standing there? "I lost my way back from the head," she replied in a credibly even tone.

"And I'm supposed to believe that?" Exhaling loudly, he placed a palm above her against the wall. "What am I going to do with you?"

"I wasn't doing anything wrong," she pleaded. "I really got lost."

When he searched her face, she met his gaze. His eyes were flecked with blue and were . . . mesmerizing. So intent, so dark, that she wanted to kiss his eyelids and then the harsh line between his brows before moving down to those chiseled lips.

She could see his expression race from anger to something else entirely. He murmured, as if in resignation, "Damn you," and then without any notice, he bent down and covered her lips in a brutal kiss. . . .

BOOKS BY KRESLEY COLE

The Captain of All Pleasures
The Price of Pleasure
If You Dare
A Hunger Like No Other
No Rest for the Wicked
If You Desire

KRESLEY COLE

The CAPTAIN OF ALL PLEASURES

POCKET BOOKS
New York London Toronto Sydney

This book is a work of fiction. Names, characters, places and incidents are products of the author's imagination or are used fictitiously. Any resemblance to actual events or locales or persons, living or dead, is entirely coincidental.

An *Original* Publication of POCKET BOOKS

 POCKET BOOKS, a division of Simon & Schuster, Inc.
1230 Avenue of the Americas, New York, NY 10020

ISBN: 0-7434-6649-7

First Pocket Books printing July 2003

10 9 8 7 6 5 4 3

POCKET and colophon are registered trademarks of Simon & Schuster, Inc.

For information regarding special discounts for bulk purchases, please contact Simon & Schuster Special Sales at 1-800-456-6798 or business@simonandschuster.com

Front cover illustration by Danilo Ducak

Printed in the U.S.A.

To my incredible husband, Richard.

How'd I get so lucky?

Acknowledgments

My deepest gratitude to my editor, Lauren McKenna, who gave me the opportunity of a lifetime. And thank you, Helena Valentin, for understanding all the work that goes into a novel (even before you had to critique it!). Many thanks go out to my wonderful writing group, Teresa Brown, Lori Johnson, and Karen Potter. The book and I are better since I've met you.

One ship drives east and another drives west
  With the selfsame winds that blow.
    'Tis the set of sails,
    And not the gales,
That tells us the way to go.

—Ella Wheeler Wilcox

The CAPTAIN OF ALL PLEASURES

Chapter 1

Nicole Lassiter's first tingle of alarm came the moment she stepped inside the squalid tap house and its fetid warmth rushed over her face.

Silence blanketed the den as the patrons inside took her measure, sensing she was out of place in the prostitute-laden tavern. She hadn't dressed to attract notice. She wore boys' pants and a shirt under an unadorned cloak. A hat covered most of the bright hair she'd prodded under it. Still they stared.

Her breath shuddered out. She was here on a mission to find Captain Jason Lassiter, Nicole reminded herself. And now that she'd arrived alone, she would merely have to do her best not to get killed. With an upcast chin and an off-hand gaze, she plowed through the throngs of roughnecks peopling the tavern. The tinny music from a badly tuned fiddle at last resumed.

Obviously, the information she'd received pertaining to Lassiter's whereabouts was mistaken; her father would never come to a place like this, a place where sailors found "company" before they shipped out. When a deckhand had told Nicole where her father was, she'd assumed the Mermaid had gone under new, less nefarious management since she'd been away.

This was certainly not the case. One last sweep over the place, and then she could go back and throttle the deckhand for his prank. One last—

Her father was here.

With a heavily painted light-skirts hanging all over him.

At least, part of her hung over him. Breasts like two hemispheres of a globe perched on the tight line of her bodice, threatening to free themselves with each of her throaty laughs. And Lord help her, Nicole thought as her face screwed up in shrinking expectation, the woman laughed *a lot*.

Nicole marched toward him through a gauntlet of human sweat, gin-spiked breath, and loose, unlaced bodies. At the sight of her, her father's jaw dropped and then snapped closed, bulging at the sides.

Here we go. . . . Jason Lassiter was a fearsome-looking man when angered. His eyes became wild and his face flushed to match his red beard and hair. That she hadn't forgotten. But she had minimized how angry he would be when she'd decided to come here tonight. There was no choice. She was running out of time.

She proceeded with a pained, set smile until she stood before him.

"Nicole," he ground out between his teeth, "what in the hell are you doing here?"

Her gaze flickered over the whore's rouged nipples,

boldly cresting her bodice. Rolling her eyes, Nicole retorted, "Just what in the hell are *you* doing here?"

With some muffled words and a pat on the woman's arm, her father shooed the prostitute away, then sharply motioned for Nicole to sit. "I came here looking for information," he answered brusquely.

"Ohhh," she said as she gave him a frown of disbelief. "Is that what they're calling it now?"

"That's *clever*," he replied with thick sarcasm, absently raising his mug. Nicole wrinkled her nose at the dented and grimy container. He looked in it, frowned, then placed it well away from him. "I'd planned to meet a man here who knows about the sabotage. It happens that he's connected with that woman." With a slightly wounded look, he added, "You know me better than that."

Nicole nodded grudgingly and gave him a small, apologetic smile. It lasted only seconds before she became serious at the mention of sabotage. Sailing in these times was perilous enough, with captains setting speed records and shipbuilders fearlessly pushing new designs. Masts rigged to snap and rudders set to be lost in the first heavy storm made it deadly.

"Tell me you have some idea who's doing this," she said. Her father's shipping line hadn't been targeted—yet—but he'd decided to take the offensive.

"I'm finally getting some good leads," he said in a manner that closed the subject. "Now, what in God's name are you doing here?"

"Well. I've been thinking . . ." But as she started the speech she'd rehearsed during her trip from Paris, with all her reasons why she should sail with him in the upcoming Great Circle Race from London to Sydney, the doxy appeared again, sidling up to her father. Giving

Nicole a nasty look, she began a provocative whispering in his ear.

Her father wasn't sending the woman packing anytime soon, and Nicole wasn't about to watch their murmured conversation. Turning from them, she dropped her chin onto the back of her chair and settled in to watch all the British tars and explicitly dressed women while they "mingled."

The earthy scenes had her wide-eyed. She imagined these sights would only add fodder to her late-night dreams, dreams in which a dark, faceless man . . . did things to her. Things that she'd seen between couples on the quay. She sighed. What would she dream tonight . . . ?

A loud thud shook her from her musings, and her gaze turned to the front door as three men marched in out of the cold.

They wore expensive and tastefully cut clothes, marking them as gentlemen. *Drunken gentlemen,* she amended as she got a better look at them. These were jaded high-steppers out for a night of cheap drink and even cheaper debauchery. Well, they'd come to the right place.

Although the men didn't attract nearly the interest that she had on her own entrance, the tavern quieted upon their arrival. Probably because the largest man was massive—over six feet and obviously well built in his tailored clothing.

But that wasn't what drew her awareness. No, it was the air of menace, seething and palpable, that reverberated in him. Even when he sat down with his long legs stretched out in front of his chair, his guise relaxed, she sensed a latent tension in him. The others sensed it, too. The parties of seamen, the crimps, the colorful doxies acted like skittish animals when forced to walk past his table.

He was the only one of the three men not noticeably inebriated, and strangely enough, when his eyes flicked over the room, a look like disgust lit his face. Why would he come to a place that offended him?

Then, as if her curiosity had drawn his attention, the man turned his intense gaze on her. After a second, his eyes narrowed. She sucked in a breath and knew: He saw through her disguise! Looked past the boys' clothes and somehow made her feel bare before him.

When the look in his eyes changed to show blatant appreciation, all rational thought evaporated like fog baked away under a southern sun. Her dark imaginings sputtered and lurched to life once more.

He looked at her as though she were the only woman in the room, a room thick with willing, half-naked women. What if she were one of them, and he called for her? What would it be like to straddle him, to envelop him in pied skirts as he absently drank, pinching and petting her bare skin beneath?

That feeling from her dreams returned—the unnamed response that felt like fear, surprise, and hunger battling inside her belly. *He* caused it now. It strengthened as his heated gaze ran over her.

"I see you've noticed Captain Sutherland," her father cut in dryly.

Nicole jerked her eyes away, her face heating furiously. But then the name sank into her muddled mind: Sutherland, the dissolute captain of the *Southern Cross,* the owner of the now failing Peregrine Shipping line—and her father's most bitter enemy.

"That's *Derek Sutherland?*" she asked in hushed amazement, staring at her father in wonder. The idea that he continually crossed this lethal-looking man was cause to make her alternately cheer his bravery and question his sanity.

"The one and only," he said as he stood. Bidding his doxy good night, he motioned impatiently for Nicole to follow him. "Looks as though we'll be leaving." Her father's face turned fierce. "Because if he keeps staring at you like that, I'll have to make good on my threats and kill the bastard."

As she followed him through the crowd, some urge goaded her to glance back at Sutherland. She gave in to the temptation, only to find his eyes on her.

Watch was too tame a word for what he did—his gaze roamed over her in a proprietary manner that defied her to walk away from him.

But she would.

Such an intriguing-looking man, despite his deeply lined countenance. What a waste, she mused acidly as she turned away.

Seconds later, long, strong fingers encircled her wrist. She knew it was Sutherland even before she turned and their eyes locked. His flesh was hot on hers—his hand was callused.

"Stay," he said simply.

From his manner, she got the impression he expected her to do just that. Did he think all he had to do was command her? The arrogance! So why did she find herself fighting a very real desire to remain?

"Take your hand off me, Captain."

When he didn't, she twisted her arm out of his grasp. In response, he gave her a mocking half-bow. How could he be so unconcerned? How could he seem bored when attraction fired hot and swift within her? Angered, she gave him a forbidding glare. "Nonchalance, Captain? How indifferent will you be when you lose the Great Circle Race by, say . . ." she tapped her cheek, ". . . a thousand miles?"

She could have sworn she saw the corners of his lips curl up before her father returned to yank her away.

"Damn it, Nicole, when will you learn?" he demanded before the toe of her boot had touched the refuse-strewn street. "Walking into the Mermaid as if you owned it! Hell, it's because of men like Sutherland that you shouldn't be in a place like that."

"I've been in worse," she countered as he anxiously led her away.

"But to attract *Sutherland*'s attention and then antagonize him?" He threw another look over his shoulder. "It's as if you're drawn to trouble."

"Well, trouble and I do go way back," she said between short breaths as she struggled to keep up with her father. He twisted around and frowned at her before slowing his progress down the quay. "If he's such a bad man, then for God's sake, why do you go out of your way to cross him?"

"I have my reasons for plaguing Sutherland. Good reasons. Besides, he's *British*." The look Lassiter gave her said he'd explained what should be obvious to anyone with American blood in them.

"Mama was British," Nicole pointed out, even though they'd been through this again and again.

"She was the only one of this whole lot I ever respected." His eyes betrayed much more than simple respect for his late wife. Laurel Banning Lassiter had been a noblewoman of English birth, whose memory was never far from their minds.

His voice hardened again as he looked at her. "That man is a wastrel and a brute and you're to have nothing to do with him. He'd use you and throw you away without so much as a good-bye. Especially since he knows I'm connected to you in some way." He paused, then added starkly, "If he realizes you're my daughter, I can't imagine what the cold-blooded bastard will do."

They walked on in silence, Nicole quiet as she thought about Sutherland. She didn't think it likely he'd recognize her since she took after her mother and bore little resemblance to her father—except perhaps a reddish tint to her hair. And, of course, in attitude.

"I don't think he'll even remember me in the morning," she finally assured him, though secretly, perversely, the idea displeased her. "After all, he'll most likely get drunk tonight."

Her father grunted. "Not so drunk that he'd forget you." He placed a hand on her shoulder, steering her around the ship debris speckling the docks. "But enough of that devil. Why aren't you in school?"

When she looked away, he asked in a voice laced with resignation, "You got thrown out again, didn't you?"

Nicole gave a delicate cough. "My leaving was mutually agreed upon." He scowled, striding on, and she added under her breath, "To the great glee of my headmistress."

When they approached the dockside that berthed her father's ship, the *Bella Nicola*, a rush of emotion brought the sting of tears to her eyes. A striking clipper with a sharp navy hull and jaunty white and red accents, it stood out among the hulks in the harbor as a diamond would amidst coal.

This is my home. She'd longed to be back aboard and had missed the ship as though she were a friend. Her breath hitched, but she didn't want her father to notice her missish reaction. To mask it, she commented in an airy tone, "Really, Father, I don't understand why you're still fuming at me."

"Don't understand?" he asked. "How did you expect me to react when you've been dismissed from the finest finishing school on the Continent? Pleased?"

"It really wasn't a dismissal like the other schools," she replied, warming to the subject. "I choose to call it a 'conclusion.'"

"Well, if this is you after your *conclusion*,"—he turned her to survey her hair-stuffed cap and boys' trousers—"your grandmother should demand her money back."

"Pssh. When I first got there, they told me I had to master seven subjects out of nine, which—I—did." He'd never know it had taken everything in her power to do so. She found it difficult to acquire graces designed to snag a rich, titled husband. Because at twenty and with her quirky looks, she was not just firmly on the shelf. She was on the top shelf—the one it took a ladder to get to.

"And I suppose it's only coincidence that you finished seven with enough time to travel back here just days before the Great Circle Race."

Nicole looked away again. She'd been planning to sail the race for the past two years, ever since reading about Queen Victoria's decree for a global contest open to sailors of any nationality. She'd decided then that nothing would stand in her way. Not slapped hands when she chose the wrong utensil nor ridiculing dance masters, and not the constant teasing about her being too old for school. Especially not a hard-as-iron headmistress bent on cramming her into a proper-lady mold and chopping off anything that remained outside.

This race would be the greatest in history—a win could catapult their line to worldwide recognition—and she wanted nothing more than to be a part of it.

When she didn't respond, he teasingly pulled her cap

down, then asked in a conciliatory tone, "So tell me, what were the two subjects you failed?"

Popping her hat back up, she feigned a grave look. "Alas, I fear that floral arrangement and playing the harpsichord are forever out of my grasp. As you can imagine, the knowledge of my deficiencies is crushing," she added as she checked an imaginary tear.

Lassiter looked to chuckle in response, his stifled smile showing her that he was happy to see her. But he made his features stern again. "Listen to me, Nicole. I want to enjoy our time together before I sail, so let's get one thing straight about the race."

Her brows drew together. Dear Lord, he couldn't be; he was opening his mouth, his face set to tell her she . . . wouldn't be sailing. "Don't say anything yet—please," she said in a rush of words. "Just give me a few days to prove to you that you need me in the race." *And every voyage after.*

"Nicole, it's not going to—"

"Please!" She grabbed his forearm and began to speak, but he held up his rope-scarred hand to forestall her.

She decided then that she couldn't win this skirmish. But this was hardly over. She had other arrows in her quiver for their next round, so she reeled in her thoughts and forced herself to let the fight lie for now.

And was even silent when he said, "I'll make this as clear as possible: Nicole, there is no way in hell you are sailing this race. And you have Sutherland to thank for making my decision easy. While I have a breath in my body, you won't be anywhere within reach when I have to contend with him."

I'm going to kill those beasts, Nicole thought grimly as she pounded her head against her forearm on the desk. When she sat up, she blew a wisp of hair out of her eyes, and looked down at her desk, presently littered with charts. She glared at all the numbers and equations fogging together.

She couldn't think, much less concentrate on plotting a course to impress her father. She didn't expect to when the livestock in the hold had been shrilling for a quarter of an hour.

Of course, this *would* happen when no one was on board to shush the puling animals. Lassiter had gone to a meeting he'd set up through the woman from the tavern, and nearly all of the crew were out enjoying their liberal shore leave.

The sounds dimmed. Holding her breath, she inwardly commanded their silence for the rest of the night. Just when she picked up her pen again, the animals erupted once more. Disgusted, she threw it down. Why weren't the two crewmen who'd drawn guard duty tonight seeing to this annoyance?

Probably asleep on the job. *She* would never fall asleep on the job.

Nicole stretched her arms high above her head before rising from the bolted-down chair in her cabin. Although she wasn't going very far, she grabbed her woolen cloak and pulled it tight.

She trotted with her clanging lamp toward the companionway, trying not to breathe too deeply of the sluggish low-tide air, but she couldn't suppress a yawn or two. She thought of the other reason she'd gotten so little accomplished this whole day—her exhaustion in the face of a sleepless night. She'd tossed and turned with sensual dreams, the sheets tangling between her legs, the fine cloth of her nightdress growing too bristly against sensitive skin.

In this dream, the man who set upon her wasn't a faceless stranger. It was Sutherland.

She reminded herself that he'd largely influenced her father's misguided decision about her sailing. And that the race would pit her father against this man again, making bad blood worse. So why could she still feel his warm, strong fingers firm on her wrist?

Shaking her head, Nicole drove him from her mind yet again. She did not have time for distractions.

At the companionway, she scanned the deck for the guards. Unable to see anyone to reprimand, she swung effortlessly down the steep, narrow steps as she had a thousand times before. When the light touched the animals, the insouciant goat merely swung its head toward her. But the wide-eyed pigs and sheep were frightened and heartily announced that fact in the echoing confines of the hold.

She puckered her lips and cooed, but they were spooked as they were when a bad storm was brewing. Muttering a curse, Nicole set her lamp on the floor and reached for the shovel to throw them more feed.

Her arm halted in midair.

The light from the lantern faintly illuminated a shape crouched on the floor, a huddled form partially obscured by one of the mighty timber ribs of the ship.

A man?

Nicole pushed her hair out of her eyes and up more securely in her hood as she squinted to make out the sailor's identity. Whoever he was, he needed to learn that he shouldn't be down here at odd hours without a good reason. Even more, if he'd upset the animals, then he should have made some effort to calm them.

"Just what do you think you're doing down here, sailor?" she demanded, each word she spoke underscored by the solid click of her boots as she marched toward him.

But as she neared him, something inside her, some oft-ignored instinct, told her to proceed warily.

He didn't answer, just rose and turned to her. Her breath leached out in a hiss.

The man bore a purplish, bubbled scar that curved over his forehead and down through a vacant eye socket. A foul odor emanated from him. It was the smell of gin, refuse, and . . . blood. She gagged, her eyes watering as she swallowed to keep from retching.

After several shallow breaths, her wits returned. This couldn't be one of her father's men. Which meant . . . which meant that she was in trouble. Again.

The play of emotions over her face must have amused the scarred man, because he grinned, revealing teeth that resembled little chunks of charred wood. She couldn't stop the widening of her eyes, or the hasty step back.

With her next step, she drew a deeper breath, regretting it immediately as his reeking form moved toward her. She managed to say, "Carry on, sailor M-my apologies."

For a second, then two, she awaited his reaction. How could she attract the guards' attention when the animals obviously hadn't? Could she outrun him? She was in trousers—she might be able to escape to the deck if he came after her. She should try . . . she really should move.

Just as she spun toward the companionway, the man called out, "Don't think we'll be wantin' 'er to go nowhere, Clive."

Appearing out of the shadows before her came a hulking second man, a man she sensed was even more dangerous than the first.

Two of them, in the hold. With her.

Nicole gaped at this new man's equally alarming appearance. She found herself morbidly fascinated by his pie-plate face, round and stamped down except for the bulbous protrusion of his lips. She watched him much like a bystander witnessing a terrible carriage accident, mouth parted, too horror-struck to move.

An instant later, the will to defend herself rose up, and her eyes darted all around to spy out a weapon. But she wouldn't be able to grab the hold's shovel or pitchfork before either of the men could get to her.

Then she spied the haphazard arrangement of tools on the floor beside the second man. The bastards were here to sabotage them! Fury spiked through her before settling like a weight on her chest, but she bit it back and said, "I am sorry for interrupting whatever repairs you're doing down here. I'll be going back up to my cabin . . . so good night."

"You ain't goin' nowhere, lady," the man called Clive said through those beefy lips. "I think you're goin' to stay with us and keep me 'n' Pretty comp'ny for a spell." His voice was guttural and his leering eyes scoured her body. Revulsion racked her. She flexed and closed her fingers as she fought for control. "You didn't think I'd let a comely piece of puss like you leave without me givin' you a good toss, did you?"

"Now, 'old on, Clive," Pretty protested from where he'd stopped, not five feet from her side. "The boss didn' say nothin' about tuppin' nobody tonight." He scratched intently in his greasy hair as he suggested, "Let's me 'n' you finish up 'ere afore we get caught, 'n' then we'll take care of 'er."

"Bugger you, Pretty," Clive said as he reached for the front of her cloak. A panicked screech burst from her lips. She kicked out at him. The stiff toe of her boot planted into his knee before she dashed around him, narrowly shimmying past his enraged lunge.

"*Help! Somebody help me!*" she screamed just once before she reached the steps. She knew no one was coming to her rescue. Tonight her survival was in her own hands.

Fast as Nicole flew to the stairs, the big brute was faster, and she managed just three steps up the companionway before he leapt for her legs. Catching her ankles in a manacle-like grip, he snatched them back viciously. She felt weightless for a fraction of a second before she crashed against the stairs in a jarring bounce. Stunned, she scarcely registered the pain as the wood shoved into her stomach and chest, wrenching the air out of her lungs.

Over her violent gasps, she dimly heard the scarred man yelling at them over the din of screaming animals. The pain ebbed and her sight blurred . . . until Clive hauled her back down, dragging her limp body toward him, one hand over the other snaking higher up her leg.

Fight, damn it, fight! With a hidden reserve of strength, she kicked forcefully, her heel catching the man squarely in his foul, soft mouth.

Blood spurt. He howled in pain, yet managed to keep one hand fisted around her leg. Another furious kick connected, loosening his hold, and she pulled at the stairs above with all the fading power left in her arms.

She'd broken free. She'd—

"I'll shoot you if you try that again." The words accompanied the rasp of a pistol hammer being cocked.

She craned her head back over her shoulder. The scarred man had a gun trained on her. Shaking, she looked back down at Clive, who rose to his feet and staggered toward her, his bloody face split into a gruesome sneer.

One glance into his pebbly eyes, seeing the frenzied rage directed at her, decided her fate in a flash.

Ignoring the gun pointed at her back, she sprang to her feet and bolted up the stairs, pumping her arms for speed, knowing she was too weak . . . too slow.

Halfway up, she felt rather than heard the click of the hammer. A shot roared through the shadowy hold.

Chapter 2

Derek Sutherland was an angry man.

Those who knew him well, and they were few, feared he wasn't many years away from becoming a bitter man. The events of the last four years did seem to guarantee his descent in that direction.

Late on this cold and bleak night, in addition to being angry, he was drunk. As was usual.

In truth, only one thing was out of the ordinary. He'd begun sobering up, an inconvenience he hoped to remedy soon in a nearby tavern. Lengthening his strides, he weaved his way through the broken crowds that populated the docks. He made his way easily even with the influx of people the race had drawn, since most wisely gave him a wide berth when he came near.

This wasn't only because he was a large man, standing a head taller than most out here. Nor was it that his hard face evinced the anger he wrestled with more and more each day. It was because he'd become a man who had nothing to lose, making him the most dangerous kind. And it showed.

He wasn't unaware of his effect on those around him—for years it'd been this way. In fact, only a handful of people didn't back down from him. One of whom was Amanda Sutherland, his mother—which was unfortunate, he thought, as he recalled this latest meaningless evening at the Sutherland London town house.

He'd been about to leave for the night when she'd summoned him into her deliberately feminine sitting room. He didn't have to guess what course the conversation would take and only wondered that it had taken her this long to approach him yet again.

When he sauntered in, he'd forgone planting a kiss on her offered cheek, and ignored the brief flash of hurt in her eyes. He moved straight to the least-delicate chair facing her and settled uncomfortably in the small seat.

Crossing his long legs at the ankles, Derek drawled, "I can't imagine why you would want to see me, Mother."

She pursed her lips at that, but after painstakingly smoothing her crisp skirts, she spoke evenly. "Will you stop by your club tonight?"

He laughed at her ludicrous question, but the sound was foreign and grated. He grew silent and fought to rein in the formidable temper that had helped bring his life to the low point he currently enjoyed.

Before he answered, he leaned forward in his seat to glare a warning. "I'll be damned if we do this again. You know bloody well that I am not going to the club or to any of your balls or soirees or anywhere else I might have to see or hear of . . . of my situation," he snapped, his face tense with resentment.

Though she should have been accustomed to it by now, his mother had looked startled at his quickening fury. Nevertheless, she said, "You have a responsibility to your title, Derek. It's time, past time, you had an heir."

"Grant's my heir," he'd said, naming his brother.

"But a son—"

"Cannot and will not happen."

His baleful tone hadn't even slowed her. No, she took a fortifying breath and proceeded to drag them both through the same old argument. She never missed a chance—they had it every time he was in London.

For what had to be half the night, he'd listened to her rant and plead, changing tactics with expert precision. Finally, he'd grown so furious he'd shot out of his chair to leave, intending to stay away from his family until he sailed.

But she wouldn't let it go.

"So which route are you sailing this time? China? South America?" she questioned before he could escape to the hall.

Reluctantly he turned back toward her, making his face cold as dead ash. "London to Sydney."

"Sydney?" she replied with mock excitement. "Oh, yes, Queen Victoria's Great Circle Race. I read about it in the paper some time back. How patriotic of you." Her brittle smile belied the sentiment of her words. "And how utterly convenient to find yet another voyage that goes so far afield."

Derek couldn't disagree.

She studied his face. "There and back should take you how long?"

"Half a year." Then, seeing the disappointment in her

flinty gray eyes, eyes so like his own, he'd once again turned toward the door.

As expected, nothing had been resolved. But her parting shot kept running through his mind: "I often wonder if you go to sea because you love it . . . or because you are a base coward."

Christ, he needed a drink.

What did that woman want him to do? And his brother Grant, who'd regarded him with awkward commiseration as Derek stormed past him and out the door? Everyone involved knew he could find no out, no possible redemption. He understood it, and damn it, he behaved accordingly.

He wondered vaguely what his mother and brother would say if they learned that something had finally pierced through the weary anger that clung to him. That a young dockside whore with soulful, dark eyes had provoked the earl to a pulse. A whore in boys' clothing working the Mermaid, of all places—

Several shrieks coming from ahead interrupted his thoughts. Curious to see what had unhinged the mob tonight, he made his way to a row of canvas-wrapped crates at the side of the walk and stepped up to get a better view. Under a canopy of large, cheaply milled hats and gathered heads, a small lad sped down the quay, running clumsily into several outraged women loitering about. With a quick lift of his chin, Derek made out two rough men beyond, plowing through the crowd after him.

Derek jumped down lightly and, with a brush of his hands, continued on his way. That boy had riled the wrong people, he mused indifferently. Those men were cutthroats—the kid didn't have a chance against one of them, let alone two. Even knowing this, he vowed to look the other way, as every other person on the docks would. He was no different from the worst sorts out here on this night.

He would just keep walking. Forget about interfering.

But when the boy barreled right past him, Derek spun around to see him get tangled in an old hempen rope coiled on the walk. The lad sailed forward, arms careening uselessly, before plunging to a stop on the slushy ground. Shaking his head, as if he couldn't quite believe he'd fallen, the boy raised himself on his arms but couldn't seem to manage his legs.

What was left of Derek's withered conscience demanded a rescue, but he easily quelled the thought. He wasn't the man he used to be. Besides, he could already see the sign of the tavern where he'd been heading. So close to a night of mind-numbing vice . . .

Judging by the sounds coming from ahead, the men were closing in.

"Watch yerself, ye bastard!" a flamboyantly dressed woman wailed as she swung her cloth bag against one of the men's heads. When he turned around to face her, she grew silent, frozen, then loped off into the night. Derek understood why—the man looked as if he were fresh from a nightmare.

Before he could stop himself, Derek turned to catch another look at the kid. Still valiantly trying to pull himself up, to get his little boots to catch a foothold on the grimy walk. Strangely, Derek had to fight the feeling of pity, a feeling increasingly unfamiliar to him.

He stalled for only a second more. The boy was probably a cutpurse and deserved whatever punishment those men handed out. Determined to turn away, he shook his head and walked on.

An affirmation, he knew, of just how big a bastard he had become.

Like a separate thing living in her, Nicole's fear grew, choking her throat. She strained to scramble up, but in her heart, she didn't know how much longer she could go on. Every movement shot pain through her exhausted limbs. Every choppy breath made her lungs burn as though she inhaled fire.

This wasn't how she wanted to go out—not sinking into the filth of a London street waiting to be plucked up by Clive.

I want to go down swinging. She bit back tears of pain and frustration, but before she was even conscious of it, a sob arose and spilled forth on a breath.

"*Bloody hell,*" a deep-voiced man grated from just behind her. A string of imaginative cursing followed; all at once she was lifted up and tucked into the side of some exasperated, angry giant. As he started toward a forgotten crack between two tea warehouses, shock rose up to claim her again; she couldn't even tell herself to fight because *he wasn't one of those men.*

Had she found a savior from the docks? Not likely, yet the man held her gently.

"Don't be afraid," he advised sharply. "I won't hurt you."

The man holding her had the clipped, precise speech of a gentleman, and her own instincts weren't screaming danger in his presence. She was strangely unafraid, especially considering that she'd just been shot at, and barely escaped with her life. *Shot at.* On her own ship, a bullet whizzing past her ear. Splinters exploding all around her head . . .

That memory crystallized her thoughts. She had

little apprehension of this man, but didn't want to be a sitting duck. No time to explain to him why—she needed to keep herself safe. She twisted in his arm and began kicking, drumming her boots against the backs of his legs.

"*I'm trying to help you.* Son of a—will you stop?"

Her blows had no effect. Thinking her attack would enrage him, she hunched her head between her shoulders to prepare for a slap or worse.

Yet he calmly redoubled his efforts to restrain her. He was easily twice her weight, huge, with unbudgeable arms. He could subdue her with laughable effort. But even as she fought, she got the strange impression that he tried very hard not to hurt her.

"Calm down! Damn it, you're like a greased cat," he uttered in a low, aggravated voice.

As she twisted to get free, she managed a fleeting look at her would-be protector. Recognition hammered past her disbelief. Even as she clawed and squirmed, her foggy mind grasped that the man holding her was none other than Captain Derek Sutherland.

If she weren't sure she was about to be killed, she might have laughed. *Out of the frying pan, and I dive for the fire.*

He struggled to rein her in, almost methodically attempting and rejecting hold after hold. It would only be a matter of time before he bested her, but she fought on. Until unexpectedly, he shifted her in his arms, one hand groping for some means of holding her.

And then . . . the unthinkable.

His hand slipped through her open cloak and up her shirt until . . . it landed on her breast.

Aside from her heavy breaths, she grew perfectly still.

She didn't know why: Because he had stilled? Or because she couldn't think of anything but his—hand?

Big, scratchy, ablaze with heat, it left an imprint on her skin. *Was that his finger tumbling over her nipple?* His hand seemed to move over her, his grip shifting from brusquely covering her breast to gently, curiously . . . cupping her. *No, now it was his thumb.*

She should begin kicking again. She should. But he'd rendered her body boneless. Captain Derek Sutherland had his hand on her breast, her mind repeated like a mantra.

His hand on her breast.

Did she hear him mutter a curse? Her skin felt chilled when he tore his hand from her shirt as if he had been burned. He spun her around, and the whole front of her body rubbed against his.

Nicole made a vain attempt to marshal her scattered thoughts. Her father's worst rival held her in a back alley, alone with him, so why didn't she fight? Because she was weak. Breathless.

Then he ran his hands down her arms and placed them on her hips. Warmth flooded her body anew and pooled in her belly.

She'd been around men most of her life, had lived in close quarters with them for extended periods of time, but she had never experienced this unexplainable yearning that seized her so suddenly and so forcefully.

Nicole shook her head, wanting to deny the feeling. She'd simply been so frightened, and he held her safely, or rather, safer, in his arms. The man warmed her, she reasoned, like a cocoon in the stinging night air. And his cleanly crisp smell tickled her nose. Male. His scent was . . . male. Not like the liquor and cheap perfume she expected from a blackguard like him, but so alluring that she wanted to bury her face in his broad, hard chest and breathe him.

Even as her face inched closer to his body, a part of her mind argued that he might not have gotten a good look at her face. Her hood was still on her head. She could run—

As if he could read her mind, Sutherland enclosed her more tightly in his arms. With a gasp signaling part disbelief, part something else she couldn't begin to name, she felt his hardened arousal pressed high against her belly. Startled, she twisted away, which only caused her to brush more closely against that part of him.

He inhaled sharply in response, and his whole body went rigid around hers. "Easy," he said. The word rumbled like lingering thunder after a storm.

"Let me go—I have to . . . go," she pleaded. She couldn't manage more than standing there panting, her body a mix of tension and a melting flow. She stared at him, this unyielding man who gave no indication that he would release her. When one of his large hands loosened its hold, she sensed he was about to remove her hood. She didn't want that, couldn't have that, but her body was immobile, drawn by the warm strength of his

Not quite in resignation, she studied his cruel-looking face, saw the skin pulled taut except where it crinkled into a scowl. His eyes found hers and held. She'd known from the night before that his eyes were cold. Now she could see more than that.

Sutherland looked like a man aboard a sinking ship— who suffered no delusions.

A whisper of air fluttered over her face when his hand sought the hood of her cloak. As he untied it and pushed the fabric back over her hair, his fingers brushed her cheek as if in a caress. Her whole body quivered from the sensuality of that sheer touch. She still trembled when he studied her face . . . and when he stroked her hair . . . and even when he effortlessly lifted her up and threw her over his shoulder.

Chapter 3

*N*othing surprised Derek anymore. He expected the worst outcome, the worst in everyone, and most times they didn't disappoint. But when he'd detected the girl from the Mermaid beneath the hood, everything inside him went a little crazy.

And outside, too. His blood-pounding erection was raw and swift, like that of a rutting animal scenting a ready mate. He didn't know if his surprise came more from finding the prostitute again or from this aggressive reaction to her.

She was dumbfounded, of course, to be draped over his shoulder with her backside pointed up in the air and her face buried in his spine. It wasn't long before she began kicking and scratching with as much spirit as before.

"Down! Now!" she ordered, punctuating each command with a swat or a kick. "Put—me—down—this—*instant!"*

He scoffed at her continued attempts to hurt him, smug because she simply hadn't the power to do so. A stab of pain pierced his moment of gloating—the Valkyrie had sunk her strong little teeth into the back of his arm.

"What the hell?" He shook her loose. "Damn it, I'm trying to help you. I don't see those men around here, but that doesn't mean they've gone."

When she had stopped struggling long enough to listen, he continued, "I'm taking you somewhere safe, and if you fight me you'll only prolong the inevitable."

She huffed, "I'll humor you. For *now.*"

His lips nearly curved at her attempt to keep her dignity even though she hung over his back with her cloak bunched around her waist. But he became tense and alert when he reached the corner and searched the area. Confident the men had run ahead, he strode in the opposite direction, toward the *Southern Cross.*

"You could let me down now. I won't run away," the girl offered after bouncing along for a few steps. He should let her walk, but he didn't want her to try to get away again. Not until she explained some things.

"We'll go quicker this way." As an afterthought, he added, "Aren't you done in?"

When she inhaled deeply and sighed, he felt it on his back. "Yes," she admitted reluctantly.

Fury fired in him as he pictured those men running down this small, defenseless young woman. Yet he became angrier with himself—he'd come so close to leaving her—and his tone was harsh. "Who chased you, and why?"

She stiffened. "That's none of your business."

"It is now, since I just saved your hide."

When she didn't say anything, he jostled her a little with the arm under her backside. "Tell me now."

"You'll have to shake a lot harder than that to get me to talk. Since I know you won't—let's not waste each other's time," she said in a nasty voice from behind him.

The girl was . . . *provoking* him?

"I wouldn't wager on that, sweet." His ire, always considerable, rapidly banked. "You obviously lack the sense to be afraid of me."

She rose up off his back. "Should I be afraid of you?" she asked in a sensible tone.

No mincing questions for this one. "That depends on whether or not you keep me happy. And right now I'm not happy."

"You don't look as if you've ever been happy," she mumbled, her cheek resting on his back again.

He slowed. "What do you mean by that?"

Derek could feel her as she took another deep breath and rose up again. "You've got a deep groove between your eyebrows from scowling, but no matching ones around your eyes like you'd get from laughing. You scowl a lot, don't you? I bet you are right now."

Hell, he was. He despised it when people analyzed him. "You don't know a damn thing about me—"

"Clearly, I know you don't laugh."

Enough. He purposely swung her down as if he was dropping her.

"Wh-whoa!" she squealed as she fell, but he caught her just before she tumbled to the ground.

After steadying herself, she pushed her thick, tangled hair out of her face and tilted her head. With a hurt expression, she asked in a genuinely confused voice, "What'd you do that for?"

He opened his mouth to speak, and then closed it. The wench had a great mane of hair. He took in the piles of curls tousled from the night, curls that couldn't quite decide if they wanted to be red or gold. They framed her oddly pretty face and curved along her slender neck. His lips itched to kiss that neck. . . .

He shook his head at such driveling thoughts. "I'm not sure I want to take you anywhere safe. You have a barbed tongue on you and don't know the meaning of gratitude. You *belong* at the Mermaid."

Her chin jerked up. "You," she said in a rising voice, "were there right along with me. Or were you too drunk to remember?"

"Lady, you're on your—" he began, but saw her eyes dart toward the sound of a fight breaking out not twenty yards behind them. Her face fell, and her body shook. For all her bravado, she was truly afraid.

Before she could run, he grabbed her waist and tossed her over his shoulder once again. Marching toward his ship, he felt a curious satisfaction as he carried her along.

He didn't know what it was about the girl. Perhaps it was that no one had ever looked at him the way she had in the Mermaid, like a siren.

Like she'd die if he didn't bed her.

Derek had told himself he wanted to find her simply to settle his curiosity. It mystified him why a young woman, a young woman who obviously sold her body at the Mermaid and consorted with Lassiter, no less, would look at him the way she had that night. First with desire, later with fury.

Plus, he'd needed to know if he could want her that badly, or if it had been the drink that night.

It wasn't the drink.

What was the matter with him? She was a sharp-tongued, insulting prostitute who dallied with his worst enemy. And she had peculiar features. Overblown ebony eyes, too dark and large for her small, gamine face, contrasted with the pout of her lips. It was as though one artist, vivid and wild, was unleashed to paint her eyes and hair, while another labored over the faultless bow of her lips. . . .

The wench began working up her pique once again. She must have thought at that point that he posed the greater danger to her, because she began writhing on his back, straining to break his hold. She weighed so little, he easily held her firm.

Then she twined her fists together and pounded his back. The force of the hit surprised him, but his stride didn't falter. It simply earned her a light slap on her shapely backside, so plainly outlined in her snug trousers.

"You! Oooh, you can't—"

He rested his hand there. "*Clearly,* I can," he said, using her word. She sputtered in outrage, and his lips crooked up. Then it was his turn to be shocked when she called him names that would make his most hardened sailors blush. It wasn't just the creativity of her curses or the venom dripping from every word that surprised him. He could expect that with her background.

No, he'd noted before that she didn't have a dockside English accent, but in her fury, her words became crisper and less like what he'd expect. In fact, he couldn't place her accent at all. With a twinge of unease, Derek realized he could determine nothing about her speech except that, barring the colorful phrases, it sounded very cultured and very affronted.

He dismissed his misgivings. He had seen her in a tap house known for its whores, leaving for the night with a man twice her age. Not exactly the nocturnal activity of a lady.

Whoever this girl was, he would take her repeatedly this night and enjoy figuring her out later, sharp tongue and all. This couldn't have worked out better, with the race in five days. Just enough time to enjoy her.

And then, as always happened with him . . . to tire of her and sail away.

With Nicole easily draped across his shoulder, Captain Sutherland stepped onto the deck of his ship and waved casually as he strode past two bewildered guards posted outside. Nicole's position embarrassed her, but the sight of the *Southern Cross* was enough to make her suck in a breath and briefly forget about cursing him. She'd never been so close to his ship, and as they boarded, she couldn't help but look around in awe.

She'd always scoffed at the sailor's fancy that a captain resembled his ship. But massive, bold, and dark, the *Southern Cross* was a credit to the idea. It was hard-planed and sharp-lined.

And forbidding.

Just when she'd decided she would attempt another escape, Sutherland reached the companionway. He dropped her to her feet and looked her over, as if making a decision about her. Finally, he said, "Go down the steps."

She answered him with a disbelieving look. Of course she wouldn't. Did he think she was insane? She didn't know why he'd taken her back to his ship, hadn't determined whether he'd realized who she was by now, and, most important, she didn't like taking orders, especially from a man like him. She was opening her mouth to decline, *thank you, no.*

"Do it now."

"No."

"*No?*"

She guessed from his look of open surprise that the word was seldom used with him. "N-o," Nicole spelled out. "Not until you tell me why you've brought—"

"*Now,*" he boomed, and all thought of rebellion ended. His tone made her jump to the stairs to get to the belly of the ship.

He didn't scare her, she assured herself; he'd just *startled* her.

Swinging down easily after her, he walked to her slowly, assessing her. He bent down deftly to miss a rafter in the ceiling, reminding her of his great height. She should be nervous after he'd just yelled at her. Afraid after all she'd heard of him. Chancey, her father's first mate, would say she had too much pluck for her own good. She supposed he'd be right, because she just couldn't make herself be wary.

Yet Sutherland didn't look as though he'd hurt her. *No, he looks like he wants to eat me for dinner.* His gaze stroked her like a physical touch, and she shivered. Those eyes, gray and dark, could easily be called cruel, but they held no anger toward her. She convinced herself that she could detect the promise of something more in their cold depths. Could that be the reason he'd taken her back to his ship? To kiss her?

For most of her life, Nicole had been uniformly rewarded whenever she'd done something forbidden. And if kissing Sutherland wasn't forbidden . . .

Irrationally, a part of her was thrilled at the prospect. But all this was crazy—Sutherland, the rogue who'd probably bedded a legion of beautiful women, desiring her, a scrawny girl with strange looks?

Nicole backed away, absurdly keeping some polite distance between them. She passed a door, and before she could prevent herself, she curiously scanned it. She did the same at the next door down, taking in the details of the ship.

He saw her flitting eyes, and then, seeming to realize what she must be anxious about, he assured her in a soothing, low tone, "Rest easy, sweet, I don't share. It'll be only you and me tonight. Aside from the guards on deck, we have the whole ship to ourselves." He reached out to smooth away a curl along her face and said huskily, "I'll reward you well for the night."

Reward her? An idea surfaced in her mind, but she shook it away.

Whatever he read in her expression made him narrow his eyes. "I will warn you once," he said in a menacing voice. "Do not think to play games with me."

She grappled with confusion. She couldn't account for what he was talking about or why he was so angry.

He grabbed her upper arm. "Why were you being followed?"

"Why did you bring me here?" she replied, tugging to regain possession of her arm.

He all but grinned. "I brought you here because I want you."

Well, that explained either everything or nothing. She had to know. "For what?"

Irritation flashed in his eyes, and she barely curbed a wince. Before she could voice another question, his other hand grasped the back of her head. "For what? *For this.*" He pulled her to meet his lips.

Nicole resisted and pushed against his chest, more out of instinct than any real desire to get away. But then he ran his hand up her neck and under her hair. She couldn't remember ever being stroked on her neck, and the sensation was so unfamiliar, so pleasurable, she stilled.

He must have sensed her surrender; his lips pressed against hers even more forcefully. Unconsciously, her whole body softened and drifted into him. His tongue stroked at her lips, demanding entrance, fueling her curiosity. *Curiosity killed the cat, Nicole.*

But what a way to go . . .

She boldly obeyed by parting them. He touched his tongue to hers and *that feeling* arose again—hot, liquid, and undeniable. His breathing became ragged. She could feel his heavy arousal against her belly—*oh, Lord,* he pressed it against her, and her head fell back in pleasure and shock, her mouth opening in a silent cry. She couldn't allow him to touch her like that. She would make him stop. . . . But she already throbbed where their bodies met. Her breasts ached. In the clash between her wanting and her will, the wanting took over. And ruled her.

She grabbed his shoulders, pulling herself up on her toes to get closer, deeper into his arms. Her body began shaking as the movement drove her breasts into his chest. She was coming out of her skin, frenzied to be near him. Was she making that low keening sound?

With a curse, he released her and deliberately set her away from him. "This will be over before it begins," he grated in a strained voice. He was out of breath, and when he ran his palm across the back of his neck, she could swear he battled surprise.

He watched her in a searching way, and even though he seemed tense as a tightly wound coil, Nicole thought that she pleased him. With the tip of her tongue, she tasted him on her lips, and brought her hand to her bruised mouth, reveling in how she could still perceive the seeking pressure of his kiss.

She studied his mouth, staring, captivated by how warm his lips had been, since they appeared to be chiseled out of stone. He fascinated her. His behavior fascinated her. And she knew there was more.

She stood there, unable to take her eyes away. Even though he was her enemy, his kisses helped her past that detail. If only for a night. Why not use him to finally know what her schoolmates whispered about in the dark?

"Tell me your name."

Wait! Sutherland didn't know her. She hesitated for just a second too long.

"Of course, I don't expect you to give your real name . . . but I'd have thought you would have picked out a working name."

Working name? What the devil— All questions ceased. He was angry again.

"Christina. My name is Christina," she hedged, supplying him with her middle name.

Was he amused? She got the impression that her "working name" was not what he'd expected.

She knew she couldn't come up with a reasonable excuse for why murderous cutthroats had followed her without letting him know her identity. Especially since all she could think of were his lips. Nervously she took a deep breath and forced a tremulous smile, though that was the last thing she wanted to do.

He, in turn, looked down into her eyes until his gaze settled on her smiling lips. Whatever he saw there had his fingers threaded through her hair, then descending over her neck, until he skimmed the backs of his fingers over her breasts. Her eyes grew wide. She grabbed his wrists to stop him, but wished she hadn't as soon as the feelings registered.

He twisted out of her grasp, placing her hands on his chest before bringing his fingers back to her body. She was dumbfounded by his actions, and her reactions. The rigid muscles in his chest moved under her fingertips, enticing her; his touch made her breasts ache.

She looked down at his hands, eyes shuttered. He didn't behave like the pinching, clutching men she'd seen on the docks. He . . . luxuriated in her, watching his own stroking movements, seemingly enthralled as he teased her nipples to hard, aching points. Her eyelids slid closed when he grasped her sides, his hands so big on her body, and rubbed his thumbs over her.

"You bring a man to his knees when you smile, but you probably know that," he told her in that gravelly tone. "Tonight, I'll have you, and I'll make you smile with pleasure." He bent down and gently brushed his lips to hers, as if preparing her, warning her, for the deepening contact of his mouth.

She became lost in his kiss with its thorough caressing. He acted hungry for her, as if he couldn't control his reaction to her, and thinking of that made her hunger for him. Heat and sensation bombarded every part of her body that touched his—her breasts, her belly, her legs.

She clung weakly to his coat, scarcely aware that she deepened the connection of their bodies by pushing into him as he'd done to her earlier. He responded by pulling her hips to his with a grinding force. She raced toward something, something she starved for. Then his hand trailed down, lighting on her thigh before kneading upward, inch by inch. Did his other hand fumble with his trousers?

She was feeling too much, closer to flying apart than she'd ever been in her dreams. Too much from this man. She stiffened. A last shimmer of sanity called to her. This was *Sutherland*. It was supposed to end with just a kiss.

Instead of holding him to her, she pushed away from him. She shook her head forcefully. For God's sake, this was Sutherland! Why did she behave like this with him? In answer, the throbbing in her body grew more pronounced.

Unconsciously she swiped at her lips as if to erase what she'd just done. Of all the men in the world, she couldn't be this attracted to *him*. She simply couldn't. Particularly since she'd never met another man who made her body rebel against her. She couldn't allow a rival, an enemy, this power over her.

A thrill, of what had to be fear, surged through her when she admitted there were a few moments back there when she probably would have done anything he desired.

More important, she reminded herself, while she was in here . . . *cavorting* with Sutherland, the two men who wanted to harm the ship and had tried to kill her were loose.

In response to her pulling away, he laughed a mirthless laugh and ran his hand through his thick, black hair. "A word of advice—in your line of work, you should at least act as though you enjoy my kiss," he said, then he stalked past her down the corridor.

Her wits were slow, simpleton slow in her desire-saturated mind, but she finally understood why he'd so heroically brought her back to his ship.

He thought she was a whore.

She wasn't offended by that in the least. She had befriended courtesans who made their livelihood from loving men. No, disappointment seeped into Nicole because during the day she had come to believe that they'd had some powerful connection the night before. The memory of that had factored into why she'd let him kiss and touch her. In reality, he'd just been surveying the women in the tavern and assumed she was part of his selection.

When he walked away, she whirled around to leave. Because that's what she should do. She hadn't even reached the deck before she started doubting her decision. Those men were out there. It was freezing out on the docks. And dark.

Nicole walked to the gangway, past the guards, who seemed uneasy around her. She tried to see each way down the quay, but only craggy, dark places abounded. Miles separated her from the *Bella Nicola*, and she had no money. And how could she be sure anyone would even be back aboard by now?

She hesitated. Captain Sutherland thought she was a prostitute. Nicole didn't attempt to delude herself that if she entered his cabin, she'd come out unscathed. Then she imagined Pretty jumping out from behind a building, his cadaverous face twisted into a grin.

Crossly, she turned and scuffed to his cabin, all the while sorting through her spiraling emotions. When she entered, his face was unreadable, but she swore he looked surprised to see her return. If he was, he promptly got over it. He didn't waste any time closing the door behind her, and she teased herself by ridiculously thinking that he didn't want her to change her mind.

He stood near enough that his warmth and his addictive scent enfolded her, before moving to the center of the cabin. He shrugged his broad shoulders out of his coat and tossed it over a chair, his every movement casual and unhurried. She had the feeling that he played with her, as if he had all the time in the world to find out her secrets.

Regardless, she would make the most of this situation. Yes, she'd just entered Derek Sutherland's cabin still shaking from his kiss. That was *bad*. *But* she needed a safe haven until she could be certain the crew had returned to her ship before she attempted to go home.

"Captain, I, uh, would like . . ." She had to stop and cough before beginning again. "I would like to stay with you for a couple of hours. For protection," she added hastily.

"Why should I protect you?"

Good question. Yet she had no good answer. "Because I'm asking you to?"

He paused, taking time to look her over again. His voice was husky when he answered, "I'll keep you here with me."

She nodded. *There. That wasn't so bad. This was a good decision,* Nicole assured herself, even as she reacted to his hungry look with another bloom of heat throughout her body.

But who, she wondered as the sensual rush turned into a deepening knot of dread, would protect her from herself?

Chapter 4

When Nicole forced her eyes away from Sutherland and surveyed his cabin, the first thing she noticed was his oversize bed. The second he'd caught her looking at it. He had the gall to smirk at her, and her face flamed as she glanced away.

The room was extremely large even for a ship of this size, but snug and warm with none of the usual drafts. She took in the tasteful colors and décor and reluctantly acknowledged that it easily surpassed her own cabin, even with all those fancy gifts from her hard-hearted grandmother crammed into it—gifts just waiting, in her opinion, for the right time to be coldly pawned.

A sizable mahogany desk rested under a large clouded-glass skylight, and scattered all over it, so like her own, were charts and scribbled numbers.

As if magnetically drawn to it, she edged over to spy out his course, straining to see in the low light. She made out many of the figures while he fed fuel into the stove and turned up the room's lanterns.

She examined his course line, knowing she was cheating, but she wanted to find out how far south he planned to sail through the Southern Ocean when rounding Africa's Cape of Good Hope. If she could determine that, then she could either meet his course or beat it with a more dangerous, but faster latitude farther south. *How low are you going to go, Captain Sutherland?*

Her eyebrows shot up. Lower than even her reckless father had ever dared.

His course ran insanely close to the perilous seas around the Antarctic, cutting the distance and sailing time to Sydney. She had to have read it wrong.

"Don't try to read that," he advised. "It will only give you a headache."

Her eyes narrowed. She'd been plotting since she was old enough to count. Indeed, she almost informed him with a sharp rap of her fingernails over the offending numbers that *he* had made a mistake in one of his calculations. But she should probably let the error stand, since it could adversely affect his course in the race. It would be a cold-blooded thing to do, but this wasn't a child's game. If he couldn't meet the challenge, then he'd fail.

When she said nothing, he scrutinized her and said, "It's a *course*—a map of where I'll sail this ship on my next voyage." *Had he explained that slowly?*

Nicole's nails bit into her palms as she quieted her arrogant pride. She managed a tepid smile as if impressed with his knowledge. Yet thoughts of the race vanished when he walked toward her in that slow, fluid way that made her belly tighten.

He reached out to her, his body so close that she would

have to move to avoid touching him. Instead, she lowered her lashes. Would he kiss her again? Did she want him to touch her with those lips once more? Nothing happened for the space of what should have been a couple of breaths.

Her eyes flashed open; he'd reached past her toward a bottle of brandy. She didn't think he'd seen her mortifying surrender, but that didn't stop her from berating herself for being so vulnerable to him. Sutherland was a cruel man. A patronizing man. He expected, lest she forget, that she would be *bought* tonight.

Well, he could occupy himself with liquor all night if he wanted, but she would not let him touch her again. As if to illustrate his matching intention, he poured a generous amount and drained his cut-crystal glass in two long draws.

Inclining the bottle toward her, he halfheartedly offered her some. She couldn't decide if this was because he didn't think she'd accept or because he didn't want to share. She shook her head in answer, the movement making her sway.

Perhaps she should have taken a drink, she thought as a sudden wave of exhaustion washed over her and chilled her. Shivering, she pulled her cloak closer and wrapped her arms around her body.

"You're cold," he said. He set down his glass and walked to a cabinet.

"I seem to be," she confessed. "I become cold very easily."

Their tones sounded so mundane that she thought of what would happen when reality claimed her. Thinking of tomorrow was like a wet blanket over all the sensations he'd produced in her, and she couldn't make up her mind whether she wanted him to kiss her or if she wanted to fall down where she was and sleep.

He turned from the cabinet and tossed a blanket at her,

and though her sore body made it difficult, she awkwardly managed to catch it. Frowning, he looked her over; then, seeming to make a colossal sacrifice, he took it from her. Without a word, he tugged off her damp cloak to wrap the blanket around her, as if she were no more than a doll he was changing.

He looked her up and down, his gaze stopping at her feet. "Since I've already started this idiocy . . ." he muttered gruffly, as he bent to untie and pull off her filthy boots. Obliged to place her hands on his wide, solid shoulders, she had to resist moving her fingers over the firm bunching of his muscles.

When he removed the first boot, his eyes narrowed. He held it up to the lantern, where they both saw that the scuffed brown leather had soaked up splattered blood like a sponge.

"Are you hurt?" he barked as he dropped that one and rushed to remove the other.

"That's not—that's not my blood." Merely thinking about where that blood came from, about the falls and the running enervated her.

His eyebrows rose in amazement, and he studied her face before returning to his task. Nicole felt foolish when he took off her socks, leaving her to furrow her toes in the cabin's plush rug. But she stood unresisting, knowing she needed his help just now. He strode to his bureau and brought back a pair of thick woolen socks. She hadn't realized her feet were cold, but when she spied those socks her body cried for them.

He jerked them over her feet, and her eyes closed in blissful comfort. "That feels so *good*," she breathed. She opened her eyes and frowned at the sound of her husky, sensual voice. When had she ever sounded like that?

He looked at her curiously, then stood abruptly. As if he needed to explain, he said, "Your feet were like ice."

Nicole nodded slowly, overwhelmed with fatigue. She took such a deep breath that her head moved with it. Her eyelids opened more sluggishly with each blink.

With something like resignation in his eyes, he placed a huge hand on her lower back and began guiding her to his bed. "Come on. You're exhausted."

"Oh. No, I can't. I couldn't."

When she resisted, he said, "I won't hurt you."

She focused on his face to tell him she absolutely could not be in his bed, but no words came. Her legs shook. She must have gone soft in the rich surroundings of her last school, because a second later they simply gave out. She sank onto his bed, bewildered by her weakness.

"Will you be all right?"

"Yes. No?" she whispered. "I'm just so tired."

"The night is catching up with you, so rest for a bit. Then we'll talk about who those men were," Sutherland said, his voice neither menacing nor kind as he lightly grasped her shoulder and pushed her down. He squeezed it firmly once, letting her know without words that he wanted her to stay put, before releasing her to walk over to the basin. He brought back a soaked cloth and began washing her scraped hands.

Nicole looked up at him one last time as he brushed at a smudge on her face, trying to decide if she could trust him, knowing she didn't have much choice. She couldn't tell anything. His face could have been made of marble for all the emotion it showed. Nicole unwillingly drifted to sleep and dreamed that Sutherland said in disbelief, *"Her eyes are blue."*

*   *   *

Derek didn't make as large a dent in his bottle as he'd intended while he sat and watched over the girl curled in his bed. He'd definitely not predicted his first night with her to be like this. Usually he was impatient to bed a woman and get her gone, but she had been afraid and possibly hurt. Still, he wasn't resigned to having her sleep here the whole night.

He was, he had to admit, proud that tonight he'd overcome his natural selfishness in order to do something considerate. Why he was being so charitable to a prostitute, he had no idea. It must have been the liquor affecting his brain, because the girl could be prickly and rude, and he certainly did not get involved with women for more than purely physical reasons.

That's just what he needed to be doing, taking on the troubles of a young prostitute. As if he didn't have enough weight on his shoulders.

Even more remarkable, he was experiencing the wholly unaccustomed feeling of protectiveness. He wanted to kill the two who'd chased her. She'd put up a good fight, which was most likely why she'd survived. Hell, the little spitfire had actually drawn blood from someone.

The idea that she was a fighter intrigued him, probably because he had let go of so much so easily.

Oddly, she hadn't behaved like a prostitute. No innuendos gone stale from overuse or practiced pouty smiles. And only minutes after she'd kissed him and made him want her with a surprising ferocity, she'd had to drag her feet back into his cabin. He'd automatically reached for a drink because she'd disconcerted him. A slip of a girl likely a decade younger had made him ill at ease on his own ship.

Derek didn't know why she didn't practice her wiles on

him, wiles he would have known how to proceed with. This girl had only looked at him with a tilted head and open curiosity, until her eyelids slid over those dark eyes, blue eyes, as she began to fade.

He'd almost experienced relief when she'd passed out. Yet that was crazy. If he understood one thing on this bizarre night, it was that he wanted to sink into her lithe body. Sink into her until she eased the ache her abandoned response had created. Damn, how she'd responded to him.

Turning his mind from that gripping image, he took a long pull of drink. The way things were going now, she'd have to spend the night in his bed. He grimaced at the thought. With him, that just wasn't done. Had never been done, in fact.

He reached over to shake her awake, but his hand stilled on her shoulder. She lay like the dead, as she had for hours. Her silky skin shone white as porcelain except for the pale lavender rings under the sweep of her lashes. But if he didn't wake her, where the hell was he supposed to sleep?

For the space of several minutes, he stared down at the girl. It wouldn't make a difference if he slept with her for the few hours left till dawn. It wasn't a monumental thing, damn it!

Decided, he slipped off his boots and clothes and slid in next to her. Her body burned like a little furnace in the bed, and being near her warmth was comfortable. Seemingly of its own volition, his arm covered her waist and brought her to him.

Derek was aware that he protected her, and on some hidden plane he felt good and strong, if only for a few hours. He pulled her small body closer still and breathed in the soft scent of her hair.

He was, though not completely—never completely—

pleased. Until he thought of the strange moment of hesitation he'd just had as he stripped off his clothes. It certainly wasn't modesty, but for some reason he had a fleeting impression that his state of undress would make her uneasy. Ridiculous, of course, since she'd probably spent most of her nights like this with dozens of different men.

His last thought before drifting to sleep was how much that fact bothered him.

When a soft ray of light flitted through the window and warmed her face, Nicole woke in a dismayed flash. Her rapidly blinking eyes spied a tanned arm sprinkled with golden-tipped black hair wrapped around her.

Captain Sutherland held her in his bed.

She slowly twisted her head back. In sleep, his face was softened, though certainly not relieved of the dark weariness that had marked it the two previous nights. She felt a tug of emotion, a pull toward him that differed from the physical attraction that had surfaced so powerfully before.

She made herself look away and took a mental inventory of her body, concluding that most of her clothes were on. Her shirt, her pants—her eyes widened and the blood rushed to her face. Sutherland pressed against her backside. At least, a very hard part of him did. It would appear that although she was clothed, he certainly had nothing to . . . restrain him.

Captain Sutherland held her in his bed with no clothes on.

Alarm quaked through her. Last night she'd been so disoriented. She'd welcomed his advances mainly because she was glad to be alive and safe. Right? So what would she do now if he awoke and touched her breasts again? If he pulled her down next to his unclothed, aroused body?

Astonished by her own answer, she understood that she could not remain with him any longer.

Besides, her father was no doubt searching for her even now, barking at people who hadn't seen her, shaking those who might have. Somehow she had to get out of this position and back to her ship. But his arm was unwieldy, anchoring her to him as if he'd never let go. Slowly, she pried it off her torso, not daring to breathe the whole time it took to lower it gently to the bed.

She grinned in relief, then jumped at the sound of his voice, deep and gravelly with sleep as he mumbled something from his dreams. After what seemed like eternity, his breathing deepened again, and she risked slipping to the floor.

Her whole body was stiff and unmanageable as she walked, but she finally found her stockings, still wet, so she drew her boots on untied over her enormous borrowed socks.

Fully dressed, she wobbled away from Sutherland, away from the compulsion to slide in next to him and have him wrap his warm arms around her again.

Before she made it to the door, her eyes leveled on his desk. The calculations. Could she leave them as they were? Although Sutherland could have done anything he wanted to her last night, he hadn't hurt her. No, he'd saved her life.

As swiftly as she could, she padded over and ran through the numbers again. Finishing in very little time, she finally walked out of his cabin and past Sutherland's openly curious crew.

As soon as she stepped off the *Southern Cross,* one of her father's search parties spotted her. As they pulled her away, the lot of them, just primed for a fight, threw aggressive remarks and lewd gestures at the *Southern Cross*'s crew. Not even half an hour later, they'd ferried her to her father, along with the story of her night's accommodations. He was livid, and he wasn't the only one, if the crew's behavior was any indication.

When her father finally cleared the nosy crew out of the chart room, he had his temper under control, at least regarding her. "I know you're tired," he began with a grimace, obviously in response to her drained face, "but I need to find out what the hell happened last night."

"I am beyond tired—"

"Please, I need to know who did this to you before you go rest."

Nicole sighed, but then smelling the pervasive scent of coffee, a tinge burned, she relented. They'd been up all night looking for her. She tried to limit her story to just the attack, focusing her tale on that part, but she couldn't steer him from the subject of Sutherland.

Nicole hoped to get a reprieve when Chancey, the big, blustering Irishman who was like her second father, ambled into the room. She gave him a beseeching glance as he dropped his immense frame in a chair behind his captain in an unconscious display of added authority.

Cornered like that, she decided to make it sound as if she'd sought Sutherland's help in absolute desperation. If not for him, she stressed, she wouldn't be here this morning—and he had not compromised her in any way. But her father seemed concerned only with the fact that she had spent the whole night on his ship. She cringed each time his hands clenched as he strode around the cabin.

"Christ, what were you thinking, going to his ship like that?" Lassiter demanded again.

Nicole imagined what he'd do if told she didn't have any say in the matter. She answered honestly, "I was terrified those two men would catch up to me. I thought I'd be safe with Sutherland."

"I can certainly think of one thing that isn't safe with a man like him," he half-muttered, slanting Chancey a knowing look. The man responded by crossing his thick arms over his chest and grunting in agreement.

"But considering the nature of the attack," Lassiter continued, "you were probably better off doing what you did. Still, didn't you wonder *why* he would help you? The man's a reprobate—hardly a knight in shining armor."

"I know, and I'll not make the same mistake again," she promised, her words a mix of raspy exasperation.

"I can't believe you stayed with him overnight," he said to himself, and turned to her, "Are you certain you weren't compromised?"

Unbelievable. Nicole glared at him. "For the last time, Father, I was not compromised and Sutherland didn't harm me." When he looked to be about to say more on the subject, she asked, "What I want to know is, after last night, with those men damaging the ship . . . we're targeted now?"

He paused, as if deciding whether he'd allow her to change the subject. Then, nodding gravely, he answered, "They'd been going to work on the *Bella Nicola* before you surprised them. But those two were just lackeys to some one directing the damage."

Her father sat down on the edge of his seat, though he would just get up in seconds anyway. "The contact I met last night wouldn't give me names, but he made it sound as if the leader was a man of some importance. Possibly a peer. He also assured me that I am a prime target. Chancey and I have narrowed the suspects down to a handful of men, but I never expected violence like this out of any of them."

She looked up as a thought occurred to her. "What happened to the guards?"

"They were knocked out. Believe it or not, they look worse than you do." Lassiter sprang out of his seat and began pacing again. "They feel horrible about what happened."

She nodded absently, becoming lost in her own thoughts.

"Nicole, you're not thinking about Sutherland?"

She jerked her head up, her face heating in a guilty flush.

He sat down again, heavily this time, as he opened his mouth to speak and then closed it. He ran a hand over his face before explaining in halting tones, "Sutherland is the worst sort of man. I understand you were scared—you had a hell of a night—but from now on you have to stay away from men like that. You're not a little girl anymore."

"Of course, Father."

Lassiter took a deep breath and rose to walk over to her. He placed his hand on her head and spoke in a tone others might think was calm, but really was only camouflaging his emotions. "Now, get some sleep. I've got half the crew guarding your cabin, including Chancey, so don't worry that those men will come back."

Because he didn't have any viable leads into who'd hired the thugs, she didn't doubt he'd go and deal with Sutherland soon. She rose and faced him, trying to keep the concern out of her eyes. "What will you do to him?"

Her father acted as though he didn't understand what she meant, but when she frowned up at him, his expression changed until he smiled benignly down at her. "Nic, I'll simply talk to him and make sure he understands he shouldn't bring young ladies like yourself to his ship." The smile vanished as if never there. "And that there will be . . . repercussions if he ever comes near you again."

As he stormed out of the cabin, she thought of all he'd said. She wasn't stupid. Her father's idea of "talking" with Sutherland meant insulting him between punches. He was a hotheaded man, her father, and she fretted that Sutherland would hurt him. Whether anyone wanted to admit it or not, he'd saved her life last night, and she didn't want him hurt either. Unfortunately for her father, Nicole didn't believe that to be the likeliest scenario.

There'd be no rest today, she thought as Chancey got up to cluck over her, to convince himself that she was all right. His concern was so obvious, the creases in his leathery face deepening, that she attempted a reassuring smile. He knew her well enough to know it was forced, but she was nervous now and would remain so until her father returned. Her mind drifted as she pictured what might happen—until she became aware of Chancey staring at her feet, at the huge socks spilling out of her stuffed boots.

"Good God, Nic! Whose socks have ye?"

Chapter 5

$\mathcal{D}$erek stepped across the threshold of the Mermaid and, as he had hundreds of times before in places just like this, made his way up to the bar.

The barmaid didn't have to ask what he wanted. "Well, 'ow do, luv?" she said with an aggressive wink before setting a mug and a corked bottle of whiskey in front of him. He pushed down a nagging irritation that not only had the woman recognized him and his drink, even though he could swear he'd never seen her in his life, she'd also easily assumed he would get falling-down drunk. Hell, why shouldn't she?

He looked over his shoulder around the lively room. For the past four years, when not at sea, he'd usually end up in one of these waterfront holes impotently railing against fate.

Turning to give the barmaid a wilting look, he slapped down some coin. He grabbed the dully clinking bottle and mug and made his way through the crowd. As was his habit, he found a corner table where he had an unblocked view of the door, and poured a drink. Once again, he thought of his prostitute.

This morning he'd awakened to a feeling that something was not right. But he was hung over, it was daylight, and he was alone in his own bed. Everything was as usual. Then the events of the night had rushed into his foggy brain.

The girl had slept with him the whole night. He was sure of it. When he woke, he could smell her sweet scent and see the indentation she'd made in his pillow. But she'd disappeared. He told himself he should be glad that there'd been no difficulty in getting rid of her.

Most of his crew had been on deck when a party of sailors retrieved her. A few thought they recognized the men as Lassiter's. The thought of him ordering a search for her was too much. And she really shouldn't have left without a word to him. Admitting that he'd done the same for all of his adult life didn't make him feel any better.

Of course, he had yet to bed her, and he'd never found out who'd chased her. He'd had a good idea that she would only lie, which would have infuriated him. So he'd decided to let it go until after he'd had her. Now he struggled with the idea of who would want to hurt her.

And just how involved was she with Lassiter?

Worse, he didn't know how to find her again. He hoped she'd return here tonight.

Derek looked down at his drink and shook his head. There was one other thing he couldn't get over, one thing that baffled him more than all the other questions swirling around her. He'd woken up to find that she'd crossed out his navigation numbers and replaced them with her own calculations. Correct calculations.

He pictured the graceful, feminine script, and winced when he remembered the patronizing tone he'd taken with her the night before. How the hell had she mastered navigation? It was a coveted knowledge that not just any sailor learned, and captains guarded it like a secret handshake. When the crew no longer depended on their captain to guide the ship, they could mutiny and dispose of him. Knowing this elite skill meant power, and he'd never met a woman who'd garnered it.

He pondered this question and poured another generous draught from the bottle. He'd wait here until she returned. It was the best he could come up with. Faces changed throughout the night before blending all together as one bottle became two.

Grant Sutherland's hope that his brother would not be among the patrons of the Mermaid, for bloody sakes, died when he found Derek ensconced at a corner table. Derek saw him immediately and glowered. Grant pushed through a crowd of doxies, his eyes widening when a couple pinched him, and joined him anyway.

"I was hoping I wouldn't find you here."

"Likewise."

Grant gave him a sardonic smile. "I wouldn't have come here, but something's come up."

"Handle it." Derek drank, not looking at Grant. "You always do."

"Not this time. This is none of my affair."

Derek turned to him then, not hiding his surprise. "Anything concerning me concerns you. You run the estates. You own half of Peregrine—"

"Lydia's looking for you."

Derek set down his mug. Damn it, Grant had wanted to tell him over coffee, not spring it on him amid the commotion of this tap house.

"What'd she want?"

"She—" Just then a man went flying over a neighboring table. Ale sloshed high and splatted, barely missing Grant. "That's it." He rose, grabbed Derek's arm, and pulled. "We'll talk about this on the way home."

Derek yanked his arm away. "I'm not leaving."

"Why the hell not? You haven't tried enough to kill yourself tonight?"

"I'm looking for a . . . woman."

Grant made a sound of disgust. "As much as it pains me to say this"—his gaze swept the room—"couldn't you have found one among the, if not clean, at least the *varied* assortment here?"

"No, she's not here yet."

Grant sat back down. "Who is *she?*"

"Redhead. Beautiful."

"Or so says the liquor." Grant flicked an empty, overturned bottle and sent it spinning on the table.

Derek shook his head. "I was sober."

"I wasn't aware you still did sobriety." At Derek's scowl, Grant said, "Well, you're not now. What do you think you could do if you found this girl again? Drink her under the table?"

Derek almost chuckled. "I'm fine."

"Then stand up."

"I will not—"

"Humor me." Grant rarely brought up the fact that he managed all of Derek's estates and investments. But all that was about to change, and Derek would find out soon enough. Grant pinned his brother with a look. "It's the least you could do."

Derek cursed and stood. And swayed.

Grant exhaled loudly. Men as big as Derek presented a hazard when drunk. Without asking, Grant grabbed Derek's shoulder and half-tossed, half-supported him out of the tavern and into a hackney.

"I left with you," Derek began as the horses' hooves clacked along the street, "now tell me what Lydia wanted."

"Money."

He pinched the bridge of his nose. "Why does that not surprise me?"

Grant wanted—needed—to tell Derek about his recent decision. He needed to tell him that he was tired of being chained to Derek's estates. While Grant was making certain Derek didn't lose everything, he himself had lost four years.

Grant was done.

But Derek looked exhausted, beaten, worse than Grant had ever seen him. Christ, he hated to see his brother like this. It wasn't in his nature to kick someone when he was down. Yet when wasn't Derek down?

When they arrived at the town house, Grant helped Derek, still insisting he was "not bloody drunk," to his room. Grant stood in the doorway, alternately amused and cringing as Derek wrestled off his boots. When Derek finally lay on the counterpane, Grant found a blanket and tossed it to him. "Good night, Derek. We'll figure this out in the morning."

As Grant shut the door, he heard Derek mumble, "Thanks. For the help."

Grant opened his mouth to answer "Anytime," but knew that was no longer true.

*   *   *

Derek woke sometime during the night. His head pounded, seeming to throb in unison with the ticking wall clock. He squinted at it. Three in the morning. Hung over, and it wasn't even dawn.

He rose in stages and lurched to the washstand. Splashing cool water on his face didn't help his head. Derek knew of only one thing that would. He started toward his study to find a bottle there, but hesitated. He didn't want Grant to wake up and see that he couldn't make it through the night without a drink. Especially not after Grant had had to peel him out of the Mermaid.

But he didn't want to stay here. He told himself it was just because he didn't sleep well off the ship. But the truth was, he didn't sleep well there either. Except for last night. His eyes opened a touch wider. He'd return to the ship to sleep, but on the way there he'd stop at the Mermaid, take one last look for the girl, and a drink for the road. Hell, he'd pay the girl simply to sleep on his ship again.

His plan set, he orchestrated dressing so that he didn't have to move quickly or lean over too far. As he walked out the front door, the thought of how much he'd enjoyed the night before made his steps brisk.

But in the back of his mind, he felt foolish for going back out. For using the girl as an excuse to go get a drink, or for using the drink as an excuse to go get the girl.

A sense of foreboding settled over him. Yet he continued, ignoring his conviction that the night would most likely not improve.

The bloody night did not improve.

Derek's only warning that he was about to be rushed was Jason Lassiter bellowing, "I'm going to kill you,

Sutherland!" He whirled around and stumbled, effectively ducking under Lassiter's meaty fist.

The bastard had blindsided him!

Lassiter roared and swung again, narrowly missing Derek's averted chin.

When Lassiter yanked off his coat, the crowd in the Mermaid retreated evenly. "What were you thinking when you kept her for the night?"

So this was about the girl.

"You must've known I'd kill you for it!"

Not that they needed an excuse to fight.

Lassiter lunged for Derek, who barely sidestepped him. If the bastard wanted a dirty fight, he'd oblige. He drew back and kidney-punched Lassiter before he could turn.

His hands clenched at the thought of Lassiter obviously being more than a little involved with the girl. From the look of him, you'd think he really cared about her. The thought filled him with rage. Of all the men in the world she could choose as a bloody protector, why Lassiter? He decided then that he wanted to provoke the older man, wanted to fight him.

When Lassiter whirled around, Derek said, "I'm sure whoever she is, she isn't worth the trip down here."

Lassiter's face twisted in fury. *"I'm going to tear you apart!"*

"Looking forward to your attempt."

When Lassiter launched another swing, Derek ducked and jabbed, landing a pounding blow to Lassiter's chest.

The man's hands flew to his chest and he wheezed frantically, but Derek knew he'd only bought time with a man that big.

This shouldn't even be a contest. But he'd never fought an opponent so livid. Although it didn't overly concern

Derek, that rage could give Lassiter added strength and deaden his pain. It would be a good fight. He welcomed it.

And it was due.

Lassiter shook his head forcefully, as if to shake the hit away, then raised his fists once more.

Derek ignored the circle of screaming patrons crowding around them in a frenzy and focused on dodging Lassiter's colossal swings. He succeeded twice. The third smashed into his face. Derek fingered the trickle of blood trailing down his cheek.

Then he smiled.

Wagers flew as everyone cheered wildly for the two captains, rivals for years, to finally battle it out.

"You can't be serious!" Nicole shrieked, having shot up from lying over her desk and now fully awake. "What do you mean, Father's in jail?"

"Got thrown in," Chancey supplied by way of explanation. "Wouldn't o' woke ye, but he don't have enough blunt in the till to cover bail." He frowned. "Don't have any blunt."

Nicole shook her head. "I spent all my money on the trip here. But I can sell some things," she added hopefully.

"That'll take time. I'll go see what he wants to do."

"I'm going with you."

Chancey studied her, and he couldn't mistake her resolve. After a moment he said with great reluctance, "If ye want to see him, get yerself dressed and meet me topside."

When he turned to go, she grabbed his arm, "Is he hurt?"

"Nothin' that won't heal. Now, git."

Darting to her sea chest, she haphazardly dragged on

clothes. She was making a hasty attempt at knotting her hair when she met Chancey on deck.

Nicole had been certain there would be a fight. She'd been terrified that Sutherland would be provoked to hurt her father, all because of her.

She'd never imagined jail.

Nicole followed Chancey blindly into the waning night, still unrecovered from her shock. They moved swiftly, and not many minutes later they arrived at the local constabulary. When she walked through the beveled double doors and into the entrance hall, the sun was just rising.

The inside was not dank and cobweb-ridden as she'd envisioned, and for that she was glad. In fact, the russet shutters outside were open to the sun's indifferent reach, and dawn streaked in to light the little dust in the air. The wooden floors were pitted but clean. All the same, she wouldn't have cared if this were a manor house. It was depressing to think of her father being kept here.

She pulled her shoulders back and lifted her chin, preparing to face him with a cheery demeanor. Then she turned the corner, and her face fell.

Instead of her father, she locked eyes with Sutherland.

"Do you want to press charges, milord?"

Derek was undecided. A part of him argued that the fight had been fair, and if he'd been released simply because of his title, then Lassiter should be free to go also.

Then he recalled how they'd gotten to this place. When the watchmen finally dragged him and Lassiter apart and out of the tavern, Derek had said, "You'll want to release me now—I'm the Earl of Stanhope." The officers had looked at him with wide, alarmed eyes. They hadn't exactly been gentle with their two prisoners.

"It's true," Lassiter had spoken up, surprising Derek, until he added, "and I'm the president of the United States."

Derek had ignored him and turned to the closest watchman. "I am Derek Sutherland, sixth earl of Stanhope. You are aware of what would happen to you if you jail me."

"I can't believe you're pulling the 'earl' stunt again."

Derek only smiled at Lassiter. "Perhaps I'll go and see to our mutual friend while you're engaged with the constable."

Immediately, Lassiter had shut up and remained silent during the time it took to convince all involved that Derek was, in fact, an earl. Suddenly the officers weren't concerned about a raging public fight that destroyed the tavern that housed it. They were outraged that an American had attacked a member of the nobility on English soil.

Now the constable wanted him to make a decision. Derek wanted to teach the cur a lesson, but . . .

At the sound of voices in the anteroom, he turned slowly and, he could admit, with some pain. He dimmed a look of disbelief when the reason for the fight tumbled into the hall, followed by a behemoth of a man right at her heels.

Her hair was falling out of its loose knot atop her head, and her cheeks were pinkened. Obviously she'd just dressed and raced down here. She was the type of woman, he thought unexpectedly, who looked beautiful when she first awoke.

She took in a sharp little breath when she saw him standing next to the constable, but aside from her slight hesitation, there was no semblance of acknowledgment. She nodded to the man with her, who stayed behind as she walked right past Derek to go to Lassiter. The rejection was like a punch in the gut, only this bothered him much worse than the blows he'd sustained earlier in the night. In her mind, he didn't warrant even a backward glance. So much for saving her.

What could she possibly see in that American bastard? He supposed women might find the insufferable Yank not absolutely unappealing, but the man was old enough to be her father. Though if Derek were honest, he should wonder what a woman like that would see in himself. He scared many women. It wasn't intentional. Some of it was due to his size, and probably a lot more to his attitude and reputation.

But she hadn't been afraid of him the night before.

Derek stood motionless, ignoring the constable and the man planted behind him. He watched her walk down the wide corridor, slim shoulders back and heels clicking lightly along, until she escaped his vision. Then he heard her gasp. Probably, he thought with a smirk, because she'd seen all the damage he'd done to Lassiter's face. When a soft sniffle followed, his thoughts sobered.

What would it be like to have a woman feel his pain, to be so close that if he hurt, she hurt, too? To have a woman care for him enough to run anxiously to a jail before dawn just to be with him? He'd always known that something vital was missing in his life, but as he stood in that cold jail, his face beaten not quite as much as that bastard's in the cell, the lack grew keen.

There was a dull scrape across the floor as she moved a chair. Backing up a step, Derek could see her sitting before Lassiter's cell. The hefty man behind him noticed his interest and made a growling noise, but Derek kept watching her. Even knowing she'd made her choice, he was enthralled with her dainty but purposeful movements. She was so intent on her protector, invisible to Derek in his cell, she seemed not to notice him staring.

She put her hands over her eyes, and Derek thought with dread that she would cry. He wasn't the type of man who was affected by a woman's tears. His mother's never moved him, nor had Lydia's the last time she'd come to him for money. But here tonight, he didn't know what he'd do if the girl wept.

Thankfully, she didn't. She dropped her small hands to her lap and knotted her fingers before she sighed sadly, "Oh, Father."

Father.

The first woman he'd truly felt something with . . . was *Lassiter's daughter.*

Bloody, bloody hell.

Unfortunately, it made sense. He hadn't been able to find her at the Mermaid, and she hadn't looked or acted like a prostitute that night. Well, she did kiss like a talented courtesan and responded like a wanton. But her bearing and accent were far from a doxy's. Now he didn't know if he should be delighted that she wasn't a whore or cringe knowing that she was related to Lassiter.

"We'll arrange for bail and have you out of here *today,*" she said to her father in a confident tone.

"How will you raise the money?" Lassiter asked slowly.

She said nothing, only stared at the ceiling, the wall, straight past Derek in the doorway, back to the ceiling.

It was as if Derek could see the sudden realization washing over Lassiter's face, because after a pause, the man shouted, "Oh, no, Nicole. I forbid it! There is no way I'll allow you to do this for me. I'd rather rot in here than take her money. If you go to her, you'll always owe her and she'll tear you apart."

Nicole's her real name? I knew she wasn't a Christina.

"Father, it's the only way—the race is in four, no, only three days now."

"No! That's final. For once in your life, you will do as I tell you—my God, when you first arrived, you certainly didn't feel this way."

Nicole took a deep breath and said in a wistful tone, "No, but I suppose fate's trying to tell me that we can't always get what we want."

Lassiter was silent. Finally he said, "I won't be beholden to that woman even if you've changed your mind."

She acted as if she hadn't heard him. "The sooner I go, the sooner we can get you out of here." She rose calmly to depart, leaving Lassiter choking on his myriad, unheeded commands.

Derek almost smiled when, on her way out, she called over her shoulder, "Oh hush, Father! My mind's made up."

When she reached Derek, she paused and looked up to him, her face grave. She probably thought this was all his doing. He felt a flush of guilt because, if she hadn't arrived when she did, it would have been.

"Listen, I can help you," he said, not caring if Lassiter heard him.

He did. "Shut up, Sutherland!"

"Go to hell, Lassiter," Derek barked before turning back to hear her response.

"Haven't you done enough?" she asked, her eyes laced with sadness as she turned to go. Derek was right behind her, but the big man who'd been waiting stepped in front of him.

"Not unless ye'll be wantin' another fight," he warned as he backed out the door.

*   *   *

It rained, the bone-chilling, lingering rain that always reminded Nicole of her last stay in this awful land. She'd been five years old. Her father was broken, her mother dead. Somehow he'd managed to get them to London from the South American port where Laurel Lassiter passed away. He would tell his mother-in-law in person that her daughter had died.

A week after the dowager learned of Laurel's death, she'd reemerged from her room as forbidding as ever. Her blond, gray-laced hair was perfectly coifed, her spine rigid. Only she looked much, much older and was clothed in black. She demanded to see Lassiter, and Nicole had been sent outside to play. But as usual, she couldn't get warm, so with frozen feet and hands she'd sneaked back into the house. She stopped outside the door to the sitting room and peeked in when she heard them talking about her.

"She'll never marry," her grandmother had predicted, her oddly dark, cold eyes taking in Nicole's poor father, her disgust undisguised. He was quiet before her.

"If you take Nicole back on that cursed ship with all those filthy sailors, you can assure yourself that by the time she's to find a husband, a husband good enough for her station, her reputation will be so shredded that no member of the nobility will want her. Not to mention the fact that she has already turned into a little savage."

Lassiter had looked as if he might argue—Nicole remembered wanting him to—but he seemed to draw deep from some inner well of patience. "I can't let her go just yet," he said, his voice toneless. "She is all I have left of Laurel. I have to keep her with me."

"Selfish as always, I see." They both turned toward the portrait of her mother above the fireplace. Laurel had been a lovely, fair-haired young woman. In the painting, she would look forever merry, as if she'd just been told something humorous and couldn't be trusted not to erupt into peals of laughter at any moment. The skilled artist had captured that happiness beautifully . . . as well as the hint of stubbornness in her mien.

"Why she ever gave up all this"—the dowager waved a hand to indicate her opulent town residence—"I will never understand." Then to herself, she added in a low voice, "The threats . . . the pleading . . . all useless once that girl made up her mind to be with you."

She rose in her extravagantly wrought day-dress to move toward a window, the rich satin gown making a muted, rustling sound with each step. Turning on him, she accused, "Staying in England wasn't good enough for you, so you dragged my poor daughter all over the world, never slowing your pace."

Nicole had watched, fascinated, as pale sunlight caught the few jewels that adorned her grandmother, throwing tiny, brightly colored prisms on the papered walls.

"And now she is . . . gone. But Laurel did as *you* wished." She returned to her ornate desk, her movements slow and dignified.

"Damn it, you know that she loved sailing with me," her father bit out, his voice hoarse. "She craved that excitement and she never regretted the life we lived . . . even in the end."

Her grandmother narrowed her eyes shrewdly. "How can you be sure the same thing won't happen to the girl? What if she were to die—"

He'd shot out of his chair to loom over her desk, his large hands knotted into fists. "You listen to me—I will *never* let anything happen to her. Do you understand me? She is a strong child, raised at sea. I will always protect her."

"I understand that you *think* you will." She looked up at him, unbowed even by the fearsome picture he presented. "But even if she were to live to be ninety," she continued, "Nicole will be doomed to spinsterhood, because she must marry a title before I'll give her Laurel's estate. And titled men *do not* marry female sailors. And were you to disregard her inheritance and think to marry her elsewhere, perhaps to some oafish American such as yourself, who will have her? She'll be more man than woman, with no grace, without the charms or the dowry to attract a decent husband."

She shook her head as if revolted at the image. "She'll be aged before her time with sun- and wind-roughened skin and hands. Do you think society will smile on such a one as she? No!" she cried as her flat palm slapped the desk, her heavy rings rapping. "Nicole will be alone because *you* will not do the right thing now."

"What would you have me do?" he asked, waving an arm. "I can't give her up, so what do you suggest?"

She leaned forward slowly and pinned him with her dark eyes. "You will send her to me on her twelfth birthday, and not a day later. She must come to me before she becomes a woman so that I will have time to undo all that you"—she looked him up and down with a sneer—"and your degenerate life have done to her. I will prepare her to assume her birthright as a leader of the nobility and marry accordingly."

Her father sank back down and exhaled slowly. "Very well. I'll give her to you then, but you must promise to marry her to a good man."

"Of course, you fool! If you do as you're bidden."

Neither of them knew Nicole was just outside the door. Nor did they know that from as early as Nicole could remember, her mother had instilled in her a powerful life-long belief. Just as Laurel had been, Nicole must be prepared to fight for control of her own destiny.

Nicole had done the best she could. When her father ordered her to wear a hat and gloves every second she was outside, she minded him. She understood his fierce over-protectiveness and obeyed his fear-driven demand that she learn navigation in case an accident befell him at sea. Learning language after language, having to beg to get the crew to teach her even the mildest of curses—she accepted all that because she was otherwise free. And when the time came for her to leave, she'd had years to plan.

She'd been about to turn twelve when Lassiter declared she was to go to England and live with her grandmother. Nicole wasn't wholly proud of what she'd done, but she'd been desperate. "Very well, Father," she'd conceded with a sniff. "I'll do as you say. But you must know that my only worry is that we would be so far apart. What would happen if you got sick? It might take me *months and months* to find out. I wouldn't be there to take care of you. And if something were to happen to me, if I got sick, or hurt, you might not be there. . . ."

That had taken care of any nonsensical talk about finishing school for about five years.

Up until this rainy night, Nicole had thought she'd done so well—she'd sailed continuously for eighteen of her twenty years and had seen the world. But as she gazed out at the docks, oily from the rain, she wondered if it wasn't all just a matter of time—if she was fooling herself by believing she had power over her own fate. She had been, Nicole decided, and resigned herself to giving up that fight.

Just not quite yet.

*   *   *

When Nicole arrived at the vast Atworth House after nearly sixteen years, she was unexpectedly composed, although the house before her was meant to be daunting. Rich marble steps led to a bold projecting entranceway, flanked by towering scroll-like columns. The wings on each side recessed from the front in too-perfect symmetry. Yet a lush cold-weather garden battled the severe effect by subtly beckoning.

Although she associated this place with painful memories, she made herself remember that her mother had spent much of her youth in this home. Had probably laughed upon these very stairs. She smiled softly at the thought. She was smiling when Chapman, the elderly butler she fondly remembered from her sole visit here, answered the door, and even when he showed her to the salon. Her grandmother awaited her there, sitting beneath a large Palladian window that dominated the room and lit her tasteful furnishings becomingly. It also highlighted her pinched face.

"Good morning, Grandmother," Nicole intoned politely as she trudged over the dense Brussels rug to face the woman. The dowager was still soberly dressed in black, her collar choking. Unhappiness limned her features. Two pug dogs had risen at Nicole's arrival and now sauntered back to their place—not at her grandmother's feet, but under a table across the room. *Smart pugs,* she thought.

"You're late," the dowager snapped, not even asking her to sit.

Nicole had chosen to wear one of the day-dresses her grandmother had sent to her school, hoping to soften the old bird, but obviously it'd take more than a polished appearance to get her within the bounds of civility.

Nothing new there. It was as if her grandmother, and this whole house, had been frozen from the time Nicole left until this return.

"I am indeed late," she responded sweetly, bravely taking a seat across from her.

"Eight years late!" The dowager studied her with a disapproving expression.

Nicole comprehended then that the woman before her, whose dark eyes were so oddly like hers, would make her crawl across glass to get money for her father. But this race would decide their future, so she'd do what she must. "I am very pleased to be able to visit with you—"

"Balderdash! Cut through the frippery, girl, and tell me what you want."

Chapter 6

*F*rom atop his mount, Derek watched Nicole Lassiter absently wind through people on the street. She clutched her cloak tighter to her neck and hiked her thick navy scarf up to her chin to battle the crisp wind whisking over the Thames. Without seeming to notice, she sidestepped a loud man hawking steaming meat pies and an intense young woman imploring her to buy a secondhand coat.

He caught glimpses of her face, and her sad expression made him react with a bothersome intensity. He gathered the reason for her mood, of course. She was walking from the direction of the jail and had probably just learned that her father's bail had been denied.

Derek had learned this information himself just hours earlier. He'd left Lassiter to stew for the morning but had returned to the constabulary to drop the charges. The constable, a different man from the night before, told him firmly that Lassiter, as an American, would have to be formally arraigned for the crime of assault and battery. Even though Derek did not want to press the charges made against Lassiter, the man told him that they had evidence against him of other crimes and expected him to be jailed for another two weeks. Derek had scrutinized the man and come away with the strong belief that he was lying.

Evidently Lassiter had made some very serious enemies in London, which was to be expected considering the man. But it appeared that Derek had given them the perfect weapon against the American.

Damn it, he didn't want to think that his strongest competition would be unable to race because Derek had trifled with his daughter. How had he ever mistaken her for a whore in the first place? And recalling the snide comments he'd made just before the fight to Lassiter about his *daughter*, well, he could understand why the man had gone mad.

It would gall Derek if he won knowing it was over lesser competition; so even though it was unpalatable to aid Lassiter in any way, he'd nevertheless offered very healthy bribes to have him freed. But with no success. Even with Derek's clout and money, the official never wavered, which led him to believe that somebody very high up had decided Lassiter would stay in jail.

The situation wasn't fair, and though Derek knew well that life rarely was, he wanted to help Nicole. He also found it strangely important that she not think he had something to do with this.

Prodding his horse forward, he maneuvered to flank her and cleared his throat, but she was lost in thought and continued walking. He noted with satisfaction that her troubled expression was rapidly dimming, replaced by one that could only be termed mutinous.

"Nicole," he called. She jumped, startled at the sound of his voice.

"Captain Sutherland!"

He touched the rim of his hat in greeting.

She flushed, and he found himself enjoying the look of her finely boned face and the way the blue scarf accented her eyes—until she turned abruptly in another direction.

Derek reined his mount around and was right beside her. "Nicole," he began in a low voice, "I dropped the charges against your father. I have nothing to do with his being held."

She froze.

Facing him again, she came closer, eyes narrowed as she studied him.

"I also know your father's bail was denied."

She reached out and stroked his horse's muzzle in what was probably an unconscious gesture. He liked seeing her small, gloved hand against the horse's black coat.

"How could you know that?"

"I think I might have information that could help you," he said, glancing around.

She leaned forward and raised her eyebrows.

"Not here, Nicole," he said with a patronizing smile. "You'll have to come to my ship if you want to learn more."

He expected her to say something cutting. She certainly looked like she would. Instead, she paused, erased her irritated look, and cast him a wide smile brimming with charm and false pleasure. "Fine. My large friend—you know, the one from this morning—and I can come around nine or so—"

His lips turned up in an indulgent expression. "Just you."

"Well, of course I won't—"

"You will, Nicole, because the curiosity will torment you."

He left her alone in the street, a baffled look on her face that was probably similar to his own. When she'd smiled before, a great change came over her face. He'd seen it the first night on his ship, but hadn't fully appreciated the effect. Now, in the daylight with her glossy hair shining around her face, all her unique features teamed up on him with that smile.

If the wind had blown at that moment, he'd have fallen off his horse.

She wouldn't go, Nicole told herself for the hundredth time. She knew better than to return to Sutherland's ship. So why was she already contriving a plan to get Chancey away for the night? As if to punctuate her guilty thoughts, he walked into the salon.

"How was it with yer gram?" he asked as he took off his coat and slumped in a large, rough-hewn chair. He'd been making all the last-minute preparations by himself, and his already wizened face bagged with exhaustion.

"She wasn't that bad," Nicole said, but then amended, "Well, she was fairly bad. But not as I've feared all these years. Of course, she bad-mouthed Father for three hours, cackled about his incarceration, and derided my manners. But she did gruffly tell me wonderful stories about Mama."

"I'm glad for that, at least. I didn't like ye goin' against yer father to go there, but it was time." He pulled out his pipe and tobacco. "Did she give ye the blunt?"

"On the condition that I marry a man of her choosing within a year, but yes, she did." She sank down in a chair beside him and briefly closed her eyes. "I tried for bail. But it was denied."

Chancey didn't hide his disbelief. "*Fer what?*"

"They told me a lot of lies about other crimes he's allegedly committed. Added on some nonsense about citizens from other countries being detained much longer."

"Well, ain't this crackin' up to be a bad day."

"What else happened?"

"Clankson came by lookin' for yer pa."

"Clankson of Clankson Emporiums?"

"That's the one. Seems he got caught up with the rest o' London. He's bettin' the race with the *Bella Nicola* to win. Bettin' heavy. And if Jason don't win, Clankson's pullin' his accounts."

Nicole's breath whistled out. Clankson Emporiums constituted half their business. "If he pulls out, our company is dead in the water." She gave a shaky laugh that held no humor. "And that would be *literally*."

She'd known how important a win would be, but until now she'd had no idea that their very existence depended on this race. Everything her father owned was leveraged to the penny, and if Clankson pulled his accounts, the shipping line would collapse like a house made of cards. And considering how Nicole's mother had died, her grandmother wouldn't raise a finger to help save their ships.

Chancey grew quiet, his pipe forgotten. "Nic, I gotta tell ye, I just don't know what our next move should be."

She swallowed hard. "Sutherland approached me today."

"And?"

"He said he'd dropped the charges against Father, and that he'd learned the bail was being denied. He told me he had information about it."

Chancey put his elbows on his knees and edged forward. "Well, go on. . . ."

"He wouldn't tell me there. Chancey, it has to be him who's doing this. How would he know otherwise?"

"It don't look good for him, I'll say that. But men like Sutherland often have their fingers in a lot o' people's pies. He probably knows just about everythin' what goes on about the quay from hauntin' the taverns as he does."

"If not him, then who?"

"Lord Tallywood," he answered. He sat back and crossed his thick arms across his chest as if defensive about his answer.

"That popinjay?" She thought of the effete dandy who for some reason liked racing clippers as much as fashion.

"Popinjay or no, he's atop yer father's list o' who's behind the damaged ships. The more I think o' it, the more me gut tells me that whoever's doin' this now is in on the sabotage, too, and it makes sense that it's one man. Yer father was supposed to be a prime target in that, too. And he's been expectin' some kind o' assault since the first one. This is as damagin' to the line—and easier, to boot."

Nicole called up the image of the pale, doughy-fleshed captain and shook her head. "I've seen Tallywood—I admit he had a shifty demeanor, but he also looked as if he'd faint being around Clive and Pretty, much less being the 'boss' they talked of." It had to be Sutherland. Tallywood's greatest crime would be wearing the same waistcoat as another fop to a soiree—*the horror!* "Why won't you even consider Sutherland?"

"Yer father hates the man, but even he don't think it's him. All that's gone on is underhanded. Sutherland may be a dangerous man, and he may not be a good man, but I'm not gettin' the feelin' that he'd do a low thin' like this."

Nicole stood and walked to the grate. She frowned— they were completely out of fuel. Were circumstances that dire here? She turned back to him, standing against the dying heat of the stove. "Father's bail is denied, and Sutherland just happens to know of it on the day it happened? He had the information before I did. I can't see why you won't believe he's a suspect. Is he or is he not Father's worst rival?"

"Aye, he is," Chancey answered reluctantly. "But—"

"And wouldn't he benefit the most from Father not sailing?"

"Possibly," he admitted, "but there're several people who'd be desperate to have yer father out o' this race. We got a whole list o' suspects."

She shook her head against what he was saying. Yes, other competitors would gain from her father's imprisonment. But none of them was in such financial straits that they depended on it.

"I believe Father told me in one of his letters that Sutherland's line was foundering?"

"Aye, it is. But that don't mean he's doin' this."

"But what if it is him?"

Chancey huffed impatiently. "If yer father hates the man above all else, and even he don't think it's Sutherland . . ."

Nicole shook her head. "I've got to meet with Sutherland and find out what information he has. I don't have a choice but to confront him."

"Ye're serious?" he asked in amazement. Then, visibly calming himself, he said evenly, "All right, so we go to Sutherland's tonight. I've done worse."

"He, uh, said it was to be only me."

"O' course he did!" Chancey roared.

She heedlessly carried on, "I don't think he'll keep Father in there if I plead our case." Truly she did think, she didn't know why, that she could have some sway where Sutherland was concerned.

However, Chancey sputtered, looking at her as if she'd lost her mind.

"Chancey, you look amazed at what is a . . . a daring idea." She pointed a finger at him. "And that really irritates, since *you* were once part of the Liverpool Irishmen. I believe that sailing enclave was notorious around the world for riotous behavior and insane exploits."

Chancey flushed. "I'm reformed!"

"Well, one day I will be, too!"

He glared at her. "First o' all, I'm not believin' that Sutherland had anythin' to do with this. And if I did, I'd be the one to confront him, not Jason's daughter!"

She couldn't understand where his confidence in Sutherland had come from. "I can't keep sitting here help-less when so much points to him. At worst, even if I can't coax him to help me, I can gain entry to his ship and snoop around for any evidence of wrongdoing." And spy for any-thing to help them in this now-critical race.

Chancey made a strangled exasperated sound; then, going into an uncharacteristic fury, he stood over her. For the first time in all the years she'd sailed with him, he used his hefty frame to intimidate her.

"I know what ye're plannin' and ye can forget it," he bel-lowed, shaking his finger at her. "Ye'll not be traipsin' after that black-hearted scoundrel!"

Nicole glanced behind him to see several of the crew lis-tening at the door. She scowled at them, and they scurried away. Everyone was accustomed to his blustering, but this was much more volatile. Still, she counted on the fact that even though Chancey's temper flared she'd wear him down in the end. Because she *never* lost a contest of wills.

"I'll not agree to it, miss," he warned resolutely as he paced back and forth. "Yer father'd not have ye doin' this for him." He took her arm and said, "Dangerous times these are—think o' it, ye were attacked right on yer own ship."

She tried to reason with the stubborn man, but Chancey held up his large, scarred hand to silence her. "Ye've grown into a lady now. Ye can't be alone with a man like that." He hesitated, looking her over once, then stammered on, "Ye're comely, and a man like him wouldn't think twice about beddin' ye."

Nicole raised her eyebrows and snorted. She wasn't comely. She had awkward features, and no matter how many times her father insisted on charitably calling her "willowy," she was much too thin. "You'll have to do better than that," she said in a derisive tone.

He frowned at her comment as if it confused him. "Listen, Nic, I don't like the man—don't like any man that gives in to his demons," he added to himself, "but whoever is keepin' Jason in jail is a cheat, and I can't see Sutherland wantin' to win like this."

She wanted to tell him that even if he didn't think the man would stoop to this, she couldn't ignore the hatred between him and her father. But she was running out of time. Instead, she backed down from the argument, resolving to attack the problem from another angle. With a staged sigh and dejectedly slumped shoulders, she said, "I'm just anxious about Father. I'm sure you're right."

She would act as if she were convinced by his logic for the rest of the day, so he wouldn't watch her too closely when she was ready to leave for the *Southern Cross*. Her heart told her it wasn't Sutherland, but she had to be certain. More was riding on his information than they imagined.

Nicole had felt as though she had an invisible noose roped around her neck when the bail was denied. After the news of Clankson's threat, it'd been raised and tightened. Without her father, there'd be no win. Without the win, there'd be no accounts. No accounts in this vulnerable time, and the line would have to be liquidated to pay off their creditors.

She would go to Sutherland, hear what he had to say, then plead their case to see if she could maneuver him into helping her. If talk wouldn't achieve the goal, then she'd manipulate him. That idea was ambitious—he didn't exactly strike her as highly manipulable. But she was adept at getting people to do what she wanted. And if that didn't work . . . well, she wouldn't think about that now.

If she was honest with herself, she'd admit that she was shamefully attracted to the man, had been since she first saw him, more so after he kissed her. He'd told her she'd be curious. Oh, she was curious, all right.

When the clock struck ten, she'd just managed to get rid of Chancey for the night. She hated lying to him repeatedly, since he truly trusted her to be as honest as he was, but it was done now.

She'd take the window left by his absence and use it to . . . simply know.

Chapter 7

I'm expecting a visitor tonight," Derek informed Jebediah Grolly, his bosun and the man who kept his ship running smoothly. "When she arrives, put her in the salon." In a sterner voice, he added, "And make sure she stays there."

"Aye, Cap'n," the aging seaman replied evenly, though his salt-and-pepper eyebrows were raised in question.

Derek understood why. A woman was coming to the ship for the second time in . . . well, ever.

"Do you think I can get a bit of shore leave after that?"

He didn't doubt how badly Jeb and the rest of his crew wanted to leave now that night was coming though during the day they certainly had no problem staying aboard. They were always visible on the ship even after they finished their duties, lingering so everyone on the quay could see that they were about to sail the greatest race of the century. But at night they were treated as celebrities in the waterfront taverns, with race followers and sailing enthusiasts buying pint after pint for them.

"That's fine," he said vacantly. Jeb walked out of the cabin with a bounce in his step and a large smile cracking his old, bewhiskered face.

Derek had never shared the consuming excitement his sailors enjoyed when about to set sail on a long route. He always thought the long trips a lesser evil for a man who belonged nowhere.

He'd at least been more involved in the past. Now all he could think of was Nicole. Even knowing she was Lassiter's daughter hadn't diminished his want of her.

He took a book down from a glassed-in shelf while he waited impatiently, but after rereading the same page four times, he tossed it aside. Just as he thought she might not show, Jeb knocked on the door.

"Cap'n! The visitor's 'ere."

He called permission to enter, and Jeb bustled in. "You didn't tell me it's the girl that strolled outta 'ere the other mornin' bold as she pleased," he chided with a sly smile. "I put her inside and ordered 'er to stay put." His brows drawn together, he admitted, "She got a bit sassy with me." Derek could only imagine how Nicole had reacted to that command.

When he entered the room, he saw she hadn't taken a seat. Instead, she was inspecting the seascapes attached to the walls.

He walked toward her, and when he was directly behind her, she said, "These are excellent, Captain Sutherland."

"I didn't know you were a lover of art."

She turned to him with a curiously self-deprecating expression. It vanished as her hand shot up to his bruised face, which had colored more deeply since the morning. She feathered the tips of her fingers over his bruised jaw, and he just managed to prevent himself from closing his eyes. Uneasy, he stiffened. At once, she pulled her hand away.

"It's nothing," he said in a gruff voice. "I assure you I've had worse."

She blushed furiously. Her touching him had been impulsive. "I'm sorry you two fought," she said in a crisper tone as she stepped back from him.

"It would've happened sooner or later." His words were tight as he watched her nonchalantly remove her cloak to reveal her unconventional attire—trousers and a fitted blouse that did nothing to hide her attributes.

It appeared to him that she had taken extra care with that splendid hair of hers. It was twisted in an elaborate style, and he could more easily see the golden strands threaded throughout. Piled atop her head, it made the rest of her form seem fragile and small.

Though she seemed so slight, she'd been soft. Soft when he'd come across what had to be the most beautifully shaped breast he'd ever held in his life. Shrugging away that too-appealing memory, he asked in a voice gone husky, "Can I get you something to drink?"

"Oh, I'm not supposed to—" She stopped, then said, "Yes, I think I would like one—whatever you're having, please."

He was having whiskey—neat—but he didn't think that'd do for the slight girl, so he added water to hers before handing it to her. "I have some questions for you."

"And I for you," she replied. "But I'd like to hear yours first."

"Very well." He moved to a chair and motioned for her to sit. She tucked a leg under as she sank into the plush settee facing him.

She took a drink, not a dainty sip but a good draw. He nearly chuckled at her watering eyes and convulsive swallowing. It was strong liquor, and since she was obviously a novice drinker, he was impressed she'd kept from gasping aloud or coughing.

When she recovered a bit, he asked, "Who were those men following you?"

As she recalled that night, her face turned fierce. Not afraid any longer, just very angry. "They'd broken aboard the ship. I stumbled onto them," she replied with a sharp look in her eyes. He thought she studied him, as if trying to see how her words affected him.

When she gathered he wasn't satisfied with her abrupt answer, she added, "That's all I can say."

He sensed that was all he'd get on the subject, so he asked, "Why were you in the Mermaid the other night?"

She brought the glass to her lips to drink again, then said, "I heard my father was going there to get some information."

"Nice way to put it."

She looked surprised before bowing her head as if hiding a grin. But when she looked up, her brows were knitted, and she appeared annoyed. "Then weren't you there for *information* also, Captain Sutherland?"

He almost grinned, but admitted, "I was there because I was too drunk to know better."

Her eyes widened. She hadn't expected that answer.

"I hadn't realized what kind of place it was either," she commented with a bright blush.

He liked the way she blushed. She had such vivid coloring, he wouldn't expect her to blush prettily, but she did. He found himself asking in an admiring tone, "Why haven't I seen you before?"

She stared at her glass and answered, "I've been away."

"Away?"

She raised her face again. "Oh, here and there."

Derek's lips tilted in a hint of a smile, but he knew it wasn't a pleasant sight. So she guarded her past? Smart girl. "Why didn't you tell me who you were?"

She took another deep pull from her glass. "I didn't know what kind of man you were. You might have hurt me just to spite my father—I couldn't be sure."

"Yet you came here tonight?"

She nodded while pushing a stray curl behind her ear. "I need to hear what you have to say. I want Father released. . . . I didn't feel I had much choice."

He knew little, and certainly not anything that could overtly benefit her. He'd just wanted her to come tonight.

He sat back and said, "I will tell you what I know. I did drop the charges against your father. In fact, I went to the constabulary personally to make sure he was released. The constable told me he had evidence of other crimes on Lassiter—"

"That's not—"

"I thought the man was lying," he said. "I don't believe there are other crimes."

She looked relieved, which was strange. Why would she care what he thought?

"I was . . . uncomfortable with the fact that your father wouldn't race because of my . . . night with you. I tried several methods to get him released," he explained vaguely. "I will say that from the way I was turned down, the person who is responsible is in a position of power or threw a considerable amount of money at this problem."

After a pause, she said, "Say you were in my position, and desperately wanted someone you cared about released.

Who would *you* target for this? And what would *you* do?"

Two thoughts came to Derek at once. One, he didn't have someone he cared about. Two, she was asking his advice, and he liked that she hung on to his words.

"If I had to, I'd say it would be a peer, someone of my rank or higher. Someone with a great deal of money, who has a stake in this race."

"Why shouldn't I think you did it?"

He found her openness refreshing. "Because I will beat your father regardless. I *want* to defeat your father," he explained simply.

She nibbled the corner of her lower lip and looked lost in thought. "I don't know if I believe you. But if you've told me all you know . . ." She stood to go, taking one last large swallow of whiskey before setting the glass down.

Derek wasn't about to let her leave yet. Though he admired her strong will, when she'd touched his face tonight her aloof facade wavered, her defenses breached, if only for a second. But it was at that instant that she became irresistible to him.

This was not going at all as planned. She was insane to think she could handle this man. Nicole wasn't daft—she'd known she could only have a measure of success in managing him if he was intoxicated, and she'd definitely not foreseen any problem in the "Sutherland gets drunk" variable. Yet here he was, facing her without a hint of a slur or any dimness in those piercing eyes. He looked as if he could see right through her and tell all her secrets.

If he was telling the truth, then she hadn't received much of a lead. Worse, it would mean he'd already done what she'd come to ask for. She didn't believe he was deceiving her; he *would* want to defeat her father.

Given the circumstances, she thought a retreat would be best. As she walked past him to her cloak, she took a last look at his face, a face so striking even with the angry mask he always wore. He looked like a fallen angel, cold and cruel, but with a lingering shadow of what he'd once been. The shadow was what was driving her crazy. . . .

Stop gaping at his face. Thank him and leave. "Sutherland, I—"

"There's more . . . ," he promised in a lower, rumbling tone. She tried to convince herself that he meant more information, but failed. When he reached out and gently ran the backs of his fingers down her face much as she had done to him, she didn't turn away.

He was about to say something, but scuffling noises and a woman's raised voice sounded from the deck. She could sense tension radiating from him, and he turned abruptly to the door. He halted before he left. "Nicole," he said as he pinned her with those silvery eyes, "do not think of leaving this room."

When the door closed, her legs went shaky. She'd been a coil of nerves, craving to be kissed again so much that she'd forgotten her true purpose for coming here.

Wait, what was my true purpose? To manipulate and spy. Oh, yes.

She hadn't expected such an opportunity to move about his ship, and she knew she should take advantage of it. Normally she wouldn't even pause to think, but the warning in his eyes bore some weight in her decision. When he'd looked at her and commanded her, he'd had no inkling of doubt that she'd do as he told her. Otherwise he would never have left her alone.

His mistake. And one she'd capitalize on. She cracked open the door to reconnoiter, but then she glimpsed the face that matched the woman's voice, and her heart inexplicably sank.

The creature heatedly gesturing in front of Sutherland was . . . exquisite. Flawless features, dressed like a fashion plate. Nicole fought the urge to look down at her own clothes, knowing she'd find thin legs encased in worn-out breeches. Strangely, her throat grew tight as she watched them, knowing he had some kind of history with that beautiful woman.

Why was she surprised? This was Sutherland, the rake who probably had a bevy of women admirers. As she took in the jet hair and voluptuous figure of the woman, she knew he'd easily choose that vision over her. Although some strange emotion stabbed at her, she steeled herself. Exhaling a loud breath, she peeked out one last time before sprinting on the balls of her feet to his cabin down the companionway.

Entering his room, she averted her eyes from the bed and rushed to his desk. She rifled through the drawers and found everything she'd expected, but nothing to help her. Then she spotted an unmarked file wedged in the back of a drawer. As she delved into its contents, her expression of excited anticipation disappeared, and her face darkened. The file contained lists of goods he'd ordered to be donated on Boxing Day to the Families of Lost Sailors Charity and to the handful of orphanages in the waterfront area.

Charities and Sutherland? The donations were staggering. If he were in straits, the last thing he'd do would be give to charity, and not even the fashionable ones at that. She knew that Chancey, curse that blasted Irishman, was right about Sutherland.

Nevertheless, she was on this ship, and she would search

every inch she could. Nicole didn't know what she would be looking for—she'd know it when she found it, she reasoned in a cavalier manner. Apparently, the liquor was beginning to hit her.

From the deck, Sutherland's scathing tone with the woman trailed down to Nicole, and a small smile broke across her face. That he didn't seem to like the woman took some of the sting out of seeing her.

As Nicole moved through the rest of the ship, she found that his clipper was in impeccable condition, his sailors' quarters immaculate, and everywhere from his cabin to the forecastle was marked by cleanliness. His ship was just as ordered as her father's obsessively well maintained vessel. Which really made her want to hate Sutherland.

She trailed a lazy finger on the wall as she made her way into the storage area. She decided she had to be drunk, because she grew distracted, dreamy even, as she thought about Sutherland. What would a captain like him feed his crew? He'd probably spend extra money to get them good rations.

She wouldn't know what kind of semiperishables he'd outfit the ship with since they wouldn't be loaded until the last minute, but she did see with a downcast shake of her head a generous stock of spirits. If Nicole didn't know he was in a race, she'd think he was trading the stuff. Not that she could talk, she thought as she bumped lightly into the wall.

Then, with eyes gone wide and a quick intake of breath, she spied a cluster of thick iron water casks in the corner of the hold. She experienced immediate jealousy. Her father still used wooden casks, and frustration gripped her from knowing that Sutherland's crew would have much fresher drinking water than her own. She walked over to inspect the layer of condensing silver barrels and knocked on the closest one, enjoying the sharp, metallic sound.

He had so many advantages over them. But that would make the win that much sweeter, she assured herself as she turned—and collided with Sutherland's unyielding chest.

"Going somewhere?" he ground out, as he gripped her arm and hauled her out of the storage hold. Slamming the door behind him, he raked his eyes over her. "What the hell were you doing down there? And do not think of lying to me!"

Think . . . think! How long had he been standing there? "I lost my way back from the head," she replied in a credibly even tone.

"Am I supposed to believe that?" He squeezed her arm.

"Of course," she lied. To distract him, she asked in a tight voice, "Who was that woman?"

He scowled. "Someone I hope never to see again," he said absently. "Now, what—"

"But why?" Nicole pressed. "She's so beautiful."

"Not," he replied in a clipped tone, "if you look her in the eye."

"I see." She didn't really.

Exhaling loudly, he placed a palm above her against the wall. "What am I going to do with you?"

"I wasn't doing anything wrong," she pleaded. "I got lost trying to get back to the salon." She could see he didn't believe her.

When he searched her face, she met his gaze. She must be drunk, because now when she looked in his eyes, she could see they were flecked with blue and were . . . mesmerizing. So intent, so dark that she wanted to kiss his eyelids and then the harsh line between his brows before moving down to those chiseled lips.

He must have recognized what she was thinking, because she could see his expression race from anger to something else entirely. In that deep, gravelly voice, he murmured, as if in resignation, "Damn you," and then without any notice bent down and covered her lips in a brutal kiss.

This wasn't what she'd come here for. She would stop kissing him. Now. *Ah, hell.* She couldn't come up with a single reason why she shouldn't enjoy him for this one last night. She was amazed that this big man, all hard planes and sculpted muscle, couldn't seem to keep his hands off her.

She wasn't about to let this chance slip by, she thought as she boldly grabbed his collar to bring him closer. Her grandmother would marry her off to some old lord, and she'd most likely never know this feeling again. In all her life, she'd never been so forcefully attracted to another as she was to him.

Realizing that it was now or never, she leaned into him, pressing her body against his as she tentatively brushed his tongue with her own. First lapping at him, then twining against his. He squeezed her hips, not quite painfully, and groaned, a low, rumbling sound that sent fire spilling through her body. His powerful reaction assured her that she should continue.

She'd learned from their first night together that if she pressed up against the front of his trousers, he kissed her more deeply. She arched toward him, her belly goading against his manhood. He moved his hands from her hips to her backside and lifted her until she was on her toes, her body more aligned against his. When her hips instinctively moved against him, he groaned again against her neck, flicking his tongue over her, flooding her with heat in that part of her he mercilessly thrust against.

Then an idea seized her, an idea so shocking . . . She hastily ran her hands down his chest, and lower. She would put her hands on him, where she was most successful in making him kiss her deeper.

Instead of being pleased as she'd hoped, he sounded distinctly pained when he grabbed her wrists. "Do you want me to spill my seed right here?"

Her passion-filled response dazed Derek. He imagined that she was just going through the motions to make him forget where she'd been, because of course she'd lied. He was angry that she'd spied on him; yet that didn't stop him from desiring her.

But he didn't want her to be with him for any reason other than her wanting him as well. Ruthlessly he shoved aside his misgivings and returned his lips to the fiery girl in his arms. He couldn't remember ever feeling so much from a kiss. Why were they burning together? Was it because he was sober, or because the little wench was matching his own surprisingly strong ardor, wrapping her arms around him and pressing her high, firm breasts into his chest?

She answered his teasing tongue by again opening for him and tasting him, as though licking him up. It made him wild. He might lose control with her, might hurt her with his big body. He set her away from him.

"God, what are you doing to me?" he rasped. He couldn't understand this little enigma, but when he looked at her face, with her swollen lips and her dilated pupils, he became determined that he would make her truly want him tonight, regardless of all the circumstances surrounding them. He bent down to put his arm under her knees and carried her to his cabin, kicking the door shut behind him.

When he dropped her on the bed, she sat up on her elbows to reach him, which only pushed her hardened nipples against the soft cloth of her blouse. He pressed her away from him down on the bed. *"Cease that now."*

But she didn't. When he yanked off his shirt, she went to her knees, her fingers sweeping over his skin, making the muscles beneath tighten and flex. She kneaded his shoulders and pulled herself up to place her warm lips on his chest. His head shot back. He couldn't prevent it, but he wanted to see her; he lowered his gaze. . . . She appeared to have truly forgotten herself in a feverish urgency. And, God, he wanted her to—hell, he needed her to forget herself—he was losing control with each second. He thought with a sudden coldness that he'd soon know if she wanted him as much as he did her.

He pushed her down on the bed and, laying one hand on her chest between her breasts, pulled off her boots with the other. Her trousers came next. He sensed a sudden hesitation as he continued undressing her, and gave her a harsh smile. "Scared I'll know if you're only feigning desire?"

Her face clouded with confusion. "Y-you could feign this?"

With a curse, he wondered at the truth in her words, words that made his blood boil to sink himself inside her.

"Take off your shirt," he commanded, and again she hesitated before removing it. What in the hell was she thinking, after what she'd been doing to him? Did she think— Then it came to him, along with a fury. Probably playing the virgin, he realized with disgust. Damn women and their perpetual games. As if a woman who whimpered and undulated her body against his like this, a woman who had been just inches away from sliding her hands down the front of his trousers, could be a virgin.

He should throw her out on her ear. When he saw her perfectly rounded breasts, tipped with light pink, he couldn't. Not until after he'd tasted her.

He sat down beside her on the bed, pulling off his own boots and trousers; her gaze fastened on his swollen cock, and her eyes widened in fascination. He watched the girl studying his body, acting as if she'd never seen an aroused man. The thought of her, a wanton, pretending to be innocent . . . goddamn it!

He'd make her remember what she was.

He slid his hand to her breasts, palming them urgently. Her eyes went wild as she gasped, but he ignored her reaction and bent his head down. He pushed the small mounds together so he had only to turn his face one way or the other to find a nipple pouting against his lips. He licked and suckled, her skin becoming wet from him. She writhed, arching her body toward his, then threaded her fingers through his hair to fasten his mouth to her breast.

She was driving him mad. He'd never responded this way to a woman before. For some reason he'd have to consider later, her own response to him mattered—mattered more than anything else.

Oddly anxious, he grazed his hand down her belly. When he halted just above the juncture at her thighs, her whole body began quivering. Even her small breasts, still gleaming from his ministrations, moved with her shaking.

He eased his fingers down to her soft folds.

Moist. Hot. He nudged her legs apart and kneeled between them, pushing her knees up. When he had her open to him, he slid a finger in slowly, edging inside. Her whole body tensed. Had he hurt her? But his finger glistened when he pulled it from her. He pushed in once more, and her head thrashed to the side as she moaned. Out . . . in . . . she began to meet his hand. His lips curled in anticipation. She was so tight.

Again and again, he drove his finger into her, fondling inside, no more able to deny that searing, hungry sheath than he could quit breathing. With each give and take, her panting breaths and little cries came more quickly. Her pale arms fell back over her head, and her legs stretched wider. She already neared her peak.

He pressed a second finger into her, spreading her, and watched, fascinated, as he pushed upward with his hand. She moaned low in her throat and shot up in the bed, legs splayed, back arched. Exquisite.

Her body gripped him hard, and as she broke over the edge her eyes flashed open with a look of disbelief and wonder.

It was a look that mirrored his own, because there, obvious to his touch, was her unbreached maidenhood.

Nicole had just come down from the most incredible encounter she'd ever experienced in her life. She wanted to savor it, to lock it away in her heart. She felt soft and languid for the first time in months. She wanted to enjoy the easing of the constant tension she battled, but that became difficult when Sutherland closed in on her with an expression that sped from bafflement to a cold fury.

"An explanation, girl."

She supposed his tone should have alarmed her, but she felt drugged. All she wanted to do was pet him and thank him and, well, reciprocate somehow. In fascination, she brought her fingers up to tease the hair on his chest, and smiled at his sharp hiss of breath when she unwittingly caressed his nipple. She'd have to remember that.

His eyes turned chilling as he roughly grabbed her wrists. "*Enough.* Is this some sort of trap?"

"T-trap?" she stammered, finally forcing herself to sit up.

His gaze roamed over her breasts, and he abruptly released her. "Cover yourself."

She dragged the sheet to her chin. She would end this now, tell him everything so he could guard himself against whoever was behind the sabotage. And then she would leave. She was deciding where to start when his next comment stopped her cold.

"A virgin seductress. You wouldn't whore something as valuable as your virginity just to get your father out of jail."

She flinched from his words but even more so when a look of dawning comprehension came over his face and with it an increasing rage. "Is that why you were so willing—because you were trying to bag an earl?" he asked menacingly, his features twisted.

Bag an earl? What the devil? Did he think she meant to trap him in marriage? She would never do something so callous. She'd known most of her life that if she did marry, it would be a miserable union to someone her grandmother chose for her.

It appeared that her silence infuriated him even more

because he grabbed her shoulders. "I will ask this once and you *will* answer me," he bit out. "What—" A muffled thud interrupted his words.

Nicole's head snapped up. She saw her own bewildered expression reflected in his eyes before they glinted in pain and then slowly eased closed.

Chapter 8

Jesus, Chancey, you killed him!" Nicole cried as she wrapped the sheet more securely around her. Flying over to Sutherland's motionless form where he'd dropped on the floor, she protectively gathered his head in her lap.

"Why then should ye care?" Chancey asked, his hands tight around the billy club he'd used to pound the back of Sutherland's head.

"Of course I'd care," she managed in a strangled whisper, as she cautiously checked his head and listened to his breathing—luckily, strong and steady. "I wouldn't want him to die. . . . I wouldn't want anyone to die," she amended when a look of rage twisted Chancey's face. "This is not as it looks," she said, wishing her traitorous face wasn't flushed red with embarrassment.

He rapped the club on his open palm. "Oh, so ye mean to tell me I find ye naked in the bed o' the most notorious rake in London, but it's not how it looks?" He turned to

Sutherland with an ominous glare. "Then tell me what *did* happen so I'll be knowin' which way to properly kill the bastard."

"No!" She threw herself over him. "I came here and eventually I, well . . . *I* seduced *him*."

"Is that so?" He snorted, clearly disbelieving, but at least he'd let go of the club, letting it hang from a strap on his wrist.

Nicole needed time to devise a way to get the furious Chancey away from the unconscious man. "I, uh, need to dress." Abruptly he turned his back. Changing the direction of the conversation, she asked, "How did you know where I was? How did you get past his guards?"

"I had a bad feelin' about ye, so I stopped by the ship to check. It didn't take a bloody genius to figger out where ye been. His guards, well, they went the way o' their cap'n," he finished in a sneering voice.

"Oh," was all she could manage. She laid the sheet over Sutherland's torso and legs and hastily threw her shirt over her head.

"Hurry yerself. More o' his crewmen'll be back soon, and I'll be needin' time for doin' what I'm after."

"Now, you just wait," she ordered as she grabbed a pillow and gently laid Sutherland's head on it. She really began to fear for him. "Listen to me. It's the truth—I initiated this. I wouldn't lie. Have I ever lied to you?" she demanded of Chancey's back. "Have I ever been anything but completely honest with you?"

"Aye, when ye vowed to me ye'd stay in school for once. Or when ye told me Cook had been eatin' his own tarts. And then tonight—when ye sent me off to look into a dead end," he countered, his disappointment palpable.

"That . . . that was an important lead. If for no other

reason than to get more information on Tallywood, *your* main suspect," she said stiffly as she bent down to finish dressing.

He let out a harsh bark of laughter at that. Truly her answer sounded weak to her own ears. It was bad, what she'd done. She'd sent Chancey out to investigate unwittingly something so nefarious as Tallywood's midnight bridge party.

"Fine, fine," she conceded crossly. "But you must believe me on this."

As she began stomping into her boots, Chancey turned and looked at her quizzically. "I might be admittin' that we can't lay all the blame at Sutherland's door. Ye're comely and ye came to him unchaperoned after slinkin' around the docks at night. Blighter probably thought that ye were fair game."

Nicole stood and met his eyes, unflinching. "I wanted this to happen, Chancey. And I don't regret it." She didn't—in her mind, Sutherland had given her a gift. Even with his harsh words and anger, she wouldn't trade her time in his bed for anything.

At length, Chancey released an exasperated sigh. "I'll let him live for now, but"—he raised a hand to cut off her next words—"only because ye'll be marryin' him."

Marrying me? Derek thought as he came to. He struggled to bite back a curse as continuous waves of stabbing pressure circled his head. His eyes opened into narrow slits as he stifled a hiss of pain, knowing that if he made a sound the giant cur with the club would just put him back out.

When he had some success in focusing his eyes, he squinted over at the arguing pair. The man was turned from him, so all Derek could see was his immensely broad back.

But considering his size, he had to be the one who'd accompanied Nicole to the jail. Derek was a big man himself, but that mammoth probably had two stone more bulk on him.

And Nicole . . . the relatively tiny Nicole openly challenged him, shaking her head furiously at his command that she marry Derek.

"He compromised ye. Even yer father would feel forced to see ye marry him, Nic."

"Sutherland? Think about what you're saying," she said incredulously. "Besides, Father doesn't have to find out."

"Ye know I'll be tellin' him, lass."

The girl's face turned ashen, and the big man's shoulders slumped in response. At once, he marched across the cabin and bent down awkwardly to pat her head with one of his huge paws. Derek had a hard time hearing what they said when their heads were bent together. Finally, the man stood up.

"So ye were able to go all over this ship?"

All over?

"Yes."

"And?"

"And I did what I came to do. You can cross Sutherland off your list."

What bloody list?

"I can't be happy with what ye've done here tonight, but at least ye've accomplished somethin'," the man said before exhaling loudly. "We can salvage the rest. We need to go and get more o' our men before the sod's crew gets back. If we have to force him to marry ye, then that we will."

Derek guessed that the big man knew the battle was just beginning because he quickly added, "I'll argue with ye on the way. But, Nic—come hell or high water, ye'll marry this scoundrel for what he did to ye."

Why was she shaking her head determinedly, telling the giant that she damn well wouldn't marry him? Nicole's reaction astounded Derek; he had difficulty keeping his eyes hooded when she glanced over at him on the floor. She was in such a dudgeon that he doubted she'd notice he'd awakened anyway. He doubted she'd notice if he jumped up and danced a jig. The chit was *fuming* at the thought of marriage to him.

As if he would ever marry a girl like her. *But, damn it, what's so bad about marrying me?* Many women had set their caps on him, praying he'd honor them with a proposal, and some, he thought darkly, had schemed to manipulate him into marriage.

But not her. This little bit of fluff quaked with anger. That simply couldn't be right. It went against all reasoning. If his head didn't hurt so badly, he could sort through all this and make some sense of her behavior.

"Chancey," she said in a low voice, "for the last time, I am not marrying him. He is a wastrel, a drunk, a—a—despoiler of women. Would you see me chained to *that*"—as if repelled, she flicked her hand in his direction—"for the rest of my life?"

Ah-ha, Chancey is his na— Wait! What the hell did she just say? Derek could feel anger pumping through him. He was not a wastrel nor a drunk. And he'd certainly never despoiled a woman. But a small part of him admitted that if he hadn't been knocked out, he would've started with her.

Still he couldn't believe what she'd said. Did that explain the look she'd given him that night in the Mermaid? Was that how she regarded him? As a drunk?

He experienced an unwelcome tinge of embarrassment, and the feeling was raw and new and most definitely unwanted. Bloody hell. He could barely suppress the urge to get up and shake her until she took back her words.

Instead, he secretly watched as she marched up to the grizzled salt with shoulders back and eyes flashing. Derek thought she looked regal when she said, "Chancey, you must leave with me right now. You know I've recently made promises that do not include him. We will leave him be," she finished warningly.

The man hesitated; then, shaking his head, he stalked to the other side of the cabin. He had to lean down to make it through the doorway. Just as they started out, he grumbled something about how she should have been sent back sooner.

Derek began to rise, but seeing blackness waver before his eyes, he dropped back down to the cabin floor in furious impotence. He might not be in any shape to go after them tonight, but it didn't matter. He would make them pay for this.

He would have her if it killed him, and he would teach that girl not to think of him as a—what ridiculous name had she called him? A despoiler of women. By God, she would beg for him.

In his anger, he strained to rise yet again, but he lay as weak as a babe. His head would not stop pounding, and his racing thoughts, although they never left the girl, were chaotic and confused. . . .

Light footsteps sounded, and he shuttered his eyes. Nicole.

But her return did nothing to help clear his confusion. In fact, he became certain he was imagining it when she swept back inside and softly drew a blanket over him. There could be no doubt he dreamed when, tenderly kissing his aching head, she whispered into his hair, "Thank you for tonight," before she leapt up and vanished.

Sixty hours. The Great Circle Race began in sixty hours, and Derek hadn't the slightest idea where Nicole had disappeared to. He'd already made up his mind when he and his crewmen couldn't locate her that he would bloody well remain in port. He'd be damned if he would wait seven months to have this situation resolved.

On his order, his men had searched every place of lodging near the water when they couldn't find her on or near the *Bella Nicola*. They'd torn apart the wharf looking for her, offered substantial rewards all over the city, but every lead stalled.

He pinched the bridge of his nose and looked down at his desk. He couldn't say he was becoming obsessed with her, because she'd already caught him in her snares. Leaning back in his chair, he again allowed his mind to revisit that night. Although he'd believed she sought to trap him into marriage, she'd definitely disproved that idea with her adamant refusals of him. And everything before that had been incredible.

Damn it, he didn't need to relive the night. As always, the memory of her abandon and the swift power of her climax aroused him to a painful degree. Even after he'd been clubbed, her kiss had been sweet and worth the pain. She'd *thanked* him. Then disappeared.

It was too much. He'd start to believe he'd made up the whole encounter if not that even now he could smell her scent and taste her on his lips. Barring the abrupt end, he wanted it to happen again.

He understood why he'd been hit, but that didn't make him any less angry about the clubbing he and his guards had gotten on his own ship. Not to mention the rest of that hazy night. He needed to know what list she'd referred to and why she'd been all over his ship. Nicole, the daughter of his worst enemy, having free rein was a disaster in anyone's books. Much less Nicole with an agenda. He had to find her and question her.

He'd left her in the salon with no doubt that she'd stay there. He couldn't remember anyone ever disobeying him deliberately. Yet the little chit probably set off the minute he reached the gangway where Lydia had slapped at one of his guards to get aboard and hysterically demand even more money.

Until Lydia had shown up, he'd been so busy brooding over Nicole that he hadn't had time to think of that witch in days, even though she'd haunted him for years....

A knock at his door pulled him from his musings.

He called out permission to enter and was surprised to find his younger brother standing in the doorway. Or rather, ducking under it. How had Derek not seen how big Grant had grown over the last four years? Grant had always been tall, but at twenty-eight, he'd completely filled out his rangy form.

Though Grant had blue eyes where Derek's were gray, and his face wasn't marred by hard living and resentment like Derek's, overall their physical differences were slight. Their personalities, however, couldn't have been more dissimilar. Where Derek appeared proud to be an irresponsible rake, given to hedonism, Grant had become a pillar of the community and had grown to be as intensely reserved as their father, the earl, had been. Still, he could remember when Grant was younger he'd been a prankster with a ready humor and a knack for finding trouble.

"Good morning, Derek." Grant sat down in the chair

facing the desk, and Derek could swear he saw power and purpose thrumming through his sibling. In response, Derek sank further back in his chair and propped his scuffed boots up on the desk.

He'd always cared about his brother, but Derek was still ill at ease that Grant had seen him so low the other night. He skipped a greeting. "What is it now, Grant?"

Grant looked around the well-appointed room before he took a deep breath. "Well, I wanted to speak to you before you sailed, but you left the house the other morning before I woke."

"Then speak."

"Very well." Grant leaned forward in his chair before he cautiously asked, "You know of Lord Belmont?"

That got Derek's attention. "Everyone knows about that crazy old bastard. What of him?"

"He came to see me this week." Grant took a breath. "He made me a considerable offer to search for his family."

"Christ." Derek shook his head. "The only reason he came to you is that he's been turned down by every other captain and shipowner in London who hasn't already signed on for that fool's errand. Myself included. I laughed him out of my office." Derek examined his brother's impassive face. "What the hell could he offer you? He's already run through his fortune on at least a dozen different attempts."

Grant appeared defensive when he answered. "If I was successful, he would give me the lands of Belmont Court when he passes on."

Derek let out a surprised whistle. "He is getting desperate, then." Rumor held that Belmont had attempted to sell the unentailed estate to finance one last search.

This conversation, Derek decided easily, merited a

drink, so he rose to grab a bottle of brandy. By way of offering, he swung the bottle in Grant's direction. As expected, Grant declined with a curt shake of his head. Although it wasn't quite noon, Grant didn't appear surprised when Derek began filling his own glass.

"You can't possibly be considering his offer," Derek said over his shoulder before returning to his desk.

"Well, I did decide against it," Grant admitted. "But it made me think—if I had wanted to go, then I should be able to."

"What's that supposed to mean?" Derek asked. "You own half of Peregrine Shipping. You can very well go anywhere you want—"

"No, I can't," Grant interrupted. "I'm too busy running Whitestone and your other neglected estates."

"Ridiculous. I have a steward—"

"Whom I fired several months ago not only for bilking you out of a pitifully large amount, but also for skimming off your tenants." His face was shuttered. "I wouldn't have stepped in, if not for your tenants."

Derek sank back, dumbfounded. Not just at the news of his steward's embezzlement, but also at the idea that Grant might not have checked his downfall. He drank deeply. "Why didn't I hear anything about this?"

Grant nodded pointedly at the pile of correspondence on the desk that had been ignored for months. "I've sent word through every channel. I'm sure if you bothered to look, you'd find that several of my letters found their way to the ship."

Derek fought to avoid looking sheepish. "Yes, well, I suppose I remember receiving some letters that I haven't had time to get to."

Grant shrugged. "My point is, if I hadn't been around to

hold everything together after you left so abruptly, then you'd be in a very bad spot. And I'm tired of it. I wasn't raised to take over Whitestone—"

"I damn well wasn't, either," Derek cut in. It had been years since their older brother's death, but he still had difficulty accepting that William was gone and that all those responsibilities now lay on his shoulders.

"*It's not mine*," Grant said in a tightly controlled tone. "Whitestone's not my estate. I want to earn my own place. Make my own way. You can't understand how hard it is to work for something that you know you have no future in."

"What do you mean, 'no future'? You're my bloody heir. Everything goes to you. And I'm not exactly living as though I plan to get old."

"One day you'll have an heir," Grant said quietly but with absolute conviction.

Derek's fingers paled on the glass he grasped. "I will *not* have an heir. We've been through this. It won't happen."

Grant ran a hand over his face. He suddenly looked tired, and his absolute self-control was slipping. "I don't accept that. I want to work in the shipping line, but it's impossible when you've taken over what was supposed to be my place in this company."

"This company is half mine."

"But think back to why it was formed all those years ago. We learned to sail so you and I would have a livelihood when William was alive and the heir. Now this earldom is yours. After Lydia, you were too . . ." Grant stopped, uncomfortable. "Well, I took the reins. But, damn it, it's been years. You've had plenty of time to adjust to your lot in life. My life is completely on hold until you decide to think of someone else for a change and free me from your responsibilities."

Derek had never looked at it like that. He'd assumed he did Grant and everyone else a favor by staying off the estates. He'd easily avoided home and all the attendant worries because his younger brother did such a good job with them.

Now, learning that Grant was encumbered by those duties, Derek understood it wasn't fair to tie him up in his affairs. But he couldn't think about that now. Besides, Grant knew better than to have mentioned Lydia and William to him in the same conversation.

"To hell with you, Grant. I have other plans. I don't give a bloody damn what happens while I'm gone. No one's forcing you to stay on."

A look of bitter disappointment flashed in his brother's eyes before he stood and turned away. Seemingly resigned, Grant walked over to the port window, studiously taking in the scene of activity on the docks. Derek wasn't fooled. This wasn't the last he'd hear about this, and the only reason it had ended now was that Grant despised emotional scenes.

Changing the subject, Grant remarked, "I am pleased that you're captaining this race, at least. We need this win." He turned to stare Derek down. "We *really* need this win. Our reputation has been compromised—whose wouldn't be after losing twelve cargoes in the last year? Yet you continually sign on the riskiest ventures. In case you haven't noticed, we've had several contracts pulled."

"Of course I've noticed," Derek said testily. And he had. Shipping contracts were based on past performance and reputation, so lost ships and the consequently damaged reputation could prove ruinous to a line.

"If Lassiter wins this race, his company will finally be on solid footing. He could easily take over even more of our business."

"I will *never* allow that to happen."

Grant's brows drew together. "Why *do* you two hate each other so much?"

Derek drank while considering his answer. "He harasses me because he has a Yank's natural aversion to the aristocracy—men should make their own way and all that drivel." He looked up when he realized Grant had said nearly the same thing, but ignored his brother's frown. "He complains to any who'll listen that I was handed everything while he works tirelessly."

"You know that's not true," Grant said. "And you? Why do you hate him?"

"Of those twelve lost cargoes you were mentioning, he's directly responsible for at least four—"

A knock on the door broke the tense conversation.

When Derek called permission, Jeb entered and said, "Cap'n, we've got goods come to be delivered. I just wanted to make sure that we're not taking on perishables until the decision to sail is made."

Whatever Grant detected in Derek's face had him clenching his fists. "Decision to sail—what bloody decision?" he ground out. "Why aren't you provisioned?"

Jeb decided this was a good chance to escape, and with a "Sorry, Cap'n," he scrambled out to close the door behind him.

"Calm down. I do plan on sailing," Derek said. "Just not yet." Seeing the uncompromising look on his brother's face, he reluctantly began filling him in on Nicole.

"Derek, don't take me for a fool," Grant said when he finished. "You don't expect me to believe you are looking for a woman. Much less Lassiter's chit."

"It's true. And it's important to me." He took a generous swig of brandy. "Lassiter, you obviously haven't heard, is in jail right now. And will be until after the race. Without him, there is no competition for the *Southern Cross*."

As Grant took in that new information, Derek continued, "And what's the urgency about sailing today? I'll win, but if I didn't, what's the worst thing that can happen? We lose a few more contracts? You know that won't break either of our banks."

Grant loomed over his desk. "Don't you have *any* pride left? Peregrine could be the most powerful line in Britain, was well on its way to being that. But then you let a woman crush you and, as a result, the company?" Grant's eyes bored into him. "I'm glad the American's picking us off. He deserves it more than we do."

"That's a little much—"

"You damn well know it's not. Think of the people we employ. What happens to everyone who works for the line? To the sailors' families? I can't tell you how much it pleased me to watch the company grow, to revive another port town. Now, without regard for anyone else, you're killing the one thing that made me proud."

Derek gave an unconcerned shrug just to irritate him.

Grant exhaled and then changed tactics. "You may shun everyone you used to associate with, but the rest of your family doesn't."

"So that's what this is about?" Derek demanded. "Your standing in the *ton*? I can see it now, you and Mother at Lady Sarah's rout hearing tales of the drunken reprobate heir. Do they whisper about me? About me ruining what was already an embarrassing foray into commerce for an ancient family?"

Both men stared at each other, neither prepared to back down.

His eyes like ice, Grant finally said, "I'll sail this ship if you don't."

Derek recognized where this was going. Yes, he could have all the time in the world to search for Nicole. But then he'd have to take up the running of the estates.

"Forget it. I'm sailing," Derek said. "When I feel like it."

Grant leveled a look of fury at him, and Derek was sure he'd charge him—actually hoped for it. But then Grant's restraint came to the fore. That worthless, damning restraint. Grant controlled himself, but did say in a scathing voice, "Looks as if you'll destroy yourself again because of a woman. Only this time you're taking everyone else down with you." He started toward the door but turned back. "You are the most selfish bloody bastard I've ever had the displeasure to know. That we're related makes the insult greater."

Chapter 9

"Chancey, will you relax?"

"Don't want to be here a mite longer," he grumbled as he threw jerky glances over his shoulder around the sitting room of her grandmother's palatial town home. Though none of the priceless knickknacks had changed location since he last checked his surroundings, the hunted look on his face deepened.

She shook her head. "As if I do?" They simply didn't have a choice since Sutherland had started tearing up the dockside looking for them. They couldn't stay on the quay, much less on their ship. "Glaring at the vases will not stop them if they truly want to charge into your hip and break."

He scowled at her. She'd never seen another person so uneasy as Chancey appeared now and for the two nights they'd spent here. And he couldn't stop pulling at his collar, which divided his neck above and below like two cogs from a gear. The dowager, who frightened Chancey more than her home did, had decreed their dress code, but it was next to impossible to find clothes to fit his great bulk. The woman couldn't be dissuaded. If they were to stay in her home or use any door other than the servants' entrance, then by God they would dress appropriately.

Abruptly, Chancey stood. "I'm gonna confront him today."

She exhaled loudly and reached for a small branch of table grapes. "We've been over this. The last time someone 'confronted' Sutherland, he landed in jail indefinitely!" With effort, she softened her tone. "I can't risk losing you, too, even if you are miserable. And think about it—we're safe here. This is the last place Sutherland would ever look."

"I'm not hidin' any longer. And he needs to pay for yer hurt honor."

"My hurt honor?" she cried. She looked around the room and dropped her voice. "One more time—I was not compromised. Even if I were, would you see me leg-shackled to a wastrel forever?"

He bunched his lips together and contemplated the ceiling before answering in a definite tone. "No, ye'll marry like ye promised yer gram."

"Exactly." Would he finally cooperate?

"Still don't like not tellin' yer pa. . . ."

They continually fought about the decision not to tell her father what had happened on Sutherland's ship. She'd ultimately persuaded him that her father would go mad not being able to get at Sutherland. And what if he did catch up with him in the future? They'd kill each other this time.

They had enough problems with that man as it was. He'd already been furious with her before he'd been knocked out, because he presumed she'd not only want to marry him, but would scheme to do so. The arrogance! She wanted to pull his ear to her lips and scream that hell would freeze over before she married him, and that Chancey had only been protecting her. As Chancey said, they'd merely "bonked his head and tweaked his nose." It wasn't as if they'd killed him.

Yet because of him, they'd gone to ground in, well, Mayfair. Even visiting her father became a concerted effort, since Sutherland's crew regularly checked the jail for her.

She was furious with Sutherland. So why did their time together remain constantly in her mind and plague her nights?

In his bumbling way, Chancey had tried to get her to stop dwelling on the man. What he told her chilled her to the core. She'd known Sutherland was a rake, but she'd thought the way he'd kissed and touched her so intimately had been . . . special.

For him, what they'd shared was a nightly occurrence. She'd been just another notch in a rake's bedpost. . . .

Her thoughts were interrupted when Chapman knocked on the parlor door. He looked apologetic as he said, "Your grandmother would like to know why you ordered a carriage brought around to the front."

"I'm about to go see my father."

Chapman nodded gravely. "If that was your answer, I am to instruct you to order the carriage to the mews instead."

Nicole crossed her eyes, and Chapman immediately had to cough.

"Tell her I will next time. And thank you," she called as he exited the room. She began to fuss with the costly veil she wore when she visited her father. None of Sutherland's hirelings would ever think the regally gowned woman arriving at the jail was Nicole.

"Listen, Chancey—"

"Christina Banning!" her grandmother shouted from the door, her black skirts rustling to a stop. Anger radiated from her, and though she was a small woman, she seemed to fill the doorway.

"My name is *Nicole Lassiter*." They'd been through this moniker skirmish a hundred times already. Her grandmother wanted Nicole to use her middle name and her mother's maiden name, so no one could connect Jason Lassiter's sailing daughter with Evelyn Banning's granddaughter until after she was safely married.

The old woman narrowed her eyes; Nicole knew the battle was on. Strangely, she was coming to look forward to these willful contests between them.

"If you can't abide by my rules, then don't bother coming back to marry because no one will have you. If they found out who you are, it won't matter that you're pretty or dowered—no man of consequence will take a woman with your history to wife."

"Do you really think I'm pretty?" Nicole simpered with what she knew was an irritating smile.

Her grandmother ignored her. "It simply can't be known. I've worked for two decades to hide your wayward life. Nicole Lassiter is a sailor—in my residence you are Christina Banning."

They argued back and forth for several minutes, until the dowager said, "Mark my words, child. I'm not doing this for me—I'm doing this for you! You do not want to enter my world with one hand tied behind your back." With a glare at Chancey, she swept out of the room.

He shook his head, his eyes wide. "Like I always said about ye—ye got more pluck than sense. She's a terror, that one."

Chancey was miserable here at Atworth House under the dowager's constant censure. Between that and his agreement to keep a secret from her father, which he didn't differentiate much from lying, he appeared near his breaking point. She arrived at her own breaking point that afternoon when they visited her father. It began when he told her he wouldn't be released in time for the race.

"So the *Bella Nicola*'s sitting idle in the greatest race ever?" The thought made her feel like crying. She glanced from one man to the other. She noted Chancey was about to buckle the small stool he covered.

Chancey cast an anxious look at her father before meeting her gaze again. "No, we've decided I'm goin' to sail the race without Jason. Yer father's worked too hard for this line to have it die for naught. I'll captain the ship."

Nicole eyed him. "You don't have papers." Chancey was a born seaman, but he wasn't certified as a captain because he couldn't read or navigate.

"I've got experience with the ship, and I'll find somebody to help me with my shortcomin's."

"Like me." She spoke arrogantly, as though it were a foregone conclusion.

Lassiter spoke up. "Forget it, Nicole."

"Then who will navigate?" she asked in exasperation.

Silence from both.

"*Who?*"

"Chancey and I have thought about it—Dennis will have to do."

"Dennis!" she exclaimed, picturing the carefree helmsman of their ship. "You can't be serious. He better have improved since I've been away, or the ship's driftwood. Surely there's someone else—someone from one of our other crews?"

Lassiter stood and paced. "No, all our ships are at sea. And any navigator worth his salt around here is already engaged."

"Father, you know I'm better than Dennis."

"No doubt of it."

"Then why not me?"

"Because you're my daughter, and these are the most dangerous seas on earth!"

"But, Father . . ." Even after her pleading progressed into threatening, neither man could be moved. She was to stay with her grandmother while Chancey and the crew made way.

"You're absolutely holding firm?"

He pressed his lips together. "I absolutely am."

She didn't know whether to cry or howl in her frustration. He could not be swayed. For someone used to getting her own way, it seemed as if the whole world had teamed to thwart her.

"As soon as I get out, I'll take you somewhere nice," Lassiter, bless his heart, promised her. "Maybe we could go to Connecticut? Stay in Mystic—check out the old neighborhood?"

"We only lived there for a few months. The *Bella Nicola* is my old neighborhood."

He exhaled loudly. "Just be patient, Nic. Only a few more days at your grandmother's—I promise."

He didn't know how right he was about that.

"The solicitor thinks I'll be out of here in a week," he said in an optimistic tone.

"Why hasn't he filed any complaints?"

Again, silence.

"Why, Father?"

"Because the reason for the fight could get out." He continued over her disbelieving look, "It's only a week more."

He was staying in here for her. *Oh, Papa.*

"It isn't a big concern, really. And it's not as though I'm without comforts." He waved a hand around the space.

The room truly didn't look bad. Like a bird, she'd feathered it with blankets, pillows, and rugs purloined from Atworth House, browbeating the guard to allow it, until her father's surroundings looked ridiculously lavish. He had cards, pen and ink, and she'd arranged for her grandmother's cook to send him food three times a day until he was released. She'd ensured that he'd be fine.

Even after she sailed.

When she said good-bye, she acted as though everything was normal, though her hug was longer than usual. Later in her grandmother's soft, crested carriage, Nicole reviewed her decision.

After this, she might be able to live on her memories when she was obliged to settle down according to the dowager's wishes. To marry a man she chose for her. To live a lie. The woman never let an hour go by without reminding Nicole that she had attempted to help her father with bail and had had a solicitor sent around. She would be *recompensed.*

Her father, of course, would have an apoplectic fit once he found out where she'd gone. Right after her grandmother did. But this was for a good cause. She reminded herself that she did this as much for her father and the crew as for herself. They expected her to stay at Atworth House, a picture of docility, while Dennis—a nice sailor, a great helmsman, but a weak navigator—was in charge of guiding the *Bella Nicola?*

Which was silly, since she'd never done what was expected of her.

She would tell her grandmother she was going to the Continent to visit friends from school and begin buying her wardrobe for the upcoming season. With work, Nicole believed she could get the dowager to commit to some type of token watch over her father while she was away.

Then there was Chancey. . . .

When she took a carriage from Atworth House the morning of the race, sea chests in tow, she dealt with only a little uncertainty and possibly a tiny bit of guilt for what she planned to do. She'd written a letter telling Lassiter that if he followed her after his release, she would always know he didn't believe in her—that he didn't trust her to get the job done. The letter had been true, even if over-wrought. Any time she heard from her conscience, she vowed he would have something to thank her for in the end.

"Good morning, Chancey," she called out to his squared back as she strolled aboard the *Bella Nicola*. His shoulders stiffened before he turned around slowly to face her.

"Tell me I'm not seein' Nicole on this deck."

"Can't do that, I'm afraid, because I'm here," she said, tapping her finger to the tip of her nose and then pointing at him in a cavalier manner. "And I'm staying, so let's get my trunks on board and make way."

He looked at her as if horns grew among the curls on her head. "Ye're touched in the brain if ye think I'm lettin' ye sail. Now, get ye gone back to yer gram's."

She walked closer and raised her face to catch his gaze. "Chancey, if you kick me off this ship, then I'm walking straight over to the *Southern Cross* and sailing with Sutherland. You know he'll take me on." She gave him a sly look.

"Bloody hell! Yer father'll have a stroke, ye just see if he won't. And he'll be comin' after ye."

"No, he won't—I wrote him a letter. He'll be fine," she said blithely, though she doubted her pleading letter would in fact keep him idle in London. "One way or another, I'm sailing this race. Since you need me, I might as well sail with you."

When he still looked unconvinced, she said, "You're always telling me to follow my gut—listen to my instincts. Well, right now my instinct's telling me that I need to be a part of this race."

Chancey looked as though that idea affected him, but then he smirked. "I'll just stay here till Sutherland sails. Then where will ye be?"

She smirked back. "If you go by his ship, you'll see that he's not sailing today, and rumor has it that he's not going to sail for a couple more days. Who knows, Chancey, he might be waiting to find me," she said. She didn't believe that, but this line of argument appeared to be wearing the man down. "I'll just go let him know where I am." She turned on her heel, astonishing even herself with how scheming she could be. But this was an exception—she *had* to sail.

She'd just made it to the gangway when he reeled off a curse. His voice gruff, he called out, "I hope all those dancin' lessons didn't make ye forget yer dead reckonin' and numbers."

Several hundred ships upriver from Nicole, Derek sat for a good part of the afternoon nursing a bottle of brandy.

The race would be starting soon, so he left his cabin to climb up on deck. He took a deep breath of air, fresher because of the high tide, and scanned the port crowded with the world's fastest moonrakers, their masts towering into the clouds. He could hear the lively music carrying over the water as an official band played. All along the Thames, shopkeepers filled the quayside with their colorful stalls, and the national flags of all the entries dotted the patchwork scene. It was a huge celebration, one he and his men should be a part of. But he couldn't think of that now.

He'd expected that the sight of his better rivals with their spotless vessels in full regalia would make him feel like a complete fool for choosing to stay in port. He'd watched and jotted down his customary observations about the ships, but he hadn't come to regret his decision. For some reason that he didn't understand, he had to find Nicole before he sailed. An urgency gripped him that he couldn't explain to himself, much less to his disgusted brother or disgruntled crew.

Remembering the astonished faces of his sailors when he'd told them his decision made his lips twitch. He hadn't missed the quick exchange of coins as bets were paid. Well, they could laugh all they wanted. The decision to find her was . . . right.

His semidrunken musings were interrupted when he noticed the *Bella Nicola* taking her place among the other ships. He knew Lassiter was still in jail, and that he hadn't even attempted the surely futile search for another captain. So who in the hell was taking the ship on?

Derek raced over the helm to pick up his spyglass. Unsteadily, he trained it on the ship.

With her glinting hair streaming out behind her, Nicole

Lassiter stood at the bow of the *Bella Nicola* and was sailing right past him. Chancey had the bridge.

Derek shook his head, unable to believe it. He ran a hand over his face; then, with an excitement he hadn't felt in years, he turned toward his crew and bellowed, *"Make ready to sail!"*

Chapter 10

Out of necessity, Nicole and Chancey made it through the day without arguing.

But that night . . .

"Damn it, what were ye thinkin'?" he bellowed over dinner. His voice boomed so loud, Nicole thought it rattled their tin plates.

She blew out a breath. "You know, I was thinking we'd make it through the whole day."

He had his thick hand stuffed into the handle of a mug that he whacked against the table for emphasis. "This is no school outin'. We're sailin' into the Forties—ye know the kind o' storms we'll see."

"I know, and I can't wait." She slathered butter on a biscuit and took a big bite.

"We'll have to adjust our course because o' ye. Hell, we shouldn't even sail this bloody race." Another bang of his mug. "We don't have a chance with ye on board."

"That's where you're wrong," she declared, tempted to bang her mug back at him. "I plan on navigating for us, winning this race, and saving the line. Unless you want to risk my father's future and ours as well, we'll stay steady and weather whatever comes, as it comes."

"What about Sutherland? We all saw him yellin' at his crew and them all scamperin' all over the deck—ye know he's comin'. What do ye think he'll do now?"

"I think he'll eat our wake for the next thirteen thousand miles," she said with a lazy grin, ignoring Chancey's vexed expression. She picked up an apple and knife and leisurely began cutting. "Really, what can he do now that we're under way? Catch us?" she scoffed.

"No, he can't catch the *Bella Nicola*. But say what if?"

"I don't know," she admitted. "I can't understand a man like that. Chancey, why wasn't he planning on sailing today? Doesn't he care that this is probably the most important race of his life?"

"Sometimes a man like that is beyond carin' about anythin'," he answered as he wrenched his mug off his hand and pushed his plate aside.

"Why?"

He reached into his pocket and pulled out tobacco for his clay pipe. "'Cause he's lost the hope in him."

"So, what happens with someone like him? Do they just stay that way forever?" she asked, then added, "Oh, don't look at me all suspicious like that. I'm not making plans— I'm just curious. I might not ever see him again."

He eyed her skeptically, but at her feigned studious look he relaxed, lit his pipe, and began explaining. "A man can change, but only when he can start lookin' forward to the days ahead. If ye dread every mornin' cause it's a new day, then ye stop carin'."

"Is that what happened with you when your wife died?"

Chancey inhaled deeply on his pipe, the air forcing his barrel chest to grow even larger, and exhaled slowly. "Aye. It were bloody hard—so hard I'd given up on livin'. But then yer father hired me aboard. Blasted Yank wouldn't take no for an answer—said he understood what I was goin' through. And I knew quick-like that I needed to help him care for ye. Ye were so wild, doin' only as ye pleased. And he couldn't naysay ye. Still can't, if ye ask me," he grumbled.

She ignored the last comment and asked, "So, we helped you get your hope back?"

"Aye. It takes somethin' to change yer life so much ye can finally see that yer days could turn out good-like in the future."

Was that why Sutherland wasted all that he'd been given in his life? He threw away so much, and it angered her. She needed to feed that anger, because she'd unforgivably developed soft feelings toward him that made her weak— soft feelings that clung even after she understood how truly despicable he was. She couldn't seem to think of him without her heart squeezing in her chest, yet for him she'd been merely a . . . diversion. The heated names she'd called him that strange night while trying to get Chancey to forget the idea of marriage had seemed harsh and overdone then. Really, they were exactly fitting.

What was so bad was that, deep down, she'd known. She'd felt the danger rolling off him. She'd seen him in that vile tap house and had learned about his exploits even before she met him.

The only thing that kept her from truly hating Sutherland was remembering that she had been using him as well. She'd needed to appease her desires and curiosity because, until that night, she'd tossed in her bed wondering about passion until she thought it would drive her mad.

Sadly, she still tossed in her bed, but now it was because she understood what passion was.

Why couldn't he be the type of man who would be as affected as she was and feel this longing, too?

"Nic, ye look like ye're gonna cry," Chancey said hesitantly as he relit his pipe.

"Huh?" She shook her head. "I was just thinking . . . and I am *not* going to cry." She was appalled at the idea. "When was the last time you saw me cry?"

Chancey thought before answering. "When ye were eight and ye fell outta the riggin' and broke yer arm. Such a wee monkey ye were." He chuckled. "I thought yer father was gonna have a fit."

The mention of her father brought Nicole's attention back to where it should have been in the first place. Since she was fairly certain Sutherland had had nothing to do with her father's continued imprisonment or the ship sabotage, she would just tuck that memory of him way back in her heart and think of him no more. The next few months would be grueling enough as it was.

"We'll just have to brazen it out," Nicole said decisively. "That's what we'll do. Father is counting on both of us, even if he doesn't know it yet. I won't let a sod like Sutherland put me off course."

Lassiter's imprisonment lasted not one week more, but two. He'd been like a madman when he'd received Nicole's letter because he couldn't do a thing to stop her. Within minutes of his release he was in Mayfair, drumming on the doors at Atworth House.

Jason pushed past the aging butler and marched down to the salon. It was a place he'd always remember. In that room, Evelyn Banning had blamed him for her daughter's death. She'd called Nicole a savage. And she'd extracted a promise to return Nicole to this mausoleum when she was only twelve. It was the only promise he'd ever broken.

He froze in midstride as he was confronted with the huge portrait of Laurel above the fireplace. No, he'd broken one other promise. In that steamy night off the coast of Brazil, he'd told Laurel that she would live.

He couldn't save his wife, but he could damn well go after his daughter.

"Nicole has sailed on my ship in the Great Circle Race," Jason announced without preamble when he stood in front of her.

Evelyn didn't raise her coiffed head from her cross-stitching. "She told me she was returning to Paris or elsewhere on the Continent. Not sailing to Australia again."

"I need to go after her, and I don't have a ship within two weeks' sailing time of here." His throat tightened. "I . . . I need passage," he ground out.

At this, she lowered her work. "Honestly, Jason! Don't be so melodramatic. I'm angry, too, but there's nothing to be done for it now. She'll be back soon enough. Chit will miss much of the season, though." Then, in a dismissing tone, she added, "Keep me updated on her whereabouts."

"I don't think you understand me. She is in danger, and I need to go after her."

The dowager stood in a huff. "Ridiculous. After all the times you've written, assuring me how safe she was, how beneficial sailing was for the girl—don't go changing your tale on me." She turned to leave the room.

"I could make sure she was safe because I was with her," Jason said as he grasped her arm. She gave him a withering look, but he couldn't be deterred. "Damn it, I wanted to spare you the realities of this trip, but you leave me no choice. I've been investigating a series of strange accidents that have been afflicting several lines. I know that my ship was targeted because Nicole stumbled across a couple of cutthroats sabotaging it. She barely escaped with her life."

He continued over the woman's horrified gasp, "She'll travel through the fortieth parallel, known as the Roaring Forties, where some of the worst weather on earth manifests itself. Thirty- to sixty-foot rogue waves, large enough to swallow a ship of much more tonnage than mine, are not unheard of. The path where they are charted to sail has literally thousands of shipwrecks on the sea floor. And if I know Nicole, she'll probably even maneuver them into the Screaming Fifties, which are much, much—"

"I don't want to know!" The cross-stitching she'd been clutching dropped to the floor. "For God's sake, why have you taken her there in the past?" she cried in outrage.

"We never sailed the more extreme course. But Nicole came across her competition's planned route. It was next to suicidal. Now that she knows how far into the Forties he'll go, she'll sail even farther south."

"I do not believe this." She grasped the high collar at her throat with shaking fingers. "This is your fault. Again!"

Lassiter drew his eyebrows together in an agonized expression. "It's usually not so dangerous. And even now, I wouldn't overly worry about her because she's in capable hands. Hell, she *is* a capable hand. But before there was no doubt about our ship's integrity—now I don't know if those thugs could have been successful. It would be a deadly combination if they timed an accident to occur in the strongest tossing of the ship."

His look was beseeching. "I've got to get to my daughter, because if she hasn't already, she could soon know a living hell."

Chapter 11

This is embarrassing," Nicole heard one of their midshipmen mumble from the deck.

What an understatement. Just hours ago, they'd lost their rudder, and the *Bella Nicola* had become completely incapacitated. Their beautiful, regal ship with its American flag pennants had been flailing around, out of control—a menace to the fishing vessels dotting the waters off the coast of Brazil.

After several hours, they'd managed to rig a makeshift rudder that would help them get closer to land and help. More important, they'd been able to get out of sight before the other gaining ships in the race had any chance to see them. Nicole knew it was shallow—but she would simply have to drown herself if Sutherland saw them like this.

She shook her hung head, only to cringe again when she looked up to the bow. They'd certainly found help.

The *Bella Nicola* was being towed by a fully stocked guano freighter.

Even in the turmoil of the Bay of Biscay's continuous storms, which Derek secretly believed was the best part of sailing, his mind had been constantly on Nicole. Evidently, she'd been spying on the competition. All of the competition, if he was part of some list.

Hell, he'd seen her studying his chart. And now that she'd learned how far south he planned to go, they'd try to beat it. He in turn would have to sail closer to the Antarctic than he'd ever anticipated.

When he found Nicole he would . . . bloody hell, he didn't know what he'd do.

For not quite six thousand miles, he'd followed patiently behind the *Bella Nicola,* rarely varying from his south-southwest course. He'd already passed other competitors and was comfortable with his position, even though Nicole led, and he was most likely steadily losing ground on her. He didn't doubt he'd make it up in the Southern Ocean—no ship was stronger than his in those seas.

As they neared the easternmost tip of South America and the waters took on the emerald green cast so common over the reefs in this area, his crew spotted some local fishing vessels about sixty miles off the coast. Anxious to confirm his second-place position, Derek closed in and signaled them. The locals approached in their log raft *jangadas* and related that the *Desirade* had already passed.

Silence claimed the deck. Word of Tallywood's lead stunned everyone. Even though the *Desirade* was an extreme clipper, Tallywood had never attained half its potential speed. With his superior airs and his negligence in captaining, he'd become a hated figure in the shipping community.

Tallywood's lead was surprising news in itself, but then Derek learned that the *Bella Nicola* had been towed into port at Recife, Brazil.

Towed?

He thought of his own strong position, of the ships he'd passed in the Bay of Biscay and down the trades. It would be a close thing to take the lead from Tallywood as they continued south, then turned east toward Africa and the Cape of Good Hope, but Derek could afford to stop. It wasn't as if Nicole would be cutting a larger lead in the meantime, and she was his main competition. Or at least, her ship was. After ordering his crew to Recife, he went to his cabin to change.

He smiled, a lupine grin, when he recalled another excellent reason to stop in Recife—namely, Madam Maria Delgado's bordello. . . .

Without warning, the dream from two nights before flooded his mind. In it, Nicole lay in his bed, completely unclothed beside him, her impatient hands smoothing over his body. He turned and reached for her, pulling her body close to press against the naked length of his own.

He tilted her head to take his seeking mouth, and she eagerly met his lips, slipping her tongue in to lightly lap at his own. His hands roamed the front of her body, only stopping to press his thumbs over her nipples.

Over and over, he brushed the peaks while he plundered her mouth, until she began writhing uncontrollably, arching her pelvis onto his swollen rod, making him want to explode against her.

The husky little moans escaping her soft lips made him desperate to possess her, to pound himself into her unmercifully until he made her convulse around him and cry his name. But each time he positioned her to take him, she moved elusively, maddeningly. At last, she allowed him to rise over her, his arms at her sides and his legs resting between hers as his mouth hungrily took hers again.

Suddenly she broke the kiss, and he sensed she would move away from him again. To keep her where he wanted, he swiftly spread his legs over hers to rest against the side of each thigh so that all of him surrounded her pinned body. But then she put her small hands on his chest and, before he could stop her, pushed against him as she inched her way down his body until he straddled her shoulders and head. He was too stunned to move—too heavily aroused to think. And when she grasped him and brought that hot, wet mouth over him, he didn't know if he could stop himself from spilling into her. . . .

Jerking upright in bed, he'd awakened from the most powerfully erotic dream he'd ever experienced. As the pressure pooled in his groin, he groaned in the dark. He gripped himself, intending to finish it off, but his rough hand sliding over his cock was a poor substitute for a woman's soft flesh, or soft mouth.

His aching erection wouldn't subside, and with each second he'd endured it, he'd sworn he would make her pay for this night. *She* had brought him to this—to experiencing more violently sensual dreams than he'd ever had, even as a green lad. Even more determinedly, he'd vowed that he would find a woman when they next stopped and use her until Nicole was placed firmly in the back of his mind.

And now he could.

When they'd docked in Recife among the many ships crowding the main harbor, Derek learned the damage to the *Bella Nicola* was nothing more than a broken rudder.

They'd be repaired and on their way in half a day. But by then he would have had a woman or possibly two, restocked his ship with perishables, and made open sea.

As he pushed through the market stalls set along the docks, he scarcely perceived the pungent odor of coffee or the sour smell of rotting sugarcane. He hardly noticed the locals gaping at his height or demeanor. His thoughts were focused inward.

He didn't actually decide to go to her ship. He just found himself walking there, and to justify his direction, he convinced himself it was on the way to Maria's. Or not too far out of the way. When he came upon the spotless vessel, he asked a crewman scraping the deck if he could speak with Miss Lassiter. The man ignored him.

Permission to come aboard was denied by another crewman. Unless Derek wanted to start a war between his crew and theirs, he'd have to back down. He inquired one last time about Nicole, and this time was answered by Chancey as he walked up behind him. Derek turned slowly, prepared for a fight.

The big man only stared at him, taking his measure. Finally, he said, "Ye touch her again—ye die," then casually walked on aboard.

Derek took one last look at her ship. He would prefer having Nicole, but at this point, he'd make do.

Decided, he made his way to an elegant Spanish-style palazzo overlooking the harbor. Casa de Delgado was the largest and most impressive home in the city, and if he remembered correctly, its inside mirrored its immaculate exterior. The rooms were spacious, lofty, and colored in the rich colonial tones that the plantations favored. Minutes after he walked through the heavy wooden doors, a guard escorted him to a tasteful study.

When he entered, Maria Delgado looked up from her account books. Unconsciously she pushed at the spectacles that made her look more like a headmistress than a madam. He'd met her many years ago when he was a young man on his way to the Pacific Ocean for the first time, and occasionally he'd remembered with pleasure his experiences in the upscale bordello.

"Captain Sutherland, how good you are to visit us once again." She smiled warmly as she rose to clasp his hand. "It has been far too long." It had been a long time, but you couldn't tell from her demeanor. She seemed completely unsurprised that he'd arrived even after all these years. And she studied him closely.

"You are, of course, welcome to enter directly." Madam Delgado unfailingly screened every potential client before allowing him to frequent her place. He recalled many regulars joking that new clients should bring Maria character recommendations just to get into her exclusive brothel.

He took her hand in his. "It is good to see you again, madam. You're looking beautiful as usual." And she was. Possibly in her early forties, she had a youthful radiance that made her dark eyes sparkle. Her thick black mane was not yet laced with gray.

"I suppose we must get you in and out as soon as possible. No?"

Derek stared at her in amusement until she asked, "You are sailing in the Great Race?"

"I'm sorry, I misunderstood. Yes, I am sailing the race, but we've got a good lead so I have a bit of time."

"I see." She smiled and tilted her head to the side as she stared at him intently. Strangely, when Maria tilted her head like that, he was reminded of Nicole.

Her curious behavior made the hair on the back of his neck stand up. He was glad he was prepared for a shock, because she mysteriously asked, "So, what would you like today, *bello?* I'm thinking you look to be in the mood for a slender, small-waisted redhead with dark blue eyes. No?"

The sun was just reaching noon when he made his way back through the palazzo to leave. Though Derek should have been running from here after what he'd just done, he was strangely reluctant to go, and his steps were slow.

"Oh, Captain Sutherland?" Maria called from behind him, and he groaned inwardly. "Captain Sutherland . . ."

He did not want to hear about his actions from her, but she didn't look like he could easily avoid her. Her bespectacled eyes blazed with a look of determination.

He stopped in the breezeway and waited for her to stroll over, wondering why she looked pleased.

"Captain, you did not have to pay Juliette so much. That is far too much for even one thousand minutes with her," she said with a sly smile, "much less five."

His lips thinned. The last thing he needed right now was to be subtly ridiculed by a Brazilian madam. "I paid Julia what I did—"

"Juliette," Maria interrupted.

"*Juliette* received that much money," he ground out, "because she wouldn't stop crying." And because he wanted to mitigate his embarrassment.

"Ah, *bello,* I only tease," she said with a laugh. "It was very kind of you. Especially since I get twenty percent," she quipped. "But now I know you must leave us. I only ask that you take the east exit, down the steps there." She pointed. "You will go through a garden past my little home, and you can see lovely blooms all around."

"I'll have to pass," he said, mustering no regret in his voice. "I have a rather limited interest in botany."

"I'm afraid you will insult me," she said in a mulish tone, her laughter forgotten. "I extend this invitation to view my private home to no man."

He eyed her, knowing something was wrong with this situation. But he had a lot on his mind and didn't want to fight with the woman, who looked to be digging in her heels.

"As you wish, madam," he said with a curt bow. "Just down these steps?" At her nod, he turned to leave, thinking this day grew odd indeed. He entered the garden and found it nice but not the earth-shattering experience Maria thought it was.

Her home consisted of a main house with two wings, separated from the palazzo by the garden as well as a sturdy gate, open now. It was pleasant, but nothing like the grandeur of the bordello. Maria's behavior from this morning on had been baffling—

His thoughts were interrupted by a conversation between two women drifting out from a cracked-open door in one of the wings.

One woman had a thick British colonial accent, Indian, he'd wager. In a crisp, businesslike tone, she said, "Now, relax, please. And unbutton your shirt further." Had Maria wanted him to stumble on something here? Curious, he slowed outside the door.

He froze at the woman's next comment.

"You have to relax, Nicole. Just trust me. When I am through with you, you'll feel like a new woman. So get your mind off your problems. Chancey will take care of your boat—"

"Ship."

"Very well, ship. Now, take a deep breath so I can finish with you before you have to leave."

She couldn't be talking to his Nicole; it just wasn't possible. But her dulcet voice, the strangely accented voice he recognized at once, replied, "Sasha, this doesn't hurt."

"Of course not, silly."

His whole body tensed as he moved closer. Was he losing his mind, or was Nicole Lassiter in this Brazilian madam's personal abode getting undressed for a woman? His hand shot to the doorknob but just as swiftly stilled. He should listen, find out more about her. Like what she was doing in there with a woman.

"I've never done this before."

"You should have," the woman confided. "It drives men wild."

"Ah, that *tickles!*"

"Stop squirming, Nic."

Derek, his teeth grinding, heard a pause, and then the more sharply commanded, "I mean it!"

"You should have more sympathy. When was the last time you had it done?"

"I do it to myself. I could teach you if we had more time." Christ, just what were they talking about?

Nicole sounded wistful. "I wish I did. I miss it here," she added before she began giggling.

"We miss you t— Nic, I can't continue until you can stop your belly from quivering like that."

Enough. His blood boiled. Jaw clenched, he yanked open the door and sucked in a breath, loudly exhaling as the scene before him unfolded. A fully, though scantily, clothed Eastern woman bent over a half-clad Nicole. Luckily, the woman snatched her hand away just as Nicole bolted up or, as he now realized, she would have had a streak of red henna going straight up her neck.

A feeling of acute relief washed over him. The woman was decorating Nicole's body with henna in the traditional Indian *mehndi*. His lips crooked up in a grin, which wasn't surprising, considering his intense satisfaction at finding her, and finding her innocently uninvolved. Maria, he thought with an inward laugh, had gathered exactly what he wanted.

"Sutherland! What are you doing here?" Nicole cried out. Could she know what her open shirt and hennaed skin did to him?

"I could ask the same of you. I was certain I'd see you again—I just didn't expect it to be in the home of a madam," he replied. Then he hitched in a breath as he got a full glimpse of the braided vine design drawn on her creamy skin. It circled her waist like a bracelet, and then, in a pattern of swirls and buds, crawled up her torso to meet in a point between her breasts. In an instant, he knew the memory of her wide eyes and wildly decorated body would stay with him his whole life.

She was too astounded to do anything but gape at him, until she saw his heated stare assessing her body. Her hands flew up to grab the sides of her shirt to pull it closed.

"Oh, no, you don't," the Indian woman, Sasha, commanded in a stern voice as she swiped at her hands. "The last bit isn't dry yet."

She gave the woman an oppressed look and moved to the side of the bed. In a huff, she turned herself from him to button her shirt.

She stopped when she received a cuff to the ear from Sasha. "I'm sorry, Nic. But you won't do anything to ruin this *mehndi*."

The woman turned to Derek, her large flattened ear-rings chiming as her doe eyes flickered over him. Then she gave a pointed, amazed look to Nicole. "He is Sutherland, the man you spoke of?"

Nicole grimaced at the question, and a furious blush stole across her face. Derek was surprised but extremely pleased that she'd spoken of him to this woman. And obviously to Madam Maria, too.

Nicole glanced down. Evidently, she thought she'd covered everything important, so she whipped around to face Sutherland. But not before flashing Sasha a look that screamed, *Are you happy now?*

Sasha looked back at Derek and gazed at him in awe, muttering something about powerful magic. As Nicole watched Derek, her expression changed rapidly from wary bemusement to outright exasperation, until she finally jerked her glance to the woman. "*What* are you talking about?"

"The *mehndi* is very powerful. It is already working."

"Already working?" Nicole choked out. "You said it would bring me luck and ward off evil. But on the contrary, Sutherland's arrival is unlucky and *he* is not being warded off, so I'd say this stuff"—she looked down her chest—"is definitely not working."

Sasha arched an eyebrow at her. "No, no, Nicole. Don't you see the lotus here?" She tugged up Nicole's shirt and pointed out a finely drawn, lacy flower on her flat belly. "I drew that for fertility and love. And then your mate just happens to walk through the door! It is most definitely working."

Nicole's jaw dropped. "Sutherland is not my mate! A-and you can count on the fact that we won't need any luck with fertility, because there won't be any—any—"

"Planting?" he added helpfully as he bit back a grin. "*Planting?*"

She was angered that he played with her, but he couldn't help it. He found he enjoyed teasing her.

"Again, what are you doing here?" she demanded.

He'd watched the whole scene between Sasha and Nicole in grinning amusement. But his grin was wiped off his face when the lapel of Nicole's shirt brushed a hardened, pink nipple just visible under the linen. Fascinated, he hardly trusted himself to speak intelligibly, so in response he smiled down at her, hoping it didn't look as predatory as he felt, and answered her question with a question. "What do you think I'm doing at a brothel?"

"Oooh, get out!" She threw a silken pillow that he easily dodged and didn't notice when her shirt gaped open even wider. "You have no right to be in here. This is private! If you came here to cart me away, you'll soon realize that won't be happening."

He might not have come here expressly for that purpose, but carrying her away was exactly what he'd been thinking of. For her to presume so . . . His half-smile was replaced by a sneer. "Don't flatter yourself, princess—I did not come here for you."

She blinked up at him, and he could swear he read a look of regret in her eyes before she turned to the bewildered woman. "Sasha, please go get Berto and see that this man is dragged out of here. Violently!"

"I'm afraid we can't do that," Maria said as she swept past Derek into the room, her silks and exotic scent trailing delicately behind her. At a nod from her, Sasha quitted the room, and Maria continued to them, "We'll have to come to some kind of agreement until he decides to leave. You are my little *bella,* but he is a good customer," she said as she pinned Derek with a pointed look.

He nearly flushed. To change the subject, he said, "Maria, I would like an explanation as to why Jason Lassiter's daughter is in this place. Now."

"This place? You make it sound awful. Though you certainly never complained before."

It riled him to see Nicole trying not to smile at Maria's set-down.

"An answer!"

Maria replied in a casually conversational tone, "She is a daughter to me."

Maria looked at Sutherland's dropped jaw and bit back a laugh. This was going to be too much fun.

"Daughter to you?" he managed.

"Yes, I have known her for fifteen years." She paused before she asked, "How long have you known her?"

Sutherland gave her a tight, impatient look. "How do you know her?"

Maria looked to Nicole in question. Nicole responded, "I don't care."

Still Maria hesitated. It was only partly her story to tell. Plus, she doubted she could conceal her feelings for Jason if she spoke of him. But what did it matter? Nicole knew. It seemed as if everyone knew. Except Jason.

And Maria sensed Nicole wouldn't mind Sutherland learning more about her. Reluctantly, she began, "I was reading here one night when a messenger brought me an urgent request. An American captain was losing his wife in childbirth."

She paused and swallowed. "No one, not even the one doctor here, would help them because a couple of cases of yellow fever had come in on an American ship the week before. I was afraid as well, but the thought of some poor woman . . . Well, I had no nursing skills, but in my business I've certainly helped birth a number of children. It was what the American thought when he sent for me."

Maria encountered the familiar sadness as she continued, "When I arrived at the ship, the screams echoed along what would have been silent docks. I hurried on, but when I saw the woman, I knew it was too late. She'd lost far too much blood. Jason Lassiter, of course, was the captain. I'd never seen a human being who was so beside himself in misery." Her voice had lowered to a whisper.

Moving to Nicole's side, she looked down at the girl she had come to love as a daughter and smoothed a curl behind her ear. In a stronger voice, she resumed, "He didn't care that I was a madam. All he cared about was his young wife. We struggled all night, and finally a baby girl was born. But they were too weak and within the hour both had passed away."

She paused when she saw Nicole's watering eyes. Sutherland saw, too, but he looked surprised, as though grasping how little he understood about Nicole and possibly Jason. Dragging his eyes back to Maria, he commanded, "Continue." She only raised her eyebrows at him until he reluctantly added, "Please."

"Jason became . . . inconsolable." She recalled that fateful night so well, it was as if she could still hear him yelling, weeping, smashing anything within reach. "None of his crew could restrain him."

She absently stroked Nicole's shining hair. "My heart hurt for them, the little mother so brave and the husband so in love. I began making arrangements for her and her baby's burial. Just when I was about to leave, Nicole, such a beautiful child, ran after me. She was terrified and crying, and when I picked her up and quieted her, she clung to me as if she'd never let go. I told a crewman I was taking her and bullied him until he let us go. She fell asleep in my arms that night, and I have loved her since."

Sutherland paused, seeming to digest all she'd told him, but then a muscle pulsed in his jaw. "This visit's over," he said abruptly as he strode over to Nicole and grabbed her arm. "You're coming with me back to the ship."

"Maria!" Nicole called, trying to twist away.

"Anything you have to say to Nicole can be said here," Maria said in an authoritative tone.

"Maria, please! You're not allowing him to stay! This man hunted Chancey and me down in London, offering outrageous rewards—"

"You knew that, damn it?" He ran his free hand through his hair. "Why did you hide from me?"

"Why? Do you think I'm daft?" she asked, finally wrenching her arm out of his grasp. "You were out for revenge."

"Is that what I was looking for?"

"What else could you want from me after that night?"

Maria watched the two interacting and knew what Nicole had just said angered Sutherland terribly. Surely if the man offered rewards for her after their brief acquaintance, he wanted more from her than that. Looking at her lovely Nicole and seeing the way the two sparked off each other, she didn't see how he could be unaffected.

Yet instead of telling her that, he simply looked her over slowly. "Yes, that would be the only conclusion."

Meu Deus, perhaps I made a mistake hoping for these two.

"Of course it is. See, Maria . . ." Nicole turned beseeching eyes toward her. "He wants to get me back for that night. You can't let him."

"She doesn't have any say in the matter," he snapped.

"Of course I do, Captain," Maria countered. "If I call, guards will come here and stop you. Or you can be civilized and speak with her here. But I warn you, if you so much as raise your voice, you are out for good. *Compreenda?*"

He looked from her to Nicole, and finally gave a quick nod.

"Well, that's just fine," Nicole fumed. "He can choose to stay here, but I don't have to. Let go of my damn arm, you beast."

"You didn't think I was a beast that night in my cabin. . . ."

Maria studied them as they argued back and forth. She'd never known two people so right for each other.

Or two people so completely ignorant of that fact.

The coldness in the captain's heart wouldn't be able to withstand his unrelenting desire for Nicole. And he wouldn't try to diminish her passion and fire because he craved it. Nicole, so full of impulse and mischief, needed the reassurance of strength of a iron-willed man. She also needed his dark sensuality to sate her.

As she had thought, the man hadn't been able to get her out of his mind. That, coupled with Derek's behavior with Juliette, rendered her decision settled.

Backing toward the door, Maria smiled. "I think, my little *amantes,* that I will just leave you two in here and let you work it out for a bit."

She slammed and locked the heavy oaken door.

Chapter 12

Yes, sweet, she's left you unattended, and I assure you I'll take full advantage of that fact." His lips curled as he slowly moved closer to her. "Unlike you, I could not be happier with our circumstances," he said in a low voice.

She couldn't believe it. He'd just satisfied his lust with one of the women next door. He'd admitted that he'd come here to visit the brothel—not her. Just how many times could a man be with a woman in a single day?

She'd be damned if she would find out this way. She could just imagine him comparing her body and face to the beautiful courtesans inside the bordello. She would fall far short.

"Stay away from me. Let me pass to the door."

"Let you go? As easy as you please?" he scoffed. "I don't think so. . . . I've waited for a month to touch you again." He reached out and stroked a stray curl. "Do you know how much I've thought about our night together?"

Before she could stop herself, she stammered, "Y-you have?"

"Of course I have. I want you."

She came close to asking whether he'd just had a good enough substitute, but she did not want him to think she was jealous. "Why can't you leave me alone? I don't want this."

He surveyed her with hooded eyes. "You might think you don't want this, but your body is telling me something different." He ran his hand over her breast, just a swift, fleeting brush, and heat bloomed inside her. She jerked away from him, stifling a gasp.

"Damn you, Sutherland. Just leave me alone."

"I can't seem to do that," he said slowly, as if he surprised himself by his admission.

"Well, you'll have to. Even if I were attracted to you—which I'm not—I could never let down my guard with you. We're opponents. Although this race means nothing to you, it means everything to my father and me."

"I know the race is important." He ran his hand through his hair. "That ass, Tallywood, has the lead."

"*What?*"

"I found out this morning. I know I should leave and go catch him, but for some reason, where you're concerned . . ." He trailed off before grabbing her wrist and pulling her to him. He bent down to give her a light kiss on her neck, a bare flick of his tongue that made her tremble. "In fact, even though I know I should sail soon, I'm still spending the rest of the afternoon in bed with you."

She couldn't stand this. Thoughts of the race, of Tallywood leading, dissipated with each of Sutherland's slight touches. She imagined what they could do together for an entire afternoon.

What kind of wanton was she? The bastard had just finished making love with someone else; yet he was kissing her a few minutes later. Hadn't she learned the first time that she was merely one woman out of a long line of many? It infuriated her because she knew, she wasn't sure how, she simply knew that she wouldn't experience the same wonder and fire with another man. Whereas he probably enjoyed those feelings every night.

She made herself remember that if she won the race, if she defeated the man holding her now, she secured her future, as well as her father's and Chancey's. She needed to get that animosity growing between them again, because she couldn't trust herself to hold firm against him.

She backed away from him, glaring at his hand firm on her wrist. He scowled and released her.

"Are you navigating your ship?" she asked abruptly.

He looked nonplussed. "Of course."

She swallowed, then said arrogantly, "Excellent. It will be that much sweeter when I beat you."

"Are you insinuating that you're directing your ship?" He gave a quick, humorless laugh, then added snidely, "No wonder you lost your rudder."

Her blood boiled again, fortunately this time from fury. "I won't be there to clean up your careless calculations again," she taunted. "You'll be lucky to get out of the harbor."

"Those were rough . . ." His words lagged as his expression turned to realization, only to be replaced by one of annoyance. But his eyes never stopped showing hunger.

"Your ploy won't work with me, Nicole. The fact that you have to contrive a fight tells me you want me as much as I want you."

She shook her head in weak denial. His long arm shot out to secure her again.

No thought, she just reacted.

Grasping a chair beside her, she simultaneously leapt away from him and yanked the chair between them. The spindle of the chair back caught him squarely between the legs.

His jaw clenched as his eyes slid closed, and he stood motionless as if waiting for the pain to set in. When it did, his eyes opened to a murderous glare. Just before he dropped like a rock.

"Oh, my Lord!" she squealed as she sank down beside him. "I'm so sorry. . . . I only wanted to get away."

This only aggravated him even more. He groaned out with effort, "You . . . will . . . pay . . ."

Nicole did not have to linger to know what he was about to say. She whirled to the door and hammered it with open palms. Immediately, the key turned in the lock.

Just before she walked out, she turned back. He was right. She'd created a fight, but she hadn't intentionally hurt him. She wanted to apologize again, but convinced herself this was just as well. Finally she said, "I'm not unaware of the pain you're feeling. . . . I wouldn't have done it on purpose." She wanted to say more, but made her heart hard. "Good luck with the rest of the race, Captain. You *will* need it."

Derek winced as he took another swig of brandy. He couldn't draw deeply because of the ache in his groin, acute even after two hours. Nicole had definitely given him something to remember her by.

When he'd been able to walk steadily again, he'd searched for her in Maria's home. He approached the bordello, but learned that Nicole had never been allowed inside. Word must have spread about him, because the women in the brothel became openly antagonistic when he demanded to know where she was. A pack of wolves wouldn't defend its cub that fiercely.

So the little chit was navigating. Before, it'd been important only to see her and finally take her as she'd wanted him to in London. Now, with her arrogant taunts, he had to best her.

With halting steps, he walked across the deck to meet the Recife port official, who'd just completed inspecting the ship for any exports. The rough-edged but prospering little port of Recife was unswerving in searching for and taxing goods. Derek had heard once that Maria Delgado was responsible for the port's aggressive taxing and collection initiative. Knowing her business acumen, he didn't doubt it.

When the man finished the record of the *Southern Cross*'s docking and inspection, Derek said, "That was quick, *senhor*. Not that I'm complaining of course," he added jovially. He'd already decided to garner some information about Lassiter's crew from the self-important little man.

"Yes, I know you are in the Great Race, so I thought I might hurry you along," he said in a magnanimous manner as he handed the papers to Derek.

"My thanks." Derek paused before asking, "Have you already checked the *Bella Nicola*?"

"Not yet." Twirling his perky mustache, he leaned closer to add conspiratorially, "I also hurry to go see Captain Lassiter's daughter."

Derek forced a benign look onto his face even though he wanted to throttle the man simply for his interest.

Apparently, Miss Lassiter had admirers everywhere she traveled. He schooled his features as a thought occurred to him. "She is beautiful, isn't she?"

After listening to the inspector's enthusiastic agreement, Derek remarked, "You know . . . you might want to be extra kind to Miss Lassiter."

At the man's quickening interest, Derek shook his head sadly. "Yes, it appears that the girl developed quite a *tendre* for me. But when she made her interest known, I had to set her down. Pretty girl, but with my being an earl—well, of course, men of my title and status can't go around marrying commoners, you understand." The man nodded as if he completely understood the myriad trials of being an earl.

Derek had a hard time keeping a sober face. "She was very distraught. So much so that she swore to me she wouldn't wait but would marry the next man who proposed to her."

"Truly?" the official asked in a voice gone higher with excitement.

"Truly. I think she might play hard to get because of her experience with me. But the fact is, the girl greatly desires to be married. And as her father is desperate to get her off his hands, I know he would be only too happy to speak at length about her substantial dowry."

"Thank you, *Capitão*. Thank you," the official said fervently. He took Derek's hand and shook it with irritating zeal.

After Derek had finally extracted his hand from the man's grip, he added, "And, *senhor* . . . Miss Lassiter greatly admires strong, I daresay, domineering men—men who aren't afraid of charting a course and following it unwaveringly. Be warned, the clever girl might try to test your dedication."

"Many thanks. I go now to see Miss Lassiter!" He confidently saluted Derek.

As the man marched away, Derek could swear he heard the official chanting to himself, "*Forte, bravo, dominante!*"

Derek took satisfaction in the thought that Nicole had no idea the hounds of hell had just been unleashed, and merrily sent panting in her direction.

"The nerve, the utter arrogance of that man! He wanted to make love to me, Maria. As if I would ever. I wanted to slap him. I will win this race, just so he will lose—"

"Nicole! If you could stop cursing the captain for just one moment," Maria began over Nicole's tirade, "I would like to tell you something."

Nicole shut her mouth, frowned, and poured tea. "Very well . . ." she mumbled.

Maria took the offered cup. "I've been trying to tell you all the way from the house that Captain Sutherland did not touch Juliette. After only a brief kiss, he told her he couldn't be with her."

Reaction exploded in Nicole's heart; thoughts roiled in her head. He hadn't made love to Juliette? Why couldn't she tell he hadn't just been with another woman?

She'd been comfortable as an adversary to the rake, especially when she thought of him with Juliette. But now that Maria had told her the truth, her emotions catapulted to the other extreme. She replayed that last ill-fated meeting between them, imagining that she'd done everything differently. Hadn't wounded him so badly.

How could she wait until after the race to tell him how sorry she was?

"Oh, God, Maria! I have *feelings* for the captain!"

"*Muito bem.* Very good." She smiled. "I'll give you my

professional opinion. The captain behaved as he did because he is already in love with you."

Nicole absently swished the end of her braid against her mouth. "No, it can't be love on his part."

"Trust me. There is something very strong between you. You two would do well together. It won't be easy, but love seldom is."

Love from the captain? Nicole shook her head. "He probably hates me now. Did you forget I assaulted him this afternoon?"

"He'll recover. You could help him with that when you next see him," she said, and chuckled.

Nicole's eyes went wide. "Maria, I need to talk to you about . . . all that. You have to tell me everything, so I won't make a fool of myself with him next time."

"Ah, *bella,* it's simple."

Nicole leaned forward in her seat.

"There's one rule. All you have to do is—"

A knock interrupted her. Nicole scowled. "What is it?" she called out.

Chancey ambled in. "Ye got a message, and the port official's here to sign off."

She rose in a huff, took the message, and tossed it on her desk. "Maria, I'll be right back. Make some more tea—I have so many questions for you."

She hurried out the door to meet the official. He was a stout little man, trollish and brimming with condescension. Even after she'd signed the papers, he lingered, hovering about her.

"*Yes?*" she sniffed in her haughtiest tone. She was dying to get back to her cabin and hear the one rule.

"Miss Lassiter—I wish to speak with you about your recent unfortunate affair."

"My what?" She froze.

"Your heartbreak. I know of it, as well as your plans to marry. I have come to offer myself."

"Sir, I have no wish to marry anyone." She strove for calm. "I'm sorry, but you should leave now."

Unaffected, he twirled his moustache. "Ah, yes, now you play hard to get. But I will overcome you."

The man was insane. Utterly insane.

Behind the official, Maria stood in the doorway and gave her a questioning look. Nicole could only shake her head. The man was now assuring her with his tubby chest puffed with pride that although he was an official of some standing, he would overlook Nicole's *basebornness* and marry her regardless.

She turned on him in a flash. "If you think I will marry you—"

The man interrupted her, "You have continued your games long enough." He was becoming piqued, and his hands, before resting on his belly, gestured heatedly. "I wish to speak to your father about your dowry."

"My father," she bit out, "isn't receiving visitors."

He demanded a meeting. At once. When she continued to deny him, he grew suspicious that Captain Lassiter hadn't appeared on deck at the high tide.

How could she explain why they sailed her father's ship without him—or any captain with papers? He could make trouble for them just out of spite.

"He can't see you because he's at Madam Delgado's," she lied. Most in Recife knew of his close friendship with Maria, so it was believable. "He won't be back until the morning."

As soon as Maria heard, she blew Nicole a kiss and then crept off the ship and back to her home to cover for her.

It seemed like hours in hell before she'd gotten rid of the man. She returned to her cabin, hating that she hadn't been able to say good-bye to Maria, hating that she hadn't learned the *one simple rule*. She sank down in her chair, weary and feeling grimy from her encounter with the troll. It was then that her eyes trailed to the message folded on her desk.

Eyebrows knitted, she picked it up and ripped it open. In harshly scratched ink, it read, *I think you two would suit.*

Sutherland, that bastard! He'd signed it in large letters, boldly, sure she could do nothing. He was laughing at her even now, she knew it.

His prank ended up costing them the better part of a day. Scared that the official was watching them, they waited for the sun to go down and then escaped in the dark. Embarking was a celebration in its own, and sneaking away was demoralizing.

He would pay for that.

She wouldn't have thought the ignominy of being towed by a guano freighter could be matched on this trip. But it had been, and all because Sutherland had a fiendish humor.

That night, as Nicole stood on deck impatient to get to open sea, she recalled she'd wanted to *apologize* to him. And the entire time, the black-hearted swine was siccing a lovesick port official on her.

All apologies were forgotten.

"Ye think we'll catch the rest of the ships?" Chancey asked from behind her, silencing her thoughts.

Her face grew hard. "We'll catch them." *Especially Sutherland.*

Hours later, when the sun broke over the water, they spotted several masts just on the horizon. It had to be the first cluster of ships. As usually happened, several were matched in speed and crew, and none could break away. Even over a thirteen-thousand-mile voyage, many would stay within a few miles of each other.

At Chancey's command, the crew raised nearly all sail, and they began to gain.

Nicole bent over the rock-weighted map on the deck's chart table, pencil tucked behind her ear. "Head south-southwest," she advised after rechecking.

"The ships are southwest."

She raised her eyebrows at him, and he complied; their course was marked even farther south of the other ships.

Nicole felt the need to explain. "They'll cover all air. We'd have to follow them for miles before we could steal a chance to break through."

Chancey thoughtfully stroked his chin. "Never bothered us before. Now ye've got us going extra distance."

"It'll be faster—"

"And harder on the crew."

She stayed silent and lifted her spyglass again, hoping to ignore him.

"This wouldn't have to do with Sutherland? Look at ye," he said with a chuckle, "it's eatin' ye alive that he got the best o' us."

She turned narrowed eyes on him. "That was a mean trick back there."

Chancey grinned and said, "It were wily, if ye ask me. And it's not as if yer father wouldn't o' done the same."

She opened her mouth to protest. But Chancey was probably right.

"And yerself. Did ye forget that ye stole his course?"

"I didn't steal it, I—"

"Put it to memory and copied it down when ye got home."

She glared at him.

"All right, I'll follow yer course," he said, relenting. "Just tell me where to go."

And then it began. The ordered chaos of activity on deck, the sound of tamed wind sieving the sails, and the crew's cheers when they passed yet another ship—she loved it all. Loved the way they all worked as one, the way they could only just control the volatile vessel, making it lurch and rocket past competitor after competitor. She had little time to speak to Chancey, except to order course alterations or speed checks, the entire frenzied time they continued to gain on Tallywood.

During a lull in the wind, the watch called out "No sign o' Tallywood." Trailing Tallywood was a slap in the face to her crew, who hated the man. Sensing the change in the men, she called out resolutely, "We can't worry about Tallywood yet. If he's anything like he was when I saw him last, he'll botch his lead somewhere on the way. We've got a closer rival to best."

Then to herself she added, "Now we sprint for Sutherland."

But Chancey heard her, and frowned. "Don't ye mean, 'Now we sprint for the *Southern Cross*'?"

Chapter 13

As Nicole raised her spyglass to view the stern of the *Southern Cross,* she felt a welling of relief that they had finally caught him. She bit back a smile.

And now we'll overtake him.

Though it didn't appear that Sutherland would cooperate. When they neared him enough to pass, he consistently stayed in front, preventing them from getting clean air.

She watched in incomprehension as he outsailed their faster, more agile ship. She whirled toward Chancey, opened her mouth to speak, then closed it.

"To answer yer question," he began with a chuckle, "Sutherland can do this because he's good and he's cold. Straight, methodical sailin.'"

"You sound like you admire him," she said in disbelief.

"Don't have to like him to admire his sailin.'"

She couldn't take it anymore. "Chancey, head north-northwest," she directed between clenched teeth.

He scowled at her. "Oh, no. Ye'll not increase our distance just to get in front o' him," he said in a low voice so the crew near them couldn't hear. "We've got thousands o' miles—ye've got to be patient."

"But I know he's got that gloating smirk on his face right now. And I know just how to wipe it off," she said in a nasty voice.

Chancey looked around him at the waves and then the sky. "The winds'll change soon; then we can cover him."

She yanked down her cap and said nothing. Chancey was right, of course. If the winds changed, the *Bella Nicola* would be between them and the *Southern Cross*. Sutherland wouldn't be able to get the full benefits. But she couldn't help thinking that her father would've done just as she'd suggested.

Half an hour later, the winds did in fact change to their customary eastward sweep, and they found themselves with the advantage.

"If we're swift, we can pass him before the straits," Nicole said. They were approaching the notorious rocky outcroppings that greeted ships following the great circle route just as they turned east away from South America. She'd always imagined that they acted as a gate that separated the lucky and the knowledgeable from the new dross at the bottom of their cold sea.

Chancey shook his head. "We'll never make that. We'll be right up beside him and have to draw back." He caught her gaze. "Sutherland isn't a man to share his sea room, Nicole."

"If we could get past, it would be us catching Tallywood instead of being jammed up behind Sutherland." She slapped the back of her hand against her opposite palm to make her point. "Calculated risks, Chancey. That's what racing is! The crew will love it. You know it'd be talked about for years if we could slingshot past him."

"There's a storm comin' soon," he grumbled. "This move might put us right in the straits with the gale on top o' us."

Nicole smiled, knowing it looked ruthless. "Then we'd better hurry."

He glowered at her. But after a muttered curse, he bellowed, "All right, men, nor'-nor'west, every stitch o' canvas set!"

"Cap'n, ship ahoy!" Derek's watch sang out.

"Where away?" he called in answer.

"Astern—I just caught sight of a ship due south of us at full sail! Looking at her flags, I'd say it's that Yankee clipper."

Derek pulled out his own spyglass to confirm that it was Lassiter's ship. His eyes narrowed at the familiar sails and pennants of the *Bella Nicola,* and he snapped the spyglass closed.

He wasn't surprised they'd caught up with him. No ship was faster than theirs in fair weather and light gales. But they had a lot of nerve to follow so closely. Nicole had most likely stolen his navigation plans even before she'd nearly unmanned him in a Brazilian brothel, and yet they sailed as though they intended to run him down. He'd never wanted a voyage to end as much as he did this one. . . .

Derek's head whipped up, his thoughts quelled, when a distant boom of thunder resounded. The storm he'd seen brewing to the south was gaining strength. Disquieting in itself. And then occasionally he could see the waves break over a previously hidden fracture of rock.

"I'm never easy in the Forties," said a voice behind him. He turned to see Jebediah approaching the rail.

"Nor am I," Derek admitted as they both looked out over the sea. He wondered if Jeb was there to assure himself that his captain was sober, and said reassuringly, "We'll get more sea room before the storm hits."

"Just don't want to join the litter of poor wrecks beneath us even now," Jeb said as he cracked his gnarled knuckles.

"What? You doubt my experience?"

"Not likely. But then, you know experience isn't a guarantee down 'ere. 'Ell, you probably like it down 'ere in the Forties since you love storms," the old man added before he shuffled off toward the galley.

What Derek considered secret was known to this man. He did love storms. Probably because they were the only things that made him feel alive. But here in the Forties, even he was anxious.

He thought of how the *Bella Nicola* would fare in this storm. The Irisher sailing her had probably handled a thousand gales. He'd be aware of the dicey channels that ran through these underwater ridges, as well as the power of the storms in this latitude.

Derek had also heard in Brazil that he was proving to be a very conscientious captain, not an unpredictable sail jockey like Lassiter. Even so, Derek thought of the jagged shoals they were even now skimming, coupled with the coming storm, and became distinctly uneasy about Nicole.

Damn it, he didn't care what happened to that ship or anything on board it, including her. She'd spied on him, lied to him, had Chancey try to brain him, not to mention her latest assault on his . . . person.

And then there were the agonizing dreams she was responsible for.

I'm only worried because I haven't had her yet, Derek coldly assured himself.

His regular musings on just what that would be like were interrupted when Bigsby, the ship's surgeon, called up from the stairs.

"Captain, a word with you, please." An anxious look pinched the man's chapped face.

Derek, seeing the doctor's worry, thought of the peculiar fever affecting some of his crew. Surely Bigsby had made certain none of the sick had worsened. Derek put his spyglass back in his coat pocket; at his nod, the first mate took over the bridge.

He followed the brisk surgeon into the chart room, waiting impatiently as Bigsby closed the door behind him. "Captain, I don't want to cause a panic among the men," he said, visibly fighting for a neutral expression, "but . . . two more galley hands and the cabin boy have come down with the sickness."

An invisible foe continued to harm his men. One Derek couldn't defend them against. "That makes eleven total." Derek scrubbed a hand over the back of his neck. "I hired you because you're the best. So why the bloody hell haven't you been able to figure out what they've come down with?"

Bigsby, his face flushing a mottled red in his nervousness, muttered uncomfortably, "I believe I have." He paused before he looked up, face somber, as though delivering a death sentence.

"The water on this ship has been . . . poisoned."

Derek couldn't believe it—but, God help them all, it made sense. He thought of the men lying in the 'tween decks, violently ill, biting back their moans of pain. He'd written it off as merely a shipboard fever, hardly uncommon as it passed among crews. But he'd never witnessed this level of gut-wrenching pain accompanying such a fever. His instincts warned him that the doctor was dead-on in his assessment.

Poison. His mind couldn't seem to get past his disbelief, but acting immediately was essential. "Are all the remaining barrels contaminated?" he asked, already knowing from the doctor's face the answer to his question.

"Yes, I'm afraid so. I opened them myself and fed a bit of water to a couple of the chickens." Bigsby frowned and looked down at the hat he'd been unconsciously mangling in his hands. "From what happened to the animals, I'm positive it is the water, and that all the water is affected."

No water? It would take them at least a week to reach the Cape of Good Hope—if his men were all able. He had a hard time making and shortening sail now, much less battling through the Forties to get to the Cape, with only a handful of sailors. And if any more of his crew got sick?

A sailor's cry broke in on his thoughts. "Look, that little ship's making full sail and closing in fast." So the *Bella Nicola* was close. He had little hope of aid from them.

"Captain, this is fortunate," the doctor exclaimed, his face opening into a relieved smile. "We can signal for help. Surely they have water to spare, and maybe a deckhand or two. . . ."

The water! Nicole in the storage room . . . Blood pumped to his head, making it pound as he sorted through the roiling thoughts flooding his mind. He hammered his hand on the table, and the physician yelped. "Get the crew on deck," Derek barked. *"Now."*

Minutes later, what was left of his able crew had been gathered. He looked at his exhausted men and another wave of rage washed over him. He forced himself to speak evenly.

"We have concluded that there is no fever on this ship." Seeing the hopeful look on some of the men's faces, he raised a hand. "I'm afraid what I have to tell you will be equally alarming. This sickness stems from our water supply."

He looked each man in the eye, never wavering. "We don't have any uncontaminated water left on board."

Agony distorted their faces.

"Our immediate need for water will, I hope, be met by the upcoming storm. But to depend on rain for such a long journey is risky." Derek wanted to run a hand over his face, but stopped himself and instead stood up straighter.

"What I am most concerned about is our lack of able hands in these waters. If none of the men on this deck fall ill, we should be able to make it."

"Cap'n, I gotta tell you," a midshipman said in a faltering voice. "I'm already feeling it—I'm afraid I'll not be able to cover my duties for much longer," he finished weakly with a look of shame.

He'd only just spoken when another man, and then another, voiced their fears about the early symptoms that already plagued them.

"Cap'n, what about the li'l clipper astern of us?" his lookout asked. "Even if it's Lassiter, surely he'll help us if we send up a signal."

Derek cut off all the excited exclamations. "We cannot count on them to voluntarily give us aid." He couldn't even begin to predict what they would do.

He surveyed his crew's bewildered looks and listened to them hope against hope that Lassiter's ship would come to their aid. He attempted to forestall that line of thinking; yet they were convinced from experience that sailors helped their own, competitors or not. Derek hadn't planned to air his suspicions, but he wanted them to suffer no illusions. He also had to prepare them for the unorthodox commands he'd be giving them shortly.

"I have every reason to believe that the person who poisoned our water is aboard the *Bella Nicola*."

Nicole closed her spyglass against her thigh and began her usual impatient pacing across the deck. It would be close, to beat him to the straits. Truthfully, one of the reasons she'd pushed to catch Sutherland was that she hadn't expected him to stick with this course. He'd charted it, but she'd thought he would back out. He took an insane risk, steering a ship of the *Southern Cross*'s size so close to these ridges with their gripping, snatching currents. Her brows drew together. *He's either very determined or crazed.* She settled on the latter.

Pulling a strand of hair from her eyes and tucking it up into her ever-present cap, she turned to look at the towering clouds of a looming storm. It would be sheer folly for him to be in these straits when the storm moved in.

But he had a good quarter mile on her. From where she stood, it looked as though he might be able to squeeze past the last of the straits before the storm broke. *Unlike me*, she thought as she surveyed the purplish clouds building.

But she felt confident in her crew and, truth be told, in

herself. She'd sailed these waters countless times with her father. And their ship was built to thrive in storms, agile even under pressure and milking every last knot from the buffeting winds. Her fondest memories were of squalls when she and her father had sailed together. They'd set all their canvas out, slicing at full speed past bulkier ships whose cowardly furled sails looked to her like tails tucked between their legs.

When Chancey gave the expected orders to prepare the ship for rough water, she padded to her cabin to fetch her oilskin raincoat. In this small break, she wasn't surprised that her thoughts again turned to Sutherland.

She'd just threaded her second arm into her oilskins when a cold shaft of fear assailed her, so powerful she sank down in her chair.

Sutherland's risk could be deadly.

Why should she care? His devilish prank had left them scrambling to get out of Brazil. She'd been furious with him for weeks now. But with the thought of the storm and the possibility that Sutherland could get hurt or killed, her anger left her as easily as a breeze deserting sail.

She had no overarching reason to hate him and couldn't seem to reignite her anger over his trick. Especially now that they were so close to overtaking him and still had half the distance to Sydney to catch Tallywood. Her anger dissipated, her emotions turned anxious and a light sheen of sweat dampened her forehead. She jumped up to race to the deck.

She stumbled to the rail and was frantically yanking out her spyglass when she caught Chancey's inquiring look. Forcing herself to be calm, she took a deep breath, even managed a small smile for him. Her foolish fears were running away from her. *After all, Sutherland was reaching the end of the straits when I last saw him.*

With a shaky laugh at her foolish emotions, she brought the spyglass to her eye.

Then promptly dropped it.

The *Southern Cross* lay dead in the water.

Chapter 14

For God's sake, what is he doing?" She didn't bother to hide her fear for Sutherland from Chancey or any of the men close by. "His sails are down—I don't understand."

Chancey grabbed her spyglass, then muttered, "Bleedin' idiot."

"Why would he—? We've got to help them!"

She had to yell the last of her words because just then, the advance winds from the storm howled over them and rocketed the ship forward, too swiftly even for the *Bella Nicola,* and all hands were needed to shorten sail.

"Stop frettin'," Chancey ordered with a chuck under her chin. "We'll take down some canvas and make our way over there."

She gave him a quick nod and assumed the helm, the one place she could physically help her crew since everyone was too afraid of her father to allow her in the rigging. Minutes ticked by as she pulled and pushed at the wheel, but she never took her eyes from the direction of Sutherland's ship. She could feel her face was tight with worry. What could he possibly be thinking?

In sudden confusion, she stared down at her hands on the wheel. She perceived an oily sluggishness as the ship became increasingly lifeless and slow to respond. The feeling was similar to having a hull full of badly stored cargo. Her mind unwillingly recognized the heavy churning, the feeling of pressure on the wheel increasing. It was as if part of her midship had just . . . given way.

Impossible. They couldn't have collided with anything, because they remained well within the channel. There hadn't been any impact, damn it! Her head whipped up and she caught Chancey's stark expression. He felt the same uneven listing.

With one hand gripping the wheel, she lifted the other palm up while frantically shaking her head. "We're not afoul of anything—I don't understand!" she yelled. He gave her a tight nod before abruptly running below decks. Chancey didn't have to go below for her to know that the *Bella Nicola* was slowly taking on water.

She bit back a frantic laugh. *Now that my own ship's in danger, I can finally stop worrying about Sutherland's.*

Chancey emerged and called for several men to work the pumps, then gazed off at the storm, at the blistering mesh of lightning hastening toward them. He called Dennis, who'd finished with the sails, to come back and relieve her. She wanted to protest, but grew silent when Chancey gave her a sad smile.

In his gruff voice, he said, "Lash yerself down, lass. We're in for a hell o' a ride."

Without argument, she did as he told her. When satisfied with her knots, he charged off to go over each detail, securing rigging, making sure the crew understood exactly what they were about to face.

Nicole strained against her ropes to see once again if she could make out the *Southern Cross,* but just as she thought she could, the clouds reached them and erupted. For what could have been hours, the rain pelted the deck and pounded in the remaining sails. It became impossible to see more than a few feet away. Until the lightning hovered directly over them.

The muscles in her neck bunched as she hunched down, away from the flashes streaming out in the leaded skies, firing closer and closer to them.

Nicole watched in horrified disbelief as a branch of lightning struck their midmast, hitting it halfway up. She wanted to shrink inside herself as the scorching intensity of heat bathed her face. A sound like sizzling grease accompanied the scoring bolt. Pain melted in her eyes from the shock of light. The immediate thunder shook not just herself and the ship but the whole black world around them.

She blinked repeatedly until she could focus on the mast. The lightning had left it smoking and splintered, held only by the rigging attached to it.

She hissed in wet air. *If those ropes give way . . .*

Then it happened. The middle of the mast kicked out to smash down near the helm, exploding all the way through the upper deck, the spars acting like claws to drag down every sail and line. She stared, stunned, as the impact shot Dennis against the wheelhouse.

For the space of two hitching breaths, she waited for him to get up. He lay motionless. With shaking hands, she dug into her knots. Just as she freed herself, Chancey reached the man and began securing his limp body to the wheelhouse. She jerked her head from Chancey to the madly spinning wheel and pressed her legs down to cross the deck to it.

With each uplifting and crash of the ship, she skidded back and forth over the timbers lying on the deck, making little progress. Finally . . . finally she reached the helm and fought to get a grip on the twirling wheel, but the pegs kept cracking against her hands. After all but tackling it, she stopped the spinning by pushing with all her might on one side of the wheel and lunging her whole body into her grip.

When she ventured a look over her shoulder, she could see Chancey's scowl as he tottered back to the helm.

"Let go! I've got to take the helm," he shouted. Without warning, a rope whining past them slashed at his face like a whip.

With a growl, he looked from her to the rope. "Tie up then, damn it. Strong knots!" He turned to find the source of the rope and scuttled off again.

She tied herself to the wheel, fighting to keep it steady as the ship continued to buck. When she'd achieved a measure of success, she looked up and scanned the ship. She bit back a scream. Chancey's great bulk crashed across the deck as another merciless wave broke over the bow and tossed him as if he were a rag doll.

Her heart thundered in her chest while she waited for him to rise. *Chancey, get up, damn you. Get up!*

As though wrestling his lumbering body, he managed to stand and trudge back to the whipping line he'd been securing. She held her panic at bay while she could see him. But masses of foam were heaving up in all directions as the wind began keening even more violently. When she finally lost sight of him altogether, the harshest, most biting terror gripped her. She choked back the screams bubbling up.

She prayed for him as she willed his return. Then she prayed for her crew's lives—for the men struggling all across the ship, yelling into the wind, laboring to prevent the destruction awaiting them. She prayed that her father would eventually remarry and get on with his life without his daughter and crew.

In the midst of the fury unleashed around them, she also prayed for Sutherland. . . .

All on board knew their lives were in the hand of an arbitrary sea, and the certainty of death drummed in every mind. Nicole knew they were lost. And she knew she had failed.

Although it had arrived like an explosion, the fierce storm lingered in indecision for hours. During that time, Derek couldn't locate the *Bella Nicola*. He'd told his men they would take Lassiter's ship and all the necessary supplies and impress the crew. Then he'd simply anchored in the middle of the channel and waited, because the Irisher would have no choice but to sail dangerously close. He'd signal them, and if they came to, so be it. If they did not, he would cannon a warning shot over their bow and force them to stop. A simple, effective plan.

He had not factored in a storm that had burgeoned into one of the worst he'd ever seen. The rain soon began battering them not from above but from the side as it seemed to rise up from the ocean. He'd had no choice but to weigh anchor and get the ship to safer waters.

With a little luck, Nicole could slip right past him in the dark of the storm. His fury grew, but he also caught himself feeling something he hadn't in a long time.

Fear.

He wanted to dismiss it at first. Yet his chest tightened

every time he thought about Nicole on a ship that could easily be ripped apart on the rocks surrounding them. He wanted to convince himself that the only thing he felt for her was loathing.

But even if she was an evil, lying witch, he didn't want her to die. If they hadn't gotten clear when this storm reached them, it would be an all-too-likely possibility. He fought not to imagine how frightened she must be, trapped down in a sloshing, freezing cabin, hearing the timbers groaning under the water's pressure.

Impatient as he hadn't been since he was a boy, he waited until shafts of sunlight finally stabbed through the dense black clouds. His own skeleton crew thankfully had weathered the storm without major damage to the ship, and when he'd gauged it safe enough, they were able to make all haste to find the *Bella Nicola*. But for hours, the only sign of the ship they found was part of a splintered mast.

Seeing that sure sign of destruction had filled him with a maddening feeling of impotence. It was as if someone relentlessly kicked him in the gut during the hours when there was no other sign of the little ship. He nearly swore he wouldn't punish her for her treachery, if he could only find her alive.

"Cap'n, the crew has started grumbling," Jeb said from behind him. "They want to cut their losses and get to the Cape."

Derek turned. "We'll search until sunset."

The salt began hesitantly, "We've covered a big patch of sea today. Do you think they'd be blowed out this far?"

"I don't know," Derek admitted, wondering how this weary tone had replaced his own. "With a mast gone, they've got to be sitting somewhere."

"Unless—"

"That's enough, Jeb," he snapped, unwillingly finishing the sentence in his mind. *Unless they went down.* "We'll keep searching. Tell the crew I'll double their rations for the next week."

"Aye, sir." The man paused and turned to Derek with a frown, then began hesitantly, "Cap'n . . . about the girl, she was—"

Whatever the man was about to say was cut off by the watch's weakened call of "Ship ahoy!"

Derek yanked out his glass. He spied a glimpse of tattered sail clinging to the one remaining mast of the *Bella Nicola* as she barely bobbed over the waves. A strange elation was overrun by surging impatience as he ordered his crew to full sail.

Though the sun continued to battle with still-laden clouds, Derek could see that the ship was dangerously low and obviously sinking. Her main mast had snapped and shot through her upper deck, where it remained in a bizarre tableau like nothing he'd ever seen before.

Groans sounded as some of the unconscious crew awakened, and he felt an involuntary twinge of pity for the hell they'd obviously been through. He stifled it. Lassiter had a core crew for this ship, the majority of whom had sailed with him for two decades. It was logical to think that some, if not all, knew of the poisoning.

Derek was also disgusted with himself to find that he scanned the decks, irritated beyond reason that he couldn't find Nicole. Did the malicious little chit still cower in her cabin? No longer could he simply call her thief or spy. By poisoning the water, she was now a would-be murderer.

No one had died . . . yet, some part of him argued, but his men continued to fall.

I simply want to find her alive so I can wring her lovely little neck.

While his ship closed in, he and his crew watched the scene unfold. A small figure was slumped over the wheel, frozen except for small, jerky movements. As they got closer, he could see what seemed like yards of hair spread out over the body. Nicole had the helm.

So much for cowering in her cabin.

Nicole lay dumbly, mute, unable to think of anything but the pain as she decided whether her bones were broken or her skull cracked.

Hearing a moan from the deck, she shook her head to try to clear it. The movement made her fall, but the ropes around her waist held her up. Squinting, she looked down in confusion. She was tied to the wheel?

She pushed at the knots, reverse threading. When free, she took a step back and collapsed, then scrambled up again. Fighting down a rising panic, she shoved her hair out of her eyes. She'd taken about ten limping steps when the unfamiliar roiling of the ship reminded her.

Her eyes snapped open in alertness as she recalled the endless hours of the storm. Water poured in below decks. *Not this ship. Not this one!* But she'd known the *Bella Nicola* was sinking even hours ago? days ago?—when they'd first encountered the gale.

She half-walked and half-crawled as fast as her flagging body could manage to where Chancey lay tied to the deck. She shook him, and he woke after a minute. After a few more, he groggily assessed the situation.

It did not look good.

"The lifeboats?" he croaked.

"One lost. One b-broken."

She knew many sailors never learned to swim. Purposely. Because being trapped on the open sea, much less *in* the sea, was worse than death. Her thoughts made her hands shake too wildly to make any headway with the ropes. Chancey had to help her with the lines that had carved deep, bloody grooves into his soaked, bloated skin.

"Signal. We might yet get out a signal." He hauled himself up and hobbled to the stern of the ship.

She lay there, stupefied. She wasn't sure she could get up again. Chancey would send up a flare. If Sutherland hadn't gotten too far, they might be saved. . . .

Suddenly, he stomped his foot and clapped his large hands in a mystifying display of energy. "Nic, buck up," he called out drunkenly. "Yer captain has come to save ye." His voice was thick as obvious relief infused him. "It's not what I'd have ordered up, but considerin' the other choices . . ."

She turned slowly, not believing, too afraid to hope.

And there he was. Lord, he was beautiful.

She'd never seen a more welcome sight than Sutherland standing on the deck as his ship slipped in beside them. She thought she'd remember forever the way his thick black hair ruffled in the wind, the way he nonchalantly rested a boot on the bottom rail with his muscular arms crossed over his wide chest. She smiled at him like a simpleton. Although her head hadn't cleared as it should have, pure pleasure thrummed through her, as strong as the despair it replaced. Not only did she know he was safe, he would save them. . . .

Grappling hooks bounced over the *Bella Nicola*'s deck.

Nicole watched in horror as they were snatched in, scraping along her already splintered deck before violently catching her recently whitewashed railing. Grappling hooks? The abuse of her ship, even though it was dying, chilled her. Why would he . . . Did Sutherland think they would fight him? She needed to think. Why couldn't she think?

Nicole stared, not comprehending, when his men skulked aboard, armed as if they were taking a resisting crew. Her head snapped up to meet Sutherland's chilling gaze. Her heart slammed in her chest. Only this time it was not from the thrill and excitement she'd experienced on seeing him a few moments before. This time it was fear.

Because Captain Sutherland looked like he wanted her dead.

Now that he was finally close enough to see Nicole, he wanted to see the guilt on her face. No, damn it, he wanted to see regret.

So he was not just surprised but startled when he looked down to find her gazing up at him with a blinding smile, as though a shutter had opened on some intrinsic light. Derek couldn't seem to drag his eyes away from the smile that used to have such an effect on him. Still had—damn her.

She seemed not to notice his intent look, and she was so pleased about . . . well, he had no idea why she would be so happy to see him. Yes, he would save her hide, but surely she must know he would have determined who'd poisoned his men. She had to know that he would exact revenge. Yet she looked up at him with her eyes shining, as if he were a hero of old come to save her.

It was unnerving.

Her gaze locked on another sight, and as the expression on her face changed, a strange feeling of disappointment passed through him. When his men threw the hooks to secure her ship, that beautiful smile guttered out, fading to a look of incomprehension.

He couldn't be sorry. He told himself it was with satisfaction that he watched her eyes follow his men. When she realized they were armed, the little fool turned to him, her chin lower than usual, her shoulders slumped. She was afraid. He'd known she would quake before him—beg him. But her next action stopped that thought cold.

Jumping up and planting her boots on the deck, her hair whipping across her face in dark, wet streams, she shook off any trace of fear. And replaced it with what could only be called rage. Then she bellowed at him. That little thing *bellowed*.

"What in the hell do you mean by this, Sutherland?"

His reply was calm even as his deep voice carried. "I mean to confiscate what's left of your supplies and impress all of your crew."

Her mouth flew open, then closed wordlessly.

He had to conceal his surprise over her reaction. Glaring down at her, he drawled, "You seem to be surprised that I am pillaging your ship and taking your crew captive"—he paused—"although we both know you shouldn't be."

She stood staring at him, bringing her hands up to her temples. She looked shaky and confused, but then it was as if a sudden realization crumpled her composure. Her face fell.

He had to strain to hear her next soft words. "You . . . all along." What did that mean?

She took a deep, ragged breath, and then louder she said, "You're right, I know exactly why you've taken us."

She wasn't even going to deny what she'd done. Had some part of him wanted her to deny it, and deny it so convincingly that he would believe her? Instead, she only looked lost and beaten. As she sank down and huddled on the deck, he couldn't help but notice how very small and fragile she appeared in her oilskins.

He involuntarily winced when one of his men hauled her to her feet again, sending her reeling. With what looked to be one last burst of energy, she turned on the man and kicked him so hard he released her. Derek watched as she unsteadily swung her head back and forth, surveying the scene to come up with some means to fight.

He knew she was a fighter. What he didn't know was why he caught himself almost pulling for her.

There was nothing Nicole could do. Nothing but become Sutherland's prisoner. Her ship lay so low, her deck nearly met the *Southern Cross*'s waterline. The . . . the end was close. Chancey and most of her crew, many of whom were still unconscious, had already been taken aboard his ship and bound. She shook free of the sailor's hand that had once again pinned her. If she had to surrender, then she would do it *her* way.

She walked with shoulders jammed back, her pride keeping her battered body ramrod straight as she marched to the steep gangway.

Sutherland had the gall to smile. He was enjoying this.

He hadn't come to rescue her. *Foolish girl.* No, she'd been right about him after all. He was behind all the accidents. And it wasn't enough to harm his competitors' ships. He had to crush them completely.

The pain in her head raced from severe to splitting, and her thoughts made it ache even more. No wonder his ship hadn't been moving; he'd simply been waiting for his sabotage to cripple her ship in the storm. And it was sabotage.

He and his lackeys hadn't been in Recife by mere coincidence.

She had to swallow hard to keep from screaming. For two days, she and the crew had known they would die. They hadn't eaten, slept, or drunk. Then to be taken prisoner by the man who was responsible for their sinking ship. . . . The realization strangled her, made her feel as though she were falling.

Yet, when forced to walk past him, she kept her head high and her gaze straight ahead.

"Look at me, damn you," he demanded in a low voice. When she didn't, he dragged her around to face him. He looked surprised by her appearance, and she hoped he could *feel* her hatred blazing out at him. When she looked at that face, still so cruelly handsome to her, she didn't know if she wanted to sink down and weep, or kill him.

When his initial surprise turned into a smug glower, she knew she certainly wouldn't sink down and weep.

The intensity of his reaction to Nicole never failed to amaze Derek. When he grabbed her arms and yanked her toward him, he had to guard himself so he wouldn't give away too much of his feeling. He hadn't seen her for weeks, and now to see her like this, . . . Her eyes drew him, with their obvious hurt and pupils black from shock. Her skin was unnatural in its paleness, giving her a translucent look. Salt had collected on her brows, lashes, and hair and glittered all around her face in the fading red sunlight. *She's still beautiful to me.*

Astonishing. With everything he'd learned about her, he still responded to her. Not in a completely sexual way, although that was unquestionably present, but he felt a tremendous pull to her just the same. Obviously, some part of him didn't care that she was a malicious little bitch.

At the memory of his suffering men, his hands shot to her upper arms. "Why?" he demanded harshly. "Why did you do it?" When she stared past him as if unseeing, he shook her. "Did someone put you up to it? Did someone make you do it?"

He dimly heard her crew protesting, and realized the men wanted to distract him from her. She stood as if mute, refusing to look at him. He gripped her arms more tightly and ground out, "Who told you to do it?" Finally, she glanced up, but she frowned as if the question had confused her.

Shaking Nicole had enraged the few conscious captive sailors, and they strained to break away from their bonds and the men who held them. They could struggle all they wanted. No one would ever get in the way of his revenge. As far as he was concerned, she'd transgressed on what was his so much that he could do what he wanted with her now.

She'd *toyed* with him. She'd definitely outwitted him. He'd believed she'd come to him about her father when in reality she was callously ensuring a win. Worse, much worse, she'd harmed his men.

Now that she was on his ship, he might as well own her. He turned to Lassiter's sailors, and his sneer told them as much. When they fought even harder to get to her, he laughed a humorless laugh before returning his attention to Nicole.

He had to know why she'd done it. He squeezed his fists around her thin arms, until she answered in a biting voice, "No one has made me do anything—I do as I will!"

Telling himself he wouldn't beat her there on the deck, he took her shoulders and shook her.

Until, with a strangled cry, she collapsed in his arms.

Fear crept up his spine when Nicole's body went bone-less. He could do nothing else but catch her and scoop her up. When he looked up, the man called Chancey caught his eyes and gave him a stabbing look that said, *What did you expect?* Derek's face flushed. He hadn't meant to hurt the girl. Damn it! He'd never been angrier with another person. Even Lydia.

Guilt assailed him, and he wanted to get her away from him at once. He strode over and handed the unconscious Nicole to Chancey. The man easily grabbed her and cra-dled her protectively in his long arms even though his hands were bound.

Derek turned to the edge of the ship and jumped down to the *Bella Nicola* to join his men in ransacking for sup-plies. Replaying the scene on deck again, cringing from his own actions, he paid little attention as he made his way, though it was hard to miss that his men had stripped any-thing not bolted down. Except in the officers' and captain's quarters in the afterhouse, which he'd ordered were not to be searched by anyone but himself.

When he rammed a shoulder against the lodged door to the largest cabin, water sloshed out around his knees. The smell of oil from a broken lamp overpowered. From the desk and the closet full of men's clothing, he determined it was Lassiter's. It was austere with no sign of luxuries.

He strode through water to the next cabin, his legs making wakes. As he scanned the room, obviously Nicole's, he took in the polished desk and the carved mahogany bed with its gilt and satin wood trimmings. Several compasses, broken barometers, and thermometers floated just above the floor. A pair of extraordinary painted landscapes and pastoral scenes attached to the panels struck him in particular.

Where Lassiter's cabin was bare, extravagances filled hers. Lassiter had spared no expense on the decor, Derek thought, taking in the rich lace on her window. He wasn't unfamiliar with the expense of the items, nor with the cost of the landscapes. No wonder Lassiter was in financial straits.

Maps floated everywhere. He didn't know if even he owned that many maps. She had a spare sail in the corner and probably made herself useful occasionally by sewing. He walked over to her sea chests, somehow feminine, and began rifling through them.

What he found in the first one surprised him. Lacy, silky underthings filled it. Womanly underthings. He'd never seen her dressed in anything other than men's clothes. But if he'd paid more attention when he hurriedly snatched her clothes off that night, would he have noticed what lay underneath? Maybe he should bring her clothes for the long journey. He remembered her skin was unusually soft and fine. What if regular cloth was too rough on her?

That was what he wanted—to punish her—wasn't it? But he'd be enjoying that skin shortly and didn't see any reason to mar something he found so attractive. At the door, he called to two nearby sailors and ordered them to unbolt the trunks and haul them to his ship.

"Cap'n, it won't be long now afore the ole girl goes down," one of his crewmen yelled.

"Make sure all the men are off this ship—I'm right behind you." A heaving motion churned beneath his feet, skidding him sideways. The death roll of the ship. He shook his head sadly and ran across the deck.

Back on the *Southern Cross*, he found Chancey and, with the help of two others, tore the seemingly lifeless girl from him. Derek considered himself a brave man, but the hair on the back of his neck stood up when he heard Chancey's inhuman growl. Derek turned with the girl in his arms to look at him, but immediately regretted it.

Because, before he could be restrained again, the man yanked his bound arm away from one sailor's grasp. Running a finger across his throat, he glared at Derek with a killing promise in his eyes.

In answer, Derek smiled, more a baring of his teeth, until like a shot, a splintering sound exploded from the dying ship.

Both men turned to watch the *Bella Nicola* rupture into huge sections as she finally broke apart just above the surface. It disturbed him to see the meticulously painted hull crack, the boards screaming as they parted. The noise was haunting. Yet even this was better than the eerie quiet as she surrendered to the greedy, bubbling waters.

Derek realized that the unconscious girl hadn't moved during the piercing rending sounds. Yet tears streamed down her face, and a desperate moan escaped her lips at the silence.

Chapter 15

An anxious Dr. Bigsby doggedly followed him as he carried Nicole to his cabin, though not close enough, because Derek slammed the door in his face.

"But, Captain Sutherland! She needs medical attention. She could be gravely injured."

Derek paid him no heed; he was certain she would awaken soon, and he could begin grilling her on what she'd put in their water. He placed her on his bed, not exactly dumping her, but close to it. She cried out in pain, and he felt his first jolt of alarm.

Working quickly, he removed her boots and oilskins. Her skin was icy—he'd never felt another human being so cold. At the sight of her abraded neck and wrists, he choked out a call to Bigsby. With his black medical case in hand, the man entered at once, since he'd never moved.

"What can you do for that?" Derek asked, holding up

her wrist. Salt had collected on her oilskins and rubbed against her skin like sandpaper.

"I have a salve, but that is the least of our concerns. I've completed a preliminary examination of her crewmates, and many suffered serious injuries. This one appears so fragile that I fear she could have internal damage. And she must be warmed without delay."

When Derek simply stood there, shaken at the anxious sound of the doctor's voice, Bigsby maneuvered him out of the way and started cutting through her shirt.

He'd only managed a small part when he said, "What the devil . . . ?"

It was the *mehndi* that still lightly decorated Nicole's skin. "*I'll do that!*" Derek snatched the scissors from the doctor's hands. He didn't like the idea of another man seeing that painted skin. Painted for him.

Bigsby stared at him with an incredulous look on his face. "If she's . . . tattooed, it makes little difference to me. I was just surprised."

With scissors in hand, Derek stood unmoving, frowning down at her.

The doctor asked in a baffled tone, "What had you planned to do with her?"

"I'm a little short on plans where she's concerned," he said as he impatiently raked a hand through his hair.

"Obviously," the doctor muttered. Then in a louder voice, he declared, "If you won't let me help her, then you must get her out of her wet clothes and get her warm."

Derek resumed cutting her shirt. But what he revealed of her body made his breath whistle out. Angry bruises ran across her chest. Without thought, his hand dipped to her skin, his fingers brushing over the livid marks.

"Captain Sutherland," Bigsby said sharply, "you

shouldn't be in here when I'm examining her. She'll be distressed when she awakens."

"I don't give a damn about that," Derek snapped. "I'm responsible for her now. She's . . . mine. I'm not leaving her alone."

Bigsby shook his head, then marched to the door to call for a bucket of hot water. When he returned and began his examination, he clucked over the girl like a mother hen. Derek could find no fault with the man's professional behavior. He removed all of her clothing, but kept a woolen blanket covering every part of her body that he wasn't currently examining.

Finished at last, Bigsby said, "She has a nasty lump on her head. I'm most concerned about that. You never know how head injuries will react. I'm also worried that she was probably in wet clothes for at least the duration of the storm. I'd be surprised if she doesn't develop a fever."

"What are you doing now?" Derek asked when the doctor directed the sailor with the hot water to set it beside the bed.

"I'm bathing her wounds," he answered.

"The hell you are! You're needed by other crew members more than you are here, and my crew comes first." At the doctor's troubled look, he gruffly said, "I'll do it."

Bigsby nodded. "Please be quick about it. She needs to be dry and warm as soon as possible. Captain Sutherland, I am not exaggerating when I say it could be life or death if you don't keep her warm. And you have to be gentle with her. Even if she's unconscious, her body registers the pain. You mustn't hurt her any more than she is."

Before he left, he added, "Since I'm not certain if she has sustained internal injuries, she absolutely cannot be moved from that bed."

Derek impatiently shoved the doctor out the door.

He turned back to his chore, grabbing a cloth out of the bucket of steaming water, and lifted it to her body. The task of caring for her proved to be punishing for him, because with every movement, she cried out in pain. Although he hated her for what she'd done, he couldn't help flinching.

Her legs and her slightly jutting hipbones were bruised even blacker than her chest. He could clearly make out where the rope had wrapped around her tiny waist, damaging the delicate skin. The lump on her head hadn't receded, and her skin was raw in several places. All in all, he'd never seen a woman in such bad shape. It scared the hell out of him.

He strove to treat her objectively but, brute that he was, he had to keep himself from imagining her skin and beautifully shaped body as they were the last time he'd enjoyed them. He was sweating when he finally finished washing the salt from her skin and wounds. He'd never tended a sick or injured person in his life, much less a sick or injured woman. He felt clumsy and inept every time he placed his rough hands on her small body.

After drying her, he looked in one of her trunks for something to dress her in, but wasn't able to solve the conundrum that was her undergarments—scraps of lacy confections, too imaginative for him to figure out. Worse was the pleasure he found imagining her in all those silks and sheer materials; he was a guilty voyeur, an interloper.

Furious with himself, he stuffed everything back in the trunk and slammed the lid in frustration. He didn't even bother with the second chest, but hastily dressed her in one of his own shirts before bundling her with every blanket he could lay hands on.

"Her bruises are worse," he informed Bigsby later that night. "And she hasn't awakened yet."

"Captain, please allow me to say for the *fifth time* that I am fairly confident nothing is broken or permanently injured. And sleep is her body's way of coping with the trauma of her injuries."

Derek stalked off again. He trusted Bigsby. Hell, he'd let him examine her even though the thought of the doctor touching her infuriated him. But it hadn't escaped Derek's notice that every time he'd approached the doctor since they'd brought Nicole aboard, Bigsby would get this ridiculously knowing look. Sometimes he appeared to feel sorry for Derek.

Still, if Nicole showed no signs of improvement by tomorrow, he'd have to find her another doctor when they arrived at Cape Town. And a magistrate. Even as the thought arose, he dismissed it. He wouldn't surrender her to Cape Town's corrupt justice system, and not just because he could guess how a girl like her would be abused. It was, he told himself, because she was his to do with as he pleased now.

When he came back to his cabin, she was just turning in the bed. She shuddered from the small movement and began crying silently in her sleep. He wanted to kill—*kill*—the Irisher for letting her sail in these waters, much less for risking her life by pushing that ship in the Forties. And her crew had allowed her to steer in a gale. Because of their stupidity, she'd obviously struck the rocky shoals and gutted her father's ship. If he hadn't been in the area, they most likely wouldn't have survived.

"Captain, you're needed on deck right away!" Bigsby called from the door.

"What is it?" Derek snapped as he ran past the doctor.

"It would appear that her crew is taking the ship."

At dawn, when Derek staggered back to his cabin in exhaustion, he found Bigsby at Nicole's bedside. During the skirmish last night, the surgeon had evidently stayed behind with her. He didn't like to think about that. He wanted to care for her as much as possible and see her through this.

So he could throttle her when she woke up.

"Is she all right?"

"Yes, Captain—"

"*Out.*"

Bigsby jumped from his seat. "Of course, Captain," the man said as he turned to leave. "I believe she'll wake up soon."

When the door closed, Derek was at Nicole's bedside. She appeared so slight, dressed as she was in one of his shirts without her cloak adding bulk to her slender form. He found himself willing her to awaken, and wondered why he was so apprehensive about her recovery. He didn't want to examine his feelings toward her. If pressed, he'd say he wanted her to wake so he could begin his retribution.

Strangely, he knew that in the next few days he would drink more than he ate and sleep little.

That night after returning from his duties, he sat at his desk, drinking heavily, and again his eyes trailed to her sea chests, the chests that he'd heedlessly brought aboard. He'd had no idea if they held things women couldn't live without, since he'd never packed for a woman or lived with one.

He surveyed them with a curious feeling of dread. They were just sitting there, those feminine sea chests. Directly beside his own. With a thread of something akin to panic, he understood that they were in his cabin and would stay there because, according to Bigsby, she couldn't be moved.

When he'd first brought her aboard, he'd strung up a hammock in his cabin, but he could only imagine the night of fitful, interrupted sleep he'd get once he could finally lie down. Damn it, he wanted his own bunk back.

She'd be in agony if he accidentally jostled her in the night, but she was small and took up little room in his large bed. He'd all but convinced himself to join her. Instead he sat debating, drinking for hours. Until she began shivering.

It wasn't cool in the room; the cabin boy constantly refilled the stove because of her. Yet there she lay, shaking more each minute. He could call for Bigsby. No, he decided, he'd take care of her himself. He stripped off his clothes, ready to sleep, and carefully slid in beside her to give her warmth.

But it made little difference. She was breathing deeply and mumbling, and he feared she'd developed a fever. Tentatively he inched closer to her and cautiously wrapped himself around her. She calmed and moved closer to him.

He felt a strange feeling of accomplishment. He'd made her shivering stop just by his presence and warmth. Unusual for him, he slept straight away.

Sometime in the night, he awoke to find her back snuggled against his chest for warmth and her head lying on his outstretched arm. His whole body tensed in response. Although she wore his shirt, it rode up her thighs, and he could feel every inch of her legs and . . . higher.

This was torture. His erection pulsed thick and rigid. Not being able to touch her when all he wanted to do was bury himself in her was maddening.

He could swear the little witch purposefully tormented him when she wriggled her bottom closer to him. He sucked in a breath—his cock rested at the press of her inner thighs. He gritted his teeth, straining to think of anything but her smell or her soft hair against his chest. But his mind kept coming back to how perfectly she fit between his hips. Their bodies meshed like two pieces of a puzzle, and he knew bedding her would bear that idea out.

Before her treachery, he would have made love to her. A thorough and selfless joining in which he would have licked her in secret places, run his tongue over the small dip between her intimate flesh and her pale thigh, and worshipped her breasts. A world away from the stiff fucking he planned for her now. The thought made him bitter—he wished he had the option to do both.

In the nights that followed, he made his way into his bunk to sleep. He awoke early, careful to leave in case she woke. Then, after he'd gone to the bridge to give out orders for the day, he'd return and check on her.

He could almost fool himself that if she wasn't aware of him spending time with her in bed, it didn't count as any kind of increased intimacy. He didn't have a choice in the matter anyway. Although he hadn't told Bigsby, Nicole shook in tremors each night. Since her skin was rarely hot, he'd concluded that the girl was gripped by what had to be hellish nightmares. Until he came to her.

Since Bigsby had finagled his way into caring for her when Derek had to take the bridge, the surgeon was with her for most of the day. Derek's only time to help her recover was in the nights, and he didn't want to stop just yet. It was a challenge to calm her.

On the third night, he couldn't stop her trembling even

after he'd wrapped himself and three blankets over her. He couldn't get any closer to her. Their skin touched in every place it could, but she continued to moan quietly and shake. In his frustration, Derek put his hand in her hair and stroked her. When this helped, he leaned close to her ear and murmured, "Shhh, Nicole. You need to sleep."

She stilled and again snuggled against him. Derek swore. A fever might be better than her continued nightmares. Nightmares of the storm, he didn't doubt. He continued petting her, and her breathing deepened and calmed. Before he could chastise himself, deride his absurd behavior, he'd whispered, "Good girl," then fallen soundly asleep.

On the fourth day, he was rewarded when her eyes fluttered open.

When she parted her pallid lips, he poured a glass of water for her and awaited her questions. After blinking several times, her eyes settled wide open. She looked as if she battled panic, so he was relieved when she was able to phrase a clear question.

"Where am I?" she rasped before she let him pull her up for a drink.

"You're aboard the *Southern Cross.*"

She drank deeply, then sank back down in confusion. "My ship . . . ?"

"Went down."

At his answer, she brought a limp hand over her face as a broken sound burst from her lips. "C-Crew?" she whispered.

"Your *crew*,"—he skewered the word—"will be hauled off to the jail in Cape Town for attempted mutiny. It would seem that not knowing about your safety drove the bastards crazy."

"Did you . . . harm them?" she asked, staring at him accusingly.

"Yes, of course they were hurt when we defended my ship!" Her face became even paler, if possible, and she looked as though she might be sick, so he added brusquely, "If you mean to ask if anyone was killed, then the answer is no."

Such a look of relief crossed her face. . . . What were those men to her?

She reached out and gripped his wrist with a frantic strength in her small hand. "I must see Chancey." Her touch was like lightning running through him. He rushed to assure himself that her skin was just hot—she might in fact be getting feverish. When her demand sank in, he became furious.

"That will not happen, princess," he pronounced in clipped tones.

Abruptly she dropped his hand as her own fell by her side, all strength vanishing. She looked desolate, with such bleakness in her eyes that he came close to taking back what he'd said.

Inwardly, he cringed at his weakness where Lassiter's daughter was concerned. Was he losing his mind to even think about letting the woman who'd poisoned his crew see the man who'd tried to take his ship? The idea was ludicrous, and it wouldn't happen.

"I've attempted to get information on the poisoning from some of your crew, but they swear they don't know anything about it." He pinned her with a flinty glare. "Now you'll tell me about the sabotage."

Her eyes widened in surprise before she hissed, *"As if you don't know."*

"What the hell does that mean? How would I know?"

Although her whole body weakened before his eyes, she spoke with increasing fury. "You know because you're responsible."

"*I'm* responsible?" He bit back a laugh as he rose off the bed and walked across the cabin. "I have no reason to hurt anyone's ship," he said with amusement, and poured a glass of brandy from the all-but-empty bottle on his desk.

"You hurt my ship," she countered while he took a large drink.

"It was dead before I even got there because you'd gutted it in the straits," he said. "You should be thanking me. If I hadn't plucked you off that sinking ship, odds are you would be dead by now."

She was silent as she obviously sought to remember and decide whether he was correct. Finally, she replied, "It's true you saved my life. But I can assure you that I didn't hit anything."

"I suppose the *Bella Nicola* just sank itself."

She exhaled in impatience. In her condition, it sounded more like a sigh. "She sank because someone sabotaged her."

"You're planning to stick to this ridiculous story? So be it." He lifted his glass to her in a mocking salute. "Here's to veracity."

She glared at him. "Will you let me go with my crew at the Cape?"

"No." Another drink as he made his way back over to the bed.

"That's kidnapping," she cried out hoarsely. She weakly moved farther away when he sat back down.

"No, it's justice, you conniving little witch." He saw her aversion and shot off the bed again. "After what you did to my crew, I have every right to punish you."

"What I did to your crew?" she asked in confusion. She feebly massaged her temples.

It was too easy to see her as an innocent young woman, alone after a tragedy. But he knew what she really was. She was the daughter of his most hated adversary, and he himself had dragged her out of his storage room right after she'd poisoned their water.

Disgusted, he turned to leave. Just before he reached the doorway, he looked back, angry and wanting to hurt her as he'd been hurt. But she appeared completely bewildered, and when a single tear trailed down her cheek, he cursed himself for a fool and stalked out. Though not before he heard her rasp, "And to think I was worried about *you!*"

Nicole woke again hours after her confrontation with Sutherland, too weak to move. A cursory survey of her body told her that she was badly off. She had never thought she'd bruised easily, but there lay her body, black and blue. And though she seldom cried, when she thought of the *Bella Nicola* scattered along the bottom of the ocean, the tears spilled forth, easily and unimpeded. She told herself she'd broken down because of the shock and injuries. The truth was that she cried because the life she had always known, had always wanted, was lost to her and her father and Chancey forever.

For what seemed like hours, she lay conjuring up memories of her ship and trying to freeze them in her mind. Her reveries were interrupted when a slim man with a crop of light-blond hair and a cherubic expression entered the cabin.

"Oh, I'm so very sorry for not knocking. I thought you'd be asleep," he said as he approached her bed. "I am Dr. Bigsby, the ship's surgeon, and I've been caring for your more serious injuries."

"How bad am I?"

"You gave us a little scare when you didn't wake for the first three days. But now that you're up and speaking, I'm sure you'll do just fine."

"*Three days* . . . I was out for three days?"

"That's correct. The rest is helping you mend." He took a small glass lens out of his medical bag and moved it to her eye. "Now, if you will look up . . . to the left, and right. Very good, with the other eye, please."

When he'd put away the tool, she asked, "What's happened to my crew since we were taken?"

He answered reticently as he took her pulse, "Well, there was that, um, trying-to-take-the-ship incident, but none of them were gravely injured. I made sure they were given adequate water and food. When you woke, I was able to assure them that you were doing much better."

"I can't believe they mutinied."

"Yes, though close, the coup was not a success."

"And Chancey? Is he all right?"

"He's prowling the hold like a caged tiger, but calmed a bit when I told him how well you're being treated."

She grabbed the doctor's hand in an anxious grip. "Oh, thank you, Dr. Bigsby. Thank you so much for that."

At that moment, Sutherland entered the room, his cold gaze settling on their hands like frost.

"Bigsby—outside. *Now,*" he barked. The doctor looked from Sutherland to her before bravely patting her hand in encouragement. "I'll be back," he said, then followed the captain out.

She couldn't make out what they said, but Sutherland returned alone.

"You will not need the surgeon's help anymore." He shut the door on the doctor still standing in the corridor.

She flinched. His voice was so severe and gravelly, so different from the placid voice of Dr. Bigsby. She eyed him warily as he started moving around the cabin gathering dry clothes. No matter how hard she fought it, how much she wanted to be on her guard with him in the room, sleep overcame her again.

Then wood crashed down against wood—her body jerked in response, but there was nowhere to run. . . .

Her eyes flew open. She wasn't on her ship? She was warm, dry . . . safe?

The door to the cabin had been thrown open. A sickly boy with ashen skin brought in a food tray and plopped it on the floor, causing the contents to slosh out over the tray.

Through locks of straggly hair that fell over his eyes, he looked down at the spilled food, mumbling something about how she "shouldn't even be given a cursed crumb."

At the doorway, he turned to give her a hostile glare with his sunken eyes before slamming the door. Then, just as Sutherland had done that morning, he locked it behind him.

What? Did they think she could escape the ship? Idiots!

After some time, she slowly levered herself up in the bed to determine whether she could bend down for the food without passing out. In the end, she decided she wouldn't even try, and not just because of her injuries. She couldn't eat when a boy she'd never seen had looked at her with such spite. She reasoned that, at worst, he would give as good as he thought he'd gotten and put something danger-ous in the food. At best, the little cur would probably spit in it. The effort to raise herself was just too daunting, and her strength ebbed away as sleep returned.

*   *   *

They made Cape Town four days later. Nicole still suffered headaches and slept for most of the day. Derek had hoped she'd sleep through their docking and the jettisoning of her crew.

As he watched his men steering the tied-up sailors on the deck, he understood that wouldn't be happening.

Because Chancey began to yell.

"Nic, be strong—yer a Lassiter!"

As he drew breath to yell again, the sailor in charge of Chancey looked askance at Derek, who nodded in reply. So when Chancey began, "Get away from him in Sydney and I'll come for—" he was interrupted by several blows to his stomach.

Derek cast an uneasy glance at the companionway. The commotion might have woken her. She could hurt herself attempting to get up. Not a minute later he yanked open his cabin door; as he'd expected, she lay crumpled on the floor, just as she'd dropped.

He swiftly scooped her up and winced at how light she'd become. She'd lost weight in the last few days. He vowed that he would make her eat more.

His thoughts were distracted when she grabbed at his collar with both hands and whispered, "Don't do this, Sutherland. Please don't do this." Her face was drawn, and it looked as if those words cost her a great deal of pain.

But he wouldn't be swayed. He couldn't. The sooner he had that crew off his ship, the safer his own men would feel. He had to think of them first.

"I have no choice."

"Then please, *please,* don't let them be hurt." Her gaze was fierce as she visibly put on a strong front, but he could see that she faded. The tension rapidly left her body, and she passed out again.

Chapter 16

"Oh, yes, yes. She's up and about," Dr. Bigsby bragged a week later to anyone who would listen. "She has blooms in her cheeks again. Strong girl, that one."

Derek marveled that the man could miss the threatening looks and harsh glares from the sailors, newly recovered themselves. They weren't exactly waiting on tenterhooks to hear about her rally.

"Captain Sutherland, there you are!"

Derek inwardly groaned when the surgeon turned his attention to him.

"How is our patient today?" Bigsby asked in a cheery tone.

"Fine."

The doctor raised his eyebrows, waiting for more information. When none came, he asked, "And her bruises?"

"Fine."

Bigsby frowned, then smiled again. "Just curious. Just

curious. Since you won't allow me to talk to her any longer, let alone examine her. Curious, you understand, of course?"

The doctor had just hidden a rebuke in that spate of bubbly speech. Derek didn't need this. "She's healing . . . fine." Really, he didn't know. She dressed and bathed herself, so he hadn't seen. Plus, he was the last person she'd tell if she was worried. He walked away from the doctor, eyebrows drawn together, and ended up wondering about her all day. Was she still sick? Was she healing readily enough? Healing at all?

He woke early the next morning, just at dawn, while she slept. Gently turning her on her back, he undid the buttons at her midriff. He held his breath as she lifted her arm above her head, tilting her face back to the pillow. When she settled, he bared her torso, noting that her bruises were fading. But so was the *mehndi*. He'd dreamed about tracing that pattern so often.

Why shouldn't he do it now? She was his to do with as he pleased.

With tentative fingers, he brushed along the design at her waist and up above her flat belly. The lines ran under her shirt, so he pulled it farther open. Heart thundering in his chest, he skimmed the pale undersides of her breasts. He'd been too long without a woman, damn it! That was the only reason for his sharp reaction to her. He wandered along the intricate tracing, following it up between her breasts.

Unfastening her shirt that far had also widened the bottom of the opening, and he could see her hips and the strip of skin just below her belly. His mouth watered to kiss her there. But under his hands, he could feel her body begin to shake from the cold. With regret, he caressed that newly bared spot with the backs of his fingers before reluctantly dressing and bundling her up again.

What had just happened? She'd dreamed that Sutherland was running his hands all over her, the rough pads of his fingers contrasting with the gentleness of his touch. The dream had been vivid and confusing, even more so when she cracked open her eyes and spied him next to her. His gaze lingered over her with a possessive, relishing look that made her body go hot and languorous, even as her mind grew outraged at his liberties.

Her first instinct was to sit up and cover herself, but only after slapping him. Instead, she secretly watched his shaking hands lighting on her body.

Soon his touch became much more than simply pleasurable. She realized she *liked* being bared for him, especially when he looked at her with such a watchful intensity. Why? Did this mean she didn't hate him? Surely you had to at least like someone to feel what she did. She knew for certain that she despised him, but when she watched him skimming her skin with those blunt-tipped fingers that had stroked her so well, she wanted to reveal more.

He must have read her mind, because he opened the shirt farther up as he moved higher between her breasts. Afraid he would notice she was awake, Nicole closed her eyes. Which started a misery unlike any other she'd ever endured.

Each sensation was heightened. She didn't know where he would touch her next. He could take her breast in his hand or touch her even more intimately, as he had before. So why wasn't she stopping him? Her body began quivering. If he continued, would she reach that peak he'd introduced her to? Right when she became dazed with wanting, just when thoughts arose that she should take his hand and press it between her legs, he pulled her shirt closed and wrapped her up in his bed.

She had no control over herself where he was concerned, and that made her afraid of him. He held all the cards now. She hated the man in one instant and wanted to give him her virtue in the next.

The next few mornings, when Derek returned from giving out orders, he found her sitting in the window, her eyes vacantly taking in the sea. Each time, a stony silence greeted him. This morning was much the same except for finding her dressed for the first time in her own clothes with her curls braided atop her head. He noted with displeasure that her clothes, boys' trousers and a linen blouse, bagged on her small body.

"I heard you were awake," he said gruffly as he closed the cabin door behind him.

She didn't answer, didn't move, just stood staring out the window. Dealing with a woman like this was disconcerting. For one thing, women always chattered around him, probably because he spoke so little. He'd never met one as eerily quiet as Nicole.

And women were usually attracted to him or, more accurately, to his money. With Nicole, it was obvious that he repelled her now. Had she ever really felt differently about him?

He didn't have the slightest clue how to deal with her. He'd wanted to punish her for what she'd done, but even he wasn't cruel enough to hurt her when she was injured. Plus, he was beginning to wonder if she would ever recover from the loss of her ship. She was being punished as it was. She was lethargic and incredibly still losing weight.

Bigsby had suggested he buy fruit at the Cape to reawaken her appetite, even outrageously suggesting a few exorbitant oranges. Amazingly, Derek had taken the suggestion. Today, the surgeon had given his blind opinion that Nicole should begin eating normally again.

"I, uh, I brought you some fresh fruit. I'll just set—"

He didn't have time to blink before she flew at him—or rather, at the fruit he'd placed on the table. She snatched three oranges and two apples, stuffing them in the crook of her bent elbow, under her chin, then attempting to take three more in a juggler's grip.

After scrambling into the corner of his bed, she apparently decided he wasn't coming to take them away. She relaxed and tore into an orange. She rolled her eyes in delight and dribbled juice down her chin.

Derek recognized what her behavior indicated, and a well of fury stoked inside him. "I take it you haven't been eating well since you've been on board."

She raised her eyebrows and gave him a look that said, *However did you guess?*

He struggled to contain his temper, and his next words sounded less harsh. "You've been brought food three times a day, every day." He pinched the bridge of his nose as he asked, "Why haven't you eaten more?"

She looked torn between answering him and eating the last section of an orange. As the orange prevailed, he had to wait for her to finish her slow, relishing chewing. Peeling another with quick, slender fingers, she asked, "You believe I poisoned your crew, correct?"

He could point out that there was no belief about it, only certainty. But she was speaking to him in whole sentences, so he nodded.

"And you sent my crew to jail because they were wor-

ried about my health?" He did not like the direction this
conversation was taking.

In a patronizing tone, she said, "I'll take the absence of a
denial to mean 'Yes, Miss Lassiter.'"

Brazen chit. Still, he grunted, and she continued, "Your
cabin boy made it clear that he doesn't think I deserve food
after the dastardly thing I've allegedly done. I'm sure your
whole crew is of the same opinion."

She began shining an apple with the hem of her shirt.
"Would *you* eat from the generous trays that keep coming
if you were in my position?"

Put like that, he probably wouldn't have, but he'd be
damned if he'd admit that to her.

She shook her head at the apple, then held it in two
hands as she lovingly took a bite with her little white teeth.

Why hadn't he foreseen this problem? Hell, he didn't
want to starve the wench. Exhaling loudly, he said, "I
promise you that your food has not been tainted at my
order. In the future, I'll make sure that no one alters your
meals in any way."

She inclined her head toward him as if in a regal
acknowledgment. Irritated at his continual softening with
her, he grabbed his hat and turned away.

"Sutherland?" she asked before he could leave.

"What?"

She ran her sleeve over her chin and took a deep breath.
"Although I find it unspeakably difficult to ask you for
anything, I find that I have to now that I finally have the
energy."

He expected she needed some type of luxury item that
she didn't already possess, so her next question caught him
completely off guard.

"How did you sink my ship?"

"*What?*"

She leapt off the bed. "I have to know!"

"I didn't have anything to do with sinking your ship. You and your crew took care of that all by yourselves!" Derek all but yelled.

"No," she said, shaking her head. "It has to be you."

"You're just trying to escape your own punishment by throwing me off the scent—"

She began to pace. "I know your motivation," she continued as if not hearing him. "After all, my father was favored to win this race. And with your reputation, the loss would be devastating to your company."

"You exaggerate."

Returning her attention to him, she said, "You know this race will make or break captains and shipping lines. All of England is caught up in it. All our reputations are at stake."

"I don't disagree with that. But, believe me, Peregrine Shipping is strong enough that a single race wouldn't run it into the ground."

She gave him a pitying glance. "I know about the company. I'm well aware that you've been losing business steadily for the last few years. You might have had some success in camouflaging that fact. But anybody who looked closely would know you're killing Peregrine."

What she'd said was only a variation of his brother's rebuke just weeks earlier but, damn, he didn't want this girl to think that.

"You can't bloody well talk, princess. You poisoned my crew so your father could win."

"How can you think I'm responsible for your crew's sickness?" she asked in an astonished tone.

"Don't forget that I found you in my ship's storage hold

sneaking around the water casks," he replied just as heatedly. "And I heard you telling that Irishman that you could cross me off the list—that you'd been through my entire ship."

"God, you are a fool. I swear the alcohol has pickled your brain."

"I am indebted to my drinking. Staying on the bottle is the only thing that prevented me from succumbing to our *poisoned water*," he thundered.

"I'll tell you again, someone else did this. Most likely the same person who crippled my ship."

"Then what were you doing in the hold?"

"Well, spying, of course."

She said it in such a matter-of-fact way, he was tempted to believe her. But he'd never had an enemy as bitter as Lassiter, and it would make sense that he would find a way to retaliate after their fight.

"I don't believe you. Your father was probably desperate to win to pay for all your frivolous luxuries."

She answered with a strangely blank look, then explained, "My father was investigating the repeated accidents occurring with the larger lines. He was at the Mermaid that night to get information because he believes someone's sabotaging them. My vote was adamantly on you. My father and Chancey thought Tallywood—"

He let out a laugh.

"My sentiments exactly," she agreed. "I also believed you had something to do with my father's continued imprisonment. We had a list of several suspects, but I was convinced you were cold enough to do it all. I wanted either to clear you or gather evidence against you."

"And which did you accomplish?"

"At the time, I thought you had nothing to do with it.

But now, after what you've done to me and my crew, there can be little doubt."

"You're lying," he said evenly. "One aspect of your tale rings false, princess. No one would suspect Tallywood over me for something like this." With a last look, he stormed out the door.

Nicole was well enough to go about on deck, but there was no way Derek could allow her out, not with the crew fuming about her being on board. Although they understood why a man would want to keep a prisoner like her, they'd hoped he would send her to jail with the rest of her crew.

Derek would be forced to escort her everywhere she went, and he didn't relish spending that much time with the taciturn girl. When she did speak, she was belligerent and insulting.

As he'd expected, she started demanding to go out shortly after they'd sailed from Cape Town.

He thought he could easily deflect her by saying, "I'll escort you topside as soon as you tell me why you poisoned my crew."

"One more time—I did not poison your blasted crew."

"So be it. When you're ready to tell me, I'll take you out."

"You don't have to take me. Just let me out! Are you afraid I'll get away? I haven't been able to take any sightings of my whereabouts, but I know we're close to the Antarctic. Do you think I'll attempt a swimming escape? Perhaps I could paddle a little chunk of ice back to the Cape," she said with a nasty smile.

He answered her smile with a patronizing one of his own. "The crew . . . dislikes you. I'm not certain you'd want to be out there without me."

She narrowed her eyes at him and looked to be gulping back whatever vicious retort she'd been thinking of. The girl had a stubborn streak a mile wide. But then, so did he. He meant it when he said she'd have to confess before he let her out. He would break her down.

Turning to walk to the window, she took a deep breath. "You must understand I can't tell you about your poisoning because I know nothing about it. You are only butting your head against an unbreachable wall."

"I think it's you who are mistaken. You'll tell me, or you'll spend the next two months in this cabin."

She shook her head and faced him with a proud look. "That statement just shows that you don't know me at all. If you think you can keep me when I want to go, then you have truly lost your senses."

She tilted her head and tapped her finger on one cheek. "Hmmm, I've heard that can happen to one if one were, say . . . a *drunk*. But I suppose that in your case"—she paused, looking him over—"it could be *age* related."

For the rest of the morning, Nicole replayed her exchange with Sutherland. She'd boldly told him there could be no doubt that it was he who'd sunk her ship. Now, uncertainty was all she felt. He wouldn't maintain his innocence for this long if he was guilty. A man with his disregard for . . . well, everything, would simply own up to it. Plus, he'd wanted to believe that Tallywood had been a main suspect. It was as if Sutherland wanted to know he wouldn't immediately be connected to any treachery in their sailing community. If he'd done it, he wouldn't be tempted to believe her.

If his sad determination that he'd be accused first swayed her, then his undiminished animosity toward her convinced her. He really thought she'd poisoned his crew. She'd been certain he'd sunk her ship. Now she concluded someone else had hurt them both. She felt a twinge of guilt over her insults that morning, but pushed it away.

So he hadn't sunk her ship—one less thing she could hate him for. And it was hard to hold his treatment of her against him when he believed she'd poisoned his men. But she could still despise him for jailing her crew at the Cape.

There was nothing for her to do but bide her time. Her injuries had healed, and he knew it. So far she hadn't pressed about wanting to go topside, but after the storm they'd just sailed through, she really would get sick if she couldn't go out soon.

When he came to the cabin at noontime, she was dressed in her own clothes and pacing.

"Captain Sutherland? May I speak with you?" She could be polite when it suited her.

He sank down on the edge of the bunk and pulled off his boots. He was soaked through and looked done in. "What do you want?" His tone was short of civil.

Lord, he was burned by her comments that morning. Captain Sutherland had some chinks in his armor. She tucked that information away for later use.

"I was hoping that you would be gracious enough to escort me to the deck today, since the storm has finally broken."

"No," he said without even pausing to consider it.

"No? Just like that?" she cried.

"Yes."

Her face burned from holding in the bitter words she was dying to say. She couldn't do it. Not another day down here. "Sutherland . . . *please.*"

Ignoring her, he walked to his chest and pulled out dry

clothes. He threw them on the bed and began drawing his wet shirt over his head. She dragged her gaze from that wide expanse of damp chest. Sutherland was a cruel, arrogant boor; so why did the sight of his body still affect her?

She averted her face so she could speak steadily. "I would ask you to reconsider. It's bordering on inhumane to keep me down here."

When he continued dressing and said nothing, she turned to him again, and couldn't say if she was disappointed or relieved to see he'd already changed his pants.

As per her plan, if he was unresponsive, she'd just have to lie. Collapsing into a chair, she raised a hand to her head. "I think that the lack of fresh air and sunlight is making the headaches come back."

For a second, she thought he looked concerned.

"Is that so?"

Damn, why did he sound like he didn't believe her? "Yes, I'm afraid it is. Please, just an hour a day. I can work. I can pull my own load."

"We don't need anyone to cook or sew for us. And we have someone who launders. You are useless to me."

"Useless? *Useless?* You only named the chores that women usually do on shore. Is that all you think I'm capable of?"

"I know lots of things you're capable of," he sneered.

That bastard!

When he stood up to leave, having obviously finished this conversation, her anger deflated. The thought of another day cooped up in his cabin made her want to cry.

She finally found her tongue when he was halfway out the door.

"But what am I to do all day?" she asked in a small, lame voice.

"I don't bloody well care what you do."

When she heard the click of the door lock, her misery once again yielded to fury. Every chantey the crew sang and every tack the ship made only provoked her more. It wasn't natural to be locked down here, especially for something she didn't do. By God, now she *wanted* to poison him!

She searched the cabin but couldn't find anything that she'd be willing to break or disfigure. Truthfully, it went against her nature to be destructive. She preferred to create. . . .

An idea surfaced. Her eyes flitted toward her sea chest, the same chest Sutherland had avoided as though it had teeth. Here, right within her grasp, was her revenge. He would regret his treatment of her. And after she'd finished, he'd never be able to forget her.

"Captain Sutherland?" Bigsby inquired with a frown when he stalked to the deck.

"What do you want?"

The man looked pointedly behind Derek. "I had hoped Miss Lassiter would be with you, since the weather's turned so fair."

"She's not." Derek made his way in the opposite direction.

Bigsby followed. "Oh. How has she been feeling? Any headaches?"

Derek's brows drew together. She had obviously been lying about the headaches. Hadn't she? Of course. She was a pitiful actress. Still . . . "Why do you ask about headaches?"

"I have always expressed worry about the blow to the head she sustained."

"No headaches."

"Oh, very well. Would you tell her I'm very pleased she's feeling better?"

Bigsby's overweening kindness almost made Derek regret his harsh manner with her. At the time, he'd thought her underhanded lying should be expected from a woman devious by nature. Yet after considering her situation, he admitted that he probably would've been driven to do the same thing.

Contrary to what most people thought, he wasn't a cruel man by nature. He turned to go to his cabin to check on her.

"Cap'n! Ship ahoy. Looks to be a homeward-bound English ship. Mail packet. They're signaling to 'speak us.'"

Derek hesitated. He was anxious to get information about the race and barter for supplies, and reasoned Nicole would be fine in the cabin for a few hours more. When they sailed in closer, he accepted the captain's invitation to row over and visit with him and his wife.

Once he was on board, the jovial, loquacious couple broke out a bottle of fine French claret and insisted repeatedly that he join them for dinner. He agreed, because the breeze that evening was light, and they wouldn't lose any time. More important, he would grasp at anything to get his mind off the woman he had locked up in his cabin.

Even so, he hadn't been able to stop thinking about her. After several hours, he'd finally managed politely to leave the neighboring ship. The claret he'd hoped would numb some of his guilt and anger toward her had only served to get him semidrunk.

He stood at the rail hoping the chill winds would clear his mind. He wanted to be in control when he faced her. Surely Nicole would be scratching at the walls by this time.

Nicole. As he gazed up at the inky sky, he thought he'd finally found the color of her eyes: the blue of a night sky at the bottom of the world. He quickly flushed at how sentimental his thoughts were. Christ, he needed to quit drinking. He was glad when Jimmy interrupted his driveling musings.

"Cap'n, you told me to tell you if anything was wrong with the girl. I'm 'ere to tell you that she ain't eaten nothin' all day."

If this was her plan to make him feel guilty, she was doing a splendid job. "Did she appear ill to you?" he said, trying to sound steady.

Jimmy shuffled his feet nervously at that question, then muttered, "I ain't seen 'er, Cap'n."

"What's that, boy?"

"She sent me away at midday and dinner saying that she wasn't dressed and couldn't let me in. So I just left the trays outside the door."

Derek guessed that Jimmy didn't give a damn about her any more than the rest of the crew and wouldn't have cared if she ate or not.

"She didn't take any of the food, but she did take the pitchers of water," the boy added, probably hoping that information would erase the hard look on his captain's face.

Although Nicole had eaten like a bird, she'd at least eaten steadily since he'd assured her of the food. Something really had to be wrong.

He stalked to his cabin, sweat lightly beading his forehead even with the freezing winds blowing. He didn't understand why he cared at all. But his crew had recovered from the poisoning now, and he found it difficult to continue wanting to hurt her.

He tamped down his visible concern as he opened the door.

She was on his bunk, bundled in his warm blankets, which was wise because his port window was open to the night air. Still, an odor like mineral spirits assailed him. He could only just make her out in the bed since her own lamp was down low, but something dark dotted her face and hair. He turned up the lantern near the door, and inhaled a whistle as he surveyed his cabin.

Which was newly decorated.

Nicole—the little witch—had painted his walls. She'd produced a pastoral scene, a landscape that was . . . remarkable.

Unfortunately, her canvas encompassed his *whole* cabin. If his shirt hung on the wall in an integral spot, she'd simply painted over it. The spines of his books, so neatly lined up, were now green and grassy. His mirror had been turned into a glassy pond surrounded by reeds. She had somehow integrated every inch of every wall panel into the scene.

He moved closer to look at the water pitchers she'd taken from her tray. Paintbrushes filled them. The gilded silver handles were engraved with the words "To Nicole, Happy Birthday, E. B." Who the devil was E. B.? More luxuries—and not from her father.

Someone, probably another man, had thought highly enough of her to give her these expensive gifts. Purposely ignoring the thought of her responding gratitude, he continued to scan the room. She'd used every drop of ink out of his wells and every ounce of bootblack. Still, she would have had to have a good supply of her own paint.

The chests. Derek inwardly berated himself for not investigating her sea chests, which were evidently filled with paint supplies.

The landscapes on her own cabin wall . . . they were hers. She was the artist he'd thought so talented. His breath whistled out as he surveyed her work. She'd done an exceptional job, but how could she have accomplished this so swiftly?

Again he felt a flush of guilt. She'd been alone in the cabin for eight or maybe nine hours. Even so, as he peered closer at the intricate details in every image, he thought she must have worked in a frenzy to get it all done in one day. Because she had painted *everything*.

She had violated all his possessions—why wasn't he feeling the familiar ire? He should be. But a part of him believed he'd gotten exactly what he deserved.

As if reading his mind, she spoke. "You told me you 'didn't bloody well care' what I did." His gaze flew from the wall to her face. Her eyes were open, watching him without interest.

"So I did," he admitted. Light purple smudges just under her eyes showed him that she'd worn herself down. What if she relapsed? Guilt twisted in his chest, surprising him with its strength, and he was about to apologize to lessen it. Instead, stupidly, he said, "You know, I should feel angry."

A moment passed. "I don't bloody well care how you feel," she said in a deadened voice, and closed her eyes.

As sleep claimed her, Derek was left to his own heavy thoughts as he lost himself in the scene surrounding him.

Chapter 17

_N_icole was sitting by the window working on her knots when a loud rap on the door surprised her. Knocking? Well, this was unprecedented with this philistine crew. She took a cursory glance down to make sure everything was covered.

Since Bigsby had been barred from her company, the door opened and closed freely without any concession to her. Luckily, growing up at sea had drilled out any hint of modesty that might once have been present in her.

Sutherland strolled in smelling of sea, salt, and freezing, crisp air. God, how badly she longed to be free of this cabin! It was so painful to her that he might as well be teasing a beggar at the kitchen window.

She'd struggled with the temptation to make up a story about the poisoning just so she could get out. But she knew next to nothing about poison and couldn't even begin to fabricate a convincing tale.

The thought of having to lie to gain her freedom galled her. If Sutherland stood there waiting for her to talk, he'd be disappointed. All she felt capable of doing was glaring hatefully at him. He in turn looked as if he wanted to shuffle his feet.

"I thought that since you've run out of canvas," he said with a pointed look around his cabin, "you might be in need of some." He laid a pile of large canvas squares on his desk as if he were placating some wild animal. Which she supposed she was fast becoming.

Then, from a small crate, he pulled out three tins. "Thought you might need some paint, also." He looked eminently pleased with himself when he presented her with the paint, as if this burst of generosity was somehow noteworthy.

Instead of responding with kind words or even a little fawning, which he seemed to expect, she simply stared at him and fingered the squares with precise, edgy movements. She stopped when her cheek twitched.

"I thought this would please you and possibly make up for yesterday . . ." His words died as she rose and marched up to him. Before he even had a clue what she intended, she'd drawn back her arm.

And punched his face.

"What the bloody hell! Why'd you do that?" Sutherland's bellow was skewed as he grasped his jaw to work it back and forth.

Her fury was so strong she shook from it. "If you think that some cut-up sail and some old paint will make me forget that you have me confined to this damned cabin"— she paused to take a deep breath—"then you are sadly mistaken. I am not some little nitwit who'll be happy with whatever diversion you throw at me! When I paint, I usually do it *after* a hard day's work!"

She'd punched Sutherland! She couldn't quite believe it, but her hand throbbed from the impact with his rock-solid face. There was a flutter of movement outside; Jimmy had been standing outside the door. For how long, she didn't know, but she did know that the boy had seen Sutherland holding his jaw, muttering a blistering curse.

She couldn't seem to dim the lazy grin that surfaced once she'd unleashed the worst of her pique. It wouldn't fade even when Sutherland made a menacing sound toward her before stalking out the door.

In fact, she grew even more pleased—the news would be all over the ship in minutes.

The next morning she received her second knock and even enjoyed a polite hesitation before the door opened. Jimmy, the little brat, padded in as if he didn't want to wake her. Each day his eyes brightened and his skin grew pinker, while she weakened. She thought she really might hate him.

As he had the day before, he examined the walls she'd painted with a marveling look on his face, then left the tray. Today, however, he placed it on the table, forgoing the floor. Instead of dispensing the obligatory scowl before his departure, he hesitated at the open door before turning back to her.

"What do you want?" she snapped. With his wind-flushed cheeks, he looked completely recovered from his sickness, and he, like Sutherland, smelled as if he'd been bathing in sunshine. The thought of Jimmy outside when she couldn't be was just too much.

This crew's treatment of her was about to change—beginning with him. She started toward the little whelp.

He backed away from her. "D-did you really give the cap'n your fives?"

She raised her eyebrows at him but didn't stop.

"Um, well, I thought you decked the cap'n."

She glowered even more menacingly. Fine. If Jimmy meant to take her to task for that one beautiful facer she'd planted, she was spoiling for a fight.

"Yes, I popped the captain. What are you going to do about it?" Tilting her head, she looked the boy over, sizing him up. He wasn't much bigger than she was. One more once-over, and she decided. She could take him.

"Wait!" He held a hand in front of him to ward off her advance, backing up to the door. Clumsily he maneuvered himself behind it, only allowing his head to peek out. "'Ow come . . . 'ow come you ain't ashamed of what you done?" he cried.

She knew he asked her not about hitting the captain but about poisoning their water. Although she didn't feel the question even deserved an answer, she was past furious now.

"Ashamed? I've done nothing to be ashamed of!" she screeched. "If you weren't as insanely obtuse as your captain, you'd have comprehended by now that I couldn't *poison* anyone. I'm not perfect by any means, but I'm not malicious enough to poison you, even though *I'm beginning to wish I had!*"

Jimmy sucked in a breath, and his eyes widened wildly before he spun around. He had to fight past the handful of crewmen who by this time had gathered by the door, most likely drawn by her screaming. Some of them nodded toward her and mumbled back and forth, but she ignored them. She supposed this was as good a time as any to bring this to a head. Because there was no way she'd spend the next month inside, and they needed to know that.

She opened the door wide and turned to the closest sailor. "So you think I poisoned your water?" she shouted.

"You're so convinced I did that your captain won't let me on deck for fear you'll do me harm." She leveled her glare at every seaman crowded about the door.

"Well, damn you all! I've done nothing but have the misfortune to be aboard with a no-good bunch of cowardly bastards!" Her fists clenched as she reached the point of no return.

"If you mean to do me harm, you better bloody well do it now, because I'm walking out that door, and I'll feel the sun on my face . . . or I'll die trying. *Do you understand me?*"

In her fury, all she could hear was the blood pounding in her head. She was barely conscious of the exhaled whistles or gruff grunts. She lunged at the door, shoving at those who were too slow to get out of her way.

Including Sutherland.

With a grim expression of realization on his face, he stood motionless. Too bad.

With all her might, she stiff-armed him to the side before she marched to the railing and looked out over the sea.

Derek didn't think he'd ever felt like such a bloody bastard. As he watched her at the rail, watched her small shoulders rise with each shuddering breath of fresh air, he knew.

She didn't do it.

He couldn't believe that she'd screamed at his crew or that she'd shoved him. But her indignant behavior was like a wedge opening up a stronghold of gut feeling. His instincts kicked in, and he simply understood. She must have been telling him the truth about what she was doing on his ship that night.

He turned from her and sought out Jeb. "Tell the rest of the crew that they are to treat Miss Lassiter as an honored guest aboard this ship."

"Aye, Cap'n. We kinda figgered things out when we 'eard she clocked you in the face."

He scowled at the sailor. "Your age doesn't give you liberty to disrespect your captain."

"No, but I can when my captain's made an ass of 'imself."

With a last menacing look, Derek turned from him and found a good place to watch her. For the next two hours, she stood at the rail. It was late afternoon when she finally laid her head on the wood. She was afraid someone would drag her back inside.

He didn't think it was wise to approach her this soon, but he couldn't let her fear him or his crew's treatment of her any longer.

"Nicole," he began when he stood behind her. She didn't acknowledge him at all. "Look at me, please," he said. He gently turned her to him, and noticed with a sharp pain in his chest that she furtively clutched the rail. "I don't believe you tainted the water."

She didn't respond.

"Did someone . . . so someone hurt your ship as well."

"Just as I've said all along."

He exhaled a deep breath. "I want to apologize to you—"

"Very well," she said tightly.

He'd apologized, and she didn't seem to care. "I am saying I'm sorry," he grated.

"And I am saying, 'Very well.'"

"What do you want from me? What do you want to set us straight?"

She looked right past him. "I want a ride to Sydney." She walked away from him, following the rail.

As seemed always the case, he was at a loss where she was concerned. Every time he believed he had her figured out, what kind of person she really was, his whole idea of her became fragmented.

He'd thought she was a prostitute and a dangerous deceiver. Now he was no closer than he'd been before. Was she a woman who wanted to sail with her father and help him build a shipping line? Or was she serious about her incredible artistic talent? Was she only sailing while waiting to find the right man to settle down with and start a family?

The thought of her marrying another man brought on a raw surge of jealousy. And it was jealousy. He wouldn't pretend any longer that she was merely someone he lusted after. He wanted to understand her; he wanted to know her.

Not that that would happen anytime soon. In the days that followed, she didn't speak to him, and he wisely didn't push the issue.

"You might as well be a gnat for 'ow easy she ignores you," Jeb told him one morning when he came upon Derek staring at her.

He scowled at Jeb, uncomfortable with being caught. He hadn't missed the fact that the crew felt sorry for him. If they spotted him looking at her, which he did for most of every day, they lowered their eyes. But not before he could see their sympathy.

"Thank you, Jeb, for your sage and unasked-for observation."

"You wish she'd scream at you right about now, eh?" Jeb observed.

He gritted his teeth.

"But, no, that one won't pour on the blame and cry."

Strangely, she hadn't done any of that to make him feel guilty. He would have, especially when he thought of all she'd lost and what she'd been through with no one to turn to. Then to be brought onto his ship, jailed, and starved, even if that last had been unintentional.

"She simply doesn't want to have anything to do with me," Derek said absently.

"I bet that bothers you like salt on an open wound," the old man said in a kinder tone.

He found himself nodding. It did, as did the fact that the only person she'd speak to out of the whole crew was Bigsby.

Like Derek, the crew had changed their minds about her, but they hadn't yet accepted her as one of their own. It didn't appear that she wanted to have anything to do with them, either. With her full run of the ship, she used the space to avoid everyone.

Especially him.

She picked up chores, not asking anyone, but simply mending or cleaning anything she thought needed it. He had no illusions that her efforts were meant to help him or his crew in any way. She worked to alleviate her otherwise obvious boredom.

The distance Nicole put between herself and everyone else was loud and jarring, and no matter what anyone did—

"Good morning, Miss Lassiter."

"Uh-huh."

—it wouldn't be breached.

Except in bed with him.

From the first night they'd slept together back in London, he'd found it . . . nice with her, and he'd continued to each night, even after her outburst. Every morning, it became harder to leave her and their unspoken—and, on her side, unconscious—truce. When he folded her to his chest, she welcomed him, even unwittingly moving closer to him.

That night, when he returned to the cabin, he looked her over. Her small hands nestled the blanket under her chin, and her thick braid wound over her shoulder. *Beautiful.* She was beautiful to him. He wanted to make love to her for more than the pleasure he knew he'd find with her. He wanted to take her, to make this clever, brave woman his.

For some reason, the want of her that never left him was more powerful tonight. He was sick with it, sick with wanting her. Tonight he wouldn't—couldn't—sleep with her. He stayed in his chair, thinking about the girl in his bed, hard drinking in hope of oblivion. When he rose to get another bottle, she awakened and rubbed her eyes.

"What are you doing?"

She didn't say, "What are you doing *in here*?" Did she know he came in each night? Did she have any idea how she affected him?

"I'm pouring myself a drink. Care for one?"

She shook her head and pulled herself up, knees to chest, bundled in a cloud of blankets. "Why do you do it? Why drink so much?"

The glass he'd filled and raised to his lips stopped. This was the first personal question she'd ever asked him, the first interest she'd shown. Yet she'd targeted his greatest weakness.

He was just drunk enough to answer her honestly. "I drink to forget. To forget what I can't change."

She angled her head. "Does it help?"

"I don't know," he said, frowning down at his glass. "I used to think so."

"I'm sad for you," she said softly, and then eased down to sleep again.

Late into the night, he thought about their exchange. "I'm sad for you" sounded more and more like "I feel sorry for you."

Damn it, he was a proud man. He wanted her to respect him, to want him. For Christ's sake, he didn't want her pity.

Even if he quit drinking—if he could—he was running out of time to win her. Each interminable night like this, they sailed closer to port, and there was more standing between them than he'd ever thought.

He could only imagine how badly she wanted to land. He himself wasn't happily anticipating arriving in Sydney, because Nicole would leave him and never look back.

Chapter 18

*F*or the next couple of nights, Jimmy brought her dinner in, setting the tray down with a flourish. The bratling had changed his behavior toward her so drastically that she suspected he had, in fact, spit in her food before and now felt guilty. He wouldn't leave her alone, but peppered her with questions. He complimented her and brought her bathwater every day, as well as choice selections of food. In fact, she'd never eaten this well this far out.

The other crewman who weren't friendly to her weren't unfriendly either and mainly kept to themselves. Which was fine by her. She already had a crew, a good crew whom she loved. She didn't need to be welcomed into the fold by this one.

Ignoring Jimmy's chatter, she scooped up a handful of raisins and thought about her situation. She couldn't continue with her grudge for much longer. She wasn't the type to stay angry; she always blew up and then minutes later forgot what the fight was about. And she told herself that under the circumstances, she probably would have believed the same thing Sutherland and his crew had.

Sutherland especially made it difficult. He anticipated her every want. Yesterday when they'd passed a home-bound French steamer, he'd signaled them and rowed over with a crewman to board their ship even though he would lose time. He'd brought back a bag full of fruit for her—apples, oranges, these raisins—for which he must have paid a fortune. She'd had to hide her open-mouthed astonishment, because he'd also brought her a good supply of ink, saying she'd probably want to *write her father*.

If she had to walk past him, which seemed to be happening more often lately, he would brush by her and put his hand on the small of her back. If that wasn't enough, he'd let it linger. She supposed that, in each of these ways, he asked for her forgiveness.

Sleeping beside him wore her down as well. Nicole was aware he came in every night, though he hadn't realized that she woke each time he entered the bed.

She should be angry at the liberty. But as long as he didn't think she knew, she could just pretend she didn't and continue to enjoy the warmth he provided in the freezing nights.

But sometimes when he put his arms around her and pulled her to him, his hand would brush her breast. She'd go still at the shock of pleasure. Each night she found it harder not to respond, and it took every ounce of willpower she possessed not to move against his body, so warm and hard against hers. His heartbeat drumming into her back relaxed her guard, lulling her.

When she was recovering, he'd sleep soon after he lay down, but now he stayed awake, tense. A night didn't go by when she couldn't feel the evidence of his arousal. He held himself in check. For her. She wished he wouldn't. She wished he'd pull her to him and touch her as he'd done in the past.

Then the guilt would overcome her. How could she desire him when he'd had her crew jailed? He himself had said that he'd given them no word of her health. Of course they would try to mutiny; they had no idea what he was doing with her. No, she couldn't let down her guard with him. Any man cruel enough to antagonize her sailors and throw them to the wolves in Cape Town when they reacted could not be trusted.

"Are you all right?" Jimmy asked, pulling her from her thoughts.

She looked down to see that her hands were clenched. "I'm fine."

Jimmy frowned as he picked up the tray. "Better get this back to Cook."

When she nodded absently, he carried out the tray.

Suddenly restless, Nicole bundled up in nearly every piece of her clothing, draped a blanket over the whole, and headed out the door. For what seemed like an hour, she stared out at the sea, where the moon's light flashed over the water. It hung above the horizon as if it were too great and heavy to rise.

"Incredible, is it not?" Sutherland said as he walked up behind her. "It's as if she's reluctant to part from the sea." He stood, making no move to join her at the railing.

She didn't answer, just battled the urge to sink back into him, into the warmth she enjoyed even now without touching him.

"I think this is my favorite part of the entire journey— these last few days so far south."

How could his voice affect her so? Why did it tempt her to turn and bury herself against his chest?

She shook her head, reminding herself that he'd hurt her crew. "That doesn't surprise me," she began in a waspish tone, "since it's *cold*." If she was cutting enough, would he leave her?

Silence followed, and she almost regretted her sharp tone. He placed his hand on her shoulder.

"You're shivering. Why don't you ever wear the warm clothes I set out for you?"

"Oh, is that why you place them on the bed?" she asked without feigning interest.

"Yes. I, uh, didn't know how to go about getting you to wear my things."

"In the future, don't waste your time."

He exhaled. "Nicole, I want you to know," he said haltingly, "that I am sorry for the way things have been between us. I would change the way I've treated you if I could."

When she said nothing, he turned her. "I know you might hate me, but we've got something between us that can't be ignored any longer. Don't you feel how right this could be?" he asked as he gently stroked her cheek. His eyes, glowing silver in the moonlight, mesmerized her with their intensity.

She looked away and attempted a casual tone. "You make it sound as if we have no say in the matter, as if it's something out of our control."

"That's how it's felt to me. Even when I believed you'd harmed my crew, I still wanted you no matter how hard I fought it."

He was describing the same feelings she had. The involuntary ones that made her forget about her crew—about Chancey.

She stiffened. "Too much has passed between us. It's too late. If you feel bad about how I've been treated here, then make it up to me. By leaving me alone."

The next morning, Derek was resolved. The night before, she'd told him, clearly told him, that she wanted nothing to do with him. Her body, rubbing against his till dawn, relayed a different want. If he had to win her on that level to have her completely, then he would. He'd use every night to overcome her objections until he could claim her days.

As on most mornings, he spent his time watching her from the bridge over a cup of coffee. Her looks charmed him, cheeks rosy from the crisp breeze, braids peeking out from the floppy hat she was never without.

She walked across the deck to Jebediah. Approaching Jeb was a first, and could she be . . . ? She was wearing Derek's sweater.

His thick, favorite, obscenely expensive sweater.

Well, he'd told her to wear his clothes, right?

These were good signs. Apparently Jeb thought so, too, because after nodding emphatically to her, he tore off to the galley as fast as his old body could creak along. Minutes later, he'd retrieved bait and fishing tackle and set her up at amidships. She said something else to him, and when he walked away his chest was puffed up in pride. A smile creased his old face.

She'd chosen to throw out a line right when the fishing would pick up again, now that they were finally traveling more to the north, and that impressed him. He was content to watch her from a distance as she took out a small fish for bait, cut it, hooked it, and then . . . slowly ran her slimy hands down the front of his sweater. He could swear that the scales embedded in the fine fabric shone in the sun. Casually, she grasped and cast her rod.

How could she—? But that was fine. He could get past cut-up fish on his clothing if it made her feel better.

She leaned over the rail. He worried, even though he knew he shouldn't. She had shown again and again how perfectly she walked the ship. So why was he storming across the deck?

As he approached her, he could hear her calling enticingly down the side of the ship, cooing down at the water.

"He-ere fishy, fishy. He-ere fishy."

His lips twitched.

"Fishy want a tow?" she asked playfully, bowing over the side of the ship.

When he reached her, he looked out to see a shark diving and swirling around her bait as if trying to decide about it.

"How will you get that thing aboard?" he asked. "It looks to be quite large."

She didn't appear surprised that he was there. She gave him an impatient sigh and pointedly glanced at the rod and reel she held. Speaking in slow tones as though answering a small child, she said, "When the fish takes the bait, I will begin to turn this crank until it's raised to the deck. It's *magic*," she breathed sarcastically.

"Fine, fine," he said with a grin. "He just seems a little large for you to reel in."

Irritation made her face tight. "I have taken a lot from you, and I'm so tired of you always underestimating—" She didn't get any further because the tip of the rod was now pointing straight down and jerking her forward.

"Damn and blast you, Sutherland!"

But he was already behind her, with one hand grabbing the back of her trousers and the other reaching over her for the rod. He steadied it against the first surprise she'd had and held it as she wound the crank. And grew amazed. She repeatedly, expertly let out line before quickly reeling it back in. She knew how to tire the shark, so it would be easier for her to pull him in.

He'd always been curious about how she'd survived in the ruthless world of sailing, and he thought her actions here were an insight. She might not have great physical strength, but he'd wager she always found ways around that.

Although he felt unneeded, he stood behind her, grabbing the rod if she got a tug, receiving a glare over her shoulder each time.

Nothing could have moved Derek at that moment. He basked in the scent of her hair in the cold air and how her body warmed his front when he wrapped his arms around her. He caught himself thinking that he should prolong this as much as possible, but he could feel her body tiring.

Surprisingly, she'd gotten the shark to the side, but looking at its size, he didn't believe she could haul it aboard by herself. He peremptorily took the rod from her, braving her initial one-handed slaps and pushes. He finished reeling the flailing shark up to where a crewman had a grappling pole ready.

When their catch lay safely on the deck, his gaze locked with hers. Then, seeming discomfited, she turned her attention to the thrashing beast, kneeling down to scan it with a wide-eyed scrutiny.

He could feel her exhilaration. She'd probably caught a hundred of them, but her eyes were snapping and bright with excitement, her lips unconsciously drawn up at the corners. And she blushed, probably after noticing the way he kept watching her.

He knelt on the other side and couldn't resist asking, "Still think you could have taken him?"

She blew a curl out of her face. "I admit, if I'd hooked it off my own ship, I would have cut line and fished for smaller."

He smiled, and could swear an answering smile shaded her lips. She stared at his face, then his lips, before appearing flustered and looking down.

Without warning, he grabbed her by the hand and pulled her up. He tugged her toward his cabin, past the seemingly uninterested deckhands, only pausing to tell Jeb to have the catch cleaned for dinner.

He'd been pleased just to be near her this morning, to share her company. After this calm weather they were enjoying, they'd probably encounter a storm before long and he'd be needed on deck soon, but holding her and then seeing her face flushed with pleasure had been too much. He wanted her. Needed her. Now.

However, he had a plan he wouldn't deviate from; he would be patient. He'd force himself to simply talk to her and possibly gain her trust.

He looked down and found her wide-eyed at his behavior. Damn it, his high-handedness had startled her. They'd had a rocky start, to say the least, and he needed to be careful with her. Easing his cabin door closed behind him, he politely motioned for her to sit with him. Seeming too curious to resist, she slowly removed her hat and edged onto the seat.

"There's been a . . . misunderstanding between us. I don't want to rehash it, but we need to come to some kind of terms," he said in a tone that was too commanding even to his own ears. Her face grew tight.

Excellent opening. Charming. No wonder she avoids you.

"Hmmm, misunderstanding." A shadow crossed her features. "You make it sound so light, when in fact it was hellish for me. Not knowing about my crew, mourning my ship." Her eyes glistened. "That ship was my home."

He moved to touch her, and though she shied away, he could swear it was less than before.

The look in her eyes tore at him.

"I spent a good portion of my life on the *Bella Nicola* and almost all of it with that crew. They were my family, since all I had was my father. And now, now it's worse," she said as she swiped away a tear that had fallen, "I *know* what you've done to them." Her voice grew choked. "Mutiny is a hanging offense."

Derek made a low growling sound as he stood. "If you are worried about your crew, I left orders for them to be freed a week after we sailed."

Her eyes opened wide, then narrowed in disbelief. "You ordered them . . . released?"

"I did." He saw her indecision. "I would've done it sooner, but I didn't want them to come after you." When her look of indecision began to fade, he said, "I swear to—" He didn't get a chance to finish because she was on him, stretching up to him, standing on her toes to get her arms around him. When he reached down to her, she grasped his head in both hands and planted smiling kisses all over his face and neck.

She drew back. "My crew's safe? They were released?"

He nodded. "Have you thought this whole time that I would have them tried for mutiny?"

She closed her eyes briefly.

"My God, you must have thought I was a monster," he said as he ran a hand over her hair. "I guess I didn't give you much reason to think otherwise."

"I do now," she said softly. "I can understand why you were so angry with me. It didn't look good. But, honestly, I was only back at the casks because I'd never seen iron drums up close."

He groaned and said in a low, chiding voice, "I can't believe you were spying in the first place."

"Well, there was that." She blushed. "But I never would have come if I didn't feel so attracted to you." She stood on her toes again to wind her hands in the hair on his nape. "And I've never regretted that night."

His brows drew together. He couldn't believe what he heard; he'd always wondered if she, like him, revisited that night. The knowledge that she did made him hunger even more for her, and he crushed her to him. Unlacing her thick braids, he threaded his fingers through her hair while running his lips down her neck. She gasped, then inhaled sharply.

Strangely, she went still, then backed away, grimacing at his chest. Absently raising a finger, she said simply, "Fish."

He glanced down at his own clothing to find transferred fish slime. With raised eyebrows, he looked up, and was answered with an endearing, sheepish smile.

He couldn't help but smile in return. "So there is. No harm done." He strode over to get fresh clothing. When he'd finished peeling off his outer layer and changing, he turned and caught her nibbling her bottom lip, hastily plucking scales from his sweater.

Grinning, he threw her a clean one. "We'll finish this tonight, sweet."

Nicole couldn't sleep with the stillness on the ocean this night. The fog, thick over the lifeless water, amplified every sound. It was that eerie stillness so absolute it presaged only the most violent weather. She dreaded another big storm, but to be honest, her anxiety tonight came not from the coming gale but from Sutherland.

He'd gone back topside today leaving her confused and wanting to sort out her powerful feelings. When he'd revealed he hadn't hurt her crew, she'd been floundering from her first glimpse of Sutherland's unreserved smile. Her flustered brain could formulate only one word. *Devastating.*

She thought he would make love to her tonight. While she was nervous about the actual act, she was calm about the ramifications of it. She'd realized today that her feelings for him went deeper than mere lust. She didn't know if she could call it love, but whatever gripped her was boundless in its strength.

The door opened and creaked closed. When Sutherland began undressing, even the mundane sounds of his disrobing made her skin tighten and heat pool between her legs. She couldn't stand another night of this; something had to give.

He'd taught her months ago what it was she desired, and now the craving, the wanting, wouldn't recede, only kept building. When he sank down next to her and put his arms around her, it took every ounce of will not to turn and place her lips and tongue against his skin.

He pulled her closer, and she worked to slow her breathing, but when his stiff arousal pulsed against her back, her breaths hitched in and panted out.

Tonight was different for him as well. Instead of lying tense beside her for half the night before exhaustion finally claimed him, he moved over her, and with a tiny flick of his tongue kissed the sensitive skin of her ear. She stifled a moan as her body trembled, quivered even more when he skimmed his lips down to where her shoulder met her neck.

What did it matter if he knew she was awake and wanted him? She couldn't hate him any longer. And without that barrier, she found her feelings rushing in a completely opposite direction. She couldn't stop this and didn't want to.

When he grazed the backs of his fingers over the nightshirt covering her nipple, she gasped with pleasure, but the sound made him take his hand away. She wanted to cry in frustration. So many nights like this, so much passion. *Not another wasted second.*

She grasped his arm behind her and brushed her fingers down it until she found his hand. Before she could lose her nerve, she placed it back on her breast. He sucked in a breath and groaned as he cupped her and thumbed her nipple.

She rubbed up against his front, gladdened by the hard feel of him, aroused by his manhood, impossibly still growing as it pressed against her. She moaned low in her throat. At once, he turned her on her back, covering her mouth and body with his own, moving his hips. When he raised himself on his arms, she looked down and saw his manhood thrust against her and then land over her belly again and again. The sculpted muscles above his groin and banded over his chest and shoulders strained, bulging under her grasping hands.

He dipped his head and ran his lips over her aching nipples, first one, then the other, wetting the cloth that covered them. It was too much. She couldn't stop her hips from rising to him. She even thought she might find that overwhelming pleasure at that second—she was so close.

"Nicole, I won't be able to stop after much longer. Tell

me now, or I swear I'll take you," he bit out. This time instead of rubbing sinuously over her, his straining flesh caught against the juncture of her thighs, pushing into the cloth covering her, demanding entrance.

She shook her head back and forth. "No, I want you. . . . I want to finally feel you inside me."

He hissed in a breath at her words. "There's no turning back from this." He lowered his head again to her tight nipples.

"I feel like I'll die. Please . . ." she breathed as she undulated beneath him, opening her legs wide for him.

Whatever tenuous restraint he possessed snapped. He groaned, a brutal masculine sound, and ripped apart her shirt. She shook. *Lord, his strength, his size*—she responded to that latent power emanating from his body even as she feared it. If he was losing control as she was . . .

He teased her with his finger.

Lightly caressing her at first, then gradually stroking her inside, with one finger, then two, and nothing else mattered. Each time he drove into her with his fingers, his whole body rose up over her, his stiff manhood probing against her thigh, as if preparing her for what he was about to do.

But her body couldn't wait. That delicious pressure gathered within her until she went senseless, sobbing out his name, head thrashing . . . eventually feeling nothing but the cold air on her tight nipples and the powerful squeezing around his relentless fingers.

"Ah, God, Nicole, I feel you—I can't stop now," he said, his voice pained as he put a hand on each thigh and opened her legs wider to him. Her eyes soaked up his every movement. His neck, his arms, even the muscles in his jaw were set with tension. He fought so hard not to hurt her that he punished himself.

"Don't hold back, don't . . ." She raised her hands to his chest and drew her nails down his rock-hard torso. He shuddered. She boldly rose up and grasped his manhood, fascinated fingers smoothing over the taut velvet heat of his skin.

"Nicole, don't . . ."

He sounded in pain, but then he made the smallest thrusting movement against her palm and she continued exploring him. She thumbed the slit at the top, and his body jerked. Her eyes widened when the thick tip grew moist against the pad of her finger, and she moaned even before he did. He threw his head back as she continued to run curious fingers over him, running his length, cupping the heavy sack beneath, until he lowered his chin, his eyes coming back to bore into her own.

He pushed her down into the mattress, brushed her fingers away, and gripped himself. Slowly, with a shaking hand, he positioned his rod, running it up and down her flesh, making her even wetter. Hot with embarrassment, she turned her face from him.

"No, Nicole. You're perfect." He kneaded her thighs. "Tonight, I'll kiss you there and show you how much I love your response."

Her mouth opened wordlessly. Kiss her there . . . ? She had only a second to wonder; then he pushed into her. The unyielding head was inside her, stretching her, coming to fulfill her. He withdrew and slowly pushed in farther.

"Oh, God. Please! Sutherland. *More.*" How many times he did this she couldn't know, because the quickening pleasure gathered again. . . .

But there was a sound from outside their cabin, dimly heard by her, a knocking, then a frantic hammering on the door. She didn't know how long someone had been outside and didn't care. Her mind was focused on the feelings cascading through her body. The tight feel of him just inside her. The coil in her belly, the beginning tremors inside . . .

Just when she thought he would give her all of himself, he pulled away and rose out of bed. He left her feeling empty, bereft, her body quaking.

"*What the bloody hell is it?*" he yelled—she had never heard him so angry. When he came back to her, he scooped up her unresisting body to enfold her on his lap. Beneath her bottom, he was hard, and she became confused, not understanding why he hadn't taken his pleasure with her.

He bent down and dropped a kiss in her hair before setting her on the side of the bed and standing. "Get your clothes on, love, and quickly." He ran his gaze down her flushed body and bit out a curse. "We've got trouble."

Chapter 19

The battered *Southern Cross* limped its way toward Sydney. Split ribbons waved in the wind where sails had once been. A bystander would swear dead men littered the deck, so dazed was the crew by the events spanning the last interminable hours.

Derek thought of all the times he'd wished for a storm, a true test of him and his crew, and shook his head. If not for this last storm, he'd already have made Nicole his. He tried not to think of how close he'd been or how unimaginably perfect she'd felt. He'd managed for most of the storm, since he'd never had time to think of anything but survival.

The life or death of the *Southern Cross* had been down to the wire. He'd fought and had made his crew fight harder than he'd ever seen men struggle to stay alive. No one slept; it was a constant, grueling vigil. He looked down at his sliced palms and was sure he had lacerations over most of his body. Strange, he didn't feel the pain.

He knew and his men had no doubt as to what had possessed him during the storm. He'd been a madman, making them struggle like animals for each quarter they could get from the waves and wind.

In the beginning, part of him had believed he'd lose his ship, and he'd labored instinctively out of the fear of death. Then he'd glanced down at Nicole. Down to where she'd disobeyed him to stand on deck. He'd seen such a blind trust in her eyes, a trust in him written everywhere in her pale face, that he'd been rocked by the force of it. She was telling him that she knew he'd protect her.

Now, he looked over to the bow where she strained to see Sydney, the hair outside her cap flowing behind her. He remembered how brave she'd been, and he recalled that he'd been proud of her. Wasn't that an emotion you saved for your family, pride in another? Yet when she'd pitched in and helped everyone, oftentimes pulling on the rigging right beside another sailor, he'd felt his chest swell. His memories were foggy after that. Hadn't his crew looked at her in wonder? Hadn't they secretly made sure some part of her was secured to the ship at all times?

"Ahoy there!" Jeb called out to an approaching fisherman, interrupting Derek's thoughts. "Any news of the Great Circle?"

"Aye," a sun-scalded man in the small dinghy answered. He pointed a finger toward Derek. "You Sutherland?"

Derek nodded, and the man called out, "Hate like hell to be the one to tell you this. The *Desirade* arrived here yesterday."

His jaw clenched. The *Desirade* was Tallywood's ship, and if he had to lose, he didn't want it to be to that worthless scrap of a man. Especially not when he suspected

Tallywood of sabotage. Though he wanted to smash something, he forced himself to thank the fisherman.

He hadn't really cared about this race, but he'd found he wanted to impress Nicole by winning. He wanted to share the victory since she couldn't have it on her own.

He felt her place her hand on his arm. It was comforting to him that she understood his frustration. His voice was toneless even to his own ears as he said, "I thought I had him."

She uttered a quick, humorless laugh. "So did I."

Her comment put things into perspective. She'd lost everything, while he'd only lost a race. He vowed then that it wouldn't matter, because he'd build Peregrine back with or without the win. She squeezed the hand he'd wrapped around her own. "We're closing in on the harbor. We don't have much time."

He frowned and turned to her.

She looked as though she was swaying a bit, but she answered his questioning look in a steady voice. "We'll start meeting more ships soon. They can't see us like this." Her eyes dropped to the deck. "I'm sorry. They can't see your crew and ship like this."

"This is exactly what they'll see. In case you didn't just hear—Tallywood won." His tone was annoyed, and she removed her hand from his.

A strand of her hair teased her lip and she brushed it away. "I heard. But you aren't sailing into Sydney like this? With your sails in tatters and rigging strewn about?"

"That's just what I planned to do." He turned from her and strode to his cabin, immediately pouring a drink.

She was right behind him. "You order the crew to trim this ship!"

He took a large swig and ran a hand down his face. "My men are exhausted. I'm exhausted. We've lost."

"So that's it?" she asked in amazement.

"I'm turning in. Do you want to join me?" he added with a leer.

She opened her mouth, and he braced himself for a blistering reply. Instead, a sad emotion flickered in her eyes. "I would have expected this of you," she quietly replied, "in the past."

When she walked out of the cabin, he followed. "Nicole, wait."

She didn't acknowledge him.

"Nicole."

When they were topside, she started hauling coarse, wet ropes to coil them neatly on a belaying pin. Slowly, one man got up and began helping her, then another, and another. He watched as Jeb purposefully looked from Nicole to him. Then, with a flippant grin, he belted out a chantey with surprising force in his scratchy old voice. Before long the rest of the crew was singing and working beside her.

A battle lost. With a loud exhaled breath, Derek handed his glass to Jimmy and began assessing their sail situation.

An hour later a spotless *Southern Cross*, with all her remaining sail out, entered Sydney's harbor. The ship looked immaculate, and even though his men were flagging, morale was higher.

Nicole avoided him and, if she glanced at him at all, it was with an undecided look on her face.

When he was better able to see Tallywood's ship in the harbor, he experienced a deep measure of disappointment. Even though he'd known the man had defeated him, seeing the bastard's ship docked there, before his own, was still a blow.

But on the heels of that emotion, he was glad that they'd

scoured the ship. The *Desirade* lay haggard and unkempt, her deck cluttered with refuse, the rigging hanging limply. The fact that a fellow countryman had arrived in front of all the crowds to claim a victory in that sad vessel embarrassed him.

Hell, people were even now lining the docks for their own arrival. The *Southern Cross* might not have won, but they would at least make it look as though they'd just completed a leisurely cruise. Thanks to Nicole.

When the ship was docked and inspected and most of the commotion of their arrival had died down, Derek scanned the decks to find her.

"In your cabin," Jeb related with a sly look in his eyes. He almost asked what the old man was talking about but decided not to bother. He was just too damn tired. And perhaps he was just too damn obvious.

When he entered his cabin, he found her in the wing chair bolted down in front of his desk. She didn't even acknowledge him. *So she's pouting?* He didn't need this right now.

"Listen, if this is about this morning, I admit I was an ass. I didn't react well to the word of our loss."

That sounded weak as soon as he'd said it. The resilience she'd shown in the last few days dwarfed his own. "Forget I said that. I know my flaws. But you don't have to hold a grudge."

When she said nothing, he grated, "Damn it, Nicole, I apologized. What else can I do? When I'm around you, I want to be a better man. Does that count for anything?"

She remained silent, and resentment sniped at him. He wanted to storm out. Instead, he strode across the cabin to face her.

And found her sleeping, her head on her balled hands

against the side of the chair. He had to grin. She didn't even know they'd just fought.

She'd bathed and dressed in one of her own wrappers. Seeing her sleeping, so completely unaware of everything, made his exhaustion more acute. Although he'd planned to make love to her at last, he wanted to ensure it would be good for her first time. He didn't think his passing out on her directly after would be ideal.

He removed his clothes, then gently lifted her out of the chair, inhaling the soft scent of her skin. He cradled her into his bed and slipped in next to her. As soon as he closed his eyes, he slept.

Sometime near sunset, he awoke to the sound of her moving about the cabin.

"What the hell do you think you're doing?" he asked in amazement as he swiped at his eyes.

She stated the obvious, he knew, just to frustrate him. "I'm packing."

"I can see that. What I want to know is why."

"I think I've overstayed my welcome. And I have business in town."

He was on his feet immediately. She blushed and turned her head from his naked body—though not as quickly as she had in the past. He yanked on his trousers.

"What kind of business could you have?" Then a look of realization colored his face. "Tallywood. You're going after him."

"That's not it."

"What else could it be? Nicole, I have two crewmen following Tallywood everywhere he goes. The rest of the crew is out gathering information in the taverns and sailors' haunts."

"I'm telling you, that's not it!"

"You plan to 'investigate' him just as you did me? If Tallywood did this to us, he'll pay." His voice was harsh. This was what he'd feared. He'd known she would want to leave as soon as they landed. At least now he had an excuse to keep her. He grasped her arm. "I'm not letting you go get yourself hurt."

"Not letting me go?" Anger pitched her voice higher. "You haven't even asked me to stay."

"You're staying." He was being irrational, treating her unfairly, but worry made his words sharp.

She wrenched her arm away from him. "What does that mean? Are you keeping me prisoner again?"

He began pacing, rubbing the back of his neck. When he stood in front of her, he said, "It means I'm not letting you go."

She was silent for many moments. "Then I am a prisoner."

"I guess you are." He didn't want to keep her against her will, but he didn't want her in danger, either. Plus, he wanted something cemented between them, something binding that would make her want to return to him. "Nicole, you're not leaving this cabin until you admit you want me as much as I want you."

Though Sutherland watched her with that dark, hungry look that made her body go liquid, she refused to succumb. She knew she needed to get off this ship. Last night in her bath, when she'd finally had time to think about all that had happened, her circumstances had become clearer in her mind.

It had occurred to her that although she trusted this man with her life, she couldn't trust him with her crew's. Every now and then, like today, like right now, she could see traces of that selfish wretch she'd met in London. She believed him when he said he'd made sure they'd be released, but could she stake their lives on it? And what if something had gone wrong?

Sutherland thought she wanted to go after Tallywood when, in fact, she wasn't planning on it. Yet. She needed to get a bank draft to a contact in Cape Town in case the crew remained jailed and the officials in charge could be bribed. Although her instincts told her to trust Sutherland, she couldn't let him know what she had planned.

For one thing, she didn't think he'd give her the substantial amount of money she planned to steal from him. She would get away from him and then handle it alone.

Even now she would have been tempted to stay if only he'd asked her to, instead of ordering her. In fact, she'd thought he would and had doubted she could resist him, which was why she'd decided to sneak out while he slept. Now, his condescension and high-handedness infuriated her.

She wasn't a woman to be bullied, she assured herself, but as Sutherland pulled her to his chest, lifting her chin to kiss her, pressing those warm, firm lips on her own, her determination wavered. She desperately wished they'd finished what they'd started the night of the storm.

She had to know what awaited her. She'd started down the path, and not knowing the destination was driving her mad. Mad enough to stay. Until he moved her against the cabin wall, pressing her lower back into the full bottle of brandy she held behind her.

"Don't . . ." she breathed. Surprisingly, he stopped.

He ran a hand through his hair. "I want you. You're staying here with me."

"What if I don't want you?"

He growled, "You'll learn to want me!"

Selfish. "I'm giving you one last chance. If I promise to come back, will you let me leave?"

"You're giving me one last chance?" he scoffed.

Memories of her time locked in this cabin surfaced, and she felt the old resentment rekindling. "You can't force me to stay here."

"I assure you I can," he said. "I can't trust that you'll return."

"*You* can't trust *me?*" she asked in disbelief.

"This subject's closed. I'll accompany you on whatever business you have in town in the morning. Now, come to bed."

Her eyebrows shot up at his resolute tone, at his decree. She made one more attempt. "You're truly not letting me go?"

"Never," he said easily as he stared down into her eyes. The realization of what he'd said obviously hit him, and he turned away as if surprised by his own words. Which was a mistake, because behind him, Nicole was bringing down the thick glass bottle, and again for Sutherland the world went black.

When Sutherland came to and found he was tied to the bed and gagged, he thrashed against the ropes. But if Nicole knew anything, it was how to tie a knot. She couldn't help flashing a proud grin at her handiwork. "Wouldn't waste your time trying to get out of . . ." She trailed off under his lethal glare, " . . . those."

He said something against the cloth she'd tied over his mouth. She could only imagine what words he used to impart the idea that he would throttle her if loose. Somehow, she prevented herself from shivering under that glacial look. She rifled through his desk and trunks for money, distracting herself from his fury. "What's that, Captain?" she asked. "Oh yes, yes, very good of you. . . . I think I *will* borrow some money." She found the bag of coins she'd been eyeing earlier and smiled over at him before glancing back.

"Most gracious of you, as usual. Your hospitality, your company . . . always so generous."

She walked over to her own trunk and began stuffing some clothing into a purloined satchel. "Pardon? Oh, of course I will write and reply to what I'm sure will be a flood of correspondence from you.

"Alas, the time has come for me to depart, and as I am sure you will no doubt make this into a long, teary goodbye . . ." She stopped when he groaned again.

Was he in a lot of pain? She hadn't hit him that hard, just in a specific spot Chancey had taught her. But that sound . . .

Any concern evaporated when she looked at him. He watched her, or rather her shirt, which gaped open as she bent down. She plucked her collar up to her neck as her face reddened. Helplessly tied to the bed, and still he looked predatory. That look was as powerful as a touch.

Could he desire her, even now? Deciding to find out, she boldly leaned down again. She made sure he had a clear view of her exposed breasts as she fiddled with something in her bag.

He groaned again. A heady sense of power flooded through her. She looked over his body and saw his arousal swelling against the cloth of his trousers. She gasped. Her mind replayed the last time they'd been intimate. In another second, he would have taken her. She remembered how desperate she'd been for him to do just that.

Doing the forbidden had always rewarded Nicole. And if making love to Sutherland wasn't forbidden . . . Slowly she padded over to the bed and sat on the edge, her hand out as she worked up the nerve to touch him.

His eyes were hooded, and his chest rose and fell quickly. She placed her hands there and lightly stroked him, loving the feel of his hard muscles and the crisp hair that came to a V. She trailed her hand down to the line of hair just above his trousers and followed it, watching his hard stomach dive as her nails grazed his skin.

She stilled. He was aroused, but what if he didn't *want* to desire her? The ropes should have dampened his need. Should she untie him? No, he'd only punish her for hitting him over the head and the embarrassment of being tied up.

Wondering how to proceed, she absently began stroking him again. Lord, this was madness. She'd knocked him out in order to get away, and although he seemed powerless, he could make her stay. She couldn't do this. She was just about to jump up and leave when she felt his body tense. Looking down, she saw her own hands petting him . . . all over. Up and down the sides of his slim hips, caressing the flexing undersides of his bound arms. "Oh!" she gasped, surprised at herself. He pulled away, twisting on his side, and refused to look at her.

Who was he to turn from her? She wanted him; would she let a few, well, ropes stand in the way?

She rose up on her knees and, using all her weight to turn him over, sat astride him above his waist. She glimpsed a flash of determination just as he rose up as far as his bonds would allow, forcing her to slide to his lap. He sported a satisfied expression before sinking back again.

He's maneuvering me? He's supposed to be helplessly tied

to the bed. Did he think he was the one in control here? Wanting to experience that heady sense of power again, she slowly unbuttoned her shirt. His eyes smoldered.

She wouldn't have thought it possible, but he became even harder and hotter beneath her. Instinctively she wriggled against him, finding the right position, getting more comfortable. She thought he cursed against the cloth. She flicked another button open as she slowly moved against him, the pressure and friction eating away any shyness she might have felt.

With her hands on the sides of her shirt, she asked before her courage faltered, "Do you want to see me, Sutherland?"

Chapter 20

Did he want to see her? He wanted to see her, and taste her, and bury himself inside her. He'd been in a living hell of wanting her and being denied her little body. All thoughts of throttling her were gone, replaced by a desire so consuming he'd never experienced the like in all his life.

He was in a less than desirable position, and he knew he'd be furious with not just her but himself later. Yet need pulsed through him, settling like steel in his cock. He burned for her, his desire overwhelming the ache of his abused head. He'd play along. Get her so aroused that she would untie him. The feelings of powerlessness and fury receded; he could bed this little wench if he wanted to, even tied up.

And, damn it, he wanted to. Under any circumstances.

He gave a short nod at the questioning look in her eyes, and she slowly, damn her, so slowly pulled her shirt past her breasts. He sucked in a breath and his cock stiffened hungrily. Her breasts, so pale and perfect, were—he'd have to use his memory—silky to touch.

He looked up to find that she'd faltered, as if she didn't know what to do next. He nodded pointedly at her trousers. She looked down and fingered the waist of her pants.

"Do you want me to take these off now?"

He gave a quick nod again. And watched spellbound as she slipped off his engorged body and stood, shyly unbuttoning her trousers. She pulled on her bottom lip with her teeth, those dark eyes grave with uncertainty. Yet even when she hadn't a shred of clothing on, she didn't shy away or cover herself. She resolutely let him look his fill.

Looking at her soft, smooth body, he thought again that he could not have created a woman who would be more beautiful to him. She fit him as no other had. Her full, upthrusting breasts had molded perfectly in his hand, and the thought of cupping them made him strain against the ropes. He tore his gaze away and ran his eyes slowly down her body, taking in the soft indentation of her waist and the gently flaring hips.

All thought left him as his eyes continued steadily down to the softly curling hair at the juncture between her thighs. His mouth watered like that of a wolf spying prey. He wanted her under his mouth. When she untied him, he would set upon her in a frenzy with his probing tongue at her wet lips. Fascinated, he watched as a blush crept up her body, as though she knew exactly what he was thinking.

When she glanced at the door and back, a feeling of unease settled over him. She could change her mind, and he could do nothing to prevent it. He nodded to his own trousers. She understood and seemed glad to have something to do. She stole across to the bed and, with trembling fingers, grasped the top of his trousers, touching his stomach. He couldn't control the sudden intake of breath or the surging hardness in his pants.

He cursed his body when she jumped back, looking at him wonderingly. *Damn.* He hadn't thought he could get even harder, and now she was even more hesitant. Before she could change her mind, he jerked his head from her to his pants. Without a word, he commanded her to undress him.

This time she pulled them down determinedly and gasped when he sprang forth. She was riveted, but he didn't want her to watch him; he needed to be in her now.

Sutherland again nodded at her and then to himself. What did he want her to do? She was afraid to untie him, yet she wanted this to happen. But he had to be on top of her, didn't he?

She moved to the side of the bed, kneeling beside him, staring enthralled at his erection. It was like its own entity, as it throbbed and grew. Beautiful, as though carved from marble, but hot. Its broad tip was moist. Before she could think, she'd placed her hands on it. The hair curling at its base was soft, the sack she hefted taut. She cupped it and weighed it in her hand, making him shudder. A sharp, low utterance escaped him. He pinned her with his stare and spoke against the cloth. Surely, he was asking her to untie him.

"I won't untie you."

He shook his head. She didn't think he'd call out to the watch because he wouldn't want them to see him like this, so slowly, cautiously, she leaned forward, untying the cloth at the back of his head and pulling it free. He took a deep breath and seemed not to know what to say. Unable to stop herself, she returned to stroking the stretched skin of his shaft, noting the sensitivity at the crown. She could touch him forever. . . .

He flinched as if she'd burned him. "*Untie me.*"

"Don't ask me that, because I won't."

"If you untie me, I can bring you even more pleasure than you found the night of the storm."

The events of that night affected her, plagued her, made her burn. But this wasn't just a memory; she could do the things she wished they'd done that night.

Her attention kept trailing to her hand gliding up and down his length. Fascinated, a moth to flame, she moved to reach him better, placing a knee between his legs. His thigh came up and pressed between her own. She drew in a shocked breath. She would move away . . . but it soothed her, like blowing on a burn. She stayed against him, still fondling him.

That was *her* hand gripping him. She was panting now, not caring that she'd grown wet against his leg. Then he flexed his hard thigh, making her rock up and down. She bit back a moan. He did it again, then stopped, rasping to her, "Use it, love. Take what you need. . . ."

And she did. She rode his leg, her right hand holding his sculpted torso, her left hand stroking.

"Nicole! Look at me."

She dragged her gaze from her busy hand.

His face was pained, his deep voice gravelly. "Do you want me to make you feel things you've never felt before?"

Shivering at the low timbre of his voice, she could only mouth, "Yes."

"Put it inside you."

She was well past the point of feeling any shyness. Her scalp tightened and her skin tingled. The yearning wetness between her legs drove her to do as he told her.

When Nicole covered him, as she had his leg, he sucked in a breath and almost exploded instantaneously beneath that dewy heat kissing his flesh. He'd been driven mad when she used his leg, almost came in her hand while she masturbated him, and now to feel her . . .

"You have to stop that," he grated. "You have to put me inside you."

She glanced down with a nervous look at where their bodies touched.

In the back of his mind, he felt like a bastard. This position would hurt her more, but he couldn't turn back. It was her fault, damn her, that he couldn't take her in a more conventional manner.

His conscience got the better of him. "This will hurt you . . . probably worse than it would if I could move over you."

She looked searchingly into his eyes. "When you've done this before, did you do anything to keep the woman from hurting?"

He frowned. "Do you mean, when I've deflowered a woman?"

"Yes," she breathed as she resumed moving against him.

He watched her eyes glaze over with passion and, feeling his body's response, he found it difficult to answer. "I've never done . . . I've never been with a virgin. But I know it helps if you're, well, if you feel desire for me, too," he tried to explain, his voice thick. "You seem to have that covered."

Her sultry eyes opened and sparkled with . . . humor?

"No pun intended?" Her lips broke into a grin as she looked down at where her body connected with his.

"Love," he said as his answering grin was replaced by a look of misery, "we've either got to do this or we need to—" Anything he might have added was lost as he watched her rise up and grasp him, feeding it in. . . .

A low hiss of breath stole across his lips as she slid over him. The pleasure was so intense, so driving, it took every ounce of will he had not to thrust upward into her.

Slowly. She needed to do this slowly.

It didn't appear that Nicole understood this. When she'd just placed the tip of him into her, she pulled away, but her body just as quickly compelled her to move down him again. She did this shallow rising and falling forever, each time lowering herself slightly more onto his aching cock. There could be no worse torture. Would he ever fit inside her?

"Nicole," he grated out, "take more of me in you—I need you to take all of me." If he wasn't fully into that tight sheath soon, he wouldn't be able to stop his hips from surging up into her.

After a pause, she pushed her hands farther up on his chest, forcing herself back until he could feel the barrier.

He never took his eyes from hers as she steadied herself, gliding lower and lower. She wouldn't look away, either. It was as if she needed him to gain courage. But when her eyes teared, he knew he needed to help her. He took a breath, dug his heels into the bed, and shoved his way into her core.

She cried out, her nails embedding themselves in his chest, before she sank over him, motionless.

"*Nicole?* Are you all right?"

She breathed against his skin. "Uh-huh."

He made himself still inside her, wanting to savor the way she clasped him so tightly, knowing she needed time to adjust to him.

How long they lay like this, he didn't know. All his muscles stood tense in agony, not being able to move inside her, but he was a big man and didn't want to hurt her any more.

Her body at last grew accustomed to the fullness and became greedy. She rose up and gingerly impaled herself. He wanted to make this last, but she began moving on him faster, sighing, moaning, wincing when she took him as fully as she could, still not to the hilt. If his hands were free, he would be running them up and down her body and maybe even encircling her waist to slow their explosive joining.

The idea of being tied up became increasingly erotic to him, and he tried not to think of the ropes lest he come too soon. With him tied, she was free to do whatever she needed to pleasure herself with his body.

Nicole was on the verge of that overriding release, and now that she recognized the feeling and welcomed it, she did everything to hasten that end. She rode him in complete abandon, opening her knees wide to pull more of him inside her. The limits of their bodies became unclear as she found herself rushing closer to her climax. She wished she had untied him so that he could touch her swollen breasts. He must have sensed what she wanted, because he commanded, "Arch your back more. Give them to me."

As she did, he leaned up, his muscles straining against his bonds so that he could rub his tongue over the swollen peaks. When he lay back, her body obediently followed him, and she felt a strange, insistent urge to hand him her breast in offering. She could only lay her right hand across her torso under her breast as she dipped down over him, but he understood the gesture and hungrily latched onto her nipple, making it harden even more between his lips.

He moved from one to the other. As though suckling her excited him, he pressed his feet down and used the resistance to reach his hips up, slamming up into her, springing her up and down in a fury. *Too much* . . . Her whole body stiffened . . . then the wave crashed over her in a fiery pulsing of wetness and gripping spasms. He followed her, her breast against his mouth as he groaned and burst forward from his own throbbing eruption.

Derek lay unmoving. Nicole had fallen asleep after he'd climaxed, lying softly on his chest, her body on and wrapped around his.

As he delved through all the emotions and questions swirling inside him, one thought stood out—he could not lose her. The feeling of wanting her so totally was mysterious to him. And alarming.

With any other woman, the idea of being tied up and unable to extricate himself after sex would have been his undoing. He'd never stayed with a woman after he was done with her. He should be experiencing the familiar panic that always came when someone was getting too close. Instead, his position infuriated him because she could choose to get up and walk away, and he couldn't prevent her. He'd never experienced anything like what continued to happen between them, and he knew in his bones he never would again without her.

How much longer would his men be ashore? Three

hours? If he could keep her here until they got back, she might think it wiser not to leave. Then, with time, he could convince her to stay with him.

He could call the watch assigned to the ship, but imagining the betrayed look that would flash down on him as soon as she woke up, he hesitated. Worse, what if she didn't move in time? He had, he thought with an inward smile, given her plenty to be worn out from.

His face tightened. The thought of his watch coming in and seeing her in the position they were in— No, he thought angrily, that wasn't an option. So now his plan was simply to remain as still as possible and hope she wouldn't wake up until his crew got back.

At least, that was the plan. Until he hardened inside her again.

She stirred in her sleep, murmuring something and lightly grasping his shoulder. Luckily she didn't wake up; if only he could say that about his wayward member.

Think of something else. Anything else. But only impressions of the sleek, warm body lying over his, breasts pressed into his chest, suffused him. He inhaled the scent of her thick hair spread over them, the smell of sex in the room. He waged a losing battle.

Struggling for an alternate plan, Derek decided he could keep her here by making love to her all night. After the second time, she might sleep again.

She moved, and all thoughts disappeared as a surge of hardness pounded below. In her sleep, Nicole squeezed his shoulder, gasping at the building pressure of him inside her. She soon awakened and wonderingly tilted her head up, blinking open her curious eyes.

She must have liked what she read in his expression, because her lips curled softly. Her upper body rubbed along his when she leisurely pressed down on him. He groaned again and lifted his head toward hers, taking her lips and tongue with his own, scalding her with a possessive kiss. She answered him, her mouth trembling and lush. As their tongues danced, her hips moved over him.

Chapter 21

*J*er daring in the face of Sutherland's killing looks astonished even Nicole. She had left him. Left him with nothing but a partially loosened knot.

"Nicole, don't you dare," he'd commanded, his voice low and menacing.

She'd explained that she had responsibilities to others. That it was her greatest wish to be with him for the time being. If she only had to look out for herself, she would stay, she'd told him, but she couldn't afford to trust him completely.

When she'd seen his reaction, seen his obvious difficulty masking his rage, she'd become afraid.

He bit out, "Where will you go? Who will take care of you?"

Take care of her? His questions had provoked her just enough for her courage to return. "With your money, I'll be able to take care of myself. Besides, I have friends in port who will give me a place to stay. Don't look for me. You'll never find me, and I believe it's for the best. . . . What good could come of this?"

That last comment angered him even more. His eyes had mocked her. "What good? Damn it, Nicole, what takes place between us doesn't happen with just anyone. If that's why you're leaving—because *no good* can come of this— then you're blind."

She'd told him in a small voice, "No, honestly, that's not the reason. Even though it's wrong, I very much want to . . . be with you again. I think spending the next few weeks in your bed would be like heaven."

He seemed to soften at her admission; she took that moment to run out the door.

The next two days of her life were as miserable as that last night had been incredible. Her nervousness that he or his crew might find her never relented. Worse, her undertaking forced her to walk among the rowdy sailors mingling on the docks. It was too warm to wear her bulky cloak, so she'd gone without. She didn't want to alarm herself, but it seemed as though men stared at her. She foolishly wondered if they could sense what she'd done. Could they see the change in her?

For all her discomfort, the time had been productive. She'd been successful in contracting with a captain to drop off a bank draft at the Cape. He would get it to a contact she had there, and she would, she hoped, have all their bets hedged. She'd also scratched off several letters to her father and Maria—even to her grandmother—and sent them through half a dozen different channels.

Nicole sat on the back of a dusty wagon, absently eating an apple she'd bought, trying to decide what to do. She'd reached a point where she didn't know if she could stay away from him much longer. Thinking about the night she left, the things they'd done . . . the things she'd done to him . . . she wanted more.

But it wasn't fair to herself or to him. He had no place in her future. It would have to end right when it began, and she didn't know if she could ever willfully walk away from him again.

Chancey would be here soon, if he had in fact been released after they'd sailed. He wouldn't leave her much choice in the matter. When she convinced herself that her future wouldn't be decided by her lack of willpower in dealing with Sutherland, but by an irate Irisher, she gave in. She had to take every second she could with Sutherland before they separated—if he'd take her back.

Decided, she flung the core into the water and began the long walk back to the ship. She hardly registered the brilliant setting sun or the dimming sound of the closing shops because she was so lost in thought. A memory from her fourteenth year kept surfacing insistently in her mind.

It was one of those days near the equator when the sky perfectly matched the flat sea and enveloped everything in a vast, blue ball. Becalmed and bored, she and the cabin boy had rigged a rope-swing halfway up the mast. She couldn't remember if it was her idea or his, but they'd pulled the swing over the water, and before her father could catch them, each had dived off from the sheer height. When she thought of Sutherland, she felt the same sharp feeling in her belly, as though she were plummeting straight from the sky. Wasn't that why they called it falling in love?

Oh, Lord, she did not need to be in love with Captain Sutherland.

She replayed her predicament. If he wanted her after the

way she'd treated him, she would have to purposefully close herself off. Although she couldn't seem to resist his bed, she had to make sure she didn't lose her heart any more than she already had. She'd promised to marry when she got back, and suffered no illusions that a rake like Sutherland would be on her grandmother's list of desirables. Not to mention her father's hatred for the man.

When she at last reached the *Southern Cross,* it was nearing midnight.

"Thank the Lord you came back," said one of the three midshipmen on deck when she stepped aboard. They all looked especially glad to see her.

She raised her eyebrows. "You boys missed me?" she asked in greeting.

"We have. Cap'n snaps at us and barks his orders."

"It's because of you," another crewman finished with a solemn look. His companions were shaking their heads emphatically, and she had to smile.

"You worried the cap'n something fierce, Miss Lassiter. He ain't ate. Nor slept more than a couple of hours since you left. Go on, then." He gestured her past. "You know the way."

When she entered his room, the lights were low. He lay in bed, facing away from her, and appeared to be sleeping. The idea of snuggling close to his long, solid body had her flying out of her clothes. She should find a shirt to sleep in, but she didn't want to wake him. No, honestly, she simply wanted her skin to touch his. Quietly, she slipped in and eased up to him.

Just as she was about to lay her head on the edge of his pillow, he said, "I didn't know if you'd come back."

She hesitantly placed her hand on his arm. His body was rigid with tension. "I didn't know if you'd take me back."

He hadn't relaxed a fraction. Exactly how angry was he?

"I looked for you—I was worried about you being out there alone."

"Is that the only reason?" She moved her fingertips down his broad back.

He sucked in a breath when the muscles contracted. "No. I want you to stay with me." He turned to face her. "Here."

"I will for as long as I can," she replied truthfully, and he seemed to accept that.

He sat up, slowly pulling the sheet off her, tugging it over her nipples, already hard and sensitive, leaving her bare. She reached up to kiss him, but he pressed her down, petting her.

He smoothed her arm back over her head, then the other, skimming the undersides, down the sides of her breasts to her waist. When she shivered, he smiled. Then he brushed his lips across her collarbone, licking and lightly nipping before descending to her nipples. She wanted to cry from the sensations when he took one in his mouth and drew on it sharply.

He enthralled her, grazing his teeth against her, pushing her breasts together to lavish one, then the other. So much so that she barely perceived he was wrapping her wrists together with a piece of cloth.

When she did, she yanked away, straining to free her hands.

He merely laughed at her attempts. "We have a score to settle," he promised her, the words harsh. Moving over her in a predatory manner, he tightened her bonds before securing her to the bunk.

"Now, I'll have you." He returned his hands to her. They were rough and burning hot. *My way.*

She had no idea what to expect from this man. What would he do to her? Alarm spiking through her, she fought against her bonds and bucked his hand away when he brushed it over her breasts again.

Sutherland continued to stroke her, rubbing his flat palm over her nipples. He changed positions, bringing his hard shaft against her leg and his skilled touch lower and lower, gentling her struggles. One hand pushed her legs apart while with the other he delved his fingers inside her.

Mindless. Teasing her inside, coaxing her wetter. Until he cruelly stopped.

His hands went to her breasts to hold them as he brought his mouth down. She raised her hips against him, searching for his giving fingers, but he ignored her. She'd been so close, and now she throbbed, on the verge of begging him to touch her again. She'd put him through this. Now she understood. He was merciless.

"Sutherland, please . . ." she whimpered.

"Call me by my name," he commanded in a low, heated voice. "I want to hear you say my name."

"Derek! *Please . . .*"

At last, he moved to place himself between her legs, but instead of pushing himself into her as he'd done before, he grabbed her bottom with splayed, clutching fingers and lifted her to his bent head. To his lips.

"I've wanted to taste you for months," he said just above her flesh, so close she could feel the heat of his mouth. Then he kissed her directly in the place she'd begged him with her body to caress, jolting her lower body off the bed, onto his waiting tongue.

This had to be wrong! She thrashed to get away.

He pressed her down into the bed, hard, then lifted his

head to catch her gaze. "You won't deny me this. You'll never deny me this." Wrapping his arms around her thighs, he dragged her closer to his mouth, clenching her down onto his shoulders. He held her imprisoned as he ran his tongue up and down her, *in* her, then higher . . . taking that sensitive bud in his mouth, wholly, sucking. She would fly apart . . .

"No, Derek, no. Not like this. . . ." She melted, flowing, wet beneath his lips. Never taking his mouth from her, he reached up and rolled her nipple in his fingers, plucking at one, pinching the other.

Without warning, the madness crashed over her, that hot rapture that made her buck her hips to his mouth, to get closer to his firm lips, to his clever tongue rubbing inside her. He was ruthless in wringing every ounce of pleasure from her. Wave after wave, first one, then incredibly another, her spasms coming with every lash of his tongue.

Dazed. She lay limp, and at last opened her eyes. His breathing was harried, and the look he gave her told her he'd enjoyed that as much as she.

He granted her no time to recover, to understand all that had just happened, before he placed her on his rod and rocked into her in one swift motion. She moaned in bliss. She wouldn't have thought she could feel it again so soon, but he knew what she wanted, what she needed.

"*Derek.* Yes!" The tightening in her body began once more, the pressure within her gathering frantically to explode. With his next raging thrust, it took her. He stifled her cries with his lips on hers.

Before she'd stopped squeezing around him, he reached forward and yanked her bonds free. Then, easing out of her, he turned her over, pulling at her hips until she was on hands and knees, forcing her legs wider. What was he doing? Why would he—

He spread her private flesh with his fingers, baring her to him. *No!* This wasn't right. She'd never felt more exposed. But dark urges gripped her. She wanted to be vulnerable, to put herself in his control.

Then he kissed her inside. She was lost. . . . She quivered, moaning, arching her back and moving her knees farther apart. He placed his hand under her, between her breasts, and ran it down her body until he cupped where his mouth had been, delving a thumb into her. He was wicked. He'd made her that way as well—too far gone to save. Just as she felt herself completely let go, he slammed that heavy rod into her.

"So tight. Wet," he growled. His big hands grasped her waist, forcing her along his length. Her back arched when he kneaded her backside.

"Yes, Nicole . . . push back. Come to me."

His words made her moan. He tugged on her hair, forcing her up against his chest, still plunging into her from below. Now his hands roamed over the front of her body, thumbing her nipples, making her gasp. "Derek, please. *Please* . . ." she begged, but didn't know for what.

Her breasts shook with each wild thrust, and he cupped them, covering them completely, pulling on them to bring her closer. To bring her ear to his lips, where he rasped, "You're mine. *Mine!*"

His hand glided down to press two blunt fingertips to her small bud of flesh. He moved it up and down, firmly, up and down . . . faster, while taking her from behind with fierce, powerful strokes.

"Derek! Now . . . I'm going to—" She clamped around him, rippling on and on as the climax took her, collapsing forward, muffling her agonized cries into the pillow. He pounded into her unmercifully, making the pleasure border on pain as she continued to convulse around him. With a brutal groan, he wrenched her hips against him one last time as his seed shot into her, filling her with heat.

Through an unspoken truce, they never mentioned her leaving or the event that led up to it. She believed Derek had made things even in his mind when she came back to him.

In that first night, he made love to her endlessly. In fact, they didn't venture from his cabin for four days, as his body tutored hers in all the different ways they could pleasure each other.

Eventually he had to leave the ship to arrange his cargo for the voyage back, but when he returned, he looked at her as if he hadn't seen her in days. While he was gone, she worked with the new paint supplies he'd thoughtfully brought her, mainly altering the erratic flow of the scene she'd created on the cabin walls.

Even so, she grew restless at being confined, especially during his absences. Just when she was about to say something, he informed her, "We're going out tonight."

She paused, her face showing her indecision. "I don't think that would be a good idea," she said, remembering the men gaping at her unconventional attire when she'd left before.

"Why not? I can sense you're restless."

She knew she looked openly surprised. She hadn't thought he'd noticed. Then she frowned. "Any clothes I'd wear off the ship were aboard the *Bella Nicola*."

He smiled down at her. "Let me take care of that," he said. With an assessing eye, he looked her over, then placed his hands around her waist. His voice had a husky quality when he said, "I'll be back by eight."

That afternoon, two boxes were delivered to the ship. She opened the first in wild excitement, then froze. Inside were three of the most beautiful dresses she'd ever seen. He'd picked deep colors and clean styles; she would have chosen them for herself. She held up a rich blue watered silk and hung it out for tonight. Simply looking at it, she could see that it would fit.

In the second box, she found a circle of soap in her favorite scent, matching slippers and small cloth boots for all three dresses, and even all the foundation accessories necessary for wearing them. While she bathed, she thought of her gifts and marveled that Sutherland—Derek, she corrected herself—that Derek had remembered she liked the fragrance of almond oil.

After her bath, she combed her hair until dry and twisted it up in an elaborate knot, allowing a few loose curls to frame her face. Before dressing, she stepped in front of the mirror, and her eyes widened at the reflection. She looked fuller. More busty even. She noted happily that the flare of her backside, the only part of her figure she'd never despaired over, was more pronounced.

She enjoyed an awareness of parts of her body she'd once thought hopeless. Now, as she spun in front of the glass, she liked flaunting her new figure. She wanted to show off those features that Suther—that Derek lavished praise on each night. After she dressed, she gazed one last time at her reflection and recognized that she carried herself much as the old headmistress had tried for months to instill in her.

When he arrived to escort her, his first reaction was to suck in a shallow breath. She panicked. Years of feeling scrawny and ungainly made her lose some of her new confidence. Although Derek made her feel beautiful, she remembered a time when she'd hated her looks.

He was silent until at last he bent down to her ear and murmured in a low, rumbling tone, "You are stunning, Nicole." Tears pricked her eyes, and she smiled to mask her reaction.

He answered with a devilish one of his own. "Even more so when you smile, love."

His open praise unsettled her, and she looked away. Some of the crew jumped back to work with smiles on their faces. Embarrassed, she changed the subject. "I know of a place we can eat, if you like." Then, feeling the soft night air rolling off the high tide, she suggested in a more casual tone that they walk.

He grinned and bowed. "Lead the way, sweet. I forget I'm not showing you a new town."

She smiled as they descended the gangway together and started walking, but after several steps, she realized he'd lagged behind. He stood there watching her.

"What? Is something wrong?" she squealed, checking her skirts.

His lips tugged up in a grin. "I've never seen you walk at length on land."

She frowned, and then her mouth made a little O at his sultry expression. In a deep voice, he said, "I like the way you walk, Nicole."

That night, she enjoyed herself far too much. Derek was attentive and demonstrated a dry wit she appreciated. Deflecting his overtures and steeling herself against him seemed more and more a lost battle. The sooner they parted, the better.

Another worry preyed on her mind. For several days, no

other ship from the race had docked. After what had happened to the *Bella Nicola* and the *Southern Cross*, she had no cause to doubt other ships had been damaged as well. But Derek could find nothing on Tallywood.

She thought that Derek sensed her uneasiness and was going out of his way to make her happy. This night he'd taken her to a play, a play she didn't remember the first line of because he'd sat holding her hand, tracing her inner palm, slowly stroking each finger. He hadn't bothered to hide his hunger.

She believed he wanted them to spend every evening in bed as they had been. She certainly wouldn't mind, but seeing how proprietary he became with her around other men was also thrilling. In his mind, she belonged to him.

One time tonight, it'd gotten so bad she'd thought Derek was going to haul her back to the ship.

Later, on their way back, she chastised him, "You didn't have to glare at that old man!"

He lifted his eyebrows and laughed. "He wasn't much older than I am. And even though he gathered you were with me, he continued to ogle your ripe, young breasts."

She blushed, not used to him speaking so frankly to her outside the haven of his bed. "I thought he was harmless."

"That's because you don't know what men like that are thinking, whereas I do. Honestly, if you had any idea, you would have run . . ." His voice trailed off. "Nicole, what is it? You've turned white as a sheet."

Her body went cold as her breath tripped in and out. She forced herself to continue walking because behind her, not more than ten feet away, came a voice from her nightmares.

"You're gonna get us lashed for this, you just wait 'n' see," Pretty whined. When Clive replied, "Bugger you,

Pretty, Cap'n can't keep us locked aboard ship for our whole stay," the blood left her face.

"Love, what's wrong?"

She'd slowed too much. The two would be abreast of them. Without thinking, she turned her back to the street and grabbed Derek by the collar to bring his lips to hers.

"Now, this I like," he murmured.

"Hush! Just keep me turned this way," she whispered against his lips.

"I take it you've seen someone you'd rather not?" he asked in an amused tone.

When she'd given them enough time to pass, she broke from him. "Those two up ahead, the wide one and the weasely one. They—they are the two men who attacked me back in London."

It was as if she could see aggression fire through his body.

"I don't know what they're doing here," she said in a shaking voice, "but maybe we should trail them and find out how they got to Syd—"

"Stay here!" he ordered, and charged toward the two men.

She hitched up her skirts to follow and got there just in time to hear Clive's nose crunch as Derek pounded him to the ground. When Pretty scurried to escape, he lunged after him, yanking the wiry man around into his other awaiting fist.

"Th-they said something about a captain," she stammered from behind him.

He looked from the barely conscious Clive slumped on the ground to the visibly quaking Pretty.

"Now, which one of you wants to tell me who your captain is?"

*   *   *

The search of Tallywood's ship took less than an hour. The watchman had arrived just as Derek learned the English earl was their captain. Upon hearing Nicole's story about her father suspecting Tallywood of being behind the damage to several ships, the Australian authorities called for a search of the *Desirade*. Word swiftly spread around the small sailing community, and crowds flanked the docks. Derek coerced his way onto the ship, and since he obviously wasn't letting Nicole out of his sight, she marched aboard as well.

"This is an injustice!" Tallywood cried, the pale, flaccid skin of his face and jowls shaking in outrage as the Australian authorities restrained him. "I'll have your positions for this, you heathens," he spat at the men who held him. "I'm a bloody earl! You're nothing but some convict's spawn."

The two officers were a brawny, rough-looking pair, and each time he whined they jostled him enthusiastically.

After picking Tallywood's safe, an officer uncovered detailed lists and intricate plans for several ships in the race.

When she spied the lists, Nicole rushed forward, dragging Derek along. "Are we in there?" she cried to the marshal. "Did he sabotage our ships?"

"The *Southern Cross?*"

Derek nodded.

"He had your water tainted before it was even loaded on the ship." He turned to her. "The *Bella Nicola?*" At her anxious nod, he said with obvious regret, "Yes, miss. They loosened your rudder and compromised a support in your hold."

She could feel her lower lip trembling. She didn't want

to appear weak in front of these men, but she had to know why. Turning to Derek, she glanced at Tallywood in question, but Derek looked as though he'd stop her. Before he could say a word, she crossed the deck to where the two men held their prisoner.

"Why'd you do it?"

He ignored her, and she thought he wouldn't answer. The second she pulled her eyes from him, the coward spoke. "You all laughed at me," he began in an eerie voice so low that she had to strain to hear him.

"Common sailors and dockside whores openly mocking me. But I won," he spewed in an increasingly violent tone. "I won the greatest race of the century. . . ." He continued ranting.

Nicole wanted to interrupt, to answer his words. But she didn't think one could argue with a man like this, a man so full of his own importance that he couldn't fathom the rest of the world wouldn't want to bring him down from his lofty position.

One of the two big officers holding Tallywood said, "You can give him something to remember you by, miss, if you like."

"Stop this, this bloody instant," Tallywood shrieked in response. He turned to Nicole. "You're nothing but a commoner. Do you know what will happen if you strike a peer?"

The other officer leaned down to her and said with a wink, "Don't hurt your hand, little bit."

It was useless to try to find some wise, reconciling words to convey that he'd won the race but lost everything else. Instead, she hiked up her skirts and planted her boot squarely between his legs.

*   *   *

With great ceremony, the Great Circle Race award had been bestowed on Derek by the mayor of Sydney. Afterward, he and Nicole walked to his ship as though isolated from the revelry around them. His hand reached down to clasp hers.

"You, uh, you . . ." he began in a gruff voice, "could have taken the race." Although he looked away when admitting that, she simply nodded.

"Your ship was unstoppable." He looked down at her now. "And you and the Irisher worked her like clay in your hands. It should have been you and your crew feted in Sydney today."

"We can never know that for sure," she assured him, but she had a good idea he was right.

"I never realized how hard this must be for you."

She wanted to deny it, but he said, "If it helps at all, I want you to know that I . . . care about you. So much that the win feels hollow." He opened his mouth to say more, but fell silent and walked on.

When they entered his cabin, he strode over to her and wrapped her in his arms, pressing his hand to the back of her head, keeping her next to his heart. She couldn't stop herself from clasping him back.

He whispered into her hair, "I'm sorry."

She cried against his chest, her tears wetting his shirt and her little hitching noises against his chest embarrassing her, until he made a vow to her with such intensity she believed it.

"No one will ever hurt you again."

Chapter 22

$\mathcal{D}$erek concluded that they couldn't continue the indefinite nature of their relationship. He needed to cement something between them, and broached the subject one night while they lay in bed relaxed and sated together.

"I want you," he began confidently, "to be my mistress." She started to speak, but he held up his hand. "Before you answer, let me tell you how I'd plan to—"

"*No.*" She extricated herself from his cumbersome limbs and jumped up to get dressed. Derek watched her in grim silence as she pulled on her last boot and briskly brushed her hands. "I don't believe I want to be your mistress, Captain."

He didn't know if he was more infuriated at her refusal or her flippant tone. She treated it as though he'd made an immature, half-cocked suggestion, when in fact he'd thought about little else since he'd realized she had nothing to do with the poisoning.

He'd never known a woman who made him so angry he wanted to put his fist through a wall! He didn't bother to hide his annoyance. "Of course not, you would want more—a title, perhaps? I'll warn you, if you angle for a marriage proposal, you're wasting your time. I won't give you more than an offer of *carte blanche.*"

"Whoa, *my lord,*" she said, dripping contempt on his title. "I don't want more—I want less. I have no desire to make any commitment to you whatsoever!"

He stared at her with thinly veiled surprise—damn it, she meant that. Her heated refusal of any tie that might bind her to him rattled him to the core.

"From what I understand about upper-class men and their mistresses, in compensation for . . . intimacy, a man keeps his mistress in a house he provides and gives her jewels and silks." She stood looking down at him, her eyes sparking. "Well, am I close?"

He agreed, impatient to hear what she would say next. One could never be sure with Nicole.

"Why on earth would I want to be kept in a house *on land,* stuck in the same place day after day for your convenience, all for some jewelry and finery I'd never wear?"

He'd only offered what had always worked in the past. Women liked to have things bought for them, to be cosseted. He'd had no reason to doubt that every female wanted fine things—expensive things—not only for her enjoyment but also for security.

Did Nicole even realize how abject her life would be once they returned to England? "In light of all that's happened in the last few months, who do you think will take care of you if I don't? Even if your father's been released, you'll have to get back to England to find him. How will you manage that?" He jumped out of bed and yanked on his clothes, his own temper threatening to boil over. "Your ship is on the bottom of the South Atlantic, and I stranded your crew at the Cape. You don't have a guinea to your name."

Her face took on a scornful, even haughty look. "I have means to survive. I'm not brought so low that I have to—oh, how did you put it that night in London?—*bag an earl,* either by marriage or by becoming your mistress," she snapped. "When you leave me here in Sydney, I'll be just fine."

During the hours that she wouldn't talk to him, he eventually cooled and considered their relationship more objectively. His desire to find some means to bind her to him hadn't dimmed, but he wouldn't force the issue. For the next several days, Derek said nothing about the future.

Really, what right did he have to offer her a future with him when his own life was so miserably set?

At first uneasily, then wholeheartedly, they forgot about the argument. To make up for it, Derek escorted her to downtown Sydney's upscale district. He could watch her excited, radiant face for hours. She had no reason to affect a bored, world-weary mien like the women he'd been around for most of his life. He might have expected it, since she'd seen and experienced more of the world than the women, and many men, of his acquaintance. But she delighted in every little detail around her.

After an hour of casual strolling, they passed a jewelry store, and something in the window stopped him. Pulling her to join him at the thick glass, he saw a pair of sapphire pendant eardrops with a matching necklace showcased in the elegant display. What caught his attention was the depth of their dark color.

Wasn't the dark color indicative of the stones' rarity? More than that, they matched the color of Nicole's eyes.

"What do you think of the sapphires?"

"They're very beautiful," she said, only half-looking at them, her attention focused on a peddler in the street. She tilted her head, wondering what he was selling.

To reclaim her wandering attention, he pressed a kiss in her hair. "Would you like—"

"Oh, Derek," she interrupted, placing her hand on his arm, "look over there. That man's selling *strawberries*. Do you know how long it's been since I had some?"

He had only a second to note the name of the shop before she dragged him away.

So that he could spoil her with strawberries instead.

When Derek awoke just before dawn, Nicole was cuddled in his arms breathing softly. As usual, the merest touch of her skin against his set him off like a randy boy. But he needed her for more than just the release. True, his body craved hers, but he wanted that closeness that came afterward, when she let down her guard.

Though she slept, he slipped his hand down to stroke her, readying her, reveling in her quick response. She awoke with a quick inhalation of breath when he entered her, then sighed in pleasure as he pushed himself in, loving her.

He thought about their morning the rest of the day while he inspected offers for him to transport goods. He caught himself whistling as he signed the numerous contracts securing the flood of business the win had brought.

Grant would be floored when he learned of their success. The ship would be loaded in two days, and it looked to be a very promising run back.

But what to do about Nicole? He was running out of time. Sometimes she acted as if she would stay in Australia and wait for Chancey when Derek sailed, but those times were becoming fewer each day. He sensed he was wearing down her defenses.

He would talk to her tonight, he decided. But before he got a chance, they made love again. Then after dinner, she began reading the new book he'd bought her in town. Tomorrow. Tomorrow, he'd tell her she was coming with him.

And if she refused? He would have to play his final card. It was unseemly, but each day he grew more attached to her. He would tell her that she could be pregnant. He hadn't been careful with her. He'd meant to; he had been careful all his life. But it felt impossible to pull away from her. It felt . . . wrong.

He didn't think it had even crossed her mind. In so many ways, she was inexperienced. She'd never had to count days, never fervently hoped for one outcome or another. He would teach her—harshly—but it had to be done. There was no way he could walk away from her.

Derek's musings were broken when he saw her scampering across the bed toward him, book in hand. She looked absorbed in thought, and he tensed while scrambling up against the headboard, certain that her knee would unswervingly connect with his groin.

Prepared for it, eyes closed and teeth gritted . . . he found only her breasts delicately pillowing across his lap. She lay perpendicular to him, the backs of her elbows touching his hip as she held the book open to read. He kept his eyes closed to better feel the luxury of her body.

He'd had her several times last night, twice this day, and still, at his age, he immediately turned stiff. When he strained against her breasts, her lips tugged up. Not in exasperation at his continual lust, not even in amusement. He knew because he ran his hand up her leg and under her gown to part her. He felt her breath catch when he touched her silky wetness. She smiled because she was ready.

And she wanted him, too.

Nicole looked down at the man next to her. In sleep, his face had at last begun to mirror the increased relaxation she'd sensed in his whole demeanor. She thought he'd grown more contented in the last few weeks. As had she. So happy, in fact, that she didn't believe she could deny Derek if he asked her again to be his mistress.

Should she accept, she would break her word to her grandmother, and the news would devastate her father. She understood this. So why did her heart tell her it was right to be with this man for as long as she could?

What would her mother do? She had always told Nicole to follow her dreams and let nothing stand in her way. Hadn't Laurel given up everything to be with the man she loved? Hadn't she lost her own mother over it? Her father would never disown her, but he would wonder why she hadn't demanded marriage. Nicole wondered herself.

She felt trapped in a curious position. She sensed that Derek was growing to love her. But she couldn't decide if he was averse to marriage in general, or just marriage to her. Yet one thought recurred. Was she unthinkable as a bride merely because he was an earl and she apparently lacked a title, fortune, or roots?

And if that was the case, why hadn't she told him who she was?

Chapter 23

The bloody man's grown larger, Chancey thought when he first arrived in Sydney and found Sutherland. Grown larger and lighter, as daft as that might sound. It was as if some burden had been lifted from his shoulders. Sutherland smiled. Often. Chancey pondered what had happened to him. Then Nicole rushed across the deck, laughing, to be swung up in Sutherland's arms.

Nicole had happened to him.

The man was their enemy, but she'd obviously forgotten that fact. Surely he couldn't be seeing her look at the man as if he alone existed for her, as if she loved him! Chancey cursed bitterly. They had to wed. From their closeness, he figured they'd have to wed very fast.

He wasn't fool enough to go storming the ship, not with Sutherland holding her, with his body language daring anyone to come near what was his. And besides wanting to kill the captain, Chancey had some bones to pick with a couple of his sailors. So he was glad to see that she had been seeing him off. Chancey's hands clenched when the bastard gave her a long, lingering kiss. But when he pulled her in again to gently kiss the top of her head, Chancey decided with relief that the man wanted her for more than one reason.

He followed behind Sutherland until they were out of earshot of the ship, then strode up to jab at his back. The man turned in a flash, his whole body tensed for a fight. Chancey just made out the slight look of surprise on his face before he concealed it behind a cold mask.

"We're gonna be talkin' now."

In response, Sutherland gave a quick nod.

The captain following him, Chancey ambled to a nearby pub, deserted at this time of morning. When they sat at a back table, he called for two whiskeys. He figured he needed one, and didn't doubt the man before him did, too.

He asked questions and, after a while, Sutherland loosened up and talked. Chancey learned of Sutherland's belief that Nicole had poisoned his crew. He listened as Sutherland told him about the storm and about Tallywood. When necessary, he prompted the man with questions about Nicole, obviously his favorite subject, to keep him talking.

When Chancey felt confident that she was safe and hadn't been mistreated, he relaxed marginally. It occurred to him that he and the captain agreed on a lot of views. If Sutherland weren't a reprobate drunk who'd seduced Nicole, they might have been friends.

Suddenly Sutherland got that cold look on his face again, and Chancey realized he'd somehow revealed that this conversation was about to change course. The blighter didn't show a hint of surprise when Chancey announced, "Ye're marryin' her tomorrow."

When Sutherland said nothing, he continued, "I let ye go once when I should o' made ye marry her, but I'll not make the same mistake again."

"As much as I would like to marry her—I can't." He ran a hand over his grim face.

"Can't or won't?" Chancey ground out as he leaned forward. "I'll kill ye if ye don't make this right for her."

Sutherland didn't back down, just spoke in a toneless voice. "I want to spend the rest of my life with her." He paused, a bleak look in his eyes. "But there are circumstances at home that make a marriage to her impossible."

"Impossible? Nothin's impossible," Chancey spat out before he swooped his glass up to his lips. After a deep draw, he added, "Ye'll just have to get around whatever obstacle stands in the way of marryin' my lass—"

"Impossible," Sutherland said, more to himself than to Chancey.

Chancey leapt out of his chair and began pacing by the table to try to get control, but his temper won out.

"Damn it, Sutherland," he snarled, "the only way that marryin' Nicole would be impossible would be if—" He broke off, then sucked in his breath as sudden understanding washed over him. His shoulders sagged. He was stricken as much by his own conclusion as by the utterly dead look in Sutherland's eyes.

With a surge of rage, Chancey heaved him out of his chair and held him by the collar. But Sutherland did nothing. The bastard wouldn't fight him.

Finally Sutherland spoke. "I want to take care of her. I can give her a house and wealth and everything else she might ever want."

Chancey hit him so hard his fist vibrated from the force of it. Sutherland didn't defend himself.

"Blighter! So ye'll make her yer mistress," Chancey spat. "Spend two nights with the missus and the children, then a few with Nicole and any bastards she might get by ye?"

"*No.* It would only be Nicole. I've never touched my wife."

That surprised Chancey, but it didn't matter. "Ye have no idea how much ye've cost her. Seems she hasn't seen fit to tell ye what she is. But I'll tell ye that ye're gonna have hurt more than her feelin's when all this mess is over."

"What do you mean?" Sutherland asked slowly as Chancey released him in disgust.

"I mean she had prospects, great ones. I know cause I seen 'em. Better than you can imagine." Suddenly, Chancey felt very old and very sad. He sat heavily with a great exhalation of air, then took another burning drink. "Ye need to leave her alone. Just pack up and sail."

Sutherland cautiously sat when Chancey did, but his whole body tensed at the suggestion. "Just leave her? With no explanation?"

"She could forgive herself for lovin' ye without marriage, but unlike ye, it would kill her to know she'd committed adultery."

Sutherland winced, but asked, "What do you think it will do to her when I just disappear?"

"It'll hurt her to be sure. But she'll get over ye." Chancey pinned him with his eyes. "Ye have to do this."

"I can't—not to her," he said firmly.

"Ye mean ye can't do this for her because all ye care about is yerself. What do ye have to offer her?" Chancey abruptly stood again. "Ye're nothin' but a shell of a man anyway—and a drunk to boot. And that's somethin' for an Irisher to accuse." He marched back and forth. "If ye break clean with her, in time she'll forget about ye. She's young enough to find another."

Chancey finally made out an unconcealable emotion on Sutherland's face, and wished he hadn't. It was as if raw pain surfaced to smother and kill any hope that had been there. It also signaled to Chancey that Sutherland accepted he was right, so he said nothing more.

His face cold again, Sutherland spoke, "I want one more night with her."

Chancey shook his head sharply. "Not a chance."

"It's the only way I'll agree to this. And you have to take money to settle on her, to make sure she has everything she needs for the rest of her life."

"Ferget it." He needed to get this drunken bastard, a married one at that, out of her life as soon as possible.

The captain stood and turned to walk away. Before he got to the door, Chancey grabbed his arm. "One night. Ye do anythin' to hurt my Nic, and I'll gladly kill ye."

Nicole could easily pass for a princess, Derek thought as he watched her sipping wine across the table from him. In fact, several people around them stared at her as if they thought she was. Their reaction wasn't simply caused by her beauty. Even among those dining in this exclusive establishment, she stood out as a royal would.

She'd dressed to perfection in one of the gowns he'd given her. The emerald patterned silk brought out her fiery coloring and made her dark eyes take on a green shade. Her ensemble had an oriental feel to it, and in her shining hair she wore the intricately carved jade combs he'd given her to match.

Seeing her at this meal, he concluded she unquestionably would have other prospects. She could make a king fall in love with her.

He'd always been amazed at her perfect manners off the ship. When not shark fishing or kicking villains to their knees, Nicole Lassiter behaved like a spirited member of the nobility. Well, a very spirited member. It was as if the minute she donned a dress, she transformed into a lady. Tonight was no exception. She handled the dinner courses and all their attendant silver better than he did. Where had she learned and perfected those skills?

She was a paradox. In his bed, she was fearless—unhesitant to partake in whatever he suggested to bring them pleasure. And after she'd apparently accepted they would be together, he'd seen a side of her he'd never imagined. When not making love—and sometimes even then—she became playful. She'd tickle him, dance away from him elusively, laughing with as much abandon as she made love.

Now, as he surveyed her across the table, another person seemed to inhabit her body. He believed she could make even his mother feel a tad inadequate at a social affair. He recognized that Chancey was right.

Unfortunately, Derek recognized this after he sensed she had let down her guard and accepted him. He believed she'd stay with him despite the less-than-perfect circumstances surrounding them. The irony of the situation wasn't lost on Derek. Just when he could finally call her his, when he had claimed more than her body, he had to let her go.

He was brooding when they exited the carriage, but as he followed her up the gangway, he couldn't prevent a slight quirk of his lips. One thing about her was completely out of the ordinary, even when she put on her polite façade. He didn't think she even realized it.

Nicole had the purposeful, exacting walk of someone always at sea, as if unconsciously she expected the ground to tilt at any moment. He smiled to see this seasoned sailor's trait in a woman. But the smile disappeared when he was reminded that her female body translated that walk into an undulating gait, a hip-swinging sweep that was incredibly erotic.

Later when they fell into bed together, he could feel her damp and ready for him. Instead of sliding into her, he worshipped her body, kissing her closed eyes, the tip of her nose, the small shell curve of her ear. Each part of her had become precious to him.

With the barest flick of his tongue, he kissed her belly and her inner thighs. Soft and lush beneath his lips, her body shook as he savored her, wringing every ounce of pleasure. When he took her, it was with an agonizing slowness, until at last he could no longer resist the feel of her core hotly hugging his flesh in her climax. Never quickening his body over hers, continuing the tormenting pace of pushing and pulling, he allowed himself to pour into her.

As they lay sated, he could feel her tears on his chest. Before she fell asleep in his arms, she sighed, "I love you."

Her words lanced his heart. He thought of all the months he'd wanted her and wanted her to stay with him. Then, just as she gave in, decided to risk all for him, to trust him, he would leave her. He bent down to press a kiss in her hair, knowing it was the last time he'd breathe in her scent.

He recalled his last words to the Irisher this morning.

Derek had turned back and asked the big man, "Why are you so bloody loyal to the Lassiters?"

The Irisher didn't hesitate. "Because the father saved my life, and the daughter saved my soul."

Derek had nodded and turned to go with a heavy heart, knowing that without Nicole, his own soul was lost.

Chapter 24

I'm going on," Jason Lassiter declared on his fourth night in Cape Town.

"*We're* going on," Maria stubbornly corrected as she pushed her spectacles farther up her nose.

"Woman! I brought you this far against my better judgment." He shook his head. "Never should have stopped in Recife. But, damn it, you won't leave Cape Town with me." Grabbing her elbow in frustration, he steered her around a pack of drunken sailors swerving down the docks. He and Maria had come down to check for word of any ships inbound from Sydney, but had gathered nothing.

Maria reminded him, "It's a simple business matter." Business *was* simple. And unemotional. Was that why she worked so hard? Because her emotions careened around this man so badly she needed a constant to ground her? "I paid for passage to Australia—you have no say."

Letting her go, he scowled, until she reached out to lay her hand on his arm. He calmed a bit. "Jason, Chancey will have gotten her by now. And we have her messages. She wrote that she is very well and told the crew to meet her here if they couldn't find a way back. And what about the money she sent them? You know the only person she could have gotten that much money from is Sutherland."

"It's just that I can't stand this feeling—he's got my little girl, Maria."

She thought her heart would break at his admission, but it didn't change her decision on the matter. "She's not a little girl anymore, and I don't care what your crew says, he won't mistreat her. I watched them in Recife, and I tell you he's in love with her."

"Then why does the crew want him dead?"

She pursed her lips, because he had a point. Then rallied. "You must trust me in this matter—he *will* take care of her."

Jason shook his head firmly. "I've got to go get her."

"If you're going, I'm going," she said resolutely. "But I think you're making a mistake. If Chancey left weeks ago, they should be on their way back here to pick up the crew. What if we miss them?"

Sometimes she couldn't understand this man. She was certain they would pass by Nicole and Chancey in this big ocean. It would be a miracle if they did meet them. She loved Jason, but she could see that often he was far too impatient, and it overruled his better sense.

"Be reasonable, Jason. You know Chancey will protect her with his life. And think of how terrible it would be for her if you weren't here when she arrived. You know she would wait here for you to return from Australia."

She sensed she'd won with that argument. Truly, it

would be awful to be stranded at the Cape. Nicknamed the Tavern of the Seas, it contained the worst sorts of people—transients, thieves, even pirates. The only nice thing she could say about Cape Town was that it was a good place to do business. There were hordes of the newly rich from the African mines who didn't know what to do with all their wealth—

Maria's eyes widened behind her spectacles. Distantly, she heard Jason saying, "I should never have pressured her to go to her grandmother's. Pressure certainly didn't work with her mother. And she's so like Laurel. If Nicole doesn't want that life, then she doesn't have to live it. I'll have to find a way to provide better for her."

Like a flash, the idea came to her. Cape Town had an abundance of capital, if you knew where to look. Sadly, Jason didn't.

But Maria did.

"Can't this thing go any faster?" Nicole asked irritably as she looked around the deck of their unwieldy steamer. Irritability had seeped into her personality until it, and sadness, defined her. This wasn't just because they hadn't been able to find a sailing vessel leaving Sydney for Cape Town and had been forced to settle on this coal-hungry monster. It wasn't even that she felt awkward and useless at sea when she couldn't work.

It was because the man she'd fallen in love with had abandoned her.

No one will ever hurt you again. Lies! He'd said the words, said them like a solemn vow. Then clawed open her chest and ripped out her heart himself.

She'd found herself able to go about four or five days without talking about him before the words clamored for release, threatening to strangle her if she didn't let them out. As always, Chancey was a patient listener. They'd been over this again and again, but she still sounded baffled when she whispered, "He didn't even say good-bye. Waited until I went to town without you, then . . . left."

The tears began, and her chin automatically rose in a futile gesture to forestall them. "Heartless . . . but he's a selfish man. I foolishly thought he'd changed."

Chancey shifted his craggy face from one sympathetic look to another.

"Looking back, it's as if he wanted to make me fall in love with him. Always trying to get under my skin and to get my attention. To get me to open up to him." She didn't bother hiding her confusion. "Then for him to do this? I was just a game for him."

Chancey looked strange, as if her suggestion had startled him. "No, no, then, that couldn't be it. He probably woke up and realized that ye deserved more than a drunken wretch," he said fervently. He'd been acting so odd lately, Nicole thought. Anytime she mentioned that she was merely Sutherland's cast-off, he defended him.

Chancey frowned and was about to say something. She waited with raised eyebrows, but he coughed and hastily pulled himself up, excusing himself to go to work. He'd signed on as a hand so he could learn as much as possible about steam-propelled ships. He and her father both recognized they were the ships of the future. She didn't begrudge him the work, but she had nothing to take her mind off those bedeviling memories.

Those crushing memories. She might deserve more than a "drunken wretch," but she'd sensed the real man under all the pain. And loved him.

Now he'd given her pain of her own.

But she would survive. All she had to do was bluster and swagger her way through this. That's what she'd done all her life.

Yet some part of her questioned whether she was strong enough to rebound from the last few months. The home she'd wanted so badly was at the bottom of the South Atlantic Ocean, along with the life it could provide. Thanks to losing the race, her father's shipping line was dying. To cap it all, she'd been left behind like rubbish by the man she had loved. Still loved, fool that she was.

At night she would cry, her mouth open from the force of her silent weeping.

Every now and then, a man came across a woman he could look at for hours, Derek drunkenly mused. Less frequently, a woman he could listen to for hours. The odds of finding these qualities combined in a woman who also gave boundless pleasure in bed was so rare it was fabled.

He'd found this woman and left her, while wondering every day when his natural selfishness would surface and he could return for her.

Yet Chancey had made it clear that they were sailing on the morning's tide after Derek left. When he'd asked where the man was taking her, he'd answered only, "Where ye won't find her if ye change yer mind." Oh, he'd changed it all right. . . .

As he sat in his cabin, drinking as he hadn't done in months, his eyes moved over the scenes on the walls, the scenes Nicole had altered and completed while in Sydney, which he'd long since memorized. He'd never thought he would admit it, but he missed her things surrounding his own. Missed a stocking thrown over his chair. Missed the scent of almond oil or paint. Absently he fingered the case of sapphires he'd bought for her in Sydney.

He'd never taken the chance to give them to her. He would never have another.

His surroundings grew unfocused, as his hollow feelings, his want of Nicole, dredged up memories. He recalled a time when, as a boy, he had walked in on a conversation among his mother, his aunt, and their friends. They were all a little tipsy, and he'd been amused.

"My firstborn," his mother had grandly begun, "shall have trouble governing his passions. His marriage will probably be one where husband and wife love and hate with equal intensity."

"Oh, dear," Aunt Serena had responded. "Sadly, I can see it."

His mother noticed Derek and smilingly beckoned him beside her. "I am talking about your and your brothers' futures. Would you like to hear about Grant?"

He'd nodded. "Well, Grant shall marry a woman completely opposite from him. As much as he is a prankster and rapscallion, she shall be a picture of virtue—a good girl with manners and money."

"Sounds stale, Amanda," one of her friends had remarked over her raised glass.

"Possibly," she hedged. "But they'll find their love in the differences. And for this one"—she'd smoothed a lock from Derek's forehead, embarrassing him—"you, son, will have a wife and family you treasure above all else. You shall love them, and they will be your strength."

"Well, he's not the heir," someone had observed. "A love match is certainly possible."

"Not just possible. Derek, you remember this. My middle boy shall be a family man."

How utterly wrong she'd been.

He was married to a woman he hated. Shortly after their farcical marriage, his friends' pity had humiliated and angered him. He'd cut them off first. Then his family, especially when they'd recognized what they had done to a man who'd always wanted a wife and children.

He'd stopped attending functions because always the bloody questions about Lydia, about when an heir would be forthcoming, surrounded him. Or, worse, the pitying looks that circulated with rumors about her latest lover.

His anger compounded itself with each adjustment he made in his life. He gambled and drank far too much. His businesses went to hell, as did his estates. He'd come to relish the freedom that attended one so far gone. No one expected anything from him. No one depended on him. For the first time in his life, he was absolutely free. And absolutely miserable, but too entrenched to bother to change.

On the rare occasions when he interacted with his family, he'd vaguely comprehended his mother's regret. As well as the fact that the lower Derek sank, the more upright and responsible the fun-loving Grant grew.

He thought about his dead brother, William. He'd been like a weight around Derek's neck for years. Then to be chained to a female version of his petty, malicious brother forever. No wonder those two had been so drawn to each other.

He remembered hearing the servants whispering about William being spoiled. But they didn't mean overindulged or cosseted, though he certainly was that.

They meant *ruined*.

Derek couldn't stand being in this room any longer. He snatched up the jewel case, shoved it in his pocket. The bottle slipped from his other hand as he slammed out the door.

Looking out over the sea, he took a shuddering breath. His knuckles were white on the railing.

"Captain?" came a voice behind him.

He turned to see Bigsby, waiting with a sour expression on his face. The man wasted no pleasantries and said only, "A word with you." The doctor sounded surprised by his own tone, but he didn't back down.

"What's this? Is a member of my crew voluntarily speaking to me?" No one approached him any longer. Sometimes he thought Jeb called him a snob behind his back, and others might add "bastard" to the list.

"We want to know why you left her. Why we were ordered to steal away while she went to town. You just . . . abandoned her," he added in a bewildered tone.

"You make it sound as if she was helpless when you know damn well she isn't. And that Irisher was there to take her home, wherever that might be."

"I know you are a peer, but she was good enough to be your wife even if her family didn't have a title."

"That had nothing to do with it!"

Bigsby looked confused. "Then what did?"

Derek shrugged, attempting nonchalance. "She can do better. Nicole doesn't need a drunk who's a decade older."

"So stop drinking, Captain. And nine, maybe ten years is hardly a notable span between you," he said reasonably. Then, as if counting down a list, he asked, "What's the next reason you left her?"

Derek couldn't believe the temerity of this man. Bigsby had chosen the wrong time to demonstrate his new spine. "You want to know?" he seethed. "I'll tell you—I am already married!"

The man's lips parted, but no words emerged.

"I can see I've shocked you. Yes, I have a wife in England. A wife I despise whom I've never touched, but a wife all the same."

Bigsby's eyebrows rose as he digested that information. Then he responded, "I'm sorry to hear that. It will be difficult for you and Miss Lassiter while you're getting divorced from your current wife, but it will pass." He looked about to say more, thought better of it. "Good night, Captain," he said, and departed.

How easy Bigsby made it sound. But he didn't know about deathbed promises and family secrets better left buried. Derek had done Nicole a favor.

Because he loved her.

A sharp, agonized roar burst from his chest as he flung the jewels into the sea.

Their ship hadn't even docked at the Cape when Nicole spotted her father and his crew among the waiting crowds at the docks. The first line was barely secure before she ran across the gangway, pushing around people in her haste.

"Father, I'm so sorry about the ship," she whispered as he drew her into a hug. "I never meant for this to happen." Tears trailed down her face.

"Hush, Nicole," he said, his voice thick. "I don't care about anything as long as you're safe."

"You weren't supposed to come after me," she admonished, then added in a derisive voice, "I'd planned to save the day for everyone."

"It's past, now. We're going to be fine." He gave her another crushing hug before he turned her to his crew. "They worried about you."

When she saw them all fit and safe, she broke into a

watery smile. "Everybody's well?" Several nodded smiles in return, some as watery as her own. Then her father turned her again. *Maria!* She stood beside her father with her arms open. Nicole's face crumpled despite all her best efforts, but it didn't matter as she ran to her.

Inside her motherly embrace, Nicole shook in what felt like a great unburdening. Maria understood unrequited love. Hadn't Maria loved her unwitting father for so long, even now loved him? She'd been through this hurt before, too.

Nicole could feel Maria sharply waving away the crew, a couple of whom patted Nicole's head as they departed. Nicole was glad. She didn't know if she could stop crying.

But even over the sound of Maria's soft Portuguese endearments, she heard her father mutter to Chancey, "He's a dead man."

"No, Father!" Nicole said, turning from Maria. "If you go after him, then I'm not finished with him. I want this finished! I want him out of my life forever." Her tears stopped as anger drummed through her. "I've decided to claim my birthright and keep my promise to Grandmother to find a husband."

Father shook his head. "You don't have to do that. Not anymore."

"I want to," Nicole said, more certain of her future than she'd been in months. "I'm going to wed. I'm going to bask in security and never be cold or scared." She gently pushed away from Maria and ran a sleeve over her eyes. "I refuse to be weak or vulnerable again."

"Well, Captain?" Bigsby asked when they'd docked in London and finished unloading the cargo. "What will you do?" The doctor didn't need to specify about what. Nicole was the only subject they'd talked about the entire voyage back.

Activity on the deck stopped. Everything fell silent. The entire crew—sailors in the rigging, men sweeping the decks—paused, waiting for his answer. Their animosity had dimmed throughout the voyage. Probably because they saw he was wearing down. He looked around at all of them, saw Jeb nodding. . . .

The last three months had introduced Derek to a new level of loathing his life. He was never without the regret that ate at him. As soon as he'd left, he'd doubted his decision. But for once, he'd wanted to do the right thing, the best thing for Nicole. Chancey was right about him. She could do better.

Then, halfway back to London, Bigsby had brought up the killing blow to his resistance: "She could do better, but could any man love her more than you do?"

No. It wasn't possible.

He resented everything that kept him and Nicole apart. That resentment had grown into a poisonous rancor so strong, it could no longer be contained.

He would divorce his wife.

And break his deathbed promise to his father. A divorce would devastate his mother and embarrass the family even more, but that couldn't be helped. He refused to imagine a life without Nicole, and she deserved to be married.

"I'm going . . . to find her." He walked away to the sound of cheers and clinking coins as bets were paid.

During the hackney ride to his London home, he wondered if she would even have him. Then the memory of their last night together flashed into his mind. He'd loved her, holding nothing back because he'd known it would be their last time together. And she'd given him everything. . . .

He looked up when the cab stopped in front of his town

house and ran a hand down his face to pull himself together. As soon as he stepped down, his mother and brother greeted him from the front door with welcoming smiles.

"Derek, you're finally home!" Amanda called in surprise, then added, "You look like hell." He smiled wryly before looking up to see his brother jogging over.

"Welcome home, Derek. We read about the win. Congratulations." He offered him a hearty handshake.

"I never thought I'd say this, but it's good to be home."

When his mother had them settled in the sitting room with tea and a light repast, Derek recounted the highlights of the race, purposely omitting Nicole from the story. But throughout the telling, his mother looked edgy, as if she couldn't stay still in her seat. He could swear Grant cast her quelling glances.

When he cut short his tale, she said in a rush, "We, um, have something to tell you."

"Mother, don't you think we can discuss this later?" Grant interrupted warningly. "As you said, Derek looks as though he's had a hell of a journey. We can wait until he's settled."

Amanda pressed her lips together. "Well, I've waited weeks to see this thing resolved, and I'm sure he'll want to know what we're talking about."

"Indeed," Derek said with a sigh as he leaned back in his seat. "What's happened now?"

With one last look at Grant, his mother grasped Derek's hand and turned a sympathetic face to him. "Your wife's pregnant," she revealed abruptly. "I see I don't have to tell you that you can by no stretch of the imagination be the father."

Chapter 25

No, you quite do not," Derek answered, running his palm across the back of his neck.

"She's three months along," his mother explained.

"Are you certain?" he asked, not wanting to get his hopes up prematurely. They'd been through this before. If she was indeed carrying another man's child, in his family's eyes he would have no choice but to divorce her. "How do you know this?"

"She's showing," she said, then added in a confessional tone, "and not prettily."

"Mother, please!" Grant interjected. "I'm sure this information is overwhelming enough as it is. Let's keep to the facts." He turned back to Derek. "She wants to dissolve the marriage to wed some foreign count. Apparently, it's his child."

His mother nodded, agreeing happily with what Grant

had said. She appeared to be struggling not to clap her hands.

"He has even more money than you do," she said, as if that explained everything. In Lydia's case, he supposed it did. Now her unprecedented visit to his ship made sense. She'd been shrieking for money, probably because she wanted to impress and snare the rich count. Poor, misbegotten bastard. But better him than Derek.

His mother sighed, "I can't wait for this nightmare to be over. You'll be able to remarry—"

"You wanted me to remarry?" he demanded sharply. In all remonstrances, she'd never said such a thing.

She paused to consider his question. "No. Not necessarily. If you'll remember, I've been ranting about your doing *something*. Anything but simply taking the disappointment and anger you've struggled with for five years. Finally, you'll be able to have those children we know you've wanted."

Had he always been so transparent? Had they known that it was what bothered him most about marrying Lydia—not having children? He'd always thought they believed it was because she was unfaithful to him. When in fact, he couldn't bring himself to care about that, since he'd never liked his wife, much less loved her.

Now children were no longer important—he wanted them, but he couldn't live his life without Nicole.

He acted calm, but the news made his head pound in time with his heart. He would end this charade so that when he found Nicole, nothing would stand in his way.

Resolved, he patted his mother's hand and slapped his brother on the back. "If you'll excuse me. This can't wait another day."

Minutes later, facing the elaborate façade of his wife's

town home, he was reminded anew of the extreme lavish-
ness of the place. Shortly after they were married, she'd
purchased and furnished it using his money, sparing no
expense; yet he'd been glad to provide it because he could
eliminate one place he might ever run into her. If he did
happen to be home from a trip, he avoided the country
estates, as well as any of the ton's gilded yet facile amuse-
ments. In their five years of marriage, he'd seen his wife on
only a handful of occasions.

"Good morning, Lydia," he said civilly as he was shown
to her sitting room. As usual, she looked beautiful, with
her blue-black hair and glittering green eyes. As usual, she
reminded him of a snake.

"What do you want?" she snapped. The only thing that
could mar her perfect face was the expression of hate that
continually suffused it. He wondered how others couldn't
see the malignity from inside that manifested itself in her
eyes, but then, he'd been fooled as well.

In the beginning, he'd wanted to ask what had filled her
with such bitterness. Though it wouldn't be a simple
answer with her. Was it her family's overweening greed? Or
the death of the man she'd really wanted to marry? But he
was long past even a token interest in his wife by now.

"No small talk? Good. We'll get right down to it. You're
pregnant," he said with a nod toward her scarcely rounding
belly. "I want a divorce."

She laughed then, a false sound. "You can't divorce me."

"I can and I will."

"That's where you're wrong," she said in an amused
tone, shifting her rich brocade morning robe. He'd most
likely paid a fortune for it.

Derek forced himself to be calm. He was doing this for
his and Nicole's future, and any anger on his part could

backfire. "I thought you desired this. You want to marry someone else," he offered reasonably.

"Actually," she began, taking a casual sip of tea, "we'll be getting an annulment."

He kept his face expressionless. With Lydia, any sign of emotion would be seen as a weakness to be exploited. He raised his eyebrows and assumed a disinterested pose. "On what grounds?"

"You are unable to perform your . . . marital duties." She looked down at her long nails. "You aren't a man to me."

"Is that what you've been telling people?"

She looked up with a chilling smile. "Yes," she hissed, looking very pleased with herself.

He tried not to laugh aloud. He'd never expected such a resolution. "And how do you plan to explain your condition?"

"I'll be gone by the time anyone suspects. My next husband's family is Catholic. He wants his child—but not a divorced mother."

"I can't believe you would do this," he said honestly.

"Believe it. It's already been set in motion. I'll be free of you in a matter of days."

"You've told everyone? There's no way to take it back?"

She gave that same eerie smile. "I've given my oath."

"Excellent!"

She looked startled.

"Bloody good idea, Lydia. I'll see that my solicitors push it through with all haste." He left the beautiful Lydia sputtering, her plump red lips gaping like those of a fish.

Prepared to be chastised, Nicole walked in to see her grandmother for the first time in more than seven months. Before the voyage, she'd claimed she planned to shop during a relaxing vacation on the Continent. Now that the dowager was aware of everything, Nicole braced herself for a martial demeanor and cutting accusations.

So she was more than surprised to find her grandmother, the Marchioness of Atworth, lovingly rubbing noses with one of her pugs, and chatting to the unmoving animal.

"Are you Mommy's wittle Pixie?" she asked. She answered for the dog with something that sounded suspiciously like "Oh, S . . . U . . . R."

The dog looked as dumbfounded as Nicole felt. Finally, she cleared her throat.

Her grandmother looked up sharply. "Why weren't you announced?" she asked, tucking the dog under her arm.

"I told Chapman I could show myself in—but if I'm disturbing you . . ." she said in an incredulous voice.

To her amazement, her stern grandmother chuckled. "Well, you caught me doing the pretty to my pug." Then she held up the object of her affection. "Pixie is such a sweet little girl, isn't she? In the past, I never told her."

In answer, Nicole only raised her eyebrows. She couldn't seem to erase the startled look she felt settling on her face. It became even more fixed when, after setting down the dog, her grandmother walked over and, with a surprising strength, hugged her for the first time in her life.

Nicole recalled the strange moment when she'd seen Maria on the dock in Cape Town. Chancey, the crew, her father—they were all there. She'd had the oddest thought and almost became embarrassed by it: *The only one missing is Grandmother.*

"Don't look so surprised, gel. I don't hold back feeling any longer. Anytime I want to express emotion, I do it."

It was then that she noticed her grandmother's collar

wasn't buttoned to choking tightness, and she wasn't garbed in black. Steel gray, yes, but at least not her usual dour attire. "What brought about this change?" Nicole asked slowly.

"When your father told me where you were going, I was saddened because it appeared that you would do anything to get away from me."

Nicole felt a swift pang of guilt and opened her mouth to explain, but her grandmother continued, "I know now how important that race was to you. So like Laurel you are. No, what really changed me was the word that your ship had gone down. I believed you were dead, and all I could do was recall with regret the times you *were* here. Regret because I should have treated you differently. I should have told you how very much you are like my own daughter," she confessed, her dark eyes shining.

Nicole sat down at the mention of her mother. "We both loved sailing. I remember hearing her laughter." She met her grandmother's eyes and said, "She was happy in her life."

Her grandmother took a deep breath and nodded. "I understand now what caused her to run away—though her choice of accomplice remains a mystery," she added dryly, and Nicole had to smile.

Then the marchioness turned serious. "I won't chase away my granddaughter as well. Circumstances will change around here. I'll never make it like that for you again," she vowed resolutely.

Nicole must have looked incredulous.

"What? You don't believe me?" Raising an eyebrow, her grandmother boldly challenged, "Invite your father to dinner here tonight."

"Father?" Nicole asked in a strangled tone. "Here? With you? Are you serious?"

"I am always serious."

"What about Chancey?" Nicole ventured to ask.

Her grandmother swallowed and allowed in a pained voice, "Very well." Then amended, "In proper attire . . ."

Nicole nodded, then dared, "Father also has a . . . guest with him."

The dowager frowned before flashing a comprehending look. "Oh, a *guest*. Well, I suppose we should invite her, too."

That night when Jason Lassiter first encountered the marchioness, he lost the ability to speak. Because she said briskly, "I was confident you'd bring her back safely, Jason." Then she mumbled, "Thank you."

When Maria nudged him to speak, he sputtered, "You should thank Chancey. He was the one who watched out for her."

Chancey didn't think, just pulled at his collar and spoke. "It weren't me that saved her. It were Sutherland."

"Oh? And who's this Sutherland?"

Nicole affected an unconcerned look while everyone around her fell silent. The dowager glanced from face to face, trying to determine why the room had grown quiet. To break the awkwardness, Maria approached her and curtsied.

The marchioness, out of long habit, looked her over, taking in every detail from the unadorned navy dress of fine fabric to the spectacles. With a decided look on her face, she declared, "You *must* be a governess."

Needed laughter bubbled up. Nicole had to fold her lips in and stare at the ceiling.

Dinner was initially awkward. But the sumptuous meal of braised duck with shallots served with an unstinting flow of wine made even Chancey stop glaring at his utensils.

By the time the footmen removed their dishes, talk had turned to the shipping company. Nicole had learned on the return voyage that Lassiter and Maria had secured financing to fund the line. Their first step, they'd decided, was to commission the construction of a replacement flagship or to purchase one outright. But they and Chancey were reluctant to leave Nicole.

"I'm fine," Nicole asserted to the table. "I know you have to take care of business. Please stop hovering over me. I'll try not to marry while you're away," she teased.

Her father smiled, though clearly unconvinced.

Nicole reassured him. "You know I want what's best for the line. After I marry, I plan to help you as much as possible." She turned to Maria. "You will make him go?"

Maria's eyes were questioning.

"Please, Maria. I'm twenty years old. We have three footmen, and I'm living in Mayfair. I'm safer than I've ever been in my whole life."

Grandmother pointed out, "Jason, it might be for the best if you two aren't seen together for a bit. I've stuck to the same story for fifteen years. If we call her by her middle name, no one in the ton should be able to connect her to Nicole Lassiter, the sailor. At least not until after she marries."

"Are ye sure about this, Nic?" Chancey asked gruffly.

"Yes. I want to be married. I want children, and I'll be twenty-one next month." She smiled at the marchioness. "Grandmother's giving me no pressure, but I'm ready. Plus, we don't have much time—the season's already begun."

The others began talking of something else, and Lassiter leaned closer and said in a low voice, "You don't have to do this. I take back all the things I've said before. Soon I'll be better able to provide for you."

She smiled fondly at him. "With Maria's help . . ."

His eyes lit up. "I think we're making it official—"

"*You're going to marry her?*" she whispered excitedly.

He looked startled and confused. "No. Officially make her a partner. She plans to sell her Brazilian, uh, enterprise. Why would you ever think we'd marry?"

"I think you could be very happy together."

The look on his face made it clear he'd never thought of Maria in those terms. "Nicole—I *am* married."

"I understand." And she meant it. But that wouldn't preclude her from trying to change his mind.

He abruptly asked, "What about Sutherland?"

Nicole deliberately chose to misunderstand him and waved off his concern. "Pssh, I'll be sure to stay out of the Mermaid and any other waterfront holes, so I probably won't run into him."

Father smiled at her bravado. "That's my girl. Always were a strong little thing."

Her grandmother heard this last comment and interjected "Perish the thought. She's not strong—she's delicate. Not another word from you, Lassiter."

Five days later, Nicole waved the trio and many of the *Bella Nicola*'s crew off on the *Griffin*, another of her father's ships, bound for Liverpool. She had no time for sadness, because Grandmother had whisked in an army of seamstresses to slave over Nicole. At the end of the week, she was prepared for her first ball. She'd complained about the extravagance of having so many women working on her gowns, but her grandmother had decreed it an *emergency*, so she'd gone along.

The marchioness would introduce her to society, secure invitations, and settle Nicole in. Then she would rest, by God.

The first ball they attended dazzled Nicole with the lights, the silks, and the beautiful, bejeweled people fluttering on the ballroom floor.

She quickly got over it.

In fact, she had been right all along. This world, this social sphere, was not her place. If she had to be on land, then she wanted to *see* the land. Not imposing mansions with a tease of a garden, or even a park to really whet the appetite, but miles and miles of land laid out in flats and swells like the ocean.

To be honest, she didn't necessarily want to return to the sea, because without the *Bella Nicola,* everything had been altered. But the ton life wasn't meant for her, either. After a few weeks of this existence, she felt as if she'd found a shining coin on the street that disappointed when found to be worthless.

The ball she and her grandmother attended this night was much the same as the others. Nicole was slowly dying, smothered by the weight of convention and the cut of her dress. The perfumes that initially had delighted her swirled in her head and assaulted her senses, as did the odor of a thousand lit candles cloying in the crowded ballroom. She couldn't get quite enough air.

Dizzy and breathless, Nicole didn't believe it when she saw *him*.

As she gazed at his broad back, his thick, black hair, his powerful form standing taller than any other in the room, the churning in her stomach intensified. Hadn't she been assured repeatedly that he was never seen at these functions? Unable to move, she stared spellbound as he turned.

She couldn't stop the knitting of her brows. It wasn't Derek.

Yet she couldn't look away. He was so similar, he had to be a brother. Though Derek had never mentioned he had one. In fact, he'd never talked about his family at all.

The man raised his eyebrows, no doubt curious about her staring. He gave her a good-natured smile that faded to a look of concern when she stood unmoving. He walked over to the earl of Allenton, her grandmother's friend who'd squired them to half a dozen functions. The man gave a nod indicating her, and he and Allenton approached her.

She hissed in a breath. Had Derek told him about her? Did this man know who she was? Know she'd made love to his brother? The panic clamoring through her body made her light-headed.

"Lady Christina," Allenton began, "it appears you have made yet another conquest. May I present Grant Sutherland, Viscount Anderleigh."

He offered another friendly smile as he bowed. She struggled to make a charming reply, to smile even, but she was frozen. This man's hard-planed face brought her ruthlessly suppressed feelings for Derek to the fore, ripping open all the barriers she'd constructed to hold her pain in check.

She was saved from an unexpected quarter. "Grant, who is your new acquaintance?" a woman asked, as she planted herself between the men.

Incredibly, Grant Sutherland, who seemed every inch the gentleman, ignored her.

"Darling *brother*," the woman began in a syrupy voice, "you must introduce me to the talk of the ton."

Nicole experienced a tug of sympathy for this man Grant.

"Lydia, don't you have some packing to do?" he asked in

an obviously restrained tone. "I heard you were taking a long trip." When she didn't move, he asked, "Where's the count? I thought he was looking for you just minutes ago. We wouldn't want him to leave you."

"He's not going anywhere without me," she said in a boastful manner, strangely undeterred by the cold anger in his eyes. "Won't you introduce me?"

His face held a look of distaste as he related in what was more an admission than a presentation, "This is my sister-in-law, Lydia Sutherland."

"Grant! Tsk, tsk. So impolite." She faced Nicole. "I am Lady Stanhope." The woman made a halfhearted motion of greeting. "The countess of Stanhope."

Nicole could have sworn Grant mumbled to her, "Not for long, *sister.*" Had his lips even moved?

Wait . . . How could she be the countess? Thoughts crept in—Nicole desperately batted them away. "S-sister-in-law?" she finally managed.

"Yes," the countess answered slowly. As she openly scrutinized Nicole, she seemed to home in on her discomfiture as though it were a beacon.

Nicole strove for a disaffected mien. "So, which brother are you married to?" she asked, even as her mind was answering her own question. She glanced over the shining black hair and cameo perfection of her face in delayed recognition. This woman was beautiful, but not if you really looked in her eyes. . . .

Lady Stanhope smiled unpleasantly. "There are only two brothers."

The lights flickered, then faded altogether. Why couldn't she get enough air? The invisible noose was back, only this time it was too bitingly tight. . . .

*   *   *

Sitting in bed considering her situation, Nicole laughed, but it was a sad, humorless sound. No wonder the hateful bastard hadn't wanted to marry her. She'd thought she would cry all night, but she had no tears left for him. This morning she'd awoken with a hollow pang in her chest and the stark conclusion that she was an adulteress. That knowledge made her want to despise herself. Instead, she directed the feeling at him. Anger had a way of making her strong.

Nicole promised herself she would go on. She would not let this get in the way of her plans. And, most important, no one would ever imagine the pain she kept inside.

"Nicole, what on earth made you faint like that?" the marchioness asked over breakfast. "I didn't see it, but I heard you dropped like a rock."

She hoped it wasn't quite so bad. In Nicole's mind, she'd more or less sunk down, cushioned by the flounces of her gown. "It wasn't that terrible. Embarrassing all the same, of course."

"Are you ill?" she queried with a look of anxiety on her face.

"I am perfectly healthy. I'm just not used to the weight of the gowns and the closeness in the rooms yet," Nicole answered somewhat honestly.

The marchioness eyed her and was opening her mouth to say more, but Nicole cut her off. "How fast could we bring one of my suitors up to scratch?"

Her grandmother looked startled. "Well, I couldn't say . . ."

"Just an estimate. A week? Two?"

"That depends on the suitor," she answered carefully. "It depends on which one you choose."

Nicole's fingers were clenched in her dress. "I choose

the one who can be brought up to scratch the quickest."

The dowager set her plate aside. "Then I suppose a week to finalize the contracts, if I put some pressure on."

Nicole caught her gaze. "Then, Grandmother, I'm asking you for pressure."

He should be elated, Derek told himself. He'd wanted to be free of Lydia for five years now. Five long years. Now he could marry Nicole as soon as he found her. But on the heels of that thought, the Irisher's words filtered into his mind for the thousandth time. Was he worthy of her?

His life was in shambles. Even with the annulment finalized, the fact remained that he'd been married before. He drank too much, and his estates would have rotted if his brother hadn't assumed his responsibilities.

But if he'd learned anything from his time with Nicole, it was that you had to fight for what you wanted. And he'd fight for her now. He'd make himself worthy.

As he sat in his study going over the runners' reports, his mother strolled in and casually wandered over to inspect his bookshelves.

Over her shoulder, she said, "I haven't pressed, but don't you think it's time to tell me what all these men are doing as they come and go from here? Won't you enlighten me as to what you do all day?"

What did it matter if she knew? She would find out soon enough when he brought Nicole here to marry him.

"They are Bow Street runners. I have hired them to search for the woman I want to marry."

Her arm shot out to the nearest chair arm for support.

"You've already met her?" Her eyes wide, she asked, "Well, who is her family? What is their title?"

He smiled. "You've never heard of her family. In fact, I'd like to forget she even has one. There is no title."

His mother sank into the chair.

There'd be no way to spare her. He might as well tell her so she at least had time to accustom herself to the idea before he came back with Nicole. He took a breath and informed her, "The woman I desire to marry is an American."

Amanda Sutherland appeared to relax at that information. Most people of her acquaintance could overlook an American without a title if she was extravagantly wealthy. . . .

"The family fortune runs in the negative at this point."

Her hand inched up to her mouth. "Could you have found someone who would be more disastrous to this family?"

How could she even dare! "Actually, I just ended my marriage to someone who was," Derek said cuttingly. "Since the family chose her, perhaps this time I'll be allowed to choose my own bride."

"We couldn't have known," his mother whispered sadly.

"Well, you might have nothing to worry about. I left the girl, abandoned her, because I was married. She'll most likely spurn me."

He turned from her and heard her rise to go. He could feel some of the frustration leaving his body. This was all in the past. He wanted to look forward. "See if you can't find Grant," he called after her. He'd get his brother to teach him how to manage everything, and he'd take care of his own obligations. "And please get every ounce of liquor out of this house."

When Grant strolled in, he was as perfectly dressed and creased as ever. "Why the long face?" he asked as he took a seat. "You should be ecstatic. The race is won, and you're single yet again."

Derek hesitated, debating whether to tell his brother everything. They had been close as boys. . . .

With a dry smile, he revealed, "Well, it appears that I am still pining over Lassiter's chit."

Grant sucked in a breath and sat back in his chair. "You don't say?"

An hour later, Grant was reeling from all Derek had told him. "Is she so beautiful?"

"To me—utterly," he said as he ran a hand through his hair. "But it's much more than that."

Grant frowned. "And yet, you just left her?"

"I was trying to be noble, to be good to her. Now I realize I was just bloody stupid. I should have brought her back here and married her as soon as I ended my marriage to Lydia."

"The man—Chancey—had a point, though, if you weren't prepared to marry the girl at the time."

"He was right then, but things have changed now."

"Are you ready to remarry?"

Derek's brows drew together. Why did Grant sound so doubtful? "I will be, with your help."

Hours later, when they'd reviewed the books and anything else Grant could think of, Derek stood and stretched.

"There isn't much left to go over," Grant said.

He'd warmed up to his brother's plans, possibly because he'd seen how serious Derek was about learning. Still, Derek wanted to reassure him. "I will handle my own, Grant."

Grant looked at him curiously, as if making a decision, then nodded. "For the first few months, it'll be learning by trial. I've got everything running smoothly, so you have a bit of time to search for your sailor before you need to dig in."

"I appreciate your help. Now, and for the last few years."

Grant appeared uneasy. "Well, don't get all sentimental on me. I drew a very large salary as your estate manager."

When Derek raised his eyebrows, Grant smiled blandly and changed the subject. "You know, it wouldn't kill you to attend one of these balls that Mother keeps harping on."

"Forget it—"

"Just hear me out. I know you're in love with this girl," he said, his eyes searching Derek's face. "God knows, I've never seen you like this. But it wouldn't hurt to at least act as though you're cooperating with her."

"Why? Because she wants me to start the search for a new bride now that the annulment is finalized? I told her about Nicole, but you know she won't give up. If I go to one of these things, she'll push a hundred women at me in the hope that one catches my fancy instead of a penniless, nameless American. If I go, she'll think she has a chance of getting me to wed someone who is not Nicole." He ran a hand over his haggard face. "It wouldn't be fair to her, because it will *never* happen!"

Grant seemed taken aback by his vehemence. "Not even a couple of nights to smooth out some of the gossip about the annulment? Your presence after so long would help stem the worst of it. The season's halfway over. It wouldn't become expected of you."

Unfortunately, Grant's arguments made sense. He didn't want to bring Nicole here and have her affected by any slurs on the family. Still, he wavered. "You know I need to be here in case I get some news."

Grant exhaled in exasperation. "You would only be

going a few blocks away. A message would be sure to reach you." When Derek said nothing, Grant continued, "When you were off gallivanting all over the world, it was Mother here who bore the brunt of shame because of Lydia." Grant stood and paced. "She's been the one most affected by the rumors, and she was the one who had to deal with Lydia's temper on a regular basis. That woman has no restraint." Grant looked as though he would shudder. Lydia's compulsive need to shock was most likely his stodgy brother's main complaint against the woman.

"And you? Did her conduct affect you?" Derek asked with concern.

"Are you kidding? It nearly made me swear off marriage. But I did feel sorry for Mother. It was extremely hard on a woman as proud as she is."

Grant's words forced him to recognize how selfish he'd been to leave them all here with her. He'd hurt more than just Nicole.

Derek threw his hands up to signal defeat. "Very well. I'll go tonight, but I can't guarantee I'll be fitting company."

"Thank you, Derek," Grant said. He walked to the door, then turned back and said in a voice that might have been just a little hoarse, "It's good to have you back."

Chapter 26

Oh, yes, he was making his mother happy. She flitted around Lady Crossman's ballroom from one matchmaking mama to the next, teasing them with Derek as if he were a slab of meat set before ravenous animals. Earlier she'd mentioned that people were surprisingly receptive to the idea of Derek remarrying. Soon, she predicted, all the new layers of gossip would bury the scandal.

People could overlook a lot when one of the wealthiest peers in London had just become available. Particularly since his mother had told everyone he was actively seeking a wife. He supposed it wasn't a lie; he was actively seeking Nicole.

He'd always had a sense of wasting time at the soirees and routs, as if he were just playing up to something that would happen in the future. Tonight was no different. He was anxious and impatient. With Nicole, he'd lived in the present. Not thinking of the future or the past, but only of his time with her. Recalling how easy he'd felt around her made it even more difficult to be civil to all the little chits pushed at him and Grant. Their vapid conversation had not improved in the time he'd been away. Not that he'd expected it to.

He thought he'd concealed the worst part of his irritation, but if the petulant little looks and huffy retreats were any indication, he hadn't succeeded. Grant knew that he'd reached his limit, because he politely removed him from the crowd. Grant looked about to laugh when Derek made a throttling gesture with his hands.

"So, little brother, am I doing my duty?"

"If not in spirit, then at least in deed," Grant replied with a grin. "You should see your scowls. You look menacing."

"That must be because I am completely bloody miserable."

Grant smiled ruefully. "I see now that this won't work for you. Well, at any rate, I appreciate all you're doing—or trying to do—for our dear, sweet mother."

As if on cue, Amanda marched over to them with a disdainful look on her face. Both sons groaned.

"Really, Derek, I did not want you to come here to scare away all your potential brides." She opened her fan in a huff. "And I mean that literally—you do scare them! Why, I heard from Lady Hanson that her daughter was too afraid to come anywhere near your glowering self."

He shrugged casually. "Ask Grant here, at least he thinks I'm trying. And I've had many ladies come up to me tonight."

"Yes, but those are the more desperate ones. Hardly good ton. Their families *make* them cozen up to win a man like you."

Grant obviously thought that was hilarious, but with watering eyes he kept his laughter in check.

Derek grinned in response. Sometimes he could see in Grant the lighthearted boy he'd been.

"Anyone for champagne?" Grant offered. "Mother?"

"That would be lovely," she replied with evident maternal pride in his manners.

He looked to Derek, and when he shook his head, Grant smiled before he turned to go. Derek then dutifully listened as his mother expounded on the merits of various young women, hinting broadly that he should choose them over *anyone*, any one woman, he might have in mind. Subtlety was not his mother's strong suit.

In fact, when Grant had accidentally let it slip that Derek was searching for a sailor, his mother had been just short of swooning. The idea that he was besotted with a penniless American who lived on a sailing vessel had become all too clear. . . .

A hushed murmur flew over the floor, distracting Derek's attention from their conversation. A curious rush of anticipation surged through him.

Amanda carried on undaunted, not discerning that he wasn't really listening. "Yes, after that debacle with Lydia, you have to marry only the best. We can't have her kind aligned with the family again," she said, pushing her point again that the American "wharf rat girl" was not for him.

"Of course," he replied automatically, his curiosity piqued by the disturbance at the door. He felt an immediate excitement; indeed, his whole body tensed.

And then . . . it happened.

Staring, with his jaw slack. He was capable of no more when he saw Nicole, Nicole as he'd never dreamed of her. She was dressed in a pale blue gown wrought of some gauzy, near-transparent material. Her coloring had always been vivid, but when set against the soft blue, it made him silently marvel. And with her red-gold braids and curls piled atop her head, her body looked small and delicate, fairylike. Yet at the same time she was softer, fuller, and she easily filled the low, straight bodice of her gown.

He wasn't the only one experiencing the pleasure of watching her, he realized with a glaring sweep around the room. As she proudly walked in on some older man's arm, all around her people stopped their conversations and stared.

She looked changed, and not merely because of the clothing. Her air was more sedate, and her regal demeanor was pronounced as her escort presented people to her. Wait, why were people being presented *to* her?

His mother did not miss his obvious reaction. "Oh, I see you've spied the talk of the ton," she commented, sounding pleased. "That's the Atworth granddaughter, Lady Christina. We'd all heard the story of the shy, retiring heiress finally coming back to London, but who would have thought she would be so lovely?"

"Lady? Shy?" he managed before he snapped his mouth shut.

His skin went cold, and his chest tightened. He watched dumbfounded as Nicole, looking like a princess, was led through the crowd. Who *was* that man escorting her?

He ran a hand over his face. Things began to make a warped kind of sense. *Put Nicole in a dress, and she transforms into a lady.* "What's their title?" he snapped.

His mother frowned at him, but said, "The girl is sole heir to the Atworth marquisate." Misunderstanding the reason for his stunned expression, she explained, "Because of some political wrangling a few hundred years ago, if there is no immediate male heir, the title will devolve on a female, and so she is the heir. She's to be a marchioness, and a ridiculously wealthy one to boot. She would have come to England sooner, but she was afraid to travel—"

"*Afraid to travel?*" She'd gone toe-to-toe with him in a grueling sailing race. How many future marchionesses understood which sailing chanteys accompanied which chores? Or knew not to tuck their thumbs in their fists when hitting someone?

Why hadn't she told him?

He'd only been half-listening as his mother prattled on, but one comment drew his attention. "She won't be on the market long. She's had a score of offers. Even now, look at all the lovesick swains."

Nicole was thronged by suitors. His hands clenched.

"Oh, Derek, I do wish you would marry someone like her," she sighed.

"Done." He gave her an absent pat on her hand.

"Done? Just like that? What's the meaning—"

"It just occurred to me that you are, as usual, absolutely right," he interrupted, never taking his eyes off Nicole, as if afraid she might disappear. "And I will endeavor to do what's best for the family. Now, if you will excuse me . . ." He stalked off, nearly knocking the glasses from Grant's hands as he returned.

When Nicole spotted him, her eyes widened in astonishment. Distress rang in her voice. "Derek!"

She caught herself, and looked around at the surprised faces of her acquaintances. "Uh, Lord Stanhope. We hadn't expected to be honored with your presence this evening," she said, her empty pleasantry more even with each word.

"Care for a stroll?" he asked, as he bent down to secure her arm.

"Well, I don't believe—" Nicole started airily, but he pulled her up from her seat on a settee and along to the terrace.

"Sutherland!" she said, once he'd maneuvered them outside. "What the hell do you think you're doing? You don't go to these things. I heard you didn't attend these functions!"

"I could ask the same of you. When did sailors start making Lady Crossman's eminence list?"

Her eyes slitted as she answered, "I have as much right to be here as you do, maybe more."

"That's right. Seems you rank above even me in the hierarchy. You must have been amused when I accused you of trying to bag an earl."

She tilted her head side to side. "Well, there was a pleasing sense of irony about it, yes," she said.

"It's the perfect cover—Lady Christina living a quiet life in finishing school on the Continent, never visiting because she's *afraid to travel,* but finally coming back to live with her grandmother. I'd wager Lady Christina's shyness makes it difficult to get any information about her because she doesn't accept many visitors."

Nicole assumed a bored pose. "So you've figured us out. Shall I clap?"

"I thought I knew you," he said with a rough smile. "You rub one foot against the opposite calf when you're nervous. You angle your head when curious." He leaned in near her ear, his voice low as he said, "And when I bring you to pleasure, your little toes curl."

She jumped away from him, shivering. "Are you quite through?"

He reached for her gloved hand, but she moved closer to the railing as though averse to his touch. A cold mask fell into place on her striking features. "Give me one reason why you feel you're entitled to even a second of my time."

He took a deep breath. "I need to explain some things—"

"*You think?*" she cut in bitterly.

This was not going as planned. He'd hoped she'd be somewhat glad to see him—hoped she'd missed him enough to at least listen to an explanation. "Do you even want to know why I left?"

"Oh, I believe I know why," she assured him as she turned to go.

When he grasped her arm again, she struggled to fling him away. "*Let me go,*" she said with such venom in her voice, he almost did.

"Not until you let me explain."

She pulled away again, trying to get someone's attention through the corridor.

"Who are you looking for? One of your young pups?"

She smiled then. "I'll most likely marry one of those men."

"The hell you will!"

"And why not? You still don't think I'm good enough?"

"That's not it."

"*Then what is?*"

Before he could stop himself, he grated, "*Because you're going to be my wife.*"

Her eyes widened, then glittered in anger. "Well, that's a rapid turnover. Word has it you just got rid of the last one."

"So you know?"

"*Everyone* knows." She looked down and smoothed the flounces on her skirt with snappish, overly crisp motions.

"Give me a chance to explain that. Please," he added at her uncompromising look.

"What's to explain? We were together for that long, and you never told me you were married."

"You never told me you were heir to one of the wealthiest houses in England."

"That's not the same! I didn't hurt you by my omission."

He exhaled and reached for her hand. "You're right."

She looked startled that he'd agreed, but masked it quickly. "I don't want to hear your excuses. Nothing can excuse the way you treated me." Her eyes became suspiciously bright. "Leave me alone," she demanded, and tried to free her hand.

When he held her firm, she brought the heel of her slipper down on his instep and jerked away at the same time, immediately fleeing to the ladies' retiring room.

He hurried after her, indifferent to the scene. At the doorway, he accosted the squat matron standing attendance.

"Does this room have another way out?" he barked.

"Really, Stanhope, the nerve—"

"Does it or not?" he ground out.

"Yes!"

He ran out the patio doors and along the side of the building to find the door to the retiring room. He didn't have to look for long before he saw Nicole, skirts hiked, barreling out into the street. He had to smile. Even dressed like royalty, underneath she was his irrepressible Nicole. His heavy footfalls echoed on the street as he gained on her.

Until she reached Mayfair, turned a corner, and ran directly up the front steps of what had to be the largest mansion on the square.

Derek stared, marveling at the luxurious home. How

had Nicole ever gotten comfortable in this place dripping with money? He followed up the steps and banged the massive brass knocker, waiting impatiently until an elderly butler answered.

"I would like to see . . . Lady Christina."

"My lady does not receive visitors at this hour," he answered on a whistling breath. "Would you care to leave a card?"

"No, I want to see her."

The man shuffled his feet. "My lady does not receive—"

"So be it," Derek interrupted, easily pushing past the old man, only to be greeted by two huge footmen who did not look happy. Wasn't that a measure of status, how large your footmen were? If so, he thought as they grabbed his arms, it would appear the marchioness was doing exceedingly well. He was fighting to shake them off when a dull thump sounded from the second floor.

She was there, rising with the book she'd just dropped. Her hand flew over her mouth until she yanked it to her side. The two footmen also turned to the noise, so Derek was able to steal a fleeting look at her. She'd risen to her full height, standing proudly and acting unconcerned.

A corner of his lip quirked up. *She was his.* The fact that she didn't even realize she would be married to him within a fortnight made him grin. He smiled even as the two men were shoving him out the doors.

"Look for me, Nicole," he called over his shoulder. "I'll be everywhere you are until you agree to talk to me. This is just beginning."

Chapter 27

*E*arly the next morning, Derek gulped down coffee, eager to ride to Atworth House, but his mother stopped him. "I need to talk to you."

He shook his head. "It can wait."

She maneuvered in front of him. "No! It can't."

He scowled at her, but she was undeterred. "I want to tell you that there's no excuse for your behavior last night. Manhandling Lady Christina like that! I saw you force her onto the balcony. I saw her trying to get away from you. I know you've been through a lot, but you have to start taking responsibility for your actions. Nothing can excuse your behavior."

"She's Nicole Lassiter."

Amanda frowned, then made a choking sound. "Wh-what? You can't be serious," she cried. "She's the little wharf rat you've been mooning over since you got back? That's impossible!"

"She spent months on my ship. I think I'd recognize her."

Grant came bounding down the stairs. "Who spent months on your ship?" he asked, pouring himself coffee at the sideboard.

"I believe we are speaking of Lady Christina," Amanda supplied in an uneven voice.

Grant frowned. "Lady Christina—"

"Is Nicole Lassiter," Amanda finished.

Grant looked as though he was choking on laughter. "Lady Christina is Lassiter's daughter? You're marrying Lassiter's daughter?" He shook his head and chuckled.

"If she'll have me."

"You'll be related to her father forever," Grant pointed out, wiping his eyes. "How will you handle that?"

With a pained expression, Derek said, "I will do what I have to do."

Amanda broke in, "These might all be empty musings—she doesn't exactly appear matrimonially bent on you."

"She found out I was married."

"Wait, I was there," Grant said. "Lydia slithered up to Lady Christina and explained that she was the countess of Stanhope."

Lydia and Nicole together? "What was Nicole's reaction?"

"She fainted dead away."

Derek ran a hand over his face. Christ, he would have spared her that. He had to see her and explain.

Amanda put her hand on his forearm. "Derek, listen to

me. I don't know everything that's happened, but you can't just run off like this."

"Like what?"

Grant was clearly pleased to answer, "You missed a spot shaving, and your boots don't match."

He scowled down at his boots but continued to the door.

"Whatever has happened between you and the girl doesn't make it right to go to Atworth House looking like that."

He could admit that he hadn't gotten very far in the planning stage, since he'd been floored by finally finding her. But he . . . missed her, and knowing she wasn't even a mile away was making him crazed.

"I've waited long enough."

"Has she?" Amanda asked.

"What do you mean by that?"

"If she is Nicole Lassiter, has she had time enough to recover from your abandonment?"

"I'm going—"

"Very well. I see my advice is neither wanted nor needed," she snapped. "I'm returning to Whitestone."

Grant pointed out, "There are several weeks left in the season."

"It doesn't matter," she said tartly, never taking her eyes from Derek's face. "I refuse to stay here when you're acting like this. I at least want to have the excuse of not being here when you embarrass yourself further."

As Derek walked out the door, he heard her exhale loudly and say, "Love has turned him into a fool. Grant, I'll throttle you if you behave like this."

When Derek stood once again on the doorstep of

Atworth House, he knocked, and after several minutes, the same wheezing butler answered.

The man masked his surprise when Derek demanded, "I want to see Nicole."

He took a loud, deep breath and announced, "She is not in at the moment."

Derek smiled as he looked down. When he raised his head, his expression was neutral. "It is seven in the morning."

"Nevertheless, she is not in at the moment."

"You're going to tell me this no matter how often I come here today, aren't you?"

He detected a slight nod just as the man said, "She's not in—"

With a raised hand, Derek shook his head. "I get the point."

Deciding not to wrangle with the footmen again, he nodded to the butler and walked down the steps. As soon as the door closed, Derek turned toward the back of the mansion, where he'd spotted an ivy-covered garden wall. He held his breath as he pushed down the latch on the gate, but it opened easily. He walked in and approached the back of the house. As soon as he stood at the steps to the terrace, he saw her.

Early though it was, Nicole sat at a veranda table under falling cherry blossoms, absently tapping the tip of a strawberry against her bottom lip and ignoring the steaming tea service and newspaper in front of her. She looked out over the magnificent garden, but was lost in thought, unseeing.

Nicole leaned back in her chair, replaying the events of the previous night. Sutherland hadn't asked for forgiveness, hadn't even asked her to marry him. He'd simply decreed it so. Again, against her expectations, the tears refused to flow.

She didn't understand what possessed the man to behave as he did. *Audacious* and *arrogant* weren't strong enough words to describe him. Outrage spilled through her. All those late-night imaginings of him on one knee begging forgiveness—yet he just expected them to retie what he had so callously severed.

As if she would marry him! She had a slew of suitors, suitors who had propped up her failing pride. She'd choose one who'd give her a nice, sedate life. She could make it work. Though not if Sutherland continued his antics. Strange how all those years her grandmother had worried about Nicole's behavior in the ton, and now a renegade earl was about to ruin her.

Suddenly, she froze. Out of the corner of her eye, near the house, she could see—no, it couldn't be him. She turned. Sutherland!

She wasn't surprised to get that inexplicable tightening in her chest at the sight of him, but fought it nonetheless. She forced her eyes away from him, rose from her chair, and began her retreat. When she had to pass Derek, he grabbed her hand.

"What are you doing, Sutherland?"

"We're going to be wed."

Not again. Panic rioted through her. *"Have you lost your mind?"*

"No, I'm thinking more clearly than I've ever done. I'm taking you to Gretna Green."

She gasped and finally sputtered, "The hell you are! Why would I wed you when I despise you?" And why couldn't she make her tone as outraged as she felt?

He reached out to stroke the hair off her forehead, and

after an initial try, she couldn't seem to fling herself away from him. Had she missed him that badly? Enough to turn docile at his slightest touch?

"Trust me—you do not want to marry one of those dandies. They're not man enough for you."

She didn't doubt that. "And you are?"

"Indeed."

The arrogance! She was embarrassed by her weakness, brought low with another stroke of her hair. She couldn't think when he did that, and he knew it.

He took advantage of her temporary calm by grabbing her hand and pulling her down the steps. "We'll talk in the carriage."

"No," she squealed as she pulled back. "I'm not marrying you. And even if I wanted to—which I do not—you can't come in here and act as if you own me. I have a family and obligations. Did it occur to you that they might want to be present when I do wed?"

"Then we'll be married twice."

"*Again,* I'm not—"

Chapman appeared at the veranda doors, politely clearing his throat. "Are you all right, my lady? Shall I get the marchioness?"

"No! No need for—"

"She's here?" Derek demanded.

With a whistling breath, Chapman inclined his head toward the door, and before Nicole could form a protest, Derek half-dragged her in that direction. What would her grandmother think when a huge man came barreling into her staid parlor?

She also questioned why she gave him only token resistance, why she was insanely going along with his high-handed behavior.

When they reached the doorway to the salon, he called to the marchioness, "My lady—"

"What do you want? I'm not hard of hearing," she interrupted without raising her head, making it plain that her cross-stitching held more interest for her.

He didn't hesitate. "I am Derek Andrew Sutherland, sixth earl of Stanhope, and I am taking your granddaughter to Gretna Green to marry her."

The dowager sighed impatiently. "If you must. . . ."

Derek paused, openly surprised. "Have her things—if you could have her things sent along to the Bickham Inn tonight?"

Her grandmother nodded, as if he'd just asked her to pass the salt.

Nicole's eyes went wide, and he took advantage of her shock by steering her toward the door again. Nicole looked back, baffled.

The marchioness had a grin on her face.

"If I didn't know better," Derek remarked as he hustled Nicole into the carriage, "I'd think the old girl might just like me." His tone was normal, as if they were having a chat over tea. It made it difficult for Nicole to sort out her thoughts. She wanted to sound rational to him, to point out logically why they wouldn't suit, but she'd sound like a fishwife compared to his even tone.

She girded herself by recalling that she was beyond irritation at his conceit, at his assumption that she would just roll over and marry him. Her thoughts bubbled up in a stammering flood. "This is kidnapping! Just like before—I won't have it—not again—not from you."

"It's not kidnapping. It's eloping," he pointed out reasonably.

"*Eloping?* I won't marry you. I won't! I can't trust you—you left me before." Her voice finally broke. Hot tears poured from her eyes, replacing those she swiped away. "Nothing ever hurt me so badly, and I'll be damned if I set myself up for that again."

Chapter 28

"Leaving you . . . nearly broke me," Derek countered as he swept a tear from her cheek. He saw her wobbling bottom lip and added gently, "But I had to go. I'll explain to you why if you'll listen to me."

She said nothing.

"Please, just let me explain. I've never told anyone what I'm about to tell you. Grant suspected, but he was never certain."

In a huff, she replied, "Well, then, go on!"

He nearly smiled at her militant tone, but instead took a deep breath. "William was my older brother and the heir, but he was not a good man. He was hedonistic and spoiled—made that way by the family and servants cosseting him and making him think he was next to God. Plus, in our father's eyes he could do no wrong."

He looked over to see if she was listening.

"Continue."

He raised his eyebrows, then said, "When William was shot in a drunken duel, a neighboring lord's daughter came to our family and told us she was carrying William's child."

When he paused, Nicole impatiently tapped at his hand for him to go on. Her tears were drying.

"My father was ecstatic that William's blood would be passed on—that his precious heir's child would inherit—"

"But wouldn't the child be a bastard?" she interrupted, clearly getting caught up in the tale.

He didn't answer for several seconds. "That's where I came in," he said tonelessly.

"Oh, no," she murmured, her face a mirror of his pain as she comprehended what he was saying.

"My mother was against the idea of me wedding her and passing the child off as my own, but in the end, everyone pitied her and pushed for marriage. Even I felt a responsibility for her. I resented William for doing this— I'd always cleaned up after him, and it appeared that I would take on his last obligation for the rest of my life. But as I said, I felt sorry for the girl, and married her."

"What about your own children? What if you'd had a son?"

"You have to understand that my father loved William above all else."

When Nicole nodded, he continued, "On our wedding night and for several nights afterward, she refused the marriage bed, saying she was ill due to the child. But on that first night, she'd asked me to stay in her chamber to allay suspicion, and I agreed.

"After a week, she indicated that she was ready to become my wife in truth, but when I arrived home that night, I received an anonymous letter. The spelling was poor, as well as the penmanship, and I didn't doubt one of the servants had written it. The letter explained that the reason she hadn't wanted to share her bed with me was because she was having her monthly cycle."

"But the baby—"

"There was no baby." Over her gasp, he resumed. "I flew into a rage and confronted her, but she denied it, swearing she was pregnant. She was very convincing. But then she began an almost panicked attempt to seduce me. I knew then. After an hour of yelling and threats, she finally admitted that she'd tricked our entire family—*gloated* was more like it. She told me of her father's financial troubles and how they'd determined she would become the next countess of Stanhope. She also said that William's death was a godsend, because they'd finally concluded that no matter how much she teased and dallied with him, he simply wasn't going to wed her."

"Oh, my God . . ."

"It's worse. She hinted, though I could never prove or disprove it, that she'd engineered the events that led to William's death, that she brought about the duel by playing one man against the other. It was then that I really glimpsed the coldness in her eyes. She's truly a . . . heartless woman. To this day, I wonder if she said those things to hurt me further or if she spoke the truth. I couldn't turn her over to the authorities, not knowing for certain. I threatened annulment, but she pointed out that no one would believe me if I said I'd never been intimate with her. She was far from virginal, and I'd spent the night of the wedding in her room. Plus, she was a celebrated beauty."

"What about divorce?" Nicole questioned, sounding outraged.

"In my family, death before divorce was the rule, but I

threatened her. She countered that it would kill my father, who'd been ailing ever since William died. In fact, it was on the eve of my father's death that he made me swear I'd always take care of William's 'love.'

"I was cornered—there was nothing I could do. I could hurt my family and break a deathbed promise to my father, or I could stay wed to her. My path was clear, but I knew I'd die before I let a woman like that be the mother of my children. I swore to her that I would never be a husband to her. And I never was. When I got back from Australia, Lydia was pregnant by some foreign lord. She wanted an annulment. She told people I was unable to perform my marital duties—"

Nicole made a wholly disbelieving sound that he felt complimented by, then asked, "But couldn't you have told me this, instead of abandoning me in Sydney?"

"I realized that I was a worthless drunk. I convinced myself that if I left, you'd forget about me and find someone more worthy of you. You deserved so much more—to be married, to have children who wouldn't bear the stigma of illegitimacy. I was trying to do what was right."

His eyes caught hers as he took her hand. "If I'd told you I was leaving and you'd given me any indication that you wanted me, I wouldn't have been able to part from you."

He saw her soften. Then her eyes became suspicious, and he could practically see her nimble mind putting everything together. "And you just happened to realize this right around the time Chancey came for me?"

Derek said nothing. He didn't want to cause any grief for the man, but he wasn't about to lie to her again.

She shook her head. "No wonder Chancey looked as though he needed to tell me something before they sailed," she said to herself. "And he appeared so guilty all the way home."

Derek remained silent.

Hesitantly, she asked, "What about the drinking?"

"I think in the back of my mind, I decided I was coming for you, even before I consciously realized it. I stopped drinking midway through the voyage back—I wanted to be a good man, a good husband for you. I haven't had a drop since," he said resolutely.

"Oh, Derek . . ." she breathed, and threw her arms around him.

"You know that you're marrying me," he said in what should have been a questioning tone, but he was confident, and it sounded more like a truth. When she leaned back and looked at him, he said, "I know you've got to feel it as much as I do, that this is right. Nicole, we are inevitable."

Nicole knew it, too. When he said they would be married, it was as if a piece of a puzzle had just shifted into place.

He must have mistaken her silence, because he declared, "I will say this once—you don't want to marry one of those lordlings. I cannot even begin to express the misery a bad union can make. You must believe me, because I've experienced it."

She looked deeply into his eyes, so grave with warning. How much he must have suffered for the last few years! Could she trust him? He'd hurt her before. But when she looked into his eyes, she *believed* that he loved her, even though he'd never told her so. She was about to kiss him in assurance, when she recalled his dictatorial conduct this morning.

They were going to have to establish some rules.

She withdrew from him and assumed her best businesslike demeanor. In a brisk tone she announced, "I will warn you, I won't be a conventional bride."

His expression turned serious as well. "I won't be a conventional husband."

"I won't abide your being unfaithful."

"I won't be unfaithful, and I won't abide it in you, either."

She gave him a quick *that's settled* nod, then said, "I don't want to live in England."

He smiled thinly. "I must. Since I'm not letting you go, so shall you." When she nibbled her lip, he said, "We can visit America as often as you like, but I believe you would like living at my estate, Whitestone. And your roots are here as well."

She didn't like his reasoning, but really, where else would they live? And it would be easier to help out her father and Maria from England.

"I don't want to have a dozen children," she announced with a tilt of her head. "Two would be nice, I think."

He paused, then said, "Agreed for now. But I reserve the right to ask you again after we've had our first child."

Our first child. Derek's child. "Agreed." This was too easy. "I want my father always to be welcome in our home, as well as Maria and Chancey."

"Chancey and Maria will be—" Derek hedged.

"Sutherland . . ." she cut in warningly. God, but her father would kill her when he found out whom she'd married.

"He'll be . . . welcome."

That was good enough for now, she supposed, and gave him a smile in conclusion.

A hungry look fired in his eyes. She read the desire in them just before he touched his lips to hers. She felt the desire in him when he slipped his tongue in to tease her to instant arousal, her breaths halting, her hands seeking. He smiled against her lips, and she pulled away. "What is it?"

"You, Nicole," he said, running his hand over her hair and face, "are a treasure."

She smiled, not knowing what prompted him to say that. His lips sought hers once more.

He tugged at the bodice of her gown to expose her breasts. "What are you doing?" she murmured.

"I'm making love to you."

She pulled back and frowned. "You can't make love to me in a carriage."

"Let me convince you that I can," he uttered in a low, determined voice that stroked her inside.

"I can't make love to you here, now." She could hear the realization in her tone.

"Don't pretend that you don't want me as much as I want you," he said, an edge in his voice.

"Of *course* I do," she said in exasperation, and he grinned. "But making love to you outside of marriage was my first mistake with you—I won't make it again," she finished, her voice becoming more determined with each word.

Derek grabbed her hand and spread it over the front of his trousers, over his rigid flesh. "Do you feel this?" he asked in a pained tone. "Four months without being inside you. Do you feel how much I need you?"

She melted with heat and want, only a shred of her determination remaining. It was just enough. "Don't do this, Derek. I want to make a fresh start with you—"

At once, his big hands were grasping her waist, pulling her off the seat. Part of her grew outraged while another became excited by the low, growling sound he made. Then his hands released her. Her eyes opened. She was sitting on the opposite side of the carriage.

"It seems I can deny you nothing," he told her evenly, though his face looked tight with strain and his hands were clenched.

She began a conversation, mainly to keep her mind off the memory of her hand caressing his straining trouser front. After a time, he relaxed and joined in. Before long, she was cuddled on his lap, with him stroking her hair. Hours rolled by as they talked about their likes and dislikes, their desire for a family. He asked her question after question about her childhood and life.

He was so attentive, just as he'd been during their time in Sydney, and she easily recollected all the wonderful times they'd had. She also recollected the nights—the wild, hot nights. To mask her discomfiture, she asked, "Why are you suddenly so interested?"

He tucked a curl behind her ear. "Before, part of me didn't want to get to know you better. I think I knew I wouldn't want to let you go."

She cast him a lazy grin. *He loved her.* He might not vocalize it, but he did.

With a returning smile, he asked, "Explain to me, please, how a young sailor with an uncanny knack for navigation can also be a future marchioness?"

"I was expected to return to England and follow in my grandmother's footsteps, but I inveigled Father into keeping me with him and letting me sail. That is, until I was eighteen and ran out of ammunition," she admitted with a frown. "During the time I was at sea, Grandmother used her influence to spread that story about me to save my reputation."

"I thought the fear of traveling was a classic touch."

"So did I!" She giggled. "It was quite funny when I told Grandmother you knew the truth. That night, she and Chapman paced the floors, wondering what to do, until she hit on an idea."

"And what was that?"

" 'Chapman,' " Nicole grated, imitating her grandmother's scratchy voice perfectly, " 'perhaps we should kill him.' "

After five days of travel and five nights of separate rooms in roadside inns, neither Derek nor Nicole was interested in celebrating their nuptials in any way but one. Within minutes after the ceremony, they were back in their room, so quickly that tears lingered in her eyes from Derek's solemn, serious tone when he promised himself to her. After they'd signed their names together, that fierce, elemental look flashed in his eyes, and they'd all but ignored the congratulatory wishes.

His passion easily ignited her own. As soon as the door to their room at the inn closed, without a word they assailed each other. She grabbed at his clothes, fighting buttons, filling her fists with his shirt, occasionally twisting her arms behind her to help him with her intricately wrought dress.

"To hell with this," he growled at her resisting clothing, ripping through enough of her bodice to get his lips on her breasts.

"*Derek*," she said his name like a prayer, with the first pull on her nipple.

"God, I've missed you," he murmured, his breath hot against her damp breast, before thoroughly attending to the other. "I can't believe you're here. With me."

"Oh, Derek . . . I want you inside me," she whimpered. "Now, can we now?"

He groaned low in his throat as his hand dove beneath her dress and slid up her stockings. Running his fingers up her thigh, he grasped the flimsy material barring him and ripped that away as well. She felt his returning hand discover her moist and hot, his fingers seeming to luxuriate in her.

"Please . . ." she moaned.

Shoving up her skirts, he moved her against the wall and hastily freed himself. Her hand shot out to grip his stiff flesh springing forth, curving around the shaft to pull him to her. Just as she was about to guide him in, he put his hand tight over hers and moved the head up and down against her wetness. Up and down once, twice. She keened his name as ecstasy spiked through her, her eyes flashing open in surprise at her swift response.

He wrapped his hand around the back of her head and plunged into her before she'd even stopped convulsing. "*You drive me mad,*" he ground out as he clenched her hips. "For months I ached for you," he rasped against her lips.

Once more she called his name; as he slammed into her again and again, she never took the ease of a climax, only continued straining toward something even more consuming.

Each time he sank into her, she flew closer . . . too intense, nearing pain. She tried to hold on. Tried to see to his pleasure with clasping, frantic hands. In that final instant when he'd grown too large inside her, when the low rumbling broke from his throat, she shattered, feeling only rapture and Derek pouring hotly into her.

Chapter 29

Though they'd spent three days in Scotland, in bed, neither Derek nor Nicole wanted to leave the shelter of their room and return to reality. Outside, rain spilled down in sheets, but inside they were warm, basking in firelight and a haze of contentment.

"Being a husband," Derek said as he lazily skimmed the backs of his fingers up her thighs, "is quite easy."

"You think so?" she sighed. She was languid, relaxed as she hadn't been since her last time in his bed. She'd needed him, needed what only he could give her. She lay on her stomach, propped up on her elbows, eating grapes from his hand.

"With the right wife," he said with a grin. "I don't suppose you have any idea what this"—he ran a finger up her cleavage—"or this"—he palmed her uncovered derriere—"is doing to your ancient husband?"

She looked down to see his thick erection tenting the

sheet, and her lips curved. She'd take care of that shortly. . . .

During the afternoon, in the time they weren't making love, they'd enjoyed a delicious lunch of medallions of veal sent up to their room in the quaint inn. Now they sprawled on the bed absently snacking on fruit and, she imagined, reviving for the rest of the night.

"I think we should go to Italy for our honeymoon. Take a couple of months—"

"Months?" She sucked another grape from his fingers. "You know I need to be back to help Father and Maria."

He frowned. "No, I didn't know that," he said, and dropped his hand. "Nicole, your father made his own troubles—he shouldn't look to you to bail him out."

"He's not." She sat up and pulled a cover over her. "He would never take a dime from me. I want to help."

"You know that by helping him, you're hurting me?" he asked her, a peculiar look on his face.

She supposed they were about to have their first married fight. Just days after the ceremony.

"What do you think you can do to help him?" he asked as he set the tray of food on the bed table. "You told me he has Maria involved now."

"They'll need someone in England. I can handle the correspondence here—"

"You mean handle the creditors. You are a countess now, and if you think I'll let my wife wrangle with a pack of those bastards, you are insane. Much less creditors bent on liquidating my main competition."

"I can't believe you'd say that." She shot him a hurt look before she jumped from the bed and slid into a shift.

He leaned forward. She'd forgotten how intimidating he could appear. In a softer, deceptively reasonable tone, he explained, "Nicole, you can't work with him because very shortly he'll have nothing to work with."

She almost blurted out that they'd gotten new, more favorable financing, but she wouldn't betray her father. She wanted to shock the world, and her disbelieving husband, when Lassiter Shipping came back stronger than ever.

"You are no longer involved with that line," he said, his jaw tight. "Period. I would have expected a little more bloody loyalty from my *wife*. Let your father figure his way out of this."

"Why can't you compromise? We can find a way around most of the direct competition—"

"Why should I compromise?" he snapped. He leapt up as well and began stabbing his legs into his trousers. "You need to decide where your loyalties lie. Every second you help him is time in which you neglect me."

"So this is about more than the companies, isn't it? You want my loyalty and think I can't give it to you and him both." The thought that she'd deliberately led Derek to believe her father was without money fluttered in her mind. When he began to say more, she interrupted, "Don't tell me to choose. You do not want me to do that right now."

His eyes bored into hers, his face tense.

"Don't ask me to choose between you, who is being overbearing and unreasonable, and my father and Maria, who were there to pick me up when you abandoned me." A tear slid down her cheek.

His eyes widened, barely perceptibly, and he reached out to smooth the tear away. "Damn it, Nicole. This got out of hand. I'm . . ." He exhaled. "I'm sorry. I don't know why I turn into an ass around you. I think it's because I'm on unsure footing with you."

"Unsure footing? When have I ever given you anything to doubt?"

"You haven't. But after what I did to you . . . I wonder how you could forgive me."

"So you want me to prove myself, my feelings for you, by choosing you over my family? Isn't the fact that I married you enough?"

"Only after I dragged you to the altar."

"If you think you pushed marriage on me, then you don't know me at all. I made a decision because I think we can have a good life together. But not if you can't be reasonable and respect my feelings."

"I'm sorry, love. Let's forget this."

"I would like to think you'd help my father if he needed it."

He shook his head slowly. "I'll give you anything, but that's something I'll never do."

The finality in his words made her realize she should just accept the hatred between the two. Why fight it? Her father had provoked Derek; she knew that. And Derek obviously wouldn't be the bigger man and bury the animosity.

Still, thinking of the blows her father had dealt Peregrine made it difficult to blame Derek. But that didn't make the sadness go away. Even when he stroked her face and her frown eased, she dreaded telling her father about her marriage to his worst enemy, an enemy content to stay that way.

Derek knew they couldn't continue like this. He'd hurt Nicole. He never wanted to do that again. She was his wife now, a beautiful, courageous woman who could love him. He didn't want to think he was the only thing standing in the way of her complete happiness.

Even now, as they rode home, he wondered about her. Was she looking out the carriage window, thinking, regretting their marriage? He knew she worried about Lassiter's company. And he knew having to tell her father about the marriage weighed on her.

After they arrived home in London and he'd introduced her to his staff, he noticed her suppressing a yawn. He flushed; he hadn't thought how the late nights and the travel might affect her.

He didn't wait, but scooped her into his arms, carrying her to his room.

"Derek!"

"I'm putting you to bed."

"It's the middle of the day. I can't go to sleep." When they entered his bedroom, she yawned again. "Well, perhaps . . ." She looked around the spacious, mahogany-paneled room. "This is your room."

She wouldn't want to sleep with him? "Is that bad?"

"No, I like it here. I just don't know why I'm so tired."

"Because I've made love to you continually for three days," he said as he set her down and began undoing her buttons. "Even a lusty woman like you has her limits." He drew the gown over her head and kissed her neck. "Anyone would need some rest after the last few nights."

She finished undressing down to her shift. "Maybe for a few minutes, but then I have to go to my father. They'll be back by now." Her voice was sad, her tone lethargic.

He pulled the counterpane over her as she snuggled down in his bed. He liked seeing her there. Kissing her forehead, he said, "I know. We'll talk when you wake up."

After he left her, he settled in his study, looking out the window, lost in thought. Damn it, he didn't want Nicole to feel like this! Yes, she acted much the same outwardly, but she wasn't happy. He'd sworn to be a better husband, a sober husband, and he knew she believed in him. But she needed more.

He sank back in his chair.

Even if he wanted to end the war between him and Lassiter, what could he do? Unlike Nicole, Derek didn't think an apology and a handshake would suffice for the bast—the man. No, some things were better left alone.

In Sydney, Derek had ceased to dismiss it when she told him he was a good man inside, but he hadn't been giving her much to believe in lately. If he didn't change, he would lose her. Period. And he couldn't imagine life without her.

Chapter 30

$\mathcal{N}$icole awoke an hour later, unable to sleep any longer. She rose and redressed, splashing water on her face and smoothing her hair before going in search of her husband in the huge mansion. A servant told her he'd gone out ten minutes before and wasn't expected back before dinner.

He must be out seeing to business. She sighed. In the back of her mind, she'd thought Derek would come around. That's why she'd let their argument drop. But he'd fled without even accompanying her to her father's ship, much less giving her a kiss good-bye. She'd be facing her father on her own.

After a short carriage ride, she boarded the *Griffin*. Chancey was there to greet her. Well, not precisely—he silently indicated with his hand that she should follow him into the room directly off the salon, then left without a word.

From the next room, she could hear a conversation just

beginning between her father and . . . her husband! Did Chancey want her to overhear what was said?

"*What do you want?*" Lassiter snapped.

Nicole heard Maria say softly, "Jason . . ."

Amazingly, her father calmed and said gruffly, "Well, why've you come here?"

Maria added, "Captain Sutherland, we are very honored to have you visit us."

"I'm glad to have been admitted," Derek replied.

Her father sounded angry again. "We're waiting—state your business and be gone."

Derek took a deep breath. "I want—I need . . . your help," he finally bit out.

Lassiter burst out laughing. Nicole couldn't believe the man cackling was related to her.

Maria spoke over his laughter. "How can we be of service to you?"

"I need help with Nicole." At that, Lassiter fell silent. Until he bellowed, "What have you done?" He must have lunged for Derek, because she heard scuffling and glass breaking. Nicole was up and not quite at the door when Maria said, "Jason!" Then the room quieted. Nicole eased back.

"I procured an annulment and married her." Again, the sound of another enraged attack. This time she heard a punch and was flying out the door. Chancey, standing in the corridor, eyebrows raised, intercepted her. Nicole whispered crossly, "Yes, I married him."

He gave her a grave, satisfied nod, then placed his finger over his lips and leaned forward to listen at the door. Nicole looked in both directions, then threw up her hands in exasperation and tiptoed closer.

"I married her last week," Derek said in an unmistakably skewed voice. Chancey gave a small punch in the air, then pointed to his nose with a questioning look. Nicole shook her head—she recognized that tone from experience, and answered by tapping her jaw.

"Perhaps you should explain what has occurred since we've been away," Maria said in a tone that brooked no denial. She somehow kept Lassiter in check the entire time Derek recounted what had happened—well, most of what had happened—in the last couple of weeks.

"And that brings me to my visit here, to ask for your help," he finished, sounding irritated that he'd had to go through the long explanation.

"Why should we help you?" her father said in a churlish tone. But did he sound less riled than before?

"Because I want to give her anything she needs to be content with me. Because I want to make it up to her for being—"

"An ass?" This actually from Maria.

"Yes, an ass." His words sounded pulled from him.

"Well, what can we do? I'm not coming up with anything as a favor to you," her father unnecessarily assured Derek.

"Nicole's dreaded telling you about the marriage, and she's worried about your company. I've told you about the marriage; you can't be angry with her about it, because I never would have given up. I would have pursued her until she said yes. And your company . . ." He paused. She could picture him running his hand through his hair as he did when frustrated. "I can think of nothing to save it unless I loan you money."

"Loan me money?"

"I know the loss of the *Bella Nicola* brought the creditors down on you. If you let me assist your company, you can stave them off until you can get it back on its feet."

"Let me get this straight—you want to give me money so my daughter will be happy?"

"She worries about you. Unless you have a better idea, that's exactly what I'm proposing." Again, he was met by laughter.

Maria's voice sounded closer to Derek. "Captain Sutherland," she began in a sympathetic tone, "Lassiter Shipping has had a new infusion of capital. We arranged for it in Cape Town. I've helped Jason with his accounting and a refinancing. I believe he's on much stronger footing than before."

"That's right, Captain. Don't want your money and don't need it."

Father!

"Jason, be understanding," Maria said. "Have you forgotten that this man saved Nicole's life?"

"He also compromised her. When he was married."

Derek spoke up, "That was wrong and I admit it—"

"But you were in love and couldn't help yourself?" Maria finished softly.

The room grew painfully silent. Nicole believed even her heart had stopped beating as she held her breath. What would he say? Did he really love her?

Then the answer, the rumble of a word exhaled on a breath: "Yes."

And she was running past Chancey into the room, straight to her surprised husband, whose arms flew open to her. "I love you so much," she sighed against his neck.

With his face in her hair, he murmured, "I love you, Nicole. More than I can say."

When Maria coughed discreetly, Nicole turned in Derek's arms until they were both facing her father. "Father. You are *bad*," she said, and he looked somewhat chagrined. "I love you both, so you'll simply have to bury the past."

"But what about that time outside Hong Kong when he ran me into the jetty?" Lassiter complained like a scolded schoolboy.

Derek scowled at him and added, "Or that time in Melbourne when you told the port officials my crew was suffering from smallpox? My crew and cargo were quarantined for three weeks."

"Enough!" Nicole commanded, looking from one man to the other. "Right now—you two, shake hands." Neither moved. Until Maria pushed Lassiter forward just as Nicole dragged at Derek. With great effort on their part, and great reluctance from Derek and her father, the men shook hands.

"I'll kill you if you don't make her happy."

"If I can't keep her happy, I might let you try."

A wedding reception two weeks hence, to be held at Atworth House.

The marchioness had decreed it so, and everyone was happy to oblige.

The evening of the celebration had been wonderful for Derek, next to perfect except for the few sarcastic comments Lassiter made. But Derek was beginning to see the humor behind some of the man's words . . . if he was very, very generous. With time, there might exist a grudging goodwill between them.

Although the festivities were still in full swing, he made his way to the door. Nicole had retired early, and he was anxious to join her.

"Derek," Grant called from the terrace. He was standing outside alone, smoking a cigar.

He'd wanted to talk to Grant ever since he'd brought Nicole home from the *Griffin*. He smiled as he remembered her that night. She was like a little general insisting they lay out guidelines and goals for their lives before they fell into bed. That part of their lives, she'd told him, needed no adjustment. The rest, however . . .

It had been unsettling to stretch himself and his beliefs to make her happy. Ultimately, however, he'd comprehended that with her fulfilled, he was fulfilled. He knew he'd been given a second chance with Nicole and with his family, and he didn't want his brother ever to worry again that Derek wouldn't meet his responsibilities.

Derek joined him at the rail overlooking the lantern-lit garden and took an offered cigar. "When will we be throwing one of these for you?"

Grant laughed. "Don't hold your breath."

"No? What about Bainbridge's chit?"

"Despite all her family's zealous efforts, I remain a bachelor."

Derek lit his cigar. "I always thought you would suit. She's nice and staid. Hard to believe you've resisted her scandal-free nature."

"She is a nice girl. She even swore she'd wait for me to return."

Derek raised his eyebrows. "Return?"

"You know Belmont's fool's errand?" Grant asked with a grin. "I signed on as the fool."

"You're serious?"

He nodded. "I went back to him and counteroffered. He's to give me all of Belmont Court at his passing."

Derek let out a surprised breath. "He must be convinced his son's family is out there to give away all he has left."

"That's because Belmont is desperate. Very emotional

man, that Belmont," Grant explained in a censorious tone. "He fears his health is failing, and the thought of them out there stranded makes giving away his home a small concession to find them."

Derek frowned. "But if he gives away the estate and you do find the family, what will become of them?"

"It didn't take you long to find the rub. If I were an intuitive man, I'd swear he dreams that I'll marry the granddaughter when I find her, and we'll all live at the court happily ever after, or some such nonsense."

Derek paused, then pointed out, "You said 'when.' "

With a sheepish grin, Grant said, "Yes, well, that damn man actually has me believing it." From his coat pocket, he pulled a fading daguerreotype of a towheaded young girl with a shy smile. "Look at her. She looks so delicate. If she did survive . . . Thinking of her, out there alone—"

Derek must have looked at Grant with surprise, because he hastily slid the likeness into his pocket, then said in a gruff voice, "Probably a waste of time. She most likely didn't survive."

"I don't know if I like this," Derek said with a wave of his cigar. "You're settling in at Peregrine. And I feel like I just got you back as my brother," he added in a mutter. His wife had asked him not to hold back his feelings with his family, but he was new to it.

"You'll just have to miss me until we come back, because it's settled," Grant advised good-naturedly. "And I figure, between you and Nicole, managing Whitestone and Peregrine for a year or so will be child's play."

Derek tamped his cigar and gave Grant an expression of absolute agreement. "I expect Nicole would like to help Peregrine, now that her father won't be a head-to-head competitor."

"Exactly so," Grant agreed. "Who knows?" he began as the corner of his lips quirked up. "Maybe I'll find some hidden treasure." He slapped Derek on the back and, with more excitement than Derek had heard from his brother in years, said, "I sail in a fortnight."

Chapter 31

*N*icole and Derek had seen a marked excitement in Grant about the upcoming expedition, though all knew it was far-fetched at best to think the lost family had survived. The islands targeted in Oceania were isolated and riddled with pirate activity, but if a voyage was what it took to make Grant happy, then they would be supportive.

On the day before Grant's departure, she and Derek went to the docks to wish him a safe journey. He was sailing the *Keveral* on the high tide, early the next morning. Embarking was a lively time, but thinking about how long Grant would be gone, and how much Derek would miss him, made Nicole's eyes tear. Lately, it seemed as though she choked up at the tiniest things.

Grant saw her dab at her eyes and said, "Don't cry, Nic." Then, in a pained voice, he urged, "No, *really*, don't cry."

Nicole had forgotten how uneasy Grant got around

emotional females and smiled to reassure him. Her smile grew when Derek moved his hand to rest at her waist. One night soon when she lay in his arms, she would tell him what she'd suspected for days.

Grant was needed to supervise the last-minute arrival of provisions, so Derek said, "Get back to work, Grant." A hearty handshake and slap on the back followed.

"Fair winds, Grant," Nicole said as she hugged her brother-in-law, nearly tearing up again. "I hope you find them."

Grant looked so very confident and strong when he said, "If they're out there, I'll find them."

As Derek escorted her off the ship, they called out a last round of good-byes and wishes for smooth sailing. Grant in turn ordered them, "Be good to each other!"

Derek put her arm through his as they made their way to the carriage. "I suppose we'll be doing this again soon," he said, sounding aggrieved.

Nicole elbowed him, and he chuckled. In another week, they would be saying good-bye to Lassiter, Maria, Chancey, and the *Bella Nicola*'s old crew as well. They were all sailing for South America to develop their newly planned routes. Nicole would miss them dearly. Even her grandmother, who'd truly become fond of her father and Chancey, and certainly of Maria, the "governess," would miss them. However, the marchioness was excited that Nicole and "dozens of great-grandbabies" would be staying in England.

Nicole was no longer worried about Maria and Father. She was confident that together they would turn Lassiter Shipping around, and she'd begun to believe that her father would finally . . . *see* Maria. The lovely, intelligent woman looked at him with such tenderness that Nicole was convinced she would win him over in the end. A love that shone so brightly would overwhelm any obstacles.

She knew. Because hers had.

As they watched Grant give a last wave before their carriage rolled away, Derek said, "I hope he finds as much happiness in his journey as we found."

"Still find." Nicole smiled and snuggled closer to his side. "And I hope we can fulfill Grant's wish by the time he returns."

"What wish?" he asked against her hair.

"To become an uncle."

Lose yourself in the passion...
Lose yourself in the past...
Lose yourself in a Pocket Book!

The School for Heiresses ❦ Sabrina Jeffries

Experience unforgettable lessons in love for daring young ladies in this anthology featuring sizzling stories by Sabrina Jeffries, Liz Carlyle, Julia London, and Renee Bernard.

Emma and the Outlaw ❦ Linda Lael Miller

Loving a man with a mysterious past can force you to risk your heart...and your future.

His Boots Under Her Bed ❦ Ana Leigh

Will he be hers forever...or just for one night?